SHARKS IN AN
INLAND SEA

BY LEHUA PARKER

Niuhi Shark Saga

Birth: Zader's Story

One Boy, No Water

One Shark, No Swim

One Truth, No Lie

Lauele Fractured Folktales

Pua's Kiss

Rell's Kiss

Nani's Kiss

Short Fiction Collections

Sharks in an Inland Sea

LEGACY OF THE CORRIDOR

SHARKS
IN AN
INLAND SEA

LEHUA PARKER

HEMELEIN PUBLICATIONS

Cover art: *Sharks in an Inland Sea* (2022) by Joe Monson
Cover design and interior layout and design: Joe Monson

Managing Editor: Joe Monson
Art Director: Joe Monson
Publisher: Heather B. Monson
Published by Hemelein Publications, LLC.
http://hemelein.com/

First Edition
First Hemelein printing, June 2022
10 9 8 7 6 5 4 3 2 1

ISBN:
978-1-64278-025-3 (case laminate)
978-1-64278-022-2 (trade paperback)
978-1-64278-023-9 (ebook)

Library of Congress Control Number: 2022934009

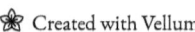 Created with Vellum

CONTENTS

LEGACY OF THE CORRIDOR

Way back in 1994, M. Shayne Bell put together *Washed by a Wave of Wind,* an anthology of short works by authors from "The Corridor", an area that covers Utah, most of Idaho, parts of Wyoming and Nevada, and stretches into Arizona and parts of northern Mexico. Sometimes, the area around Cardston, Alberta, Canada, is included, too. For those unfamiliar with this area, it was settled by Mormon pioneers, members of the Church of Jesus Christ of Latter-day Saints.

Shayne's anthology highlighted science fiction and fantasy works by authors from the area, as The Corridor contained an unusually high number of successful authors—for the population in the area—both genre and non-genre, both members and non-members of the predominant religion. That legacy continues today with an impressive list of authors such as:

Jennifer Adams
D. J. Butler
Orson Scott Card
Michael R. Collings
Michaelbrent Collings
Ally Condie
Larry Correia
Kristyn Crow
James Dashner
Brian Lee Durfee
Sarah M. Eden

Richard Paul Evans
David Farland
Diana Gabaldon
Jessica Day George
Shannon Hale
Mettie Ivie Harrison
Tracy Hickman
Laura Hickman
Charlie N. Holmberg
Christopher Husberg
Raymond F. Jones
Matthew J. Kirby
Gama Ray Martinez
Brian McClellan
Stephenie Meyer
L. E. Modesitt, Jr.
Brandon Mull
Jennifer A. Nielsen
Wendy Nikel
James A. Owen
Ken Rand
Brandon Sanderson
Caitlin Sangster
J. Scott Savage
D. William Shunn
Jess Smart Smiley
Eric James Stone
May Swenson
Howard Tayler
Brad R. Torgersen
Nym Wales
Dan Wells
Robison Wells
David J. West
Carol Lynch Williams
Dan Willis
Julie Wright

That's a big list of names, and it only barely scratches the surface. Hemelein Publications created this publication series to highlight authors from The Corridor, both well-known and lesser-known. We think Shayne did a wonderful job drawing attention to these amazing writers back then, and we want to continue what he started.

You can learn more about the series at:

http://hemelein.com/go/legacy-of-the-corridor/

Joe Monson
Managing Editor
Hemelein Publications

SWIMMING WITH THE SHARKS

JOE MONSON

I may have discovered Lehua Parker differently than most of her readers. The first story I read by her was "Pua's Kiss", a romance story set in her Lauele Universe. Most other people I know discovered her stories through the Niuhi Sharks Saga, which is set in the same universe, but targeted at a younger audience.

At this point, I should probably share that I like reading romances. And watching them. I'm weird that way. I'm picky about which ones, but I've dabbled in most of them. A couple of my aunts have poked fun at me for it, especially when I went with them and my mom to see *Sense and Sensibility* in the theater several years ago. What can I say? I enjoy a good story, especially with a bit of romance thrown in for good measure.

My wife finds it humorous that I like romantic comedies and romances in general, while she loves the blow-'em-up action adventure stories. I guess we make a good pair that way.

Back to the topic: By far, my favorites of her stories are those in the Lauele Universe. The characters are interesting, and I get to catch peeks of the mythology I've read about since I was quite young. I remember reading all the mythology books I could find on the Bookmobile that visited my small town back in the day during the summer. During the school year, I read through all of them in the school library, too.

There was something special about the the mythology from places like Hawaii, Japan, China, and other far away places. It was quite different than the "classical" mythology taught in schools. It was even different than the Native American mythology I'd read about. So, seeing that mythology I'd read about decades ago in stories like Lehua's was a double treat.

Not all of these stories are in the Lauele Universe, and some are significantly different. There are stories that fall under dystopia, cosmic horror, dark fantasy, several with adaptations of Hawaiian mythology, interesting takes on fairy tales, and alternate history, and all of them have some form of humor in them. There's a novella, a bunch of short stories, some flash fiction, a couple creative non-fiction / memoir stories (stories written to appear as fiction, but which are simply a creative retelling of an actual event), and a couple essays.

There's even a one-act play, and it's really fun.

The one thing all of these stories have in common is Lehua's solid grasp of entertaining an audience. Her characters are interesting (I mentioned that before!), and their stories are told in interesting ways. There's something here to fit just about any reader's tastes.

So, sit back in your comfy chair, make sure the lights are on (remember: some cosmic horror and dark fantasy, not to mention the occasional shark), and enjoy these tales. I know I'll be reading this collection again, and again, and again.

Joe Monson
Managing Editor
Hemelein Publications

INTRODUCTION: AN INLAND SEA

Stories bubble up from my subconscious like a sliver of carrot or taro in Sunday's kitchen sink stew. Or maybe more like a shark fin's shadow glimpsed from the corner of a salt-splashed eye.

No lie; I owe my current writing career to Honolulu's horrific traffic and mascara.

Writers start as readers. Growing up, I devoured books like potato chips. During my tedious and convoluted commute from home to school and back again, I passed the time by reading anything I could get my hands on, including a lot of books considered too scary, romantic, intellectual, or avant-garde for kids. I didn't care what the books were about—if they were available from a library, I brought them home. Every Friday, I would scour the shelves for the thickest books, books that might last me through the weekend. It's no wonder I hoard eBooks now.

Omnivorous and voracious reading first turned into writing when I was eight and ran out of books one Saturday afternoon. I had some early publishing and award-winning successes in my teens and early twenties, but... I... stopped. Life took me in different directions. It wasn't until 2010 after a decades-long break from writing fiction that I started publishing stories again.

It kickstarted with a dare.

Knowing I was bored and between projects, my sister Soozy challenged me to write a story for a local Halloween contest. "Like what?" I said.

"Write about something a kid knows is true, but adults don't," Soozy said.

I dusted off my keyboard and imagination, submitted, and won a fantastic dinner for two. Seeing a manuscript in print again, the smoke and salt of prime steak still on my tongue, I began to wonder *what if*. What if I hadn't chosen to be a responsible adult with a career, mortgage, bills, and a desire to eat? What if I had written stories instead?

What if I could do both?

I started scribbling again in fits and starts, dreaming of Hawaiian beaches during snowy Utah winters. At first, I was writing simply to amuse myself and avoid housework. As the bits and pieces came together, I realized I was writing a novel, probably a series of novels. Set in imaginary Lauele, Hawai'i, a place that looked nothing like Hollywood's version of aloha, a place where the fantastical was right under the surface of every day, I was certain no publisher would be interested.

But like humpback whales, some stories cross oceans to give birth.

One evening back in 2011, a publisher came to a local bookstore to talk with aspiring writers. I convinced myself to go simply because I'd already put on mascara that day; why waste it just doing dishes? I stayed through the entire presentation because I was sitting in the far corner and didn't want to climb over people to leave. But because I flicked mascara on my lashes that morning, I was in the room when the publisher announced, "Pitch me your stories." The rest, as they say, is history.

Reading widely and deeply embedded story structure in my bones, but it's my mixed-plate of life experiences seasoned with an overactive imagination that fuels my writing. As much as I read, I also did all the regular things kids do growing up in Hawai'i. I went to the beach, bodysurfed, and got sunburned. I was on soccer, volleyball, basketball, and softball teams. I played the flute, danced hula, and spent late nights with calabash cousins watching subtitled kung fu movies and passing bags of lychee, crackseed, and kakimochi. I only *sorta, kinda* always had my nose in a book.

As a blond, blue-eyed Hawaiian at The Kamehameha Schools, I sometimes wondered why my outsides didn't always match my insides. Every few years, I'd travel to Utah to spend time with my mother's family. In Utah I looked like more of the people around me, but in many ways that only highlighted how different I was. I didn't see or move through the world like my Utah cousins did, and I certainly didn't talk like them, either.

For me, Hawaiian Pidgin English and standard American English are switches I flip in my brain and mouth. Pidgin is how I express deep emotion. My kids famously judge how much trouble they're in by whether or not I scold them in Pidgin or English—and there's a lot of truth in that. With Islanders, Pidgin immediately creates connection; through its rhythms and phrases island life-blood beats.

Fo'real.

Some of the works in this collection unapologetically contain Hawaiian and Pidgin phrases. There's a glossary in the back for those who are unfamiliar, but I think most of the meaning is clear through context. It never occurred to me that writing Pidgin and Hawaiian phrases wasn't allowed in American literature, no more than other authors who have written and published works expressing their own southern, urban, or mix-heritage dialects. I never felt I needed permission to use my authentic voice, but this is one of the things about my Lauele stories that shocks, delights, and surprises island kids most.

But not all of the stories I publish blossom from my Hawaiian roots. There's a lot of Utah in my writing, too.

In many ways, this collection is a stewpot of hopes, dreams, and fears bubbled up from a rich mixed-genre broth where Hawai'i and Utah simmer. There are stories about people you know—a broke 'ōkole old man and his poi dog, an unscrupulous mortuary director, a desperate televangelist, and a bored insurance adjuster. There are kidnappings, monsters, sandwiches, and things that are not at all what they appear to be. Sharks swim in these waters, sharks with teeth and bite, who hunt in an inland sea.

But no worries, gangies! E komo mai! The water's fine!

But keep an eye on the shadows in the corners. You never know.

Aloha no,
　　Lehua

TOURISTS

In the calm waters off Keikikai beach, a thin crescent moon bleeds silver into the ocean as it cruises along the horizon like a shark's fin. Drifting beyond the reach of lights on shore, Kalei and a woman he met in the bar across the street skinny-dip in dark anonymity. The woman flicks her wrist, delighting in the little blue sparks that fly from her fingertips.

"Magic," she whispers.

Kalei's chuckle bubbles to the surface as he circles, gliding through the water as effortlessly as a seal. Splashing, he sends ripples of electric blue in every direction.

"Not magic," he says. "Bioluminescence."

"What?"

"It's plankton. Bioluminescence. You don't believe in magic."

"No. But out here in the ocean with you, I might change my mind."

He grins, his teeth gleaming like stars.

Kah-lay, she thinks, *remember his name is Kah-lay. Like the strings of flowers at the airport.*

"Cold?" Kalei asks.

"No, the water's wonderful. It's like silk."

"Good."

"I've never seen the ocean glow like this," she says. "It's spectacular."

"It doesn't happen very often."

"You were right. I wouldn't want to miss this. I don't know what that guy's problem was."

"Don't think about him," Kalei says. "We left him back at the bar. He's long gone."

"I can't believe he grabbed my arm." She rubs the spot.

"What did he say?"

"You didn't hear?"

"No. He pulled you away, remember?"

"I could barely understand him," she says. "He slurred something like, 'No go in da wah-dah.' I think he knew we were headed across the road to the beach."

Kalei nods, bobbing in the current. "That makes sense. I've seen him around. He's a part-time lifeguard. Probably wants to enjoy the evening without his pager going off."

"Funny," she says. "I can swim and so can you."

"He's just trying to keep you safe. The ocean's tricky at night."

"You mean he wants to keep this place to himself." She shakes her head. "Locals. Never want to share. Think everything belongs to them."

"Sometimes," he says, rounding to her side.

"Without tourists this island would fall apart in a week."

"Hmmmmm," he says, trailing a lazy fingertip from the point of her shoulder down to the delicate spot on her wrist. Her pulse quickens; blood leaps to the surface. *Beautiful,* he thinks. *I can trace the veins by her heartbeat.*

Like wax on a surfboard, he eases his body behind her and rests his fingers lightly on her shoulders. Despite her words, she doesn't swim well, and he wants her relaxed, not struggling to stay at the surface.

"First time?" Kalei asks.

She flinches. "What?"

"In the islands."

"Oh. Yeah," she says, turning and pulling away. "First, but not last. I'll be back next month."

"Another Hawaiian vacation? Lucky." He cocks his head. "Or spoiled. Trust fund baby?"

She laughs. "I wish. I'm a senior location scout for Miramax. We're in pre-production." She lifts her chin and looks down her nose, waiting for the obligatory star-struck moment.

Kalei says nothing.

A little miffed, she fills in the blanks herself. "I can't tell you the title or the director, so don't even ask. It's all hush-hush. I've been here a week, hiking from one mosquito hell to another."

"Hiking? Whatever for?"

She splashes a perfect arc of blue stars. "Like you don't know what a location scout does!" When he doesn't laugh, she hesitates. "Wait. You really don't?"

Kalei shrugs.

"Miramax? The movie company?" she says. "*Working Girls; Kill Bill; Don't Be Afraid of the Dark; Sex, Lies, and Videotape?*"

He tilts his head to the side. *She really is lovely.*

She narrows her eyes at him. "You've seen those movies, right?"

"I've heard of them. I don't get out to theaters much," he says.

"Unbelievable. I keep forgetting this isn't L.A. You Hawaiians spend all of your time at the beach."

"Only when the urge strikes. You Angelinos have beaches, too. But as you said, you prefer movies. Easier to control the story."

She bites her lip. "I'm not a writer or director," she says. "It's my job to find the right place for the story to happen. It's not up to me to tell it." Tossing her head, she turns and regards the moon.

Jerk, she fumes. *'Come swim with me in the moonlight, and I'll show you real Hawaiian magic.' How did I fall for a line like that? It's straight out of one of Trudy's beach movie marathons. We're in a scene from* Gidget Goes Hawaiian *or* Blue Hawaii. *Next he's going to say he's a real* Soul Surfer!

Leaning forward, her bangs drip ocean into her eyes, but she remembers in time to flutter her lashes like Esther Williams until the salt washes away. No rubbing—no matter what.

He's got to be messing with me. Who doesn't watch movies? She catches his eye and tries not to frown. *He was better looking at the bar,* she realizes. *Out here in the water his smile's too wide; his teeth are too big.*

Who cares if I have raccoon eyes? This saltwater sucks. She gives in and rubs her eyes, kicking harder to stay afloat.

She's off the hook, Kalei thinks. *Time for a new approach.* He circles, considering. "I hate hiking," he says.

She shrugs.

"Hiking through the rainforest is hard work even if you know what you're looking for."

She purses her lips.

"I bet you found it, though," he says, capturing her hand with his. He lays her palm flat against his bare chest. "To be a senior location scout so young you'd have to be really good at it."

"I'm not that young," she snaps.

"What? 25? 26?"

She softens. "You think I'm 25?"

"Only because you have to be at least 25 to rent a car here. And you have all that Miramax responsibility. But you look much younger."

"Now you're flattering me."

"Truth," he says, raising a hand to the sky. "You said you've been hiking. Tell me what you found."

"It wasn't easy."

"Of course not. Anybody can do easy," he says, squeezing her fingers and stroking her wrist.

"It took me a week and a hundred-dollar tip to the guy at the hotel desk, but I found it—it's perfect. There's no hint of civilization in sight—no telephone poles or paved roads—and the tree canopy is straight out of the Amazon."

"Amazon? You were looking for Brazil on O'ahu?"

"Of course! Hawaii's great. All the modern conveniences with a third world vibe. Exotic without the hassle of diseases and currency exchange. Hawaii can be anywhere in the world. Production crews love it."

"Hmmmm," he says, releasing her hand.

As she drones, Kalei's attention wanders. *There's nothing better than being in the ocean as the moon slips into the sea and the lights on shore wink out,* he thinks. *When the sky and water are the same inky black, impossible is effortless.*

"It's all good," she says, laboring a little in the water. "I've got three of my four locations under contract," she says. "All but the murder scene."

His attention snaps. "Murder scene?"

"Don't worry," she says, "It's a revenge story with a twist, not a boring whodunit or a slasher flick. We'll shoot most of it on sound stages in L.A."

"But you don't have the murder location. Maybe I can help."

She brushes his cheek. "You're sweet, but this afternoon I found what I was looking for. The only problem is getting the permit."

"Pink malasada boxes," he says.

"What?" She laughs. "Mala—what?"

He shakes his head. "Nothing. Just a saying: if you want something done, bring a box of malasadas—they're like doughnuts, but better—to the secretary or clerk of the guy who signs the permits. Any permit."

"Business 101," she says. "I thought I'd greased the local wheels, but when I called to register my murder scene's location, Marie—that's my contact at the Honolulu film commission—Marie Wong? Wang? Something like that—Marie Whatevers, my new best happy hour friend all last week—she stiffed me over the final location permit because of a pile of rocks."

She kicks harder, rising a little in the sea.

"That doesn't make sense," Kalei says. "Films bring a lot of money and tourists here."

"I know, right? Who holds up a multimillion-dollar film over a heap of moldy lava that some old guy claims is sacred?"

"Sacred?"

She feels him twitch; his movement sends a signal through the water to her brain. Something niggles for her attention, tugging her subconscious. *Catholic school guilt*, she thinks. *Like Trudy says, I have to let go. But don't think about Trudy now.* She waves her hand, banishing that train of thought.

"Who said sacred?" he repeats.

"Some cultural advisor claimed the area was an ancient Hawaiian hey-ow temple." She rolls her eyes. "But it's only a pile of loose rocks. It's not like it's Chichén Itzá or the Great Wall of China." She kneads the water faster.

She swims like she's churning butter, he thinks, drifting away to give himself room to breathe. No matter how tantalizingly she splashes, the confession must come first. "A *heiau* temple? Around here?"

"Next valley over. Maybe two. I dunno; I can't keep anything straight. Not even the locals know which direction is north."

"*Mauka* and *makai* are easier," he says.

"That doesn't even make sense. Nothing islanders say about the land sense. That's why I rely on GPS and survey maps."

Kalei blinks. "What are you talking about?"

She bristles. "Get this: after Marie Whatevers tells me no, I try to explain that I've been all over the island. There's no place else like this perfect spot—it's crucial to the film. Right in the middle of my explanation, she hands the phone to the cultural advisor who just cuts me off. He demands to know where I am. I read him the GPS coordinates, and he announces that I'm trespassing."

"Trespassing?" Kalei asks. "He used that word?"

"Yes! I say the GPS and survey maps say it's public land. Fair game. He says it's not, and I have to leave. Now. Like I'm some child he can boss."

"But he can't," Kalei says.

"Hell, no. I tell him it's not posted no trespassing, and he says to look for a sign saying kah-pooh, k-a-p-u. I'm standing under it. Kah-pooh means no trespassing. Why don't these people just say what they mean instead of being all wink-wink with the Hawaiian? It's still America, damn it."

"That's rough." He cups a hand and strokes, pulling his body through the water to circle behind her.

This time she doesn't turn with him and keeps her eyes on the last sliver of moonlight. She leans back in the water, shaking her hands and sending blue plankton twinkling from her fingertips like the Fourth of July. "Superstitions." She slaps at the water. "It's all a game. When enough green shows up, the spirits change their minds. I've seen it a million times."

"Green?"

"C'mon, this ain't my first rodeo."

"Senior location scout," he says.

"I'll get the permits. We'll shoot there. I just need to figure out which native support group gets the generous donation."

"That's frustrating."

"Don't worry; it's built into the budget. It's not like it's coming out of my pocket."

Time to calm, he thinks. *All this agitation leaves nothing to savor.*

With one finger he lightly brushes her shoulder. When she doesn't move away, he rests his palms; when she sighs, he begins massaging, rolling her muscles in slow circles under his thumbs.

She closes her eyes, thinking back. *At the bar in his ratty aloha shirt and swim trunks, he probably couldn't afford to buy me a drink. That's why he wanted to go to the beach. He wanted the fun without buying the rum.* She lifts a shoulder, and he obliges by digging deeper. *He's got blue collar hands. Rough. They're better than loofah at scratching an itch.*

Trudy won't understand. She'll be jealous if she finds out. Meal ticket, she'll say; he's hoping you'll be his sugar mama. But the joke's on him if he thinks I'm good for more than breakfast in the morning.

As her breathing slows, he gentles the massage. His hands rasp lightly, just enough to warm and pink her tender skin. "Securing the perfect spot for your murder scene shouldn't be this hard," he says. "You're too tense."

She shrugs. "Par for the course. It's all about money and control." Stretching her neck, she swivels her head like a hula dancer's hips. "Ummm," she says. "Feels good."

"It's supposed to."

"I'm glad I let you talk me into going for a midnight swim. So much better than that sorry excuse for a bar. I feel like I can be myself out here," she said.

"Me, too."

"That bar! What's it called?"

"Hari's"

"That's it. Hari's, with an i. Can't believe I even walked into that place, let alone used the restroom."

"The TV's nice."

"The bar is missing an entire wall! It's open to rain, rats, roaches; I don't even want to think about what crawls over the tables. Who eats in a place like that?"

"Locals," he says. "Who else?"

Oh-oh, she thinks. *I've offended him. Time to play nice.* She reaches back to touch him, but he slides away again, curving to her side. Fighting the undertow, her hands flutter in the water like a bird with a broken wing.

For a beat he watches her struggle, amused.

Water is so foreign to her, he thinks. *She needs to just let go. You can't make a wave change its course.* He reaches out and steadies her.

"Thanks," she says, clinging to his arm.

"No problem."

She clears her throat. "I can see why some people like the open wall. It's breezy, quaint. Definitely gives the bar an authentic *Gilligan's Island* feel. Do you go to Hari's often?"

"Not really. I don't have many friends there."

"You don't?"

He smiles.

Braces, she thinks. *He could really use some. Why didn't I notice his snaggle teeth before?*

"I don't have a lot in common with the people who live in Lauele now. I'm more of an old fashioned guy."

"I knew it!" She beams. "You have that real, what's it called—oh! It's on the hotel brochure—"

"Brochure?"

"Don't tell me; it's on the tip of my tongue! Aloha—"

"Aloha? Are you going somewhere?" he teases.

"Ah, spirit! Aloha spirit."

"I have a real aloha spirit? You can sense that?"

"Yeah. It shines in your eyes." *Better,* she thinks, but she knows she's fooling no one, not even herself; they've both read this script long ago. She cuddles closer, her body warming the ocean between them.

"My aloha spirit," Kalei says. "No one's noticed before."

"How could they if you're always lurking in the shadows? You were sitting at a table practically hidden in the jungle. The light from the bar didn't even touch it. If I hadn't been coming from that horror of a restroom, I would have missed it completely."

"It's my usual table," he says, a little off-script. "When I'm in town, I sit there."

"Whatever for?"

"Out there people leave me alone. And it has a great view of the TV."

"But when I saw you, you weren't watching the TV." She tilts her head, coy in the water, determined to get them back on track.

"No," he says.

"You were watching me."

"Yes."

"It's my long, red hair, right?" She touches it. "All the island boys love it. So different from what they're used to."

He arches an eyebrow. "There is something special about you, something that attracted me to you, but it's not your hair."

"Oh?" she wavers. He's off-script again. She has no idea where this ship is sailing.

"That specialness is the reason I asked if you'd join me in a swim. It calls to me."

Reassured, she smiles. "Now you're feeding me a line. I won't take the bait."

Kalei shakes his head. "No line. It's true. Tonight I only have eyes for you."

"That's so romantic." She unspools the love scene in her mind. *Will it be* From Here to Eternity *or* Blue Lagoon? she wonders. *Damn. We don't have a beach mat. Sand could be a problem.*

"I really am here just for you," he insists.

"I can tell."

In the water? I've never done that, she thinks. She splashes him, sending more blue embers into the night. He doesn't duck away, but lets them rain down on his head. Touching her cheek, he brings her eyes to his, the perfect Tom Cruise moment.

"Good," he says. "I want you to remember, to believe, that tonight I'm here for you. Only you."

She swallows. "You said that before."

"I mean it." He squeezes her hand as the last lights on shore blink out. The darkness gathers and nestles close, the stars blazing like diamonds against black velvet.

"Mean what?" she whispers.

"Let me show you."

Ocean slick, Kalei eases around her body, coming to rest behind her. As she bobs in the current, he gently rolls his thumbs in the tight spot where her neck joins her shoulders, easing away the tension.

"I'm sorry for your troubles," Kalei murmurs.

She barks, her laughter shattering the moment.

"Don't be. Back in L.A., I'll dine out for a month on this story. I even picked up a small souvenir from that heap of stones to use for show and tell."

"A rock? You took a rock from the *heiau*?"

"Just a little one from the top of a pile. No one's gonna miss it," she says.

"The rock," he persists. "Where is it?"

"Relax. It's in my pocket on the beach. I'll show you; you'll love it; it's covered in moss like some ancient relic from a movie set. So *Indiana Jones*."

"I feel like I know it already," he says. "It's small and round like a perfect lichen-covered golf ball."

"Exactly!"

"It fit into your pocket. That's why you took it. Simple to show off."

"See, you get it."

"I do," Kalei says. "Completely."

"The islands need more people like you. If you were in charge, I'd have my film permit!"

"I'm not a cultural advisor. Those things aren't up to me." He pinches harder, grinding her skin against her bones.

She exhales, releasing stress in one long breath.

That's more like it, he thinks. *Just relax. It will all be over soon.*

"There's some good in all this," she says. "If the cultural advisor hadn't threatened to call the cops and report me for trespassing, and if I hadn't been desperate for a restroom, I never would have stopped at that bar. I'd be back in my hotel room in Waikiki. I wouldn't have met you, and we wouldn't be here now."

"You're right. I don't get to Waikiki often. Too many tourists."

He presses his palms down into the meat of her shoulders and uses his fingers to tap a rhythm along the ridge, calling the blood to the surface and sending tingles down her spine. Her breath swells in her chest as she melts into his touch, the last of her anxiety slipping away.

I deserve this, she thinks. *I will not allow myself to feel guilty.*

"Let go," he says. "Let me do all the work." He cradles her head, rocking it from side to side, loosening the joints and sinews. The water laps over her collarbones, brushing her chin.

"You know what this is?" she asks.

He leans close, his breath tickling her ear. "I know exactly what this is," he whispers. Moving deftly, his hands work their magic deep into tissue and fiber along her spine, soothing away her concerns.

"You should know I can't promise you a part in the film. A little Hawaiian holiday, that's all this is. I'm headed back to L.A. and my girlfriend in the morning."

"Lie back," he says, placing one hand in the small of her back, the other supporting the nape of her neck. "I want to see all of you."

She sighs and brings her toes to the surface, floating. Baring her face to the sky, her breasts and hips are islands in the sea, her hair a coral fan of red and gold in the starlight.

"You are truly lovely," he says.

"You're not so bad yourself."

"Look at you. So luscious in the water, full and ripe and sweet." He smiles without showing his teeth.

"Flattery will get you everywhere," she giggles. "Want a bite?"

"I thought you'd never ask."

She senses him slip under the water, gently sliding his hands away as her toes dip below the surface, her body settling upright. His tug on her ankle is first, just a little lover's nip sparking a shiver of anticipation.

In the water, then, she thinks. *It's the perfect location for our happy ending.* Lolling her head back, she floats, closing her eyes, holding her breath for his next caress.

His skin, rough and cold, his beard perhaps, she isn't sure, chafes along her thigh. A nuzzle, a nibble, then sudden warmth floods, sending dark red blossoms rising around her in the sea.

Confused and off balance when she tries to kick, she opens her eyes and throws her arms wide, blue sparks shedding from her fingertips, the only sound the blood pounding in her ears when she recognizes the impossible: a dorsal fin behind the lei of shark teeth lovingly embracing her neck.

"It's GOT to be over here, 'Ilima. Poor thing's been calling all night."

Old man Kahana and 'Ilima, his four-legged companion, pick their way down through the bushes to the beach. In the predawn light, Kahana pauses to survey the scene: women's clothes piled above the tide line, no beach mat, and two sets of prints disappearing into the water, one dainty, the other larger and missing part of a toe. Farther down the beach the larger prints return, heading toward Piko Point.

Kahana shakes his head and rubs his whiskery chin.

Auwē, he thinks. *Last night Kalei came to Hari's, but not to watch TV. He was hunting. All 'Ilima and I can do now is try to make things as pono as possible. How I don't know. Making this right is not going to be easy.*

He eyes the lump in the pocket of the shorts and grimaces. *It's in there,* he thinks. *I need to get it out, but I'm not doing this alone.*

Raising his arms above his head and facing the sea, he chants a short prayer asking the gods and ancestors for their forgiveness and protection.

Satisfied he has their attention and approval, he wiggles his fingers into the pocket and pulls out the small lava rock whose terrified calls kept him awake all night. Turning it in his fingers, he notes which sides are mossy and which are plain so he'll know exactly how to replace it later on the *heiau's* altar. In safe hands, the rock promptly goes to sleep. It's been a long night.

From the beach, Kahana glances back across the street toward Hari's, scanning the parking lot. He easily spots the new white Avis rental next to Mrs. Espinoza's orange pinto.

Bingo.

'Ilima whines as she paces, looking out to sea.

"It's okay, 'Ilima. Kalei's gone. We'll take proper care of the stone. Kalei won't have a reason to come back," Kahana says.

'Ilima turns and noses through the woman's clothes, uncovering a leather purse.

"Good thinking. We're going to need to take care of that." Kahana opens the purse and takes out the wallet. He flips through the credit cards and stops at the driver's license. "From California. Pretty. Whatchu think?" Kahana holds out the card.

'Ilima chuffs.

"Nah, she's not sick. All the L.A. girls want to be that thin."

'Ilima lifts a brow and tilts an ear.

"Old? No, thirty-six is not too old for tank tops!"

'Ilima snorts.

"You're just jealous." Kahana thinks for a moment. "We better take the credit cards and shred them. I don't want somebody finding them and running up a big bill. We'll leave the ID for the cops to find, though. Wow, there's a lot of cash."

'Ilima yips.

"You're right, waste not, want not," Kahana says, pocketing the bills. He scrambles through the crumpled tissues, hair ties, and lipstick, digging through the purse for the rental car's keys. "We'll leave the rest in the car in Waikīkī. Won't take long for somebody to find it, especially if we park it in a handicap spot. It's an easy bus ride back to Lauele, but that means you gotta fake service dog again."

'Ilima licks her nose and pouts.

"Only on the bus, I promise. You can wear your pretty pink leash and collar with the bling. Sharp, that. I'll wear the extra dark glasses and stumble a little. It'll be fun. We'll make a day of it. *Heiau* first, drop the car in Waikīkī, bus, home." He pats his pocket. "We even have lunch money."

'Ilima perks her ears and wags her tail.

Stooping, Kahana rolls everything into a bundle, then plows his feet through the sand, erasing all traces. As the sun rises over the mountains, 'Ilima prances along the shore break, dodging waves and smudging the last of Kalei's footprints.

Kahana stands for a moment at the water's edge, looking out to sea.

"Tourists," he sighs.

BRIDGES

Sister Morgan's eyes glistened as Tomás bore his testimony. The Spirit confirmed what the sister missionaries hoped: Tomás was *ready*. The witness was so strong, so sure, that Sister Morgan gave up trying not to blink and let the tears roll down her cheeks. These were the moments she prayed for when she left Montana for the front porch of a modest home in Pueblo Árido, Chile.

Sister Hernández, the senior companion, beamed. "Yes! Christ makes all the difference. Thanks for sharing that. Oh, Tomás! We're so happy for you. When can we schedule your baptismal interview with the district leaders?"

Tomás' face fell. The sisters exchanged a look.

"Tomás?" Sister Morgan asked. "It everything all right?"

A small Chilean man in his mid-forties, Tomás Maximiliano Silva swallowed hard. "The elders?"

Sister Hernández smiled assuringly. "Yes. It's nothing to worry about. Just tell them what you told us. The Spirit will be there, too."

Seated on the porch steps between the sisters, Tomás wiped his eyes. The sisters exchanged another look. Sister Morgan shrugged. Sister Hernández gently asked, "Is there something you haven't told us?" Sister Morgan held her breath.

Tomás met their eyes, a ghost of fear and sadness haunting his face. "I've talked with elders before."

"You has?"

Sister Hernández winced. "Have, Sister Morgan. You *have*, not you *has*."

"Ah. Thank you. Your help makes my Spanish strongest."

With great restraint, Sister Hernández didn't roll her eyes. A native speaker from Hermosillo, México, her rapid-fire Spanish and vague distain for soft Americans could be...*challenging*. Transfers weren't for another month.

Not that anyone was counting.

Sister Hernández turned to Tomás. "You've spoken with elders about *baptism*?"

"Yes, many times."

Sister Hernández flipped through her book. "When, Tomás? We don't have a record of that."

"The last? About four years ago, in Santiago. My brother Paulo and I went to church there for a year, but...." He shrugged.

Sister Hernández closed her book and leaned against a post. "When we knocked on your door—"

"I knew who you were. I've read the Book of Mormon many times, met with dozens of missionaries, but you are the first sisters."

Sister Hernández glanced at Sister Morgan. "We should've known."

"Golden," Sister Morgan muttered. "They exist."

Sister Hernández bit her tongue, counted to three, and said, "Tomás, why didn't you tell us this before?"

"Every time I wanted to be baptized, the elders said no. I thought sisters might be different."

"But the gospel's the same."

He closed his eyes. "Sisters are softer."

"Softer?"

"Humbler. More accepting. I hoped you'd see how much I want to be baptized and have compassion for my situation."

Sister Morgan shifted in her seat. "Situation? What sit—"

Sister Hernández cut her off. "Tomás, you don't have to—"

"I'm allergic to water," he said.

Sister Hernández blinked, then burst out laughing. "Oh, Tomás!" she whooped, "You're such a tease. I was actually worried for a second."

Sister Morgan leaned forward. "Excuse me, what does *allergic* mean?"

This time Sister Hernández rolled her eyes. "Ah, poor Sister Morgan; she doesn't get it!"

"What is *allergic*?" Sister Morgan hissed.

Sister Hernández waved her hand. "A joke. Too complicated to explain."

Tomás got up and went into the house.

"Sister," growled Sister Morgan, "whatever *allergic* is, it's not a joke to Tomás."

"He's kidding!"

"No. I saw his face. Whatever it is, it's serious."

As Sister Morgan glared, Sister Hernández paused, reconsidering. Quickly, she repented, calling, "Tomás! I'm sorry. If going underwater is scary, we can help. The water isn't deep, and you're only under for—oh."

Tomás reappeared holding a glass of water in a kitchen-gloved hand. "This is allergic," he said, pouring water on bare skin.

"OH MY FREAKIN' HELL," shouted Sister Morgan, leaping to her feet.

Tomás' wet hand sizzled, blistered, and hissed. Healthy brown skin sloughed off to reveal rough grey scales, iridescent and shiny in the sun. Tomás quickly brushed his hand against his pants, stopping further damage. He held out his hand.

"Tomás," breathed Sister Hernández. "Oh, Tomás!"

He spoke matter-of-factly. "Everyone in my family has the same reaction when water touches our skin."

Sister Morgan crept back. "Does it hurt?"

"A little."

"You mean a lot!"

He shrugged. "You get used to it. See? It's already starting to heal." Sister Hernández took the glass of water from him and sniffed. "It's plain water," he said, slipping off the glove and stuffing it into his pocket.

Cautiously, she tipped a bit into her palm. When nothing happened, she dumped the rest onto the dirt. "It *is* just water," she said. "But Tomás, the elders were right. For you, baptism is death."

Tomás' shoulders slumped, defeated. "I understand. Baptism's not for me."

"Hold on," said Sister Morgan. "We all felt the Spirit. Christ is for everyone, right? Membership is for everyone. Baptism is for everyone."

Sister Hernández shook her head. "No, it's not. Some people—"

"Not Tomás! He knows right from wrong. He's repented. His life's in song—"

"Harmony," sighed Sister Hernández.

"Harmony! Harmony with God and the gospel," Sister Morgan continued undaunted. "We can't just assume it's impossible."

"But the elders said no to Tomás' baptism many times," Sister Hernández said. He nodded. She pointed to his hand. "I'm sorry, Tomás. I don't see a way to bridge this gap."

Sister Morgan ground her teeth. "What is *bridge*?"

Tomás said, "A bridge connects two things over an obstacle, like two towns across a river."

"A bridge over water, that's it!" Sister Morgan turned to her companion. "Sister, God prepares a way for all his children. He knows and loves Tomás. The Spirit witnessed we're here at *this moment* for a reason. I think God expects us to find the bridge connecting Tomás to the church."

"God's bridge?"

"Yeah. It exists. I'm sure of it."

"But we're just Sisters. Why—"

"We're *missionaries*. Christ's hands."

Sister Hernández regarded the mud puddle at the bottom of the stairs. "Tomás, how do you bathe?"

"Coconut oil and sugar. I scrub my skin and wipe it off."

"A barrel of oil? Would that work?" Sister Morgan asked.

Sister Hernández wrinkled her nose. "Two men in one barrel?"

Sister Morgan snickered. "Not if one of them is Elder—"

"Sister!"

"C'mon, you were thinking it, too."

"Regardless, oil isn't water," Sister Hernández sniffed.

"Something else, then." Sister Morgan snapped her fingers. "Tomás, what do you drink?"

"Bilz. Pap. Mote con huesillo. Leche con plátano. I don't know why, but sugary liquids don't blister or burn."

"We could fill a font with apple juice, maybe," Sister Morgan mused. "Easier than oil."

"Juice isn't water."

Sister Morgan shrugged. "People get baptized in ponds, rivers, the ocean. Juice has as much water as those kinds of places."

"Juice is *sticky*," Sister Hernández said with a shudder.

"I used to drink coffee," Tomás said. "That's not sticky."

"But it stains," said Sister Morgan. "Can you imagine? A coffee ring around the font?"

"Yeah," Sister Hernández muttered. "We're not going there."

Nervously twisting her CTR ring, Sister Morgan spotted the glove peeking out of Tomás' pocket. "Does the water have to touch him?"

Sister Hernández snorted. "It's a baptism by *immersion*, Sister."

"But what if we put him in—*you know*—clothes that keep water away when people go under the sea—"

"A *dry suit*?" Sister Hernández raised an eyebrow.

"Yeah, what if Tomás wore a dry suit in the baptismal font? Plenty of room. Not sticky. No stains."

"But how will my sins wash away if water doesn't touch my skin?" Tomás asked.

Sister Hernández closed her eyes. Dreamily, she said, "Christ had no sins to wash away. Baptism's a witness, a covenant with God. It's faith in Christ and his atonement that washes away sin, not water."

"Do they make white dry suits?" said Sister Morgan.

Sister Hernández flicked her wrist. "Unimportant. Christ didn't wear white." She bit her lip. "At least I don't think so." She nodded. "I think we found Tomás' bridge."

"Sisters," Tomás whispered, "baptism's possible, even for someone like me?"

Sister Morgan's tears spilled again.

"Yes, Tomás," said Sister Hernández. "We don't know how, exactly, but we're sure there's a way for you to be baptized. God has not forgotten you. He built a bridge to His church for you. We just need to work out the details with President Baird—and the elders."

Tomás bowed his head. "Oh, Sisters! You are God's answer to my prayers!"

As they were leaving, Sister Hernández turned back. "Your brother."

"Paulo. In Santiago."

"Would he come to your baptism?"

"Maybe. If I asked."

"Paulo attended church with you!" Sister Morgan gasped. "We should send missionaries!"

"I—"

Sister Morgan gushed. "This is perfect! Paulo's not baptized?"

"No, but—"

"We found your family's water-bridge! Like you, Paulo can be baptized."

"No, Sister," Tomás sighed. "Paulo married José. That's a bridge too far."

"Oh," said Sister Morgan. "But there's always a bridge. Where have you looked?"

HAWAIIAN ON THE INSIDE

(AN ESSAY)

I was walking through Dick's Sporting Goods in Salt Lake City, Utah when I saw it hanging on the back wall: a ski jacket with the same electric bird of paradise print my tutu had on her couch in the '70s. It called to me like poke with a side of poi.

My teen daughter was appalled. "You are NOT wearing that, Mom. Don't even try it on."

I put it on.

"See, it's reversible," I said. "Plain brown on one side and bright Hawaiian print on the other."

"No. Just no, Mom."

"I like the print side out."

"Mom!"

My husband shrugged. "At least we'll be able to find Mom in a crowd."

I bought it.

And I wore it. For about a week it clashed with everything and everyone, as out of place as an aloha shirt at—well, a ski slope. When you're an ex-pat Hawaiian living in Utah, it can be hard to find the aloha sprit in January. It didn't help that my daughter is a serious winter athlete. At her competitions, I was running around dressed in prints more suited for Waikiki than a winter Olympic park. It made her uncomfortable in that teenage *yeah, that's my mom, she's not from around here* kind of way.

I tried not to care. I ignored the stares and snickers and carried my childhood wrapped around me like a blanket. But one day I caved and reversed it.

"What's up with your coat?" my son asked.

"It's like me. I'm wearing my Hawaiian on my inside."

He tilted his head. "Yeah, but unlike your coat, you're not even brown on the outside."

Ouch.

Through a genetic quirk my youngest sister and I inherited our mother's super fair northern European coloring while my other sister and brother have our father's mixed Hawaiian heritage of medium brown hair, eyes, and skin.

I'm not going to lie to you. As the only blond, blue-eyed kid in the entire school district in Kahului, Maui, it was rough. No one, not even a teacher or librarian looked like me. Unlike every other Hawaiian family I've known, my dad was an only child—and from Oahu. I didn't have a huge *'ohana* of cousins calabash or otherwise on Maui to vouch for me. It was easy to be the target from the teachers and principal on down.

No lie. People go to jail now for what they did to me in elementary school. But Maui was a different time and place back then. At least I like to think so.

There's a disconnect that happens in your head when you're beaten for being an outsider by kids who are descendants of sugarcane and pineapple workers from Asia when your ancestors farmed taro in those same fields for hundreds of years. But on the playground, nobody cares about those kinds of distinctions. It's all about freckles and the need for sunscreen.

For a year or two around second grade, while waiting for my mom to get off work, I went to a house afterschool where the father carved traditional *ki'i*—tiki statues—and the grandmother spoke beautiful Hawaiian with her friends under the shade of mango trees. They were patient with me—the gangly *haole* girl who watched with big eyes and listen to the melodious voices rolling like water over her head. Sometimes they would tell me stories about Hawaiian history, culture, legends, and traditions. I soaked them up like a sponge.

After my family moved back to Oahu, I was accepted into The Kamehameha Schools, a private school for native Hawaiians, and that changed my life. I didn't have to fight so hard to belong because everyone knew I wouldn't be there if I didn't. At Kamehameha I learned more about what it means to be a modern Hawaiian, and like my classmates, promised to perpetuate our culture in positive ways. Our princess Bernice Pauahi Bishop had given us the precious gift of an education; we therefore have an obligation to be her hands and pass aloha along.

I write The Niuhi Shark Saga and other stories for island kids who never see themselves or their families in popular literature. So much about Hawai'i has been rewritten or completely fabricated by Hollywood that even islanders get confused. There is a need for authentic Pasifika voices to tell our stories, and I hope to add to the conversation in my small way.

When people read the words, they hear a Hawaiian voice. But when I show up at a book signing or appearance that disconnect happens again. "You're Lehua? A Kamehameha grad? No way!" I don't think anyone ever gets used to being called a liar within the first few minutes of meeting a stranger, but I smile and roll with it. I've thought about putting my dark-haired sister's photo on the back of my books and sending her to out into the world as Lehua, but I know that wouldn't be *pono*. And for a Hawaiian, living a life that's *pono*—a life in harmony with what is good, noble, and true in thought, action, and deed—is our deepest aspiration.

Like many of my classmates, I went to the mainland for college and stayed to raise a family—a family of towheads like me with looooong Hawaiian middle names. And I worry about that.

Every year I grind my teeth when the local grocery store hosts its Hawaiian days with samba music from Brazil, masks from Papua New Guinea, paper flowers from India, and calls anything with pineapple Hawaiian. In the summer, neighbors are keen to throw luaus where they wear cellophane grass skirts, fake coconut bras, and serve Hawaiian haystacks—a truly vile concoction of shredded chicken, raw veggies, coconut chips, long-grained rice, and Campbell's cream of chicken soup. About the time they bring out the limbo stick and form a conga line is when I sneak home. I know I should be more gracious, but it's hard.

I insist my kids call flip-flops *slippahs*, snow cones *shave ice*, and understand that true aloha comes from within. I wonder if I'm going to be the last generation in my family that remembers how Maui captured the sun, when the *makahiki* season starts, and why *hāloa* is the staff of life. But then I hear about how my son called out his AP World Geography teacher about comments he found derogatory and inappropriate about Polynesians—and insisted on an apology. When the teacher balked and called him a poser, my son told his teacher to look at his middle name and offered to have his mother come in and explain real Hawaiian history to the class.

Pono.

Maybe I won't be the last after all.

RED

With each bump, the puppy's head lolls in the wagon bed, one ear limp and the other bloody. Jammed between a carpenter's box and coils of pulleys and ropes, Elise studies it in the fading afternoon light.

Dead, she thinks, remembering how Highway Man casually twisted the dog's neck and tossed it in the back next to her. She dry swallows around the gag, the taste of axle grease and lye soap tickling the back of her throat. With the calico scrap riding like a bit in her mouth, it's hard to breathe through her swollen nose.

Don't upchuck, she prays. *Highway Man says if I upchuck, I'm dead.*

It's hot the back of the horse-drawn wagon, but the puppy doesn't smell like death, just like iron nails in a blacksmith's pocket. Elise takes shallow breaths and shifts her weight off the sore spot on her hip. The wagon slows and takes a hard right.

We're headed toward the old sheep camps above Deer Creek, she thinks.

Her guts grip.

No one will hear the screams.

THE PUPPY WAS A NICE TOUCH.

Walking alone along River Road in the waning afternoon light and carrying a satchel, twelve-year-old Elise's thoughts flittered like a mountain chickadee, bright with excitement and expectation. Tonight was her first Harvest Moon, and her eyes scanned the meadow for deer. She didn't think anything of the weathered buckboard and horses standing in the shade until a flash of yellow caught her eye. A Labrador puppy with a bright green bow around his neck scampered over the side rails and down beneath the wheels.

From behind a tree a man called, "Chester! Chester! Come back, you naughty dog. Hey! Sweetheart! Yes, you! Thank goodness, you're here. Help me, please! Don't let him get away."

Elise sprinted, her feet slapping against the ruts in the dirt road, knees pumping high and hard, her lucky red cloak billowing out like a sail.

"Here, Chester," she said, dropping her satchel and bending down. The puppy crawled out, pushing his eager nose against her, tail wagging. "You're not naughty, just playful," Elise laughed. "Hey, Mister, I got your dog," she said to the black boots rounding the wagon.

She tipped her head back, her eyes sweeping from the worn boots to the canvas pants and no-nonsense workman's belt to the homespun shirt, all the way to the bandana covering his face. *But it's not dusty,* she thought just before his fist landed in her face.

Stunned, she rocked back between wagon wheel ruts, deep grooves in the hard-packed dirt that cradled her pain while the puppy licked her cheek, her bleeding nose, her swelling lips.

"All the better to kiss you with, my dear," purred a new voice in her head.

"Don't, Elise!" shouted her mother's voice from deep within. *"He's just a common Highway Man. A kidnapper and a thief. It's not what you think. Scream. Fight. Yell. Don't let him take you."*

But when Elise opened her mouth to scream, fight, yell, Highway Man kicked her in the gut.

Lying in the dirt, all Elise's mouth could do was open and close like a fish on the dock. Air flowed weakly into her lungs as through a crack in a winter-tight door. While she struggled to breathe, the Highway Man moved.

Forcing her wrists together at her stomach, he looped them with a piece of rawhide and cinched tight. "Those earbobs are perfect, Honeybun. I love how them gold hoops shimmer along your throat. Very grown-up." Her hands tied, he reached up and chucked her chin, ignoring the teakettle protests that wheezed past her lips. "But I what I really wonder about is the color of your bloomers." She stilled. He held her eyes. "Cornflower blue, I'm guessing," he mused. "But don't tell me. I'll find out soon enough."

With a magician's flourish, he pulled a scrap of bright yellow calico from his pocket. "Ladies and gentlemen! Nothing up my sleeve! For my first trick, I'm going to make a child disappear." He shook the rag in her face. "Now you, young lady, have the look of a sensible child. I can just gag you if you're sensible. Far less bruising if we do it that way, but I have plenty of rope if'n I need it."

This can't be how I die.

"Well, Cherry Pie, I'm waiting. Are you sensible?" Highway Man stood and drew back his foot for another kick.

Still no air to speak, to yell, to scream. Elise clamped her lips and nodded.

Highway Man's foot stopped mid swing. "Good girl. That's what I figured. Gag and hands only. But keep your guts in order, hear me? If you yak, you'll choke and die. It's happened before. And that's a sad thing for both of us."

Highway Man twirled the calico scrap between his hands like a cowboy's kerchief, then tucked it between her lips, knotting it tightly behind her head. "Bruises are bad," he said. "You're makin' the right choice, Johnnycake."

With his gunslinger's hands he picked her up and half-threw half-dumped her into the wagon like a sack of potatoes. The handle of a shovel bit cruelly into her hip, but she ignored it and scooched like a worm, moving as far from him as possible.

He snickered, shaking his head. "They always do that."

Highway Man scooped up Chester and her satchel, flinging her bag next to her. "Can't leave that lying around now, can we?"

Cradled like a baby in the Highway Man's arms, Chester wiggled, frantic to reach anything a puppy's tongue could love.

"Good boy. But I won't need you any longer now that I've got Angel Cakes to play with."

Ruffling his ears, Highway Man snapped Chester's neck and dropped him boneless to the wagon bed. "That's better, Plum Puddin'. You won't be lonely with Chester to keep you company."

Highway Man swung up to the front and raised the reins. "Hup," he called to the horses. She felt him crack the reins, once, twice. Moving at a ground-eating trot, the horses stepped out from the trees, aligned the wagon's wheels in the ruts, and vanished down the road.

Chester.

Elise screws her eyes tight.

I won't cry, he can't make me cry, not over a silly puppy, but tears spilled anyway. *With his hands on the reins he can't hurt me. I'm okay. I'm getting through this.*

Elise tips her chin, sucking bloody snot back up her nose, swallowing the lump down her throat.

All the better to smell you with, my dear.

Cautiously, she wipes her nose along her sleeve.

Swollen and hot, but not broken. Teeth still tight in their sockets. Bottom lip thick, but not split. Blood on my new cloak, red on red—forget it. Forget about the dog, too. Don't get distracted. Stall. He doesn't know.

An hour passes like kidney stones until the wagon rocks a hard left, turning off the main country road. Her satchel tips.

Oh, no. Please, don't let it roll onto Chester. I'll never use that satchel again.

More twists and turns, and by the sharp scent of the pines Elise knows they've passed all the low-lying meadows and fields.

Into the woods.

Trapped in her winter cloak, sweat beads on her forehead and runs dust and dirt into her eyes. Using the sides of her thumbs, she smears black streaks.

War paint.

SQUIRRELED AWAY in Elise's hope chest, the gold hoops were her grandmère's legacy. She'd never worn them before.

"Earbobs, Elise? Really?" Maman frowned, turning from the stove to serve dinner. "Do you see what your granddaughter's wearing?"

Grandpère caught Elise's eye. "She looks fine," he smiled. "Sophisticated. Like her grandmère."

"Merci, Papi!" said Elise, taking her place at the table.

"It's the truth," he said, kissing her cheek. "I'm so proud of you. It's your Harvest Moon!"

Maman clenched her jaw as she set the meat platter next to the butter. Shaking her head, she said, "She'll lose one in the woods and then what? Some things you can't undo."

"Maman. I'll be careful. Promise."

"Uh-huh. Heard that before."

Elise picked up the serving fork and snatched the biggest steak.

"What big eyes you have," Maman tsked, guiding Elise's hand to Grandpère's plate.

As the steak dropped, Grandpère said, "She's a growing girl."

"Who needs to keep light on her feet."

Grandpère shrugged. "You're right, of course. It's better that way."

"She needs to stay sharp. Earbobs are a distraction."

"My Harvest Moon's tonight," Elise said. "I'm old enough."

Maman snorted and flipped the smallest steak onto Elise's plate. "That's not what I'm worried about."

Elise picked up her fork and prodded the meat. "It's not like I haven't eaten deer my entire life."

"It's different when you hunt it yourself."

Grandpère raised his grizzled head. "She'll be fine."

"Of course I will."

Grandpère slipped a forkful of steak past his lips. "Mmmm. I remember your maman's Harvest Moon." He waved his fork. "Big buck, too."

Elise set down her fork and drank from her cup. "I don't want big; I want tender."

Maman rolled her eyes. "Doesn't matter what you want. You won't choose your Harvest Moon."

"Of course I will. The hunter always chooses."

Maman slipped her serviette onto her lap. "Not your first."

Elise paused, a bite halfway to her mouth. "What?"

"During a Harvest Moon, the prey offers itself. That's why it's called a blessing."

"That's crazy."

"It's tradition."

"You'll see," Grandpère said. "Young, old, big, small—it won't matter. You'll know your blessing when you receive it." He smacked his lips. "You may have eaten deer your entire life, Elise, but this one will be special. Nothing tastes as good as something you brought down yourself."

"I just don't see why I have to do this alone. Why can't you and Maman be there?"

"Tradition," Maman said. "Now eat. Your food is getting cold."

"Ugh. I can't eat now."

Grandpère nodded. "Nerves."

Elise set down her fork and pushed away her plate. "I'm heading out."

Maman glanced out the window. "Now? It's so early!"

Elise stood. "I'll eat later."

"The confidence of youth," Grandpère chuckled.

Maman sighed. "Be mindful of the time."

"Oh, Maman. As if I could forget!" Elise turned from the table and lifted her new cloak from a peg near the door.

Maman rounded the table, reaching for her. "Don't wear that, Elise. The deer will see you from miles away."

"But it's cold in the woods at night," she said, twirling it over her shoulders and fastening the clasp.

Maman clucked her tongue and shook her head, her eyes lingering on the twinkling golden hoops. Sighing, she smoothed Elise's hood flat against her shoulders. "Your first Harvest Moon. My baby's all grown up. Wear your red cloak if you must, but stow it in your satchel. Don't leave it too late. You don't want to ruin it."

"I know, Maman. You've told me a million times."

"And I'll tell you a million more. It's what mothers do." Maman smiled and pressed Elise's cheek. "Good hunting!"

"Bonne chance!" Grandpère called.

"Merci, Papi! I'll get a nice, tender yearling for you." Elise slipped out the door. Through the window they watched as she checked her satchel one last time to make sure she had everything she needed.

Maman sat next to Grandpère and leaned close. "She's really doing this alone?"

"Didn't you?" He smiled and slid Elise's steak onto his plate. "Tradition!"

Elise didn't look back as she strolled down the path to River Road, her red cloak swirling like blood down a drain.

THE LONG SCREECH of a scrub oak branch trails down the side of the wagon as it sways to a stop. Highway Man hops down and starts unhitching the horses. Elise's heart beats faster as she tries to suck in more air around the gag. Her nose is throbbing and too crusty to be much use.

She glimpses the blue of his shirt as he disappears around the side, leading the horses to a nearby stream. The cool evening air seeps in, taking some of Chester's iron and leather smell into the aspens. She hears tuneless humming, then the sound of leaves crackling and wood popping. *Smoke,* she thinks. *Highway Man is building a campfire.*

It doesn't take long for the first fly to come.

She flinches, thinking a bee has come to sting her. She's deathly afraid of bees—any insect that buzzes, really—and this more than anything makes her want to scream. The gag is soggy now; ribbons of blood-salt and lye coat her tongue.

She feels her gorge rise and her stomach heave. *Don't upchuck, don't upchuck, don't upchuck.*

Don't.

Highway Man's head pops over the side of the wagon. He pulls the bandana off his face. "Don't need that anymore," he says. Without the mask, his face goes from outlaw tough to saggy and middle aged, the face of a guy who dry farms forty acres and prays for rain Sundays at church. The mask is better. Ordinary is harder to swallow.

He grabs the shovel. "Going to need that next." Wrinkling his nose, he hooks a finger under Chester's ribbon and slings the dog's body to the ground. Catching her eye, he smiles. "Don't worry about Chester. He's a good dog. He'll keep you company long after I've gone." He jerks his thumb toward the trees. "There's hot chocolate and marshmallows waiting for good girls at the fire. If you come out, I'll take off your gag. You'd like that, right?"

Highway Man waits a beat, then hefts the shovel and turns. "Suit yourself." He strolls back to the campfire, whistling. Soon Elise hears sounds of digging in the trees.

The night deepens. In the underbrush crickets sing love songs in the darkness. More flies come, but preferring Chester near the wagon wheel, they don't settle long next to Elise. The glow from the fire is rosy and homey against the trees. Leaves drift slowly from the aspens, raining yellow and red and pooling in her lap. The mountain air is apple crisp. Elise strains her ears.

Nothing.

I'm leaving.

Elise rolls to her knees. Ignoring the pins and needles shooting through her legs and the dull ache in her hip, she creeps toward the front of the wagon. She inches quietly, thinking of mice and cats and cheese. At the bench where the driver sits, she pauses, stretching her neck and spine tall like a prairie dog. Peering through the gap between the backrest and the wagon seat, she looks toward the firelight.

Facing the wagon are two stumps with rough backs notched with a hatchet. There are sticks with marshmallows leaning against them. A coffee pot warms near the fire.

"Boo!" shouts the Highway Man from behind.

Elise shrieks and hits her head on the backrest. Stars and supernovas collide behind her eyes. She barely keeps from pissing herself when she feels him grab her arm.

"Gotcha!" he chortles. "Bet ya didn't see that one coming." He wraps his arms around her and lifts her over the side and to the ground. She doesn't want to, but she leans against him. When she finds her toes and balance, he releases her and steps back. "What nice hair you have," he says. "So shiny." He sniffs. "Ummm. Smells like lavender, too."

Head down, Elise blinks rapidly. Moving hurts, but she can't let him know that.

"You can't run," he says. "Well, you can, you just won't get far. We're way up in the woods here and there are monsters in the dark. If you run from the fire, they'll get you." He gives her shoulder a nudge toward the fire. "Come. There's chocolate waiting for good girls."

It's better than the wagon, she rationalizes, trying desperately to ignore

Chester's new friends buzz-buzz-buzzing near her feet. After the second step the vertigo eases and she shakes her head to bring her hair forward to hide her face, one earbob swaying gently, the other lost in the darkness. Her eyes scan the campsite and catch a glimpse of the shovel among the aspen trees. She follows the handle down to the ground and discovers it's sticking out of a big pile of dirt.

He's right. He doesn't need the mask anymore.

At the campfire, he plops down on a stump and picks up a marshmallow stick. "The coals have to be just right," he says. "Most things in life work that way. With marshmallows, it just takes a little patience and planning. If you rush, you roast them alive." He jams the end of his stick into the heart of the fire; the marshmallows blaze and blacken. He pulls them out, the end of his stick burning blue and bubbling. He sighs. "Charcoal. Patience was never one of my virtues." He blows them out, then tests with his fingers. "Take off the gag."

Elise waits for the punchline, but it doesn't come.

"Go on now," he encourages, licking white melted crème from his lips, "give 'er a try. Your wrists are tied, not broken. Tug on the end of the knot behind your head. I know you can reach it." He rummages in a sack hidden in the dark and fishes out fresh marshmallows to spear.

Elise slides her hands along the back of her neck and pulls. Like magic the knot disappears. She peels the gag out of her mouth and takes her first full breath in hours.

I could've done that at any time. What else am I missing?

He motions to the log next to him. "Sit. Let's get acquainted." Elise gingerly sits. "Here." He hands her the other marshmallow stick. "Give 'er a whirl. Patience, remember? You look like a patient girl to me."

Elise thrusts the marshmallows into the fire and there's a savage joy that rises within her as she watches them burn.

"Patience, Cream Puff," he says. "You don't want to flame out too soon."

Elise ignores him as the white end of her stick collapses into molten black tar.

Good. No one will ever eat these.

"You can call me Kid," he says. "My own private joke. What's your name, Muffin?"

I have a weapon. I can take my stick and poke Kid in the eye—

"No, you can't," Kid says. Startled, her eyes dart to his. "You're thinking you can use your stick, but you can't. It's too flimsy, and I'm much bigger than you. I'm your only hope. I'm the only one who can keep the demons away."

"Demons?" It's her first spoken word since she found Chester.

Kid nods. "Didn't your mother tell you not to go into the woods alone?" She looks to her lap, hiding again behind her hair. "Thought so. You're much safer here with me by the fire." He pokes at the coffee pot with his foot. "Chocolate?"

"No chocolate," she says. *Chocolate is for good girls.* "Just water."

He snatches the marshmallow stick from her hands, lifts a canteen from behind a log, and sets it in her lap. He tilts his head, then reaches over and twists off the cap, dropping the chain to the side. "What do you say?"

Elise sits dumbfounded. There are too many words in her head to choose.

"What do you say?" he prods. "What's the magic word?"

Abracadabra? Open Sesame?

He leans forward in his seat. She feels energy coil around him, a snake about to strike.

Untie me, you madman? Please? Oh.

"Thank you," she mumbles.

His shoulders slump as he sits back. "That's right. For a minute there I thought you were one of those rude ones who didn't have any manners. But you're not. I can tell your momma taught you proper. What's your name, Gumdrop?"

She stalls by taking a long swig, feeling the blessed coolness brush her tongue, fall down her throat, and land in the pit of her stomach. She means only to sip, but the water washes away the horror of axle grease and snot, and she guzzles most of the canteen.

Kid grunts and wrinkles his nose.

Elise comes up for air and gasps. *I can do this.*

Kid's lips thin in disapproval.

Ladylike. He likes soft, polite, and ladylike.

"Thanks for the water, Mister."

He pushes his feet to the fire and relaxes. "Now I told you to call me Kid. Say it."

"Kid."

"What's your name, Gingersnap?"

"Elise."

"Elise what?"

"Rougarou." She clears her throat and takes a dainty sip. "Elise Rougarou."

"Roooo-gah-rooooh." He rolls the word around his tongue and kisses the last bit with his lips. "Sounds foreign. You one of them emigrants? Russian, maybe?"

She shakes her head. "American."

Kid narrows his eyes. "Don't sound American. Where your people from, Cupcake?"

"Grandpère says France. Before the war." She pulls against the rawhide, hiding the movement with the canteen.

Too tight. Patience.

"Grandpère, huh? Your grandfather, you mean. French." His eyebrow quirks. "I heard me a lot of stories about Frenchies in the war." Kid picks up the coffee pot and fills a mug with rich hot chocolate. "'Course, nothing fit for young girls' ears." He stirs his drink absentmindedly with a finger then licks it clean. "Still, apples don't fall far from trees. I'm gonna have to consider other options. Might not be a cornflower blue girl after all."

He paws through the sack and plops a marshmallow into his drink. "Hot chocolate and marshmallows. Best thing ever." He fills his mouth, swallowing the marshmallow whole. "Well, second best thing."

The horses snort and stamp near the trees. Through the flames Elise spots Grandpère leaning against an aspen. Elise shifts her eyes to Kid, but he's busy with another marshmallow.

Grandpère points to the glow on the mountain ridge, bright against the diamond scattered sky. He holds her eyes until she nods. It's still her Harvest Moon.

With her bound hands Elise tugs on her lucky red cloak and sighs. *No way to take it off. Maman was right. I should've left it home.*

Kid picks up the sack and dumps, piling chocolate bars, jerky, and hard tack onto the ground. When the horses whinny again, Grandpère disappears like smoke.

"French," Kid mutters. "That explains it. The scarlet cloak. Them bright earbobs. Can't help tarting yourself up now, can ya?"

Moonlight rolls down the mountainsides and puddles in the valleys like fog. Energy coalesces. She feels it humming under her skin, swarming around their camp like a hive of angry bees.

"You're too young for earbobs."

No longer afraid, she breathes the bees in. "But I wore them just for you, Kid," she says.

He stills, caught in the moment of unwrapping chocolate. Slowly he drops his hands to his lap, his eyes never leaving her.

"I thought you'd like them, Kid. See how they shine? Don't you like them?"

He breaks off a piece of chocolate and slips it between his teeth. "What, Sugarplum? What are you trying to say?"

"Chocolate's my favorite. Can—I mean, *may* I have a piece?"

Kid tosses the broken bar from his lap and she catches it, bringing it to her lips to nibble. "Thank you, Kid," she says.

"You're welcome, Elise." He polishes off the last of his drink and slides a finger across another candy wrapper, splitting it seam to seam. "You're different from the other girls."

"What girls?"

"You're not crying or begging."

"I can if you want me to."

Kid stands and walks to the woodpile. He lifts a hatchet and chips a few pieces off a log and tosses them into the fire.

"Red," Elise says.

"What?"

"My bloomers. Red. Not blue. Blue is for babies."

He hefts the hatchet in his hands. Elise sees how he likes it when the blade tips forward, eager as ever to bite. With a flick of his wrist he pulls the head back and buries it in a log. Returning to his chair, he contemplates the fire.

"You're a baby," Kid says.

"Not really. I'm small for my age."

"How small?"

Elise shrugs and drops the canteen to her side.

"I picked you, you know."

"I know," she says.

"I watched you walking all by your lonesome. Not home safe eating stew meat and corn bread by firelight, but wandering the River Road in a scarlet cloak, your earbobs shining like fishing lures. Like the others."

"What others?"

"The seven. My special seven. You're eight." He crosses his arms and regards her in the firelight. "But number eight should be special, too, just like the first. I like to be first. First and only is best." He squints. "I think I've misjudged you, Lollipop. I'm not your first."

"I don't know what you're saying."

He nods. "French. Of course you do. The hunter always knows its prey, Apple Dumplin'. You like games."

She draws a lungful of autumn air as the tingle spreads from the pit of her stomach. In her mind she hears Maman's voice. *There's nothing to be afraid of. One quick flash of red in the woods, and it's over. No reason to think twice. All creatures have a purpose and a place. You're just fulfilling yours.*

"Who?" He chucks a woodchip into the fire and watches it flare.

"Who?"

"Are we pretending to be owls, now? Who was your first, Peppermint Stick? Uncle?"

"What?"

"Brother?"

"I don't—" The first pain, sharp and biting, knots her hands and spine. She gasps and looks to the ridgeline. The light of the full moon hits her like a locomotive.

Another chip. "I know," he says to the fire. "Like my Annie. You're a daddy's girl."

"No," she manages. "You've got it all wrong. You're my first." Her bones twist, snapping the rawhide like candy floss. Another deep breath and this time she tastes iron, sweat, and fear. The horses squeal, eyes wide and rolling. Rearing, they break their highline and bolt. She runs her tongue over her too long teeth.

Canines. All the better to eat you with, my dear.

She swings her shaggy head away from the fire, searching for Maman and Grandpère. She howls and two wolves answer. She knows they're there, watching. But this is her Harvest Moon.

A blessing of red in the woods. And no one will hear the screams.

THE CHAMPION

"You're certain there's a maiden up here?" Sir Baskel puffed as he waddled up the thin hunter's trail that switch-backed along the hillside. "It's a long way to come for nothing. If I'd known it was this far, I would've ridden my horse."

Padwit glanced at the sun. *Five minutes,* he thought, *I have to get the lordling in front of the dragon's lair in five minutes or all is lost.* He glanced back at the portly knight in full armor struggling up the wooded rise and shook his head. *We're doomed.*

"Just a bit further, my Lord. We're nearly there," said Padwit.

"Are you sure, boy? And I must insist. A maid and a dragon; it has to be both."

"Yes, my Lord," Padwit called over his shoulder. "There's both. But we must hurry!"

Planting the tip of his sword in the ground, Sir Baskel leaned against it like an old woman on her cane, stretching his aching back. "Tell me about the maid again. She's pretty?"

Padwit scampered back. "Of course, my Lord. It's a standard village-dragon bargain. The maid must be as beautiful as the sun and innocent as the day she was born."

"Uh-huh," said Sir Baskel, picking a bit of beef from his teeth. "So she's blonde?"

"Um—"

Sir Baskel wiped his nose on the lining of his gauntlet and inspected it absently. "You said as beautiful as the sun. Suns are golden."

"I think that's metaphorical, sir. Eye of the beholder, and all that. Some redheads are quite pretty, too. Then there's the miller's wife—a brunette. Some find her fetching." Padwit leaned close. "I've heard the stable boys talk."

"Hmmm. I suppose whatever she is will have to do. How far is she, this maid in need of rescuing?"

"Just over this last rise and through the trees. She's chained between two posts and standing on a stone platform at the mouth of the dragon's lair."

"Chained? Doesn't seem very sporting."

Padwit sighed. "I don't think that's the point, my Lord."

"Let me get this straight." Sir Baskel mopped sweat from his brow with the edge of his cloak. "In exchange for peace, your village elders struck a deal with the dragon S'blath for one unblemished virgin on the night of each new moon."

Faintly beneath their feet the ground trembled.

Four minutes.

Padwit lunged for the knight's arm. "My Lord Baskel, the sun is setting; S'blath awakes. We must hurry!"

Sir Baskel pushed him aside and reached for the wineskin tucked in his belt. He poured a healthy slug down his gullet, then pursed his lips. "Just a common virgin? Not a princess? Not the daughter of a Duke or even a Guild Master?"

Padwit swallowed his impatience. "No, my Lord. All sacrificed or married off years ago. But we must—"

"But your village still has virgins to spare? That's what—twelve or thirteen maidens a year? Your village center is no wider than a grease spot on a mountain trail bookended by a tavern and a well. Tell me, this damsel in distress, does she still suck her thumb?"

Padwit closed his eyes and counted five seconds he didn't have, then simply got behind Sir Baskel and pushed. Hoisting him over the last rocky ledge, Padwit led the knight through the scrub oak to the open glade in front of a large cavern set deep in the hillside. "See for yourself, my Lord."

Sir Baskel's jaw hit his collar guard.

That'll leave a mark, thought Padwit.

Chained and abandoned to her fate, the young woman stood in the last shaft of sunlight, her hair spinning a golden spider-silk halo about her shoulders. The simple white of her gown was stark against the gore-streaked stone beneath her feet. Tapping her foot, head bowed, her outstretched arms were looped through chains tethering her to wooden posts.

"Oh, good," said Sir Baskel, "a blonde. That makes things so much easier."

"Elsbeth!" Padwit called.

Her head snapped up as she glared into the brush. "Cutting it rather fine, Paddy," she barked.

"But Ellie! I brought you a champion!"

Sir Baskel leaned against his sword, a hand on his hip. "That's no virgin, boy. She's the tavern wench. The dragon will know in an instant. No wonder you need me to defeat it."

"That's my sister," Padwit hissed.

Sir Baskel cleared his throat. "No disrespect, boy. But she's not a virgin and not a princess. The deal's off. No ballad's going to come of this."

Elsbeth fluttered her lashes. "Not so, my Lord Champion! Sing it, Paddy!"

"Tah-dah-dum-tah-dah-dum-tah-dah-dum-dum-dum," sang Padwit.

"There it is!" Elsbeth said. "Hear the bard's heroic tale as it rings through your father's hall! It practically writes itself."

"Tah-dah-dum-tah-dah-dum-dum-dum!" Padwit thumped the rhythm against his chest.

"Tah-dah-dum-tah-dah-dum-dum-dum," Elsbeth trilled. "All the courtly ladies swoon as they hear of how your mighty sword was no match against the black dragon S'blath—"

Sir Baskel blinked. "Black? No, I distinctly remember Padwit saying S'blath is a silver dragon."

"Ah, she is," Padwit sputtered.

Sir Baskel stepped back. "She? S'bath is a *girl* dragon?"

"He, she, who can really tell anymore," said Padwit. "Dragons these days! Am I right?"

"I'm not fighting a black she-dragon. That's ridiculous."

"S'blath is a silver dragon with shiny black talons. And definitely male," Padwit affirmed. "Not that there's anything wrong with that."

"But the tavern wench said—"

"Padwit's right! Just her—*his*—*its*—talons are black," Elsbeth called. "Don't listen to me; I'm a little confused right now."

"Because there's no way I want it getting around that I fought a silly black she-dragon for the dubious honor of a maybe maiden. No offense."

"None taken, my Lord," Padwit murmured.

A subterranean moan rose from dragon's lair.

Elsbeth shrieked and yanked her chains. "S'blath awakens! Hurry, my champion! Save me!"

"I don't know about this. It feels sketchy. Not a lot of honor here."

"My Lord," Padwit stammered, "only we three will know for sure what transpires. It's a heroic battle against a ferocious silver he-dragon! A maiden will be saved. You'll have the undying thanks of the village—"

"And me!" shouted Elsbeth.

"How thankful?" Sir Baskel asked, adjusting his braise.

Padwit paled. "My Lord!"

Elsbeth fluttered her eyelashes again and gave her hair a toss. "Very thankful, very grateful, my Lord. I'll prove it."

The ground trembled. Small rocks rolled down the hillside, a shower of gravel, stone, and dust.

"My Lord!" Padwit slipped behind Sir Baskel and pushed. "There's no time! You must step up and meet the dragon!"

"Right," Sir Baskel said, hitching up his sword and striding to the entrance. "I'm on it."

A deep-throated sizzle rumbled as a thin trail of steam wafted from the cavern's maw. *Less than a minute,* Padwit thought. The sizzle rolled into a humid roar, scattering twigs and leaves into the air.

Sir Baskel held his cloak to his nose. "Ugh! Dragon farts! Worse than rotten eggs!"

"That's the dragon's breath, my Lord!" shouted Padwit. "It's time to fulfill your destiny! Step to the mouth of the lair and hold your sword high! Finish S'blath off with one quick stroke before her—*his*—wings are free!"

"Wings?" Sir Baskel turned his back to the cave and started walking toward Padwit. "You didn't say anything about wings! At the tavern, you said a noble deed worthy of a ballad."

The rock crashed down on Sir Baskel's helmet with the fury of a woman scorned. Padwit winced as Sir Baskel's eyes rolled to the back of his head and his boneless body crumpled.

Elsbeth dropped the rock as she snatched off her blond wig. She nudged the unconscious lordling with her toe. "Really, Paddy? Do I have to do everything? You had one job—get him standing at the entrance. If he's not there when the geyser erupts, the whole gig falls apart."

"So grab a limb and help me!" Padwit wrapped his hands around the unconscious knight's ankles and dragged him toward the cave. He spared a glance at Elsbeth. "The wig was a nice touch."

Elsbeth scratched her head. "I'm not sure it was such a good idea. I know blondes are all the rage, but I got this blonde bit of fluff from the tinker's daughter."

"The one with the—"

"All the dogs? Yeah." Elsbeth looked suspiciously at the wig and shrugged.

"Elsbeth, I could use a little help here," grunted Padwit. "If you're not too busy."

Elsbeth grabbed Sir Baskel's arms and tugged. "Oh, good grief! Did you have to pick the fattest knight in the kingdom?"

"Beggars can't be choosers. It was down to him or Sir Willie."

"Blind Willie'd be missed," sighed Elsbeth.

"Exactly," said Padwit, squaring the body to the cave's entrance. "Sir Eats-A-Lot was our only option." Bits of leaves fluttered on the ground the mouth of the cavern, then mounted to the sky in a hurricane storm as heat thundered to the surface. "She's gonna blow. Run!" shouted Padwit.

Elsbeth tossed Sir Baskel's sword across his body, hiked up her skirts, and scampered after Padwit to the safety of the trees. Like a sideways waterfall, hot steam erupted from the cave, swallowing Sir Baskel whole.

"That never gets old," Elsbeth grinned.

It was full moon before Sir Baskel's armor cooled enough from the geyser's spray for Elsbeth and Padwit to drag his body back to the stone platform. After rummaging through his pockets, prying the ruby from his sword hilt, and finding the hidden pouch of gold in his boot, Padwit went to work with his special three-bladed tool.

Elsbeth lit the torches, signaling the stable boy to bring the wagon.

"What'da'ya think?" Padwit asked.

Elsbeth cocked her head. "Lots of dragon-red blisters from parboiling in the tin suit." She sniffed. "Nice brimstone bouquet, but no charring. Hand me a torch; I'll fix that. I like what you've done with the claw marks across his arm and chest."

"Not too much?"

"No, no!" She kissed her fingertips. "Perfect. Don't change a thing."

"I left his face bare."

"Exactly the right call. Mothers like them sleeping."

"Remember Sir Elsemere?"

"Couple of months ago? Little guy with a blue cloak and a thing for dragon scales?"

"Yeah. His family sent us a nice bit of cheese along with a note." Padwit rubbed his belly. "Sir Baskel didn't miss many meals. Maybe his parents will send a ham."

"A ham would be good," said Elsbeth. "Is the ballad ready?"

"I just need to cross out black and write in silver. Tah-dah-dum-tah-dah-dum-tah-dah-dum-dum-dum...maybe, *silver flashed in the pale moonlight—*"

"Won't that mess up the rhyme?"

Padwit shrugged. "Not so it matters."

CARDINAL ALIGNMENT

Once again, I'm lost in Provo.
They said, "Go south one block, then turn east. Entrance faces north."
Growing up Hawaiian, Utah's as foreign as Mars. North? East?
    Only tourists navigate this way.
Here I'm perpetually adrift, wandering the desert like Moses.
Utahns say look at the sun.
But it's night.
My pioneer ancestors collectively face-palm. Utah's an ancestral
    home, but my roots feel too thin.
Suddenly, there's warm Waikiki sand under my feet. My Hawaiian
    kupuna, navigators who easily crisscrossed the vast Pacific, raise
    my chin toward Utah Lake and whisper, "Think makai."
    Toward the ocean.
Timpanogos. "Mauka," they say. Toward the mountains.
Left. "Diamond Head. Payson. South."
Right. "'Ewa. Salt Lake. North."
Aligned to land, not sky, I'm grounded.
And never lost again.

FOUND

(HOʻOLOAʻA)

Editor's note: This story is presented in two versions here: this one in English, followed by a version in Hawaiian Pidgin English.

Goosebumps

Early Sunday morning, old man Kahana walked toward the ocean at Keikikai beach, his rubber sandals flip, flip, flipping sand behind him. His yellow dog, ʻIlima, bounded ahead of him, sniffing around old soda cans and cigarette butts.

"Careful where you put your nose, ʻIlima. I bet jellyfish washed up on the beach last night."

ʻIlima looked back and whined. Jellyfish hid their sly nature behind pretty blue bubbles. Instead of trading sniffs or licks hello like a proper being, they stung her tongue and nose, making them swell and ache for days. Peculiar herself, ʻIlima understood the advantages of hiding in plain sight and the power of striking when least expected. But she didn't like it when it happened to her. Narrowing her eyes, she glared suspiciously along the shore.

"Nah, ʻIlima, don't worry. I have meat tenderizer," Kahana said, patting his bag. "Takes the sting out in nothing flat."

'Ilima chuffed and went back to work.

Overhead, an albatross called as it headed out to sea. The sun was finally over the mountains, the pale shell colors of early dawn replaced by brilliant blue sky. Hefting his spear and throwing his ratty beach towel over his shoulder, Kahana settled his sandals deeper into the night-cooled sand and surveyed his domain.

To the right was an ancient lava flow that jutted out into the ocean, dividing Keikikai and Nalupuki beaches. Nalupuki was a famous surfing spot, but only small waves kissed the shore. *No wonder the parking lot's empty,* he thought.

In front of him, Keikikai's shallow bay was crystal clear to its sand bottom, perfect for spearing parrot fish or octopuses along the reef's edge.

"We lucked out, 'Ilima. Everybody's still sleeping or on their way to church. We're the only heathens worshiping at the beach this early."

'Ilima scanned the empty beach and sneezed.

"Yeah, it's perfect. Another beautiful day in paradise. Time to catch breakfast. Maybe lunch or dinner, too."

Still, as eager as he was to dive into the ocean and stroke out along the reef, Kahana paused. He slipped his towel off his shoulder and stood looking at Piko Point, the farthest tip of the lava flow stretching into the deep. Something wasn't quite

HUNGRY!

right.

Kahana shook his head. *Hungry?* He rubbed his belly through his tee-shirt and shot a quick glance at 'Ilima. *I could eat,* he thought, *especially Hari's breakfast special with extra gravy or maybe scrambled eggs, Spam, and rice, but I'm not ravenous. That thought wasn't mine. Something else is here.*

It had been a long time since he'd heard a Voice. He cleared his mind and opened his heart, inviting whatever needed to Speak.

I hope I remember how to listen.

Keeping his breathing slow and even, Kahana tried not to count each wave that sloshed at his toes, tried not to think of his father or his grandmother or 'Ilima at his feet or the way his pulse beat like a hula dancer's drum in his temple. He set his eyes on the small band of churning sand that separated the ocean from the shore and felt the gentle breeze, saw how the ocean reflected the impossible blue of the sky. It was the perfect day for spearfishing. So why

C'MON, OLD MAN!

did he feel like a crab inching into a baited trap?

WHAT'RE YOU WAITING FOR?

There it was again, a strange alien thought drifting like seaweed in the currents of his mind. Something wanted him to hurry. Something hungry.

Kahana shaded his eyes and scanned the horizon. Whatever it was, it was out in the water.

'Ilima wandered back from the ocean's edge and sat at Kahana's feet, ignoring the waves sweeping back and forth as she scratched behind her ear.

"What do you think, 'Ilima? Is this a good day for spearfishing?" Kahana asked.

EH, OLD MAN, DON'T BE SCARED. THE WATER'S FINE.

There was that Voice again! But who?

'Ilima whined and leaned against Kahana's leg. Short of tugging on his tee-shirt, she knew nothing she did would make Kahana leave. It wasn't a *who* that she feared, but a *what*.

In the hot sun, Kahana shivered, goosebumps rising. "Yeah, I know, I know. I feel it too, 'Ilima. Something's out there, something that wants to eat a skinny old man. Maybe we better stay on the rocks today. Pick seaweed and limpets. Maybe we'll get lucky and find a glass fishing float all the way from Asia. We can give it to Hari to sell in the shop. Tourists like those glass balls as souvenirs. Better than taking rocks, right? But don't worry; I'll only sell small glass balls; we'll keep the big ones for ourselves. Can you imagine? I'd hang a big one near the sliding glass door. That way we could watch the rainbows it made when the sun shines through, like it's still part of the ocean. It would be nice."

Kahana rubbed his arms, but the goosebumps wouldn't settle. He hefted his fishing spear and settled his towel back on his shoulder.

Even the thought of rainbows doesn't chase away the sinking pit in my stomach.

He jerked his head. "Come on, 'Ilima. Let's walk along the reef. No swimming today."

Shark Taunt

KAHANA AND 'ILIMA headed along the shore toward the lava flow. It curved like a long fingered hand, shielding Keikikai from the wild open ocean.

As they strode across the rocks, from the corner of his eye Kahana saw something flash: a quick, angry flick of a tail near the far edge of the reef at Piko Point. Using his hand to block the sun, he saw a dark bullet shape cruising along the inside reef.

It was headed for Keikikai beach.

Spotting the tail fin, Kahana grinned. It was Kalei-O-Manō, a Niuhi shark.

Even though it had been years since they last met, Kahana knew it was Kalei's Voice that had tempted him into the water. With Niuhi, biting humans was never about hunger. It was always personal.

Always.

"I knew it, 'Ilima!" Kahana narrowed his eyes as the shark cruised along the Keikikai side of the reef, nosing into pockets and hollows as if searching for a snack. "That's Kalei. See the piece missing from his tail? That's how I know it's Kalei-O-Manō." He cocked his head to the side and bit the end of his thumb. "But why is Kalei headed towards a kids' beach? Niuhi hunt around the outer islands near Respite Beach where there's better game and fewer people. But there he is, swimming past Piko Point in broad daylight. That's bold, even for him. This can't be good."

'Ilima gave a quick jagged yelp, then growled low in her throat. She understood better than most Kalei's true nature. Live and let live sounded good in theory, but in practice only the good got hurt.

Kahana's vision blurred as he remembered the way Keikikai beach looked the last time Kalei hunted here, the water heavy with red lehua blossoms of blood staining the sand.

"Remember how Kalei got tangled in the big fishing net? Daddy jumped into the water to cut him loose and accidentally sliced his tail. That's why he's missing a chunk." Kahana shook his head. "I've never seen a shark that angry; I thought he was going ram our boat and sink it, but he didn't. We should've died that day, 'Ilima. You, me, and Daddy, too."

Kalei-O-Manō circled closer to the edge of the reef and rolled to his side, his black Niuhi eye watching Kahana and 'Ilima on the rocks.

"Whoa, 'Ilima, Kalei's gignormous now! Bigger than Jaws, I think!"

Knowing better than to shout Kalei's true name, Kahana called out to sea, "Eh, Jaws Junior! Long time no see! Let's keep it that way, okay?"

At his shout, the enormous shark surfaced. Raising his massive head and barring his teeth, Kalei sent the thought straight to Kahana where it rattled around his brain.

ANOTHER TIME, OLD MAN. YOU CAN'T STAY ON THE REEF FOREVER.

Like a freight train disappearing down a tunnel, Kalei sank back into the water.

Safe on the rocks, Kahana waited, scanning the water and reef. Sharks are ambush predators, and like the ocean, it was never a good idea to turn your back on them.

After a moment or two of nothing but calm water and a light breeze, the feeling of dread released its grip on his guts. His goosebumps relaxed into regular skin, a sure sign that Kalei had moved on.

No confrontation today.

He's headed home to Hohonukai.

Kahana let the air out of his lungs with a whoosh and pretended his knees weren't wobbly.

At least, I hope.

Peeling a bit of thumbnail off with his teeth and putting the sliver carefully into his pocket, Kahana reached down and patted 'Ilima's head.

"Kalei doesn't do anything without a reason, 'Ilima. He's hunting something, but what? All the big fish are out past Nalupuki's second surf break. Nothing on this side of the reef would make a mouthful."

'Ilima shrugged, then stood and moseyed along the rocks, looking for something interesting to roll in.

"There's nothing big here except *people*," Kahana said. "But biting people causes more trouble than it's worth. Nobody knows that better than Kalei." Kahana clicked his tongue. "Remember when we had shark hunts and bounties? No one wants that again. Bad for the ocean, tourists, and sharks."

'Ilima chuffed and yawned. Even though Kalei was gone, it sounded like Kahana wasn't going in the water. That meant it was time to find somewhere else to eat. Who cares about shark hunts and bounties? In her opinion, humans always made things far too complicated.

"Maybe we should forget the whole thing."

'Ilima smiled her doggy smile. Finally!

"We should leave the beach and go vegan."

'Ilima whipped her head around and whined.

"Don't be such a baby. I meant vegan for the day, not forever. I think there's some ripe papaya by the Nakamuras' back fence. Plus we have a ton of green mangoes from Liz. They're really tasty with a little soy sauce."

Kahana absentmindedly scratched his chest and watched the water flow over the reef and onto the sand.

Nope. Not a day for spearfishing; not a day for anything near the ocean. Everything's a little bit...off.

Lassie to the Rescue

KAHANA AND 'ILIMA turned toward the pavilion, heading away from the beach. 'Ilima dragged her feet. Even with soy sauce, mangos were not as good as fresh fish with lemon and butter.

Riding the breeze like a surfer, the sound so soft that at first Kahana thought he imagined it, came the last thing he expected to hear: the weak cry of a newborn baby.

"What the…"

In a flash, 'Ilima took off for the farthest fingertip of lava at Piko Point, the one that pointed the way out past the reef and into the deep, deep, deep.

"'Ilima! Careful! If you slip and fall in the water, you'll end up a Niuhi Scooby snack! Kalei's sly; it might be a trick to get us into the water! Slow down!"

Kahana hustled after 'Ilima, his rubber sandals wrapping around sharp points of lava, sliding over seaweed-slick patches, and splashing through puddles of warm, salty water. A hard knot formed in his stomach and pushed into his throat.

What horror cries like a newborn baby and lives on the reef?

In the distance, 'Ilima wagged her tail as she ran her tongue over and over something, pausing only to bark at him to hurry, hurry, hurry up.

"So what, you think you're Lassie now?" Kahana puffed.

Climbing over a jagged bulge of lava and skirting the last tide pool, Kahana bent down and pushed 'Ilima away. It was small, very small, with two arms, two legs, and a mouth that was no longer crying. Its eyes were scrunched closed against the bright sun, and part of the umbilical cord was still attached to its bellybutton.

"A boy? A newborn boy, naked, no blanket, no diaper, all alone out here? Can't be more than a day old, maybe only a few hours! Thank goodness it didn't rain last night!" Kahana pushed 'Ilima away again. "Enough, 'Ilima! Your licking will give the baby a rash!"

'Ilima chuffed excitedly. This was better than rolling in forty dead fish!

Kahana dropped his fishing gear, slung his towel off his shoulder, and gently lifted the baby off the hard lava rock, wrapping him securely in his towel.

You forget how small they are until you hold one in your arms again.

'Ilima whimpered and nuzzled the small bundle.

"I know, I know, he looks a little gray. I think he's cold, and salt's no good for baby's skin. Look how rough, how chapped it is. No, 'Ilima, no more licking! Hey, Lassie-wanna-be, you want to be useful, be a hero and find this baby's mama."

From the far fingertips on the deep ocean side of the lava outcrop to the coconut trees on the shore, Kahana scanned the beach in front of him. For miles he could see it was empty. Behind him was the deep ocean, above him the sky, and beneath his thin rubber soles was hard, cold lava, shiny with pockets of salt and dotted with the cast-off shells of crabs.

Wherever this kid's mother is, it's not here.

Portents

CRADLING the baby against his chest, Kahana walked to the last sliver of land at the end of Piko Point and stared down into the dark blue water of the open ocean. Below the surface, shadows crawled and darting streaks of silvery light flashed, but there was no towel on the rocks, no tee-shirt, no shoes, no blood. It didn't make sense.

Deep water. I bet it drops 500 feet or more, and late last night the current ran out to sea.

"Hey, 'Ilima, you think this baby's mama gave birth then just jumped in the ocean? A lot of crazy Californians come to Hawaii to commune with the dolphins. We've seen them out on the reef, wearing sarongs and raffia leis, chanting as dawn breaks over the mountains, so confused when it didn't rise from the sea. Remember the silly one who shrieked when I came up from the bottom of the big saltwater pool with the eel on my spear? Called me a murder." Kahana pursed his lips, his memory sharper than a spear point. "If he only knew."

Unimpressed, the baby squirmed and kicked. Kahana wrapped him tighter, tucking the end of the towel under his toes.

"I bet this little one's mama is one of those new age nuts chasing primordial authenticity. She came here ready to have her version of natural childbirth alone in the dark on black lava rock. Then, feeling one with the universe, all connected to her maternal ancestors, she went for a rejuvenating swim and ended up a shark snack. Maybe that's why Kalei's hanging around here. Maybe something about her Called to him, and he came. What do you think, 'Ilima? Plausible?"

'Ilima sniffed around the biggest saltwater pool, then sat down and whimpered. It wasn't Kalei that she smelled on the rocks or the baby. The truth was much stranger, and she didn't like it, not one bit. She looked back to Keikikai beach and pulled her ears tight against her head.

"I think you're right, 'Ilima," Kahana said. "I don't think Kalei came through the open tunnel under Piko Point and into this pool. If he had, Junior-boy wouldn't be here." He lifted his chin toward the deep water. "Whatever happened, happened out there."

He looked down at the baby.

"I don't know where or who your people are, little one. Your skin is kinda gray, but not European fair. Your hair is so dark and curly, I bet you have some Hawaiian or Samoan or African blood. You a military kid? Is your father overseas on temporary assignment, leaving your mother all crazy and lonely in a small high rise apartment? Maybe she's from Manila or Seoul and no speak good English. Was your mother all alone in the world when you came? That's hard."

Kahana's eyes traveled over the horizon in all directions, searching for anything, any clue that might lead to the baby's mother. He turned slowly, sweeping his eyes over the beach again and again, back over the rocks and out to sea.

He shrugged. "Maybe you're a local kid whose mama was too scared to let anyone know about you. Maybe she left you here because she couldn't handle it." He gripped a sandal tight with his toes and stepped over a puddle. "Well, whatever. Don't worry, Little One. Uncle Kahana is going to help you."

Tucking the baby into the crook of his arm and hitching his shorts up, Kahana left his fishing gear on the rocks and headed back to the beach. Tail high, 'Ilima scouted the way.

Nestled in the towel, the baby began to warm enough to complain.

He's hungry, and I don't have any milk. This will have to do.

Wiping his pinky on his shorts, he slipped it between the baby's lips.

"Shhh," he cooed, "I know it's not what you—ouch!"

Snatching his finger from the baby's mouth, he examined the small slice across the tip.

"Whoa! Kid, what did you do to my finger? It hurts worse than a paper cut! 'Ilima, look!"

'Ilima glanced back and yipped. What did Kahana expect from a child such as this? Humans!

Gently, Kahana separated the baby's lips and looked in his mouth.

"You have a tooth!" Gingerly, he touched it. "Whoa, it's sharp!"

Annoyed and hungry, the baby fussed.

"Ah, don't cry, don't cry. Everything's going to be okay." Swaying like a drunken tourist trying to hula, Kahana moved off the lava and onto the sand.

Thoughts churned like driftwood in an eddy. *A baby abandoned on a reef. A tooth. Fair skin. Dark curly hair. A Niuhi shark hunting off Keikikai in daylight.*

At the edge of the pavilion, it clicked.

"Wait, just wait a second, Grandmother Kaulupali told me about this. Sometimes babies are born with teeth—milk teeth, she called them. Aunty Lei, her sister, was born with one. Grandma said...she said...ah, no way, this can't be!"

'Ilima chuffed. Finally!

Kahana gently rolled the baby over. There, in the middle of his back between his shoulder blades was a tiny blue-black birthmark in the shape of an upside down triangle. A shark's dorsal fin, the mark of Niuhi.

Eyes wide, Kahana turned the baby back over.

By all the ancient Hawaiian gods, Kalei was hunting for you!

The thought left him reeling.

Did the mother know? Did she leave you there for me to find or as an offering for Kalei?

Kahana scanned the ocean horizon, his heart hammering out of his chest.

Should I put him back? What kind of hell am I unleashing by getting in the business of gods?

"'Ilima?"

'Ilima cocked her head, listening.

Kahana sank to the ground and leaned against a coconut tree. The long ago words of his father came to him, words and practices he'd denied for decades.

Center, his father's Voice said. *Remember to breathe. Na akua, na 'aumakua, our gods and ancestors, cannot speak to a mind confused like water boiling in a pot. Stillness. Peace. Breathe.*

Kahana held the baby against his shoulder and pulled salt air deep into his lungs.

In.

Out.

In.

Out.

He closed his eyes and counted his breaths until his mind was still like water resting in a wooden bowl.

From the bottom of the ravine behind the pavilion, a Voice like stone called out to Kahana's mind.

HE IS YOURS. HE IS YOUR RESPONSIBILITY. HE IS FAMILY.

In a blinding flash, Kahana had his answer. It was his duty and responsibility to see this infant raised in love and safety. The whys and hows of the baby's existence no longer mattered; like gravity or the moon, the baby's pull on those around him was inexplicable. Kahana knew arguing or fighting against fate was futile; you might as well stand on the shore and shout at the waves to roll back. But the gods didn't demand unless they prepared a way; Kahana would just have to find it.

'Ilima whined and licked the tear that leaked down Kahana's cheek.

"Thank you, gods and ancestors," he whispered before opening his eyes. "'Ilima, they've come back," he said.

'Ilima chuffed and wagged her tail. Of course, she knew the gods and ancestors never left Kahana; how could they? Kahana, like so many of his generation, had simply forgotten how to listen. She perked her ears. Things were finally getting back on track.

HOʻOLOAʻA

(FOUND)

Chicken Skin

Supa early Sunday morning, makule Kahana wen walk to da ocean at Keikikai beach, his slippahs flip, flip, flipping sand all kapahaki. His yellow poi dog, ʻIlima, waz bounding ahead of him, sticking her nose in stuffs like old soda cans and cigarette butts.

"Ho, ʻIlima, careful where you put your nose, yeah? Bettah watch out for portagee-man-o-war! I bet da buggahs wen wash up on da beach last night."

ʻIlima wen look back and whine. Jellyfish waz sly, making all nice-nice behind pretty blue bubbles. All a time dose sneaky buggahs sting wen she only like lick hello. ʻEʻepa herself, ʻIlima stay akamai about da advantages of hiding in plain sight and da power of striking when nobody looking. But she nevah like it when it happen to her. Narrowing her eyes, she glared suspiciously along da shore.

"Nah, Sistah, no worry. I get meat tenderizer," Kahana said, patting his bag. "Take da sting out in nothing flat."

ʻIlima chuffed and heleʻd on.

Overhead, a mōlī called as it headed out to sea. Da sun waz finally over da pali, da pale puka shell colors of early dawn wen come brilliant blue. Hefting his spear and throwing his hammajang beach towel on top his shoulder, Kahana settled his slippahs deeper into da night-cooled sand and surveyed da ʻāina.

To da right and past da ancient lava flow dat divided Keikikai and Nalupuki beaches, only manini waves rolled on shore.

No wondah da parking lot empty, he thought. *Surfers no like waste time ovah hea.*

In front of him, Keikikai's shallow bay waz crystal clear all da way to da sand on da bottom, perfect for catching uhu or heʻe along da reef's edge.

"We lucky, ʻIlima. Everybody still hiamoe or on dere way to church. Only us makule heathens on da beach dis early."

ʻIlima spoked out da empty sand and sneezed.

"Perfect, yeah? Jess another day in Hawaiʻi nei. Come, we go spear breakfast. Mebbe lunch and dinnah, too."

Still, as eager as he waz for dive into da ocean and stroke out along da reef, Kahana paused. He slipped his towel off his shoulder and stood looking toward Piko Point, da farthest tip of da lava flow dat jutted into da moana deep. Something wasn't quite

HUNGRY!

right.

Kahana shook his head. *Hungry?* He rubbed his ʻōpū through his tee-shirt and shot quick side-eye at ʻIlima.

I could eat, he thought, *especially a Hari's loco moco with extra gravy or maybe scrambled eggs, Spam, and rice, but I'm not starving. Dat thought wasn't from me. Something else stay heah.*

It had been since hanabata days dat he'd heard one Voice, especially one so loud and nīele. He cleared his mind and opened his heart, inviting whatever needed fo' Speak to talk.

Chee, I hope I remembah how fo' listen.

Keeping his breathing slow and even, Kahana tried not fo' count each wave dat sloshed his toes, tried not fo' tink of Daddy, Tutu Kaulupali, ʻIlima, or da way his pulse beat like a paʻu drum in his temple. He set his eyes on da small band of churning sand dat separated da ocean from da shore. Da breeze waz gentle and soothing. Da ocean reflected da impossible blue of da sky. It waz da perfect day for spearfishing. So why

E HELE MAI, KANAKA MAKULE!

did he feel like a crab inching onto an ahi head?

WHATCHU WAITING FOR?

There it stay again, one strange alien thought drifting like limu in da currents of his mind. Something wanted him fo' hurry. Something hungry.

Kahana shaded his eyes and scanned da horizon. Whatever it stay, it waz out in da water.

'Ilima wandered back from da ocean's edge and sat at Kahana's feet, ignoring da waves sweeping back and forth as she scratched behind her ear.

"What you tink, eh, 'Ilima? Good day for spearing one uhu?" Kahana asked.

EH, OLD MAN, NO BE SCARED. DA WATER'S MAIKAʻI.

Dat Voice! Again! But who?

'Ilima whined and leaned against Kahana's leg. Short of tugging on his tee-shirt, she knew nothing she did would make Kahana leave. It wasn't a *who* dat she feared, but a *what*.

In da hot sun, Kahana shivered, chicken skin all over his arms and chest. "Yeah, I know, I know. I feel 'um too, 'Ilima. Something's out there, something dat wants fo' kaukau a skinny kanaka makule. Maybe mo'bettah we stay on da rocks today. Pick limu and 'opihi. Maybe we lucky and find one pōpō aniani from Korea or Japan. We can give 'em to Hari fo' sell in his shop. Tourists like dose glass balls. But no worries; I only going sell da manini kine. Da big kine's for us. I like da way dey look on da lānai with da sun coming through. Like rainbows in da ocean. Nice."

Kahana rubbed his chicken skin arms, but da bumps wouldn't settle. He hefted his fishing spear and set his towel back over his shoulder.

Pau already. No sense chance 'em.

"Come, 'Ilima, we go. No swimming today."

Henehene Manō

KAHANA AND 'ILIMA headed along da shore toward da lava flow dat curved like one rice paddle, shielding Keikikai from da wild open ocean.

Striding across da rocks, from da corner of his eye, Kahana wen spak one flash: a quick, angry flick of a tail near da far edge of da reef at Piko Point. Using his hand fo' block da sun, he checked out one dark bullet cruising inside da reef.

It waz headed for da beach.

Spotting da tail fin, Kahana grinned. It waz Kalei-O-Manō, a Niuhi shark.

Even though it had been years since they last met, Kahana knew it waz Kalei's

Voice dat had invited him into da water. With Niuhi, biting humans waz never about hunger. It waz always personal.

Always.

"I knew it, 'Ilima, dat buggah waz jess waiting for me!" Kahana narrowed his eyes as da shark cruised along da Keikikai side of da reef, nosing into pockets and hollows as if searching fo' one snack. "Dat's Kalei. See da piece missing from on top his tail? Dat's how I know it's Kalei-O-Manō." He cocked his head to da side and bit da end of his thumb. "Now why come Kalei stay around one kids' beach after all dese years? Niuhi hunt around da northern islands near Respite Beach. More remote out dere, better game. But heah he stay, swimming past Piko Point in broad daylight. Das bold, even for him. Big pilikia, fo' sure."

'Ilima wen yelp quick and jagged, then growled low in her throat. She understood better dan most Kalei's true nature. Live and let live sounded good, but everybody knew only da good got hurt.

Kahana's vision blurred wen he remembered da way Keikikai beach looked da last time Kalei hunted heah, da water heavy with choke lehua blossoms of blood staining da sand.

"Remember how Kalei stay all tangled up in da hukilau net? Daddy jumped into da water fo' cut him loose and accidentally sliced his tail. Dat's why he's missing a chunk." Kahana shook his head. "'Auwē, I never seen one shark so huhū; I thought he waz going ram our boat and sink it, but he never. We should've make-die-dead dat day, 'Ilima. You, me, and Daddy, too."

Kalei-O-Manō circled closer to da edge of da reef and rolled to his side, his black Niuhi eye watching Kahana and 'Ilima on da rocks.

"Ho, 'Ilima, check it; Kalei's gignormous now! More big dan Jaws, I t'ink!"

Knowing better dan fo' shout Kalei's true name, Kahana called out to sea, "Eh, Jaws Junior! Long time no see! Let's keep it dat way, hah?"

At his shout, da enormous shark surfaced. Raising his massive head and barring his teeth, Kalei sent da thought straight to Kahana where it rattled around his brain.

BUMBAI, OLD MAN, BUMBAI. YOU NO CAN STAY ON DA REEF FOREVAH.

Like one sugarcane train disappearing down one tunnel, Kalei sank back into da water.

Safe on da rocks, Kahana waited, scanning da water and reef. Sharks are ambush predators, and like da ocean, it waz never a good idea fo' turn your back on 'em.

After a moment or two of nothing but calm water and a light breeze, da feeling of dread released its grip on Kahana's guts. His chicken skin relaxed back into regular skin, a sure sign dat Kalei had moved on.

No beef today.

Hele on home to Hohonukai, Kalei.

Kahana let da air out his lungs with one whoosh and pretended his knees no stay wobbly.

Please, Kalei. Just go. Mahalo nunui!

Peeling a bit of thumbnail off with his teeth and putting da sliver carefully into his pocket, Kahana reached down and patted 'Ilima's head.

"Kalei never like do nothing without one reason, 'Ilima. What's he hunting? All da big fish stay past Nalupuki's second break. Nothing on dis side of da reef would make a mouthful. Odd, yeah, 'Ilima?"

'Ilima looked up, shrugged, then stood and moseyed along da rocks, looking for something interesting fo' roll in.

"Nothing big heah except for people," Kahana said. "But biting people causes more trouble dan it's worth. Nobody knows dat better dan Kalei." Kahana clicked his tongue. "Remember da shark hunts? Da bounties? Nobody wants dat again. Bad for da ocean, bad for da tourists, and bad for da sharks."

'Ilima chuffed and yawned. Even though Kalei stay gone, it sounded like Kahana wasn't going in da water. Dat meant it waz time fo' find somewhere else fo' eat. Who cares about shark hunts and bounties? In her opinion, humans always made things way too complicated.

"Chee, maybe we should just bag da beach entirely."

'Ilima smiled her doggy smile. Finally!

"Mebbe leave da 'opihi on da reef and da fish in da sea. Go vegan, yeah?"

'Ilima whipped her head around and whined.

"Don't be such a diva-lani. I mean go veggy for da day, not fo'evah. I tink get some ripe papaya by Nakamura's back fence. Plus we get plenny green mangoes from Liz-dem. 'Ono with a little shoyu."

Kahana absentmindedly scratched his chest and watched da water flow over da reef and onto da sand.

'A'ole day for spearfishing; 'a'ole anything near da ocean. Everything stay a little bit...off.

Lassie to da Rescue

KAHANA AND ʻILIMA turned toward da pavilion, heading away from da beach. ʻIlima dragged her feet. Even with shoyu, mangos were not as good as fresh fish with lemon and butter.

Riding da breeze like one surfer, da sound so soft dat at first Kahana thought he imagined it, came da last ting he expected fo' hear: da weak cry of a newborn baby.

"What da..."

In a flash, ʻIlima took off for da farthest fingertip of lava at Piko Point, da one dat pointed da way out past da reef and into da deep, deep, deep.

"ʻIlima! Careful! If you slip you gonna be one Niuhi Scooby snack! Kalei's one sly buggah; it might be a trick fo' get us in da water! Slow down, confunit!"

Kahana hustled after ʻIlima, his rubbah slippahs wrapping around sharp points of aʻa, sliding over limu-slick patches, and splashing through shallow tide pools of warm, salty water. A hard knot formed in his stomach and pushed into his throat.

What horror cries like one newborn baby and lives on da reef?

In da distance, ʻIlima wagged her tail as she ran her tongue over and over something, pausing only fo' bark at him fo' hurry, hurry, hurry up.

"So what, you tink you Lassie now?" Kahana puffed.

Climbing over a jagged bulge of lava and skirting da last tide pool, Kahana bent down and pushed ʻIlima away. It waz small, very small, with two arms, two legs, and a mouth dat waz no longer crying. Its eyes waz scrunched closed against da bright sun, and part of da umbilical cord stay still attached to its piko.

"A boy? A newborn boy, naked, no blanket, no diaper, all alone out heah? Cannot be more dan a day old, maybe only a few hours! Good ting never rain last night!" Kahana pushed ʻIlima away again. "Enough, ʻIlima! Your licking will give da baby a rash!"

ʻIlima chuffed excitedly. Dis waz uku times mo'bettah dan rolling in forty dead fish!

Kahana dropped his fishing gear, slung his towel off his shoulder, and gently lifted da baby off da hard lava rock, wrapping him securely in his towel.

You forget how small they stay until you hold one in your arms again.

ʻIlima whimpered and nuzzled da small bundle.

"I know, I know, he looks a little gray. I tink he's cold, and salt's no good for baby's skin. Look how rough, how chapped it stay. No, ʻIlima, pau licking already. Eh, Lassie-wanna-be, you like be useful, go be one hero and find dis keiki's mama."

From da far fingertips on da deep ocean side of da lava outcrop to da coconut trees on da shore, Kahana scanned da beach in front of him. For miles he could see it stay empty. Behind him waz da ocean, above him da sky, and beneath his slippahs stay hard, cold lava, shiny with pockets of salt and dotted with da cast-off shells of crabs.

Wherever dis keiki's mother stay, it's not heah.

ʻŌuli

CRADLING da baby against his chest, Kahana walked to da last sliver of land at end of Piko Point and stared down into da dark blue water of da open ocean. Below da surface, shadows crawled and darting streaks of silvery light flashed, but there waz no towel on da rocks, no tee-shirt, no slippahs, no blood. It didn't make sense.

Deep water. I bet it drops 500 feet or more, and late last night da current ran out to sea.

"Eh, ʻIlima, you tink dis keiki's mama wen give birth den just jump in da ocean? Get plenny pupule tourist from California come to Hawaiʻi for commune with da dolphins. You know da kine—da ones out heah on da reef wearing lava-lavas and raffia leis, chanting as dawn breaks over da mountains, so confused when it never wen rise from da sea. Remember da tilly dude who shrieked when I came up from da bottom of da big saltwater pool with one eel on my spear? Called me one murder." Kahana pursed his lips, his memory sharper dan one spear point. "If he only knew."

Unimpressed, da baby squirmed and kicked. Kahana wrapped him tighter, tucking da end of da towel under his toes.

"I wonder if dis little one's mama wen come heah thinking she like be one with da ocean. Have one real natural childbirth in da dark on black lava rock, all alone like some new age lōlō. Then, wen she feel all one with da universe, she wen go for one swim and stay come one manō meal. Maybe dat's why Kalei's hanging around heah. Maybe something about her Called fo' him, and he wen come. Whatchu tink?"

ʻIlima sniffed around da biggest saltwater pool, then sat down and whimpered. It wasn't Kalei dat she smelled on da rocks or da baby. Da truth waz much stranger, and she didn't like it, not one skosh. She looked back to Keikikai beach and pulled her ears tight against her head.

"You right, ʻIlima," Kahana said. "I no tink Kalei came through da open tunnel under Piko Point and into dis pool. If he had, Junior-boy wouldn't be heah." He lifted his chin toward da deep water. "Whatever happened, happened out there."

He looked down at da baby.

"I dunno where or who your people are, little one. Your skin kinda gray, but local kine ashy, not fair like one haole. Your hair is so dark and curly, I bet you get some Hawaiian or Samoan or pōpolo blood. You one military keiki? Is your father overseas on temporary assignment, leaving your mother all futless and lonely in one small high rise apartment? Maybe she's from Manila or Seoul and no speak good English, hah? Waz your mother all alone in da world when you came? Hard, dat."

Kahana's eyes traveled over da horizon in all directions, searching for anything, any clue dat might lead to da baby's mother. He turned slowly, sweeping his eyes over da beach again and again, back over da rocks and out to sea.

He shrugged. "Maybe you one local kid whose mama stay too scared for let anyone know about you. Maybe she wen leave you heah 'cause she no can handle." He gripped a slippah tight with his toes and stepped over a puddle. "Well, whatevahs. No worries, brah. Uncle Kahana going help you."

Tucking da baby into da crook of his arm and hitching his shorts up, Kahana left his fishing gear on da rocks and headed back to da beach. Tail high, ʻIlima scouted da way.

Nestled in da towel, da baby began fo' warm enough to complain.

He's hungry, and I no mo' milk. Dis will have fo' do.

Wiping his pinky on his shorts, he slipped it between da baby's lips.

"Shhh," he cooed, "I know it's not what you— auwiiii!"

Snatching his finger from da baby's mouth, he examined da small slice across da tip.

"Ho! Kid, what you wen do to my finger? Buggah hurts more worse dan one paper cut! ʻIlima, look!"

ʻIlima glanced back and yipped. What did Kahana expect from one keiki li'dis? Humans!

Gently, Kahana separated da baby's lips and looked in his mout.

"You get one tooth, hah, little one?" Gingerly, he touched it. "Ho, da sharp!"

Annoyed and hungry, da baby fussed.

"Ah, no cry, no cry. Everything's going be okay." Swaying like a half-drunk tourist on stage at a Waikiki luʻau, Kahana moved off da lava and onto da sand.

Thoughts churned like driftwood in an eddy. *A keiki abandoned on da reef. A tooth. Fair skin. Dark curly hair. A Niuhi shark hunting off Keikikai in daylight.*

"Wait, try wait, Tūtū Wahine Kaulupali wen tell me about dis. Sometimes babies born with teeth—milk teeth, she said. Aunty Lei, her sistah, stay born with one. Tutu said...she said...ah, no way, cannot be!"

ʻIlima chuffed. Finally!

Kahana gently rolled da baby over. There, in da middle of his back between his shoulder blades waz one tiny blue-black birthmark in da shape of an upside down triangle. A shark's dorsal fin, da mark of Niuhi.

Eyes wide, Kahana turned da baby back over.

Oh, na akua, Kalei waz hunting for you!

Da thought left him reeling.

Did da mother know? Did she go leave you dere for me fo' find or as one offering for Kalei?

Kahana scanned da ocean horizon, his heart hammering out of his chest.

Should I put him back? What kind of hell am I unleashing by getting in da business of gods?

"'Ilima?"

'Ilima cocked her head, listening.

Kahana sank to da ground and leaned against a coconut tree. Da long ago words of his father came to him, words and practices he'd denied for decades.

Center, his father's Voice said. *Remember fo' breathe. Na akua, na 'aumakua, cannot speak to a mind confused like water boiling in a pot. Stillness. Maluhia. Breathe.*

Kahana held da baby against his shoulder and pulled da salt air deep into his lungs.

In.

Out.

In.

Out.

He closed his eyes and counted his breaths until his mind waz still like water resting in a koa wood bowl.

From da bottom of da ravine behind da pavilion, a Voice like stone called out to Kahana's mind.

HE IS YOURS. HE IS YOUR KULEANA. HE IS 'OHANA.

In a blinding flash, Kahana had his answer. It waz his kuleana fo' see dis infant raised in love and safety. Da whys and hows of da baby's existence no longer mattered; like gravity or da moon, da baby's pull on dose around him waz inexplicable. Kahana knew when nestled in da hands of na akua and 'aumakua, arguing or fighting against fate waz futile; you might as well stand on da shore and shout at da waves fo' roll back. But da gods didn't demand unless they prepared a way; Kahana would just have fo' find it.

'Ilima whined and licked da tear dat leaked down Kahana's cheek.

"Mahalo nui loa nā akua, nā 'aumakua," he whispered before opening his eyes. "'Ilima, they're back," he said

'Ilima chuffed and wagged her tail. Of course she knew nā akua and nā kūpuna never left Kahana; how could they? Despite her companionship, Kahana, like so many of his generation, had forgotten how fo' listen. She perked her ears. Things waz finally getting back on track.

VOICES

"Kari, if you miss the damn school bus again you're walking."

"I won't, Mom," I call through the bathroom door.

"Like I haven't heard that before."

In the mirror, I hold a razor blade next to the new black hole the size of a freckle on my cheek. Its mosquito-pitched whine is the sound of a hurricane through a crack in a door. My hand shakes. If I don't get this right, missing the school bus is the least of my problems. I close my eyes.

Troops, I call to the people in my head. Report.

Just do it, Big Frank says. *Cut quick like we did on our thigh, a single long stroke to let the pressure out.*

But it's on our face, Bunny sighs from her burrow. *And the others didn't whistle.*

Exactly, Big Frank says. *We need to nip this crazy in the bud.*

I open my eyes and tilt my chin. As I move, the hole shimmers, twinkling like glitter or diamonds. It's the smallest of the four, smaller than the pea-sized hole on my thigh, the pinkie nail hole on my toe, or the hole hidden in ink on my arm. I put the razor down and touch it. Air flows out colder than star-breath. I gasp and stick my finger in my mouth, sucking hard. Pulling it out, I see subzero blisters where my fingerprints should be. The holes in my body oozed cold before, but this ferocity is new.

I peer into the mental space where Granny Roz lives. Granny? What should I do?

Plug it, Granny Roz says.

With what? Big Frank sneers.

Bath tissue. Bum-fodder. The old t.p., Granny Roz says, scratching her corn-rows. She purses her lips and spits tobacco juice into an empty Dr. Pepper can. *Cover it up with face-spackle. Ain't no one gonna see.* She shifts her tobacco wad to the other side. *Nobody ever do.*

Plugging didn't work yesterday, Bunny says.

This hole ain't but a baby, Granny Roz replies.

Cut it. Get rid of the cancer, Big Frank says.

Spoken like a true military man, snorts Granny Roz. *Why fix what you can beat into submission?*

It's a hole in our face, Bunny says. *It's making noise. It needs to stop.*

The voices in my head advise, but the final decision is mine. I tug some tissue from the roll and lean so close to the mirror that my breath fogs it and I have to pull back a little to focus. I press a tiny piece of toilet paper against the shrillness. It doesn't stick.

Wet it, Granny Roz says.

I take a drop of water from the tap and roll a needle-sized plug. I twist and jam it into the hole. Like a teakettle lifted off the heat, the whistling stops. In the silence, time speeds up.

"Kari!" Mom calls. "I'm not driving you if you're too stupid to catch the bus."

I dab a bit of concealer over the lump and lean back from the mirror. The area looks red and swollen, a blemish about to erupt.

Good enough, Granny Roz says. *Don't forget our backpack. Put it next to you on the bus so none of Them can sit there.*

Big Frank growls, but doesn't say anything, just grabs his binoculars and heads to his lookout post. Bunny runs down her burrow to make sure all the dolls are tucked into bed. Bunny hates school.

Switch it on, Granny Roz says. *Let me see it.*

Mentally, I reach up to my master control panel and flip the switch that reveals a soldier's thousand yard stare. Big Frank taught me that last year when I first went into battle with Them.

Now you're ready. Granny Roz settles into her rocking chair, picks up a bowl of peas, and starts shelling. *We're here if'n you need us.*

As I walk out the bathroom door, I tuck a tube of concealer into my pocket.

Might need a touch up later.

Not that anyone will notice.

I get to the end of the driveway in time to watch the bus pull away from the corner. Through a window, Becca Jameson points at me and laughs. Charlotte Hanamoto, that cow, joins in. Without thought, my arm raises and my finger flips them off. They laugh harder as the bus rolls out of sight. Big Frank, I say.

What, he says. *They deserve it.*

I look toward Mom's car.

Big Frank shudders. *Let's avoid that crapfest.*

How?

Granny Roz shakes her head. *You got two feet, Chile. It's not but a twenty minute walk.*

I'll be late.

Better late than getting into Mom's car, says Big Frank.

Bunny? I think.

Walk, she says, *you'll still make the second bell.* She curls her ears over her face and closes her eyes. In the background the shadow troops stand silent.

Walking gives me time to think.

The first black spot—holes I call them—appeared a week ago on my littlest toe. Covering my entire nail, it looked like a Goth pedicure gone wrong or the aftermath of a hammer's kiss. The rest of my toe was warm, but the arctic draught of air coming from the place where my nail had been froze my sock to my shoe. Walking across polished cement floor of the library, I'd slipped and barely caught myself before tumbling into a spinning rack of paperbacks. Ignoring the glare from the librarian, I eased into a study carrel and pried icy laces loose.

WTF?

There was something familiar about the hole and the thin thread of bitter air leaking from it.

The swan, Granny Roz said.

That's it! It reminded me of the inner tube with the swan's head that I'd gotten for my sixth birthday. Something about its beak or eye. Maybe it was the way the swan was supposed to keep me safe that day at the Great Salt Lake, but slowly leaked until I was floundering, unable to keep my head above the wakes and splashes of the other kids.

That day the miracle of Granny Roz's voice saved me. I remember floating in the too thick water, salt sticking in my hair, not paying attention as the swan carried me away from shore and toward a diving platform. Bobbing in the lake, I watched bigger kids cannonballing and lying in the sun, white spots of salt pooling in the hollows of backs and knees.

"Watch this!" a boy's voice called. I didn't see the giant tsunami of a splash that knocked me sideways, only heard the girl next to me snap, "Carl! Knock it off or I'm telling!" as she brushed water off her face.

Slip. Struggle. Slip. I remember the sound of wet plastic rubbing against skin. Slip. Splash. I felt a hand grab my ankle as I slowly sank like a pocket full of rocks. Instead of buoying me up, water seven times saltier than the sea pulled me down, filling eyes and ears, gurgling in the back of my throat, burning like hellfire.

My toes touched mud, feet burying themselves to the ankles in slickness.

Raising my arms to the surface, I watched the deflated swan lift past arms, wrists, fingertips—buoyant only enough to save itself. Bubbles rose, trailing fish kisses against skin as the darkness closed in.

Jump, commanded a new and wonderful voice in my head.

I jumped. Only my fingertips broke the surface.

I said, jump, Chile! Jump like a frog in bucket of cream. Jump with all the might God give you!

When my feet touched mud again, I pushed harder and swung my arms, this time rising high enough to catch a quick mouthful of air before sinking back into the lake.

Good, said the voice. *Now not just up—you gotta jump toward something. Jump toward salvation, Chile. Jump like you're playing hopscotch.*

What's hopscotch? I thought.

Eyes screwed tight against the salt burn, I saw a young girl in cornrows and a hand-me-down dress, the blue faded by harsh lye soap rubbed across scrubbing boards and the heat of the sun. The girl tossed a pebble at a line of squares scratched in the dirt. Glancing over her shoulder, she giggled, then jumped one, two, three.

Like that, said the voice.

Is that you?

A deep rumbling like the sound of gravel in a wheel well rolled through my head. *No, Chile. That's not me. At least not how I am now.* Hopscotch girl smiled, then dissolved into a sturdy middle-aged black woman in a white kitchen apron standing on a sharecropper's porch.

Who are you?

Call me Granny Roz. Now jump!

I jumped.

Bouncing from the mud to the surface and back again, my six-year-old legs finally walked up the shore, feet crunching through the thin salt crust over mud.

Mom looked up from her book. "Where's your swan?"

I sniffled, sucking snot and saltwater up my nose. "I—"

Mom shook her head and held up a hand. "Kari, I don't want to hear it. You lost it five minutes after you got it."

"That's—"

"Tough titty said the kitty. I didn't bring you all the way to the Great Salt Lake to listen to you cry. Go play with the other kids like a big girl."

"But—"

She flicked her hand in dismissal. "Go. You're dripping all over my towel."

I didn't want to play with the other kids. Instead I sat in the shallows and listened to Granny Roz's stories about a life spent on a dry farm in Kentucky.

Always save tater water for gravy, she told me, *and be sure to set the water a boilin'
before pickin' the corn.*

Later, as we walked past pavilions and balloons pointing the way to another
girl's pretty pink princess pony party, Mom muttered about waste. I ignored her
and watched Granny Roz crimp a scalloped edge on a piecrust.

"Don't expect another one," Mom snapped, grabbing my arm and twisting.

"What?"

I said you can lick the bowl. Granny Roz smiled.

Over the years when things got bad, I made my way back to the Great Salt
Lake. I'd wade out until I could slip my head under the water. Holding my breath,
I'd think about a trouble that couldn't be named and a new voice would appear in
my head with answers.

Big Frank taught me about the power of no when one of Mom's boyfriend's
hands wandered where they didn't belong. Bunny held me after the scary voices
shouted in the night and the fires started. There are others; shadow troops I call
them; they lurk in the background, waiting for I don't know what. Only three keep
me company: Granny Roz to guide, Big Frank to fight, and Bunny to comfort.

For the past week, my pinky toe hole has been easy to hide under a sock and
tennis shoe. Out of sight, out of mind as long as I pay attention to the differences
between grass and tile, carpet and cement. As I walk to school, I glide my foot like
an ice skate or rollerblade.

My eye catches the ink running over my left hand, lines smeared by soap and
scrub brushes. Bunny pulls blankets over her head. *That wasn't one of our brighter
moments.*

It's fine, says Big Frank. *You're over-reacting.*

We got in trouble, Bunny mumbles. *I got us in trouble.*

Not trouble, I soothe. Dr. Susan gave us hope. Despite the holes, there's a
chance we might get out of here in one piece.

Granny Roz clucks her tongue. *You better hurry, Chile. You gonna be late.*

I pick up the pace, but the ink still catches my eye. I push back my sleeve and
remember how just yesterday morning the world changed again.

I was cutting a pattern on a square of linoleum in art class when the second
hole appeared on my left arm, the size of a silent dime.

Trouble at seven o'clock, Big Frank shouted. *Prepare for attack.*

Bunny's head popped out of her burrow, her nose wiggling furiously. Her eyes
darted left, right; her head swiveled front, back, up, and down. *No,* she said. *We're
good.*

Granny Roz rested her broom against the kitchen table and walked out her
front door. *Show me,* she said.

I raised my arm to my eyes. The hole appeared shiny, like water on asphalt, black ice on a bridge. I could see the edges where skin ended and the hole began, but no blood or bone or sinew; there was no sense of looking through or into. The hole was a void, an abyss that led nowhere and was filled with nothing.

This is our arm, Granny Roz said, her words knocking the air right out of me.

Nothing. I am filled with nothing.

As my warm breath rushed out, it coalesced as mist and frosted the tiny hairs on my arm.

Just like reeds in truest winter, Bunny shivered.

Granny Roz shook her finger. *Don't you touch it, Kari. Hear me. This is the devil's work.*

I'll smash whomever is doing this to us. Big Frank put down his binoculars and picked up his sniper rifle. He chambered a round.

It's not Her, Granny Roz said. *She's not even here.*

It's somebody. I'm going to find 'em and make them pay.

No, Bunny said, throwing her paws wide, the pale pink of her ears standing tall. *We don't know why. It's better to watch and wait.*

The best defense is offense. We hunt. Big Frank slipped his buck knife into its sheath and pulled his canteen snug against his shoulder.

A sharpie is better than a bullet, Bunny said.

What are you up to, Rabbit? Granny Roz crossed her arms.

A picture formed in my mind. Tossing the x-acto knife back into the pencil box, I picked out a thin sharpie marker. A flick and a twist, and hole was now part of a butterfly's wing. I drew flowers and vines wrapping my wrist; leaves tickled my knuckles. I put the black ink down and picked up red, blue, silver, and green; highlights and shadows—

"What do you think you're doing?"

Lost in creation, I looked up, startled. Mr. Harcourt loomed. The design sprawled from elbow to fingertips. "I—"

"That's what I thought."

Near the pottery wheel someone tittered. "Crazy Kari."

"She's cuckoo for Cocoa Puffs."

"You think?"

Mr. Harcourt sighed. "That's enough. To the counselor's office, Kari. You want to tattoo yourself, do it on your own time."

The student chair in the counselor's office was wider than normal and squishy. It wrapped around my hips and sucked me deep into the padding like a hug. Big Frank squirmed. *Metal folding chairs are more honest,* he groused. *Give me a three legged stool any day.*

The light from the big picture window framed Dr. Susan in silhouette, highlighting bits of fly away hair rising from her scalp like a crown.

L'Oreal number 8g, Golden Summer Sunshine. Granny Roz rolled her eyes. *Just look at them eyebrows. Who does she think she's foolin'? No way that color's anywhere close to natural.*

I think it's pretty, said Bunny. *Like Goldilocks or Cinderella.*

More foolishness, Granny Roz said.

Dr. Susan tapped her keyboard. "How's this week been, Kari?"

I tugged on the edge of my sleeve, squinting.

Dr. Susan glanced up. "Sorry," she said, twisting the blinds closed. "It's that time."

I tugged some more on my sleeve and tried not to stare at the hole in my arm.

Relax, Granny Roz chided. *It's not getting bigger.*

The mouse double-clicked. My eyes darted to Dr. Susan's face.

"So tell me about this week. How're things, Kari?"

I shrugged.

Dr. Susan waited several beats. I fiddled some more with my sleeve. "Kari?" she prompted.

"What?"

"I asked how things were."

With a finger, I traced the edge of the butterfly. "Good," I managed.

Mouse click. Big Frank adjusted his binoculars. *She just checked a box labeled lack of eye contact.*

"When you say this week has been good, what do you mean?"

"Good," I said.

Mouse click. *She checked disengaged,* Big Frank said. *We're heading into the danger zone.*

"Are you getting your school assignments in?"

I nod.

"How are you sleeping?"

Another shrug.

Big Frank gasped. *Incoming! The cursor is hovering over parental consultation. We have a red alert situation, people. Mobilize.*

Sit up! Smile! barked Granny Roz from the porch. *You wanna get us locked up in the nuthouse?*

I sat up and forced my lips back. "I mean, I'm sleeping better. The pills seem to be working."

"No more nightmares?"

"No."

Yes, Big Frank said from the tree blind. *But you're right, stick to name, rank, and serial number. Everything else is strictly need to know.*

Dr. Susan peered over the rims of her glasses. "Kari, I'm concerned about the way you've drawn all over your arm."

"It's just ink."

"It's a lot of ink. What are you trying to cover up?"

Bunny's eyes widened. *Careful. There are wolves about.*

"Nothing."

"Bruises? Did Charlotte or her friends hit you?"

I have bruises, yellow, purple, and green, but not from Charlotte or her friends. Mean girls punch with their words.

Say nothing. Bunny pressed her lips tight.

Dr. Susan nudged a box of tissues closer. "Did someone shove you into a locker?" Bunny hid her head. "Kari? Talk to me. This is a safe place."

Big Frank placed the laser dot in the center of Dr. Susan's forehead. *Target acquired,* he rumbled. *Just say go.*

"Is it bruises, Kari, or something worse?"

Say something, Chile. Anything, Granny Roz said. *Silence is becoming her truth.*

"It's not bruises. It's nothing. I just felt like drawing."

Dr. Susan leaned forward. "Is it cuts? Are you cutting, Kari?"

Cutting? Bunny held her breath.

"It's okay. Lots of girls like you cut themselves. They think it relieves the pain. They think it gives them control."

I blinked. "What?"

"Kari, if you're cutting, I need to know. Cutting is dangerous behavior."

Slow, Chile. Relax. Think about flowers and vines. Butterflies. You're too tense. She thinks you're lying.

"Girls who cut need help, Kari. They can't do it on their own."

You're not alone, Big Frank said. *You got us.*

"I know you want to stop, but you can't. Let me help." Dr. Susan reached out to touch me. I jerked away.

"I'm not cutting. I don't even know what that means."

Dr. Susan leaned back, considering. "I get it. You don't trust me."

"I'm not cutting."

"Okay. You're not ready for this."

"I'm not cutting."

"All right. I believe you." She tossed a pamphlet at me. "This can help."

I slipped it into my backpack and stood. "We done?"

"Not quite. I've been talking with YWF."

"YWF?"

"Young Writers of the Future. I sent them your essay."

"I didn't say you could do that."

"Sit down for a minute. Mrs. Miranda thinks you're a gifted writer."

Wary, I dropped my backpack and flopped onto the chair.

"You've heard of the YWF's summer programs?"

I shrugged.

"They were impressed."

"I can't go."

"Yes, you can."

"There's no way—"

"They're offering you a full-ride scholarship. You just have to show up ready to work."

I bit my lip and studied my knees. There's no way Mom'd ever let me go.

"Things change, Kari. You won't be in high school or living with your mother forever. Remember that."

I flinched.

She's not a mind reader, Chile, Granny Roz said. *It's just a lucky guess.*

Play it cool, said Big Frank.

"Do you want me to talk with your mother about it?"

I shrugged.

Don't cry, don't cry, don't cry, Bunny chanted.

"Kari, you're a smart girl. High school isn't the end. You have a bright future ahead of you. Like that butterfly on your arm, you can be anything you want to be."

"We done now?" I stood up again.

"Yeah, we're done. Let me know about the summer writing program. You know I care, right, Kari? Come back anytime. I'm here for you."

And so are we.

Later that same afternoon, the third hole the size of a pea appeared on my inner thigh. I was hiding in a bathroom stall with my regular clothes stuffed in my backpack. Everyone knew Coach Jensen did one shower check each gym class. Skipping the shower was easy if you changed in a stall.

As if gym wasn't awkward enough.

Unlike the hole on my toe or arm, this one wasn't streaming cold. I sat on the closed toilet seat and poked at it with a pencil. No pain; no pressure. I pushed harder and watched as the pencil slid inside my leg all the way to its nubby eraser. With a flick of my finger I let go. It disappeared.

WTF?

I pressed along the edges of the hole like it was an over-ripe pimple needing a little encouragement. No bulge of a yellow number 2. I kneaded my thigh like bread dough.

Nothing.

How many pencils and pens could I stuff in? Rummaging around in my pencil case, I found my x-acto knife.

Linoleum carving was such a bore.

I popped the safety cover off the blade and considered. I felt the troops stir.

Power, Big Frank said. *Control.*

Pain, Bunny said.

Freedom, Big Frank said, *for girls like us.*

Foolishness. At her kitchen sink Granny Roz peeled carrots lickety-split. *There's only one good use for a knife.*

I listened to a locker slam followed by the sound of running feet. The tardy bell rang. White noise filled my ears, ebbing and flowing as I sat like a stone in a river. I rolled the x-acto knife between my palms, then held it to my cheek, drinking in the coolness of metal against hot flesh.

Granny Roz shook her head. *Lord, grant me strength. Chile, you done wore me out.* Dropping her paring knife among the carrot shavings, Granny Roz left the sink and sat in her rocker on the porch. In no time she was napping, head back with a little bead of drool pooling against her lips. Bunny was curled like a kitten in her burrow.

Against my skin, the blade warmed.

From his hideout in the trees Big Frank nodded. *Power,* he said. *Control.*

I cut.

It was hard at first, rubbery like the surface of an egg or a squishy piece of steak. The blade teetered on edge, then bit, catching the lip of the hole. My skin split, popping like the seal on a jar of pickles. Red, sticky blood welled, filling the hole and flooding my thigh with warmth.

Relief.

Stupid Dr. Susan was right about one thing.

One cut was enough. I stopped the bleeding with a wad of toilet paper pressed flat against my thigh. It wasn't much, a teaspoon of blood at the most, but it cleared my head. Colors were brighter. The taste of lemons and grass filled my mouth. Exhaustion swept over me.

Sleep, Kari, we're here.

I curled around the toilet, resting my flushed cheeks on the tile, inhaling the faint scent of bleach and pee.

Writing camp. I'm getting out of here and going to camp. I'm going to college. I can break free and be my own person. Another little slice and I can feel like this again and again. The empty holes mean nothing. I closed my eyes and didn't wake until the janitor's bucket bumped against the door. I—

Kari, watch out! Big Frank yells.

Breaking from the memory, I leap back to the curb as a car swooshes around the corner and into the high school. "Stupid kid!" the driver yells. "Watch where you're walking. You got a death wish?"

Yeah, right back at ya, butt-head.

Keep it together, Granny Roz says. *That's the second bell.*

I'm late to biology. All eyes are on me as I slip into my seat.

"Let's get started," Mr. Cooper says. "Homework out, please."

"What's that on Kari's face?" Becca snickers under her breath. "Looks like toilet tissue."

"Probably cut herself shaving," Charlotte says. "She's such a troll."

"Yeah, Troll, where's your bridge?" Becca taunts. "Go live under it."

"No, go die under it," Charlotte says.

Bitches. My eyes start to water.

"Oh, look. She's going to cry! Charlotte, you made her cry." Becca holds out her knuckles for a bump.

Sticks and stones, Chile, Granny Roz clucks. *Don't fret. I'll make you a cherry cobbler.*

They can't actually hurt you, Bunny says. *Not here in front of everyone. Mr. Cooper won't let them. All they can do is talk.*

Charlotte bumps Becca's fist with a laugh. "Now watch. Right after class the little loser is going to scamper back to Dr. Susan. That's what you do, right, Loser? Tattletale about the mean girls. You're such a troll."

I open my notebook and pick up a pen. *Ignore them,* Big Frank says, running a bore snake down his barrel. *I got your back.*

When Mr. Cooper walks by, I don't bother handing any papers in. He doesn't even break stride. Head down, I concentrate on drawing intricate spirals, circles, and loops between the ruled lines. As long as they're small it looks like I'm taking notes.

"Baby scribbles," Charlotte mocks. "You're so retarded."

I'm going to writing camp. I've got a scholarship. This is just a way stop on my way to a much better place.

With the homework stacked on his desk, Mr. Cooper clears his throat. "Jonah, you're up," he says. "Now I need all of you to pay attention to the presentations. I'm going to be marking participation grades, so don't think you can just check out when you're not up here with your PowerPoint. I want questions, class. Let's engage our brains. Tiko, dim some of the overheads, please."

It's warm and stuffy in the room. *Chicken coop. Incubator,* Granny Roz mutters. *Do we need eggs?*

Jonah drones on about energy and life coming from the sun. In the darkness, eyelids droop as graphics of leaves and cells blur across the screen. After ten minutes the class is comatose. It takes Mr. Cooper longer that it should to realize Jonah is finished.

"Very good. Any questions?"

No one can muster the energy to think let alone raise a hand. My notebook is filling with ink.

"Thank you, Jonah. Eric?"

Eric bounces up like an over-caffeinated kangaroo. He rubs his hands and bubbles like a salesman making the pitch of his life. "My topic is how parasites rule the world. There is no free-will. It's awesome."

Granny Roz stands up. *Chile, we need to leave. Now.*

It's the middle of class.

Now, says Granny Roz.

I can't leave. I can't risk a zero for participation.

Mr. Cooper rolls his eyes. "Eric, we discussed this."

The class perks up. Eric is smarter than the teachers. Everyone but Mr. Copper knows that.

"But Mr. Cooper, I have proof! Check it—this ant lives in South America." Two large black ants, one with a cherry bulb for a butt fills the screen.

We have to go, Big Frank says. *You have to go.* Suddenly my stomach rumbles and cramps. *Or there'll be trouble.*

Mr. Cooper is annoyed. "Eric—"

Eric advances his slide. "And here's another ant that's controlled by a liver fluke. At night it makes the ant climb up a blade of grass so a cow can eat it."

"That makes no sense."

Kari, says Bunny, *if you love us, you have to leave now.*

We love you, Kari. From the shadows the troops surge; there are more than I can count.

At the front of the class Eric grins. "It's the cycle of life. Climbing trees and grass to get eaten is not natural behavior for these ants. They're being controlled. If it can happen to ants—"

"People are more complex than ants," says Mr. Cooper.

"It's not just ants. It's spiders—"

"Insects are not human."

Kari, Kari, Kari, the voices call. The cramps are unbearable. I'm going to barf.

"—fish, grasshoppers, worms, crabs—" Eric won't stop.

"All lower creatures, Eric."

"How about rats, Mr. Cooper? We use rats to test human drugs, right?"

"Eric."

The voices are a bandsaw in my brain, drowning out Eric and Mr. Cooper. I can't think, can't breathe.

"There's a single-celled parasite that changes the behavior of rats in ways that increase the likelihood that an infected rat will get eaten by a cat. You know why it does this?"

The situation's critical, Bunny says.

"Eric—"

"The parasites need to do it in a cat."

The class roars.

"Principal's office, Eric. Move it."

Now? Big Frank asks.

Not here, Granny Roz says. *Too many witnesses.*

I fall out of my chair as the world fades to black. I can't see, only hear Skylar say, "Uh, Mr. Cooper? I think there's something wrong with Kari."

The whole ride home is torture.

"You made me miss work again, Kari." Mom whips the car into the driveway. "You're not a baby anymore. If you've got a headache, take medicine like a normal person. Don't go whining to the school nurse."

"I'm sorry. I didn't—"

"Yeah, you never do. Get out. I'm late." I grab my bag from the floorboard and open the door. "I want the laundry and dishes done before I get home. If you're not going to school, you're going to work."

"Okay."

"Take chicken out of the freezer for dinner. And if you put my nylons in the dryer, I swear I'll—"

"I won't."

"You're not too big for the belt, Kari. Maybe you need a little reminder."

"I won't forget," I say.

Mom cocks her head at me. I don't like the look in her eyes. "Somebody's getting uppity. Thinks she's better than everybody else."

"I'm not," I say quickly. This is headed nowhere good.

"I got a call from that counselor of yours this morning. Something about a writing camp."

"She talked with them, not me," I say.

"So you don't want to go? Dr. Susan said it's free."

I take a deep breath. "I want to go."

"What?"

"I want to go to a summer writing camp."

Mom leans over and slaps me across the cheek. "Yeah, and I want to be a size six again. Forget it. Neither of us is getting what she wants."

The pain makes my teeth ache. For once the voices are silent. I don't care. This is my life, and I'm breaking free.

"I'm going to a summer writing camp."

Mom laughs. "Oh, look at you. Think you can take me? Go on, try little girl."

I can't meet her eyes.

"That's what I thought. You're not going to camp. I told Dr. Susan you're not well. You need to be here with me. End of discussion."

"When I graduate next year, I'm leaving and going to college."

"Not with those grades. You'll live here with me. You know you can't manage alone. You'll see when I die."

"I—"

"Why are you still sitting here with your mouth open like a retard? Get out and shut the door. It's your fault I'm late." I push the door closed and step back. Mom shakes her head. "I said, shut, not slam. College? Right. Only if they hire you to scrub toilets."

I stand in the driveway watching the car roll past the stop sign. The sun feels good on my face.

In the kitchen, I lift each glass out of the dishwasher and put them upside down in the cupboard. Dr. Phil is nattering on the TV, telling a woman with smeared mascara that she is on a journey to find her authentic self.

I'm going to writing camp. I'm going to college. I'm not going to be anyone's slave any longer. I'm going to tell Dr. Susan about Mom. There are places in the world for girls like me. I don't have to live like this anymore.

My stomach growls. First, I'm going to eat. I get out the bread and make a peanut butter sandwich. There's no milk. I make do with water.

When I sit down in the living room I feel it—an itching, burning sensation under the delicate skin of my cheek. The slap.

Fire ants, Bunny says.

No such thing, silly, Granny Roz says. *Eczema. A little dry skin.*

Poison ivy, says Big Frank.

Hush, now. You'll frighten her. Go wash your face, Chile. Things will be better, you'll see.

I rise and head to the bathroom. When I flip on the light switch, I see terrible crackling lines spreading along my hand, arm, leg. In the mirror I see fine webbing on my face, neck, shoulders. "Crazing," I say aloud. "In pottery it's called crazing."

With a whoosh, the tissue cork in my cheek pops out. The hole tears and widens, but there's no pain, just the sound of a freight train's whistle.

It's time, Granny Roz says.

We're coming, says Big Frank.

Hello, says Bunny.

I lean closer to the mirror. The hole on my cheek is no longer empty. An eye peers out.

Aunty Mitzy's Helpers

Standing outside her house, Aunty Mitzy fumbled in her purse. She took out her spare glasses, a crumpled tissue, new tissues still in their pack, gum, a thimble, the ace of spades, a fortune cookie, and her comb with one tine broken off the end and set them on the chair next to her front door.

Still no key.

She sighed.

Guess she'd have to get the spare.

If only she could remember where she hid it.

She walked over to the coffee cans of orchids hanging from her chain link fence.

Something about *makai*.

Renton, her nephew, was all the time trying to give her little tricks to help her remember things, things like one, two, grab your shoes, tree, four, lock da door.

Mo'bettah she jus' write 'em down.

But *makai* and keys. Maybe ocean breeze? Were her keys hidden where the trade winds blew through her lānai in the afternoon?

Nope. Not there.

Confun it, she thought. I really need to get in the house. 5-4-4 was calling and the call was urgent.

"Hey," she said, "I need my keys. Hui! Can I get a little kokua? I no like shishi in da bushes! Shame, you know."

THWACK! CHING!

It was the sound of her keys bouncing off the front door and coming to rest on her front step.

"Ah, there they stay," she said. "Mahalo plenny! Jess wait one skoshi, yeah?" She rushed through the door. "I get cookies for you guys, but I, ah, gottah take care of something first."

The hibiscus bush twitched.

"Shhh," said Moke.

Giggles.

Moke rolled his eyes. "You guys more worse than kindergarteners. Like you never."

THIS ONCE WAS A SEA

From the safety of her rented SUV, Leticia Greenbaum watched rain fall in sheets, obscuring the sign over the main doors of a big industrial building painted in shades of deep-sea green. Squinting, she could just make out the logo for Salt of the Earth Inc., and the words Field Operations Center, Gilgamesh, Utah.

This must be the right place, she thought, throwing it into park and cutting the engine. *What a shithole. Nothing but sage brush for miles.*

A senior account manager with Bountiful Insurance, it had been more than a minute since she'd last done an onsite appraisal. Back in Seattle, most of her time was spent wining and dining big corporate clients and signing off spreadsheets, but this claim was too big to leave to junior adjusters.

Damn Janice. This is her account. She should've been the one to drive to BFE Utah. What a baby. Appendectomies are no big deal.

Leticia unplugged her phone from the console and slipped it into her briefcase. *Whatever. Just get through it. Take a few statements, snap some photos, and put it all in the rearview. Easy-peasy.* She checked her Fitbit and scowled. *Too much sitting. But if I hurry, I can make the last flight and get more steps in at the airport.*

Fiddling with the keys, Leticia was looking down when something struck her window. She looked up. Sasquatch waved. She shrieked, the sound rising like a chainsaw through a brick wall.

Sasquatch jumped back. "Whoa, there! Sorry, ma'am. Didn't mean to startle you. I'm Barry, Barry Giles. You the adjuster?" Barry was six foot six in stocking feet with a barrel chest and beard that rivaled Santa's. When he was sure she wasn't going to pull a gun, he shifted his golf umbrella to his other hand and leaned forward, peering through the SUV's window.

Not Sasquatch, but maybe his cousin.

Leticia swallowed her heart back into her chest and nodded.

"Oh, good. You found us." Barry hefted his umbrella. "It's raining." *No shit, Sherlock.* "Thought I'd come get you."

Yeah, not getting that close to you, buddy. Nice try. "Thanks, but I'm fine." Leticia pulled the door handle. The dome light flashed on.

"You sure? It's coming down cats and dogs—"

"Yes." She tried to ease the door open.

Barry raised the umbrella higher. "It's no trouble, ma'am."

"Could you back up a little? The door—"

"Oh, sure. Careful, it's—" Leticia swung her leg out, stepped down, and sank, cold sludge filling her Miu Miu loafers. "—muddy."

"What the actual—"

"Yeah," Barry sighed. "Parking lot's six inches deep. Look, you got boots or something? Hip waders, maybe?"

Rain ran from the edge of the umbrella down the collar of her shirt. "No."

"They told you this was a flood claim, right?"

"I—"

Barry shook his head. "You can't walk in those. Just slip them off and leave them. We'll find you something else inside."

Standing in the lobby and dripping on the cement floor, Leticia began questioning her life choices. Icy red clay oozed between her toes, her oyster-colored nail polish looking like rotting teeth in a charnel-house mouth. Her pants were soaked and muddy to the knee, and her hair hung in wet tangles, smearing her glasses.

"Found 'em." Barry came back with a pair of irrigation boots, a Tyvek suit, and a couple of shop rags. "Best I could do." Leticia took a shop rag and blotted her hair. He held out the boots. "They'll be big, but better than barefoot. I tucked a pair of socks in them." Leticia blinked, her eyes wide through her streaked and spotted glasses, her mascara bleeding like a bruise. Barry looked away. "Don't worry," he said. "They're clean."

Leticia set her briefcase on the reception desk and took the clothes. "Where is everybody?"

Barry shrugged. "Corporate sent them all home. Salt's not worth anything wet."

"You're claiming total loss?"

"Millions of years ago, this was an inland sea. Cut off from the ocean, the water dried up and left rich deposits of pure salt just below the surface. We're a shaft operation—rooms and pillars, the deepest less than 300 feet. Our mining operation is a matter of scooping and loading trucks. All the salt gets sent to our packing facility in Price—easiest thing in the world." He eyed her ruined power suit. "They really didn't tell you how bad it was?"

"I'm not from the Utah office. I'm from Seattle."

"Oh, good. So you know about rain." Leticia looked at him, nonplussed. Barry cleared his throat. "Like I said, I'm Barry, the Operations Supervisor. I didn't catch your name."

"Leticia Greenbaum, Senior Account Manager."

"Well, Letty—"

"Leticia."

Barry paused, then nodded. "If you'd like, you can change in my office, Ms. Greenbaum. I'll wait in the back. The main entrance to the mine is through there."

She picked up her briefcase. "There's paperwork. Forms and interviews—"

"Of course, and we'll get right to them. But there's something you need to see first."

"Barry, I know what flooding looks like. This ain't my first rodeo."

He bit his lip, careful not to catch her eye or look at her muddy bare feet. "Didn't think it was," he said, shaking his woolly mammoth head. "But nothing I say will make sense unless you see it first." He turned and pointed. "Office is that way, first door to the left." The overhead lights flickered. "Power's iffy. The lines are unstable. I left you a lit lantern on my desk. Bring it when you come back. You won't need your briefcase where we're going. You can leave it on my desk."

"I need photos."

"Up to you, then."

As she turned to head to his office, the big picture window in the lobby flexed; the cement beneath her feet trembled.

"Whoa! That was a big 'un," said Barry.

Leticia smiled. "Not really. I've felt worse." Like two furry caterpillars, Barry's eyebrows raised. "Dad was in the Air Force," she added.

"Sonic boom?" Barry asked. "You think that was a sonic boom?"

She lifted her chin and looked down her nose. "Of course. I grew up around them. They're no big deal."

"Nope," said Barry. "Not a sonic boom. That's coming from the ground beneath us, not the sky." Barry paused. "Feel that one? That one's just a little baby."

If she hadn't been paying attention, she would have missed the slight sway beneath her feet, like standing with your toes on the end of the dock on a warm spring day. "What—?"

Barry shrugged. "Things shift in a salt mine."

"Even before the flood?"

Barry cocked his head as if listening to something far away. "They're more frequent now. Water's filling spaces it hasn't in aeons. Things bubble up." He stepped back, rubbing his face and smoothing his beard. "You're shivering. I can see the goosebumps from here. Why don't you get changed? Sooner begun, sooner done." He spun on his heel and headed deeper into the building. "Don't forget the lantern," he called. "We're going to need it."

Alone in Barry's office, Laticia rolled her eyes. *All he needs is a framed photo of the company picnic.* On the wall next to his desk were his geology diploma from the University of Southern Utah and a framed certificate of mining safety training. On the bookcase behind his desk were rows of heavy three-ring binders lightly coated with dust and a photo of the Giles family on vacation, three strapping boys and an uncomfortably tall girl at the beach. But what really caught her eye was the crystal ball paperweight glistening in the lamplight. There was something in the middle bigger than her fist. She picked it up.

Heavy. She rolled it between her palms. *Smooth. Polished.* She peered closer. *WTF? Is that a bug?* She counted. *Eight legs and two lobster claws. Not a bug. Some kind of crab, maybe? And what are those things coming out of its head? Antennae? Mandibles?* She tipped it into her other hand to see it from another angle. She held it closer to the lantern. *It looks like a flea mated with a king crab. What's that on its belly? Some kind of octopus sucker?* She shuddered, remembering how her father lit a match to burn leeches off her legs the summer her cousin pushed her into the pond.

Soulless. Eyeless. A monster. Who keeps a monster on his desk? She dropped it back on the pile of papers.

As she turned away, shadows flickered and danced in the crystal. *Did it twitch? Was the right claw now higher than the left?* Leticia closed her eyes. *Stop. Just stop it,* she thought. *You're letting Sasquatch and the creepy mine get to you.* The hair stood on the back of her neck. She slapped at it. *It's just water dripping. Nothing's crawling down your spine. You're freaking out over nothing.*

She glanced at her watch and made a promise to herself. *It doesn't matter how late it gets. I'm not staying around here. I'll drive to Vegas to catch a flight if I have to.*

Leticia slipped off her wet pants, wiping the mud off her feet as best she could. She slid into the jumpsuit, zipped it up, and rolled the sleeves to her elbows and the hem to her ankles. Big wads of rough cloth bunched around her body, rustling like a tarp in the wind whenever she moved.

As much as she tried to ignore it, she kept glancing at the paperweight.

It's probably a fancy prop from a movie like Jurassic Park *or some D&D gamer crap. What a surprise. Sasquatch is a twelve-year-old nerd living in a salt mine in the desert.* She pulled on the boots, three sizes too big. *All I need is a red clown nose. What a shitshow.*

She looked at her beautiful alligator briefcase and shook her head. *I'll just take my phone and snap a few photos. Barry can email me the claim forms later. I'm not staying one second longer than I have to.*

Another thought crossed her mind. *I'm going to have to fly home in a Tyvek suit and irrigation boots.*

Screw it. There's always a Walmart. Nobody will look twice if I walk in like this. No matter what, you're never the weirdest person in a Walmart.

When Leticia waddled up to the entrance to the mine, phone in one hand, lantern in the other, Barry held out a hardhat. She just looked at him. "Regulations," he said, taking the lantern.

Leticia jammed the hardhat on her head. Too big; it wobbled. Barry held the lantern high as she tried to adjust the fit. It was useless. To keep the brim from covering her eyes or knocking her glasses down her nose, she had to keep her head tipped up.

Perfect, she thought, *just perfect. I'm ready for the cover of* Vogue. *Hillbilly-desert Chic.* Barry shifted his weight, swaying a bit as another wave buckled beneath them.

Leticia glared. *He's enjoying this. Making the city girl feel small.*

Barry said, "Did you see the thing on my desk?"

Leticia narrowed her eyes. "The picture of your family on vacation? Cute kids."

"Not the photo. The thing next to the lantern. It was round." He jiggled the lantern as if to jog her memory.

Nope. Not going to feed the fanboy. Leticia pursed her lips and shook her head.

Barry said, "It was in a clear salt ball sitting on a pile of papers."

"Like a paperweight?"

"Yeah, that's it." His eyes sparkled.

"No, I didn't notice anything like that." Like butter wouldn't melt in her mouth.

"Oh. Well." Barry frowned. "I really hoped you would."

"I'm not into gaming," she said.

He perked up. "So you did see it."

Throw him a bone. Get this show on the road. "I might've. What was in it?"

"We don't know."

"What?"

Barry rubbed the back of his neck. "We find them sometimes in the salt. Most are like the one on my desk, encased in a flawless salt crystal. They're perfectly round and usually the size of a quarter. The guys saved that one for me because it's so big."

"How...thoughtful."

"I'm not explaining this well," said Barry. "Look. We used to sell them for a couple of bucks in the gift shop."

"You have a gift shop?"

"Behind reception. For school kids and tour groups. People like big machines."

Leticia adjusted her glasses. "Who doesn't?" she said, like someone who really doesn't.

"It's a goodwill thing. We give them a little bag of salt at the end. We don't charge admission, but we do use the proceeds from the gift shop to support the local Sub for Santa. Me and some of the guys do the local Christmas Eve deliveries. It's fun."

"Of course," Leticia said, swallowing a yawn.

He held up a hand. "We're getting off track. None of this important."

She tipped hardhat off her glasses, saying, "It's your story. I'm just here for the ride."

"Here's the thing." Barry swayed as another shockwave rolled by. Leticia let it pass through her. It was surprising what you got used to.

Barry said, "About a month ago, I got an email from a grad student from USU's School of Paleontology. His nephew'd showed him one of our salt-bug balls, and he wanted to come see the mine. He thought the salt-bugs were related to trilobites—or were at least that old. But the lower levels had already started to flood, so I put him off and just sent him a couple of samples. We continued to email and text. I sent him some photos. He was curious why the salt-bugs balls weren't squished like trilobites or fish fossils. He thought they were...I dunno, too *plump*. He was running tests. Yesterday I got another text. The salt-bugs are not related to trilobites or crabs. They're even older."

Leticia opened her mouth, but before she could say a word, another not-sonic boom rumbled, sending ripples through puddles like a crocodile's wake through the bayou. "Are we safe here, Barry?" she asked. "All this shaking and booming makes me anxious. I feel like it's all going to collapse."

Barry adjusted his grip on the lantern. "Don't worry. The mine won't collapse, even if it fully floods. The supports are designed for this. *Over*-designed if you ask me. You should know—it's one of the riders on the insurance policy."

The ground rumbled again, sending shockwaves through her toes to rattle her too loose helmet down over her eyes. "You sure about that?" she asked, pushing it back.

"Yeah. The ground's already saturated. It's been raining for forty days and forty nights in the mountains north of here."

"Forty days? That's—"

"Biblical?"

Leticia grimaced. "I was going to say *a lot*."

"I forgot you're from Seattle. Maybe it's not so unusual for you."

"Barry, I'm trying to make a flight."

"Let's get to it, then. This way." At the small side gate to the mine's cavernous entrance, he paused, looking back at her. "You're insured, right?"

"Hilarious, Barry. Now open the damned gate."

He unlocked the gate, swinging it wide, and walked to an electric panel. "Leave it open," he said as he threw the main light switch. The high bay fixtures overhead flashed once, twice, then sizzled. He slapped at the panel, flipping breakers. "Son of a bitch!"

"Barry?"

"Yeah, that's what I was afraid of. Here, let me—" Barry reached over and turned on the headlamp in her hardhat. The warm yellow glow hit Barry squarely in the chest. "That's better. Follow me. Watch your step. It angles down from here."

At the entrance, the first thing Leticia noticed was the smell—salty, briney, like kelp beds at low tide along the shores of Puget Sound. She tipped her hardhat back, the light shining more on the ceiling than the walkway and followed Barry into the gloom.

Barry walked out on a platform and stood by a railing. He motioned her closer. "This is the observation deck. From here you can see all the way down into the center of the mine, about 100 feet to the floor. From there we have a few main shafts that go deeper. A conveyer belt runs along the right. Normally, we back the trucks in over there."

"Oh my God," she whispered. "The water is level with the platform." She took out her phone and snapped a few pictures, the red and white walls twinkling in the flash.

"Yeah. It's a giant pool. Let me light it for perspective." From his pocket Barry pulled out a flashlight tied to a thin rope. "Waterproof," he said as he turned it on and chucked it into the water like a fishing line. The light spiraled down, bouncing crazily as it pushed past pink clouds of semi-dissolved salt. Leticia leaned over, snapping as the light drifted down, down, down.

"This can't be from rain," she said. "Noah's flood wouldn't account for all this water."

Barry shook his head. "I don't think so either. Ever heard of Howard Reservoir?"

"No."

"It's about two miles upstream from us. The state owns it. Forty years ago, guy by the name of Philips got a lease and started, well, *diverting* local tributaries."

"That's illegal," Leticia said.

"Yeah, but who's looking? We're out in the desert. Philips created campgrounds, boat ramps, the works. Brought tourist and tax dollars in. Good for the local economy. Nobody's asking questions."

"Typical," she said. "But..."

"But he used embarkment dams. Soil's not right for that."

"You suspect the reservoir's leaking?"

Barry scoffed. "I know it is. Channeling under bedrock and through salt pockets. This is where it's collecting."

"That's great!" Leticia said. Barry leaned back. "I mean for your claim. If the state owns the land, but wasn't making sure improvements weren't up to code, they're liable. We'll look into that. States have deep pockets. That's good news."

Barry sighed. "Litigation take years. I don't think we have that long."

Another tremor rippled across the water. The light in the pool winked out.

In her Tyvek suit, Leticia stood taller. "There are federal aid programs. Low interest loans. Salt dries; it's not completely ruined when it gets wet, not like silk or wheat. This is just a pause, Barry, not the end of the world."

"From your lips to God's ears, Letty," said Barry. "But all this water isn't what I wanted to show you." Barry swung the lantern to the left. Encased in the salt wall was the same creature as on his desk, but this one the size of a horse.

Leticia gasped.

"This is Oscar. He's the biggest salt-bug we found, but he wasn't encased like the little ones. Kids on fieldtrips used to dare one another to lick it. The crew called him their good luck charm." Another boom echoed through the cavern; this time waves splashed over the edge of the deck, salting her boots and stinging her nose.

"There's more. The text from the grad student said the salt-bugs were eggs. He thinks Oscar's a juvenile."

"A juvenile? That means—"

"We don't know what that means. But these creatures aren't like trilobites or crabs. They're closer to cicadas."

In the flickering lamplight, Oscar twitched.

Another boom. Chunks of salt rained down from the ceiling.

Boom, boom, boom.

Stillness.

Barry turned to Leticia. "What do you know about cicadas?"

BOOM.

Splash.

They turned. From the middle of the caldron rose a red beachball stuck to the top of a yellow flagpole. It split open, the green cat-eye pupil locking on the lantern held high. Around it the water roiled, hissing like cicadas rising in a storm.

Leticia dropped her phone, shattering glass into a million pieces. Barry stepped between her and the leviathan, his Sasquatch body bold as waves crashed around his knees. "Run!" he screamed, pushing her toward the gate. She turned and fled, high-stepping in the too big boots, the toes catching and tripping. Lying on her back in cold, red earth, she watched the creature emerge from the brine, *boom, boom, boom,* one eye stalk, two eye stalks, a claw, and a terrible beaked mouth undulating in the center.

The last thing she smelled was salt.

DOORS

When the trauma nurse leaves them alone for a moment, Kyle grabs Shae's hand, yanking her close. She ignores the flaring pain in her hip as a hospital bedrail digs a deep bruise and fights to keep her feet. He's stronger than he should be, lying like a mummy in loose saline-soaked wrappings, his vitals and pain managed by machines and tubes.

Her ear next to his lips, Kyle's breath is ashes and sepsis as it wheezes from his lungs. She tries to smile as she holds her breath, eyes watering. "Kill me, Shae," he whispers. "Kill me now before she comes back."

At his words, an infinite number of doors erupt in the universe of possibilities all around Kyle's hospital bed. Shae doesn't want to believe it, but the whirling thresholds are impossible to ignore. This hospital room is a critical life nexus, one of three power-filled moments in her lifetime that change everything.

Clarity blazes like wildfire; she's leapfrogged through future possibilities once before, racing against that moment when the doors lock tight, the future narrowed to one inevitability. There's no way to explore them all.

Choosing the future is both a gift and a curse.

Oblivious to the doors swirling around his bed, doors only Shae can see and pass through, Kyle's morphine-hazed eyes beseech her. "Shae, do it. Take the pillow and put it over my face. Please. I don't want to live like this."

Shae steps away from the bed and flees through the nearest, most likely possibility.

From the doorway she watches this version of the future unfold like a movie, a future where she doesn't smother Kyle with a pillow or slip extra morphine into his drip. Two nurses, Chubby and Thin, debride charred flesh. Kyle moans and tries to jerk away, but experience has taught them to tie his arms to the bedrail and strap his legs to the bed. Thin soothes him, touching the island of healthy skin on his shoulder. "It will be over soon, Kyle. Just try to hang in there."

With the ointment's first kiss, Kyle shrieks and gasps in short quick bursts like a fish pulled from the lake to the dock. Thin is swift with a numbing spray, but there's really no other way but to gut through it. Raw flesh is scrapped clean or it's slow death by infection, a suffocation of pus.

Chubby reaches for a fresh scrubbing pad and catches Thin's eye. "I'm never going near a campfire again," she mutters.

Thin nods. "So stupid," she whispers. "So unnecessary."

Blinking back tears, Shae realizes Kyle is deep, deep, deep into his pain. The nurses' words are less than ripples in a sea of agony.

"Tragic." Chubby runs a pad delicately over Kyle's cheek, flicking away dead skin as she goes. Kyle arches his back, but it's no use. The nurses are skilled and relentless in their care. Kyle will heal.

Moving forward, Shae crosses another threshold.

Kyle sprawls on their couch, the skin on his face red and puckered, drawn upward in a jack-o-lantern's grin. He's wearing long sleeves and cotton gloves, a far cry from the mummy wraps at the hospital. A pale, exhausted version of herself walks in and places a plastic cup with a straw on the coffee table. Kyle eyes it for a second before batting it across the room.

Pale Shae scrambles after it.

"Leave it," he slurs.

"You promised to drink more. It's good for your skin."

"Whatever."

"It's important, Kyle."

"Like you care."

"Of course I care!"

"I'm hideous," he says.

"No, you're not."

"I'm a monster."

"No," she sighs, mopping at the water puddles with her sleeve. "You're not."

"I am."

"Then you're my monster, and I love you."

"I hate you."

"Kyle—"

"This is your fault, Shae," Kyle starts.

From the doorway, Shae watches herself grind her teeth and realizes this conversation is their version of *Ninety-nine Bottles of Beer.* Pale Shae says the second line. "You wanted to fish, Kyle,"

"I'm never fishing again."

"The doctors say you can. Let's go. We can head up to the lake right now."

"The hell I'm fishing with you."

"What about—"

"Bobby? Skeeter? Slim Jim? None of those guys can stand to look at me. You heard what Hunter said. Said I'd scare all the fish."

"He was kidding! Remember when you used to call him Whiffle? The whole team chanted that every time he got up to bat—his *own* team. And Skeeter? What about the summer you guys called him Two Dunk because he got hammered at the basketball game? Trash talk is bro-love language. Call 'em up. Bet someone's ready to head to the lake right now."

"I ain't fishing again."

Second verse, same as the first. She says, "You're alive. That's the important part."

"Freddy Kruger," Kyle mumbles. "Halloween. Every damn day."

"If you want a movie, I'll make popcorn," she jokes, but the smile doesn't reach her eyes.

At the chorus, he says, "This is your fault, Shae."

He's right, Shae thinks as she watches herself set the cup on the table. *There's no plastic surgery, no ointment, no faith-healing cure for Kyle. Buck Up Li'l Camper is not his style, and there's no Pollyanna sunshine miracle moment ahead in this timeline.*

Shae steps backwards and shuts the door. This is not the future she'll choose.

Around her doors to future possibilities whirl like wild leaves in an autumn sky, a few stuttering in flight just long enough for Shae to cross their thresholds if she chooses. By now most are shut, and she wonders about the futures behind those doors, oak doors, iron doors, doors made of glass, doors that are gossamer curtains, and doors carved like stone. She bites her lip and plunges sideways along an alternate track.

A doctor consults his charts. "We're going to have to amputate. The infection is too deep."

Shae starts running, leaping through open doors as future possibilities blur like an old fashioned newsreel.

"We'll try more hyperbaric treatments, but you'll have to prepare yourself—"

"The cadaver skin grafts didn't take. We're going to have to harvest healthy skin from—"

"Phantom pain is often—"

"With therapy, he might be able to walk—"

"Hospice care—"

"Our grief counseling services are available—"

Which doorway, which one? Near the edge where the future is born, Shae closes her eyes and remembers Kyle hiking up the mountain trail. Healthy and strong, he laughed when her pack got snagged by a tree branch.

"You spaz," he said. "I can't believe you walked into it."

All around her Shae feels doors locking, the tumblers spinning on futures no longer viable. *I'm taking too long,* she thinks. *My indecision is choosing the future without me.*

Two long jumps backward and Shae passes through a doorway marked with a skull and crossbones. Over the threshold she watches herself slip a trash bag over Kyle's head and twist it tight.

A final sigh, the alarm bell of a hospital monitor, and the door disappears behind her. Darkness flashes as Shae feels time bend around her like a hula hoop. There's the sound of wings rushing and a tug in her gut as Kyle's soul passes through her. She closes her eyes, holds on, and refuses to throw up.

The sound of bowling balls rolling a strike startles her. Her eyes blink open. She's surrounded by pine trees and aspens that reach like cathedral spires. The air is filled with the scent of daylilies and cinnamon. Her backpack leans against a tree.

Our campground? Am I back where I started?

As she gathers her bearings, there's a haze in the air that softens the lemon-yellow light. When she tries to fill her lungs to clear her head, she realizes she's not breathing. She's in the place where all doors eventually lead.

Along the dock freshly gutted trout glisten, ready for the frying pan. Shae turns to see Kyle standing near a roaring campfire. He charges, arms waving over his head.

"You don't even give me a chance!" Strong and whole, Kyle's voice is jagged lightning and rolling thunder.

Shae begins weeping in ugly, snotty gulps as Kyle towers over her like the judgment of God. She pulls her heart raw and bleeding from her chest and offers it to him. "You beg me. You say you don't want to live like that."

Kyle takes her heart and throws it into the fire where it hisses like water in a skillet and disappears. "No, Shae. It's *you* who can't stand to live with *me* like that."

"That's not true, Kyle. I love you no matter what."

"You make a fool out of me, Shae."

Shae scrubs her eyes on her sleeve, the bloodstains from her heart streaking her cheeks. "I make a choice."

"A choice." Kyle scoffs and looks toward the fire. "You play the victim, but you're really the puppet master. You pull strings and people dance. You cut strings when it serves you best."

"I can't see every possibility—no one can. We all die, Kyle. I spare you—"

"You spare me nothing. Stop lying and admit it. You kill me to be with James."

Shae's head snaps up. "That's impossible. I don't even know a James," she says.

Kyle's chest puffs with righteous indignation. "But you do meet him, don't you, the nice man who helps you fix your flat tire—and in the rain, no less. Who does that, Shae?"

"I don't know what you're talking about."

"Trust me. You meet him."

"You're not making sense."

"You meet him because you kill me. You choose a golden door that leads to a family and a white picket fence."

"I don't—"

"Yeah, you do. After you kill me, I wait here alone by our campfire every damn day and watch."

"If you watch, you know she cries." A tall young man with light brown eyes walks up and takes Shae by the hand.

Shae flinches. "Who—"

Kyle's eyes narrow. "What're you doing here?"

"I'm here for Shae."

"You're here because you have skin in the game."

The stranger shrugs. "Maybe."

Shae pulls her hand away. "Who are you?"

Kyle balls his hands into fists and leans forward. "Leave."

"It's not up to you," the man says.

Kyle drops his hands and glares, his breath hot and hissing in her ear. "No matter what you say, it's selfish, Shae. And when you kill me we can't ever be together." Kyle spits at the stranger's feet and walks away.

"Kyle—" Shae says.

"Let him go," the stranger says.

"But—"

"Can't change the past, Mom," he says. "Not even you."

Only the future, Shae thinks, spinning away. She sprints through the archway on her left, leaping back the way she came.

Slam, slam, slam.

Only two thresholds left. Shae leaps through the tallest, pulling the door closed behind her. She prays she still has a choice to make.

"Shae?" Kyle upends a can of gasoline, splashing big slugs of fuel everywhere. No wussy charcoal lighter fluid for him. "Shae!"

Shae starts. "What did you say?"

He shakes his head. "Scattered-brained idiot. Can't you focus for one damn minute? Get your head out of the clouds and stop mouth-breathing like a retard." He reaches over and adjusts a sopping piece of wood. The pile in front of him is heaped high and deep enough to roast a pig. "I said, I'll get the fire started. Go get my bait from the cooler." Shae hesitates. "Or is that too complicated for you?"

Near the tent a golden door shimmers. She's back to nexus prime.

She watches as Kyle lifts a lighter from his pocket. "Why don't we skip the campfire tonight," she says in a rush.

"You know if I don't start it now the coals won't be ready in time for the trout."

"I'm not in the mood for fish tonight."

Kyle tilts his head to the side. "Not in the mood."

"Trout's not my favorite."

"Funny. You ate the ones Skeeter caught last week easily enough. Said they were the best ever."

"Let's skip the fire and go on a hike. I'll make sandwiches. We'll eat by the lake."

"Why? You think I can't catch any?" Slamming the gas can down, the last of the liquid erupts like a geyser, splashing Kyle's jeans and hiking boots, soaking the cuffs of his shirt. He throws his arms wide. "Son of a—! Look what you made me do!"

"I'm sorry—"

"Yeah, you are!" Spinning on his heel, he stalks off. "Whatever. I'm going fishing. Something good better come out of this day and fast. What a waste."

"I—"

"I'm eating fish for dinner." Kyle flings his lighter over his shoulder, striking Shae in the face. "Let me know when you change your mind."

Just past the tent the golden door flickers; the future possibilities are coalescing into stone.

The lighter lands in the dirt. Shae stares at it for a very long time.

BROTHERS

Drifting in our small fishing boat off the coast of the Big Island, Hawaii, I look toward the Naʻiwi shore. Our family's tents are on the campground above the sand, but I don't see my cousins Haley, Kade, or Jace. Uncle Jeff took them cliff jumping. Too dangerous, my parents said. Come fishing with us. We'll catch something good for dinner.

I don't even like fish. It's so unfair.

"Kekoa," Dad says. "Why aren't you wearing your life jacket?"

"Hot," I say. "Itchy."

Mom says, "You know the rules."

"In a minute," I say, leaning over the safety railing.

On shore, I watch my cousins Roxi and Maile practice hula in the shade. While Tutu and the Aunties talk story and play cards, Uncle Josh tends the grill. Fat dripping and juice sizzling onto kiawe coals, the smell of the huli-huli chicken reaches all the way to the boat.

So ʻono. And I'm so hungry. I want to go back to camp where the fun is. Where the food is. We haven't caught anything all day.

"Do we really need to catch fish? Uncle Josh is cooking chicken," I whine.

"Put your jacket on now, Kekoa," Mom says. "Stop stalling."

But before I can, a breeze steals my hat.

"No!" I swing my arm to catch it, but it falls into the water, the current teasing it just out of reach.

Dad says, "I'll get the net."

"No, I got it, Dad." I jump up and rest my thighs against the rail. Balancing with one hand on the boat, I stretch out like I'm playing first base. My fingers brush the brim.

"Kekoa," Mom warns.

Just a tiny bit more—

I fall.

I don't even have time to scream.

Underwater, I sink like a stone, my shoes dragging like anchors. My ears pop as the ocean sucks me down, down, down. Water swims up my nose. I open my eyes and blink through the salt sting. Bubbles escape my lips, tickling as they rise.

I kick and kick, but the ocean won't let me go. Down I sink, faster than I can swim. I cover my mouth with both hands, trying to keep my breath in.

Drowning.

It's a terrible way to die.

Out the corner of my eye, something flickers.

I'm not alone. The hair rises on the back of my neck. I spin in the water, trying to spot the new danger. Rising fast out of the darkness and spiraling like a torpedo, death comes.

It's a shark.

He's big—at least six feet long. He circles past me; his alien black eye peering into mine.

I kick harder and swing my arms like I'm climbing a ladder, but I'm not going anywhere. My bubbles race past me to the surface.

Only ten yards away, the shark shakes his head, flashing his teeth.

It's no use. I can't swim away. I make a fist and face him. I'm not going down without a fight.

He rounds in a tight circle and charges. I pull back my fist. The pressure wave hits a split second before I swing, a moment when time slows and I can count each gaping tooth. I punch and punch until his head snaps back, eyes wide. He jerks away.

Holy cow. That worked.

I tip my head to the surface. The boat's miles above me. I ditch my shoes. Anchors gone, I start to rise. I swim, pulling my arms and legs like a frog.

Twenty feet more. I'm going to make it.

WHAM!

The shark hits me in the back, propelling me through the water like a rocket. I reach back and rip at his tender gills. He jerks away again and circles to the front. He lowers his head.

He's not giving up.

My lungs burn. The ringing in my ears is louder than the recess bell. I'm dizzy. Around the edges, my vision blurs. There's no way I can make it to the surface now. I shake my head and try to think.

If I breathe in water, it will end. Just one giant breath of saltwater, then darkness, no pain. But my lips refuse to open. My lungs won't swell. I can't bring myself to do it.

I'm not giving up.

This time, the shark comes cautiously. As he sidles along my stomach, I punch and punch, my knuckles tearing against his sandpaper skin. To him my fists are nothing more than the buzzing of a fly to a bull. When his nose nudges my ribs, I screw my eyes tight and scream my lungs empty. I feel him thrash, burrowing his head.

For an eternity, I wait, but I don't feel teeth.

Maybe you don't feel what kills you.

The shark flicks his tail, once, twice, three times.

Faster than the bubbles, I rise.

My head breaks the surface. Gasping, I open my eyes, expecting to see red lehua blossoms of blood in the water, but all I see is my shredded tee-shirt floating around me. Thirty yards away in our boat, Mom and Dad frantically scan the water. Dad's about to jump in. The shark nudges me one last time, then turns away.

"Mom!" I yell, but my head goes back under.

"There!" Mom points.

"Kekoa, I'm coming!" Dad says.

"No!" I scream, flailing to stay at the surface. "Shark!"

The shark's dorsal fin cruises to the boat and passes along side. Mom looks down. "Oh, Ke Akua, look at the stripes! Kamalei! It's Kamalei!" she shrieks.

The shark wheels and circles toward me. The boat's too far. Dad's too far. Treading water, I brace myself. This time I'll go for the eyes.

Mom shouts, "Kekoa! Grab the shark!"

Grab the shark? Is she crazy?

"Do it!" Dad yells.

As the shark brushes by, I grab his dorsal fin. In an instant, the shark glides over to the boat. Dad reaches down, pulls me out of the water, and dumps me on the deck. I cough and cough all the water out of my lungs, but Mom and Dad don't hug or scold me. They don't even hand me a towel. They're both leaning over railing.

"Mom?"

She turns to me, tears in her eyes. "Come," she says.

I peer over the side to see the shark resting alongside our boat. Mom leans down into the water and strokes his back. Dad's crying, too. Mom takes my hand and places it on the shark. Along his back are delicate stripes of black, gray, blue, and red, checkered and crisscrossed like sunlight through water. I've never seen anything like it.

Mom whispers in my ear. "Kekoa, thank your brother."

I whip my head at her in disbelief. She's not joking. Dad kneels next to me and puts his hand on the shark, too. He says, "It's true. Before you were born, Mom and I went camping at Naʻiwi." He gestures to the shore.

Mom says, "I was seven months pregnant."

"Wait. You had a baby before me?"

She nods. "The doctor told me everything was fine. The baby was strong and healthy. But in the middle of the night, I went into labor. Your brother was still-born." She takes a deep breath as the memory slides across her face. "I named him Kamalei for the star that shone when he was born. In the moonlight, I washed my firstborn in the sea and wrapped his body in a checkered blanket." She traces the shark's stripes with her finger. "This pattern. This towel." Beneath sandpaper skin, shark muscles twitch. "I'd know it anywhere."

"But—"

Dad says, "Just listen. In the morning, we dug a grave near the beach and buried Kamalei."

"You left him? Is that even legal?"

Dad smiles. "Naʻiwi is a beautiful place. Peaceful. No matter who owns it, it's been our family's land for generations. It seemed like the right thing to do."

"Dad and I spent three days watching the tides and stars and telling Kamalei how much we loved him. We knew he needed to meet the rest of his ʻohana, so we left for a few hours to bring them."

"Everybody came—the entire ʻohana. Grandparents, great-grandparents, aunties, uncles—everybody. We brought a stone to mark the grave, but when we got here, something had torn open the ground. The blanket, your brother—every-thing—gone."

"Gone? I don't understand."

Dad caresses the shark as his tears roll into the ocean. "We failed our son. We left him alone to be eaten by animals."

"I couldn't bear it," Mom says. "My precious baby was gone, and I didn't even have a place to lay a lei."

Dad says, "But then my great-grandmother Tutu Kalamaonamano told us not to cry. 'We are people of the sea,' she said. 'Look with your ancestors' eyes. Feel with your ancestors' hearts.' She took your mother by the hand and showed her the trail in the sand that led from the empty grave to the ocean, saying, 'No animal dragged him from his grave. See? He crawled. Don't mourn. Your child born early and bathed in the sea simply returned to his ocean home.'"

Mom says, "And as a shark, this shark, your brother remembers his family."
Dad pulls me close. "And loves us, too."

RELL'S KISS

Chapter 1

The rental agent in the beige cargo shorts and electric green polo shirt shakes his head. "No matter how hard you cram, it's not going to fit."

I'm standing in the parking lot of Aloha Island Rentals at the Honolulu International Airport and trying not to cry. Next to me are twin stacks of boxes piled higher than my shoulders, each stamped with Watanabe Global—Rush Delivery—Extremely Fragile.

Looking at the orange Mini Cooper convertible in front of me, I'd be hard pressed to fit even my single carry-on in the trunk.

I have less than two hours to get everything across the island before my wicked stepmonster erupts and rains hot lava all over me.

Who am I kidding? Even if I pull off this miracle, she'll still blow her top.

Rental Dude waves his sales tablet over the mess like a magic wand and says, "You're going to need something much larger. Why'd your company reserve this car?"

I sigh. "Because I asked for it."

"A Mini?"

"A convertible. I had this image of driving through paradise with the top down."

"You didn't know about the boxes?" he asks.

"Nope. This is Regina's way of getting back at me."

"Regina—"

"Regina Watanabe."

"Of Watanabe Global?"

"Yep."

"You're her assistant?"

"Stepdaughter."

He checks his tablet. "The reservation is for R. Watanabe."

"That's me. The R is for Rell, not Regina."

"Got it. You're here for the auction?"

I nod.

"The whole island's talking about it. It's a big deal," he says.

Somehow, this is all going to be my fault.

Don't cry, don't cry, don't cry, I tell myself.

Out loud I say, "The Mini isn't going to work. Talk to me about renting a truck or van."

He tippy-taps on his tablet for a moment and frowns.

"We don't have anything available on the lot. I have a van due back later tonight, but that's not soon enough for the auction." A few more taps. "Looks like none of the other agencies have trucks or vans available, either."

I feel tears start to well again, but there's no way I'm going to let something Regina did make me cry. When Daddy died six years ago, I swore whatever happened, I'd never give her that satisfaction again.

She thinks banishing me to a tiny all-girls prep school in North Dakota is torture, but I know the Christmases and summers I spent on campus with the headmaster's family were warmer than any celebration at home.

Wherever that is.

I almost feel sorry for my ten-year-old stepsisters, Zel and Ana.

Almost.

Today's date is just a coincidence. I should've known when Regina sent me the ticket to Hawaii that this trip wasn't about me. The car and boxes prove that.

Stepmonsters never change their stripes.

I bite my lip hard. *There's got to be a way.*

"What about a delivery service? Can I hire someone to take the boxes to La...La...?"

"It's pronounced *Lau-el-lay*. Lauele."

"Lauele," I say. "Thanks."

He pushes back the brim of his cap with his stylus. "The auction's not really in Lauele, though. It's at a pavilion above Keikikai Beach. That's where they're setting up the tents for the auction and luau. Is that where the boxes need to go?"

I nod.

He looks at the ground for a moment, then makes a decision.

"Hey, I know we just met, and I don't want you to think I'm some kind of creeper—"

Said every creeper ever.

I take half a step back.

He sees the look on my face and laughs. "Which is exactly what a creeper would say?"

I shrug.

"Just hear me out. You don't have many options, and there are a ton of boxes."

"What do you have in mind?"

He points toward the monkeypod tree in the employee lot. "Take my truck."

What? He can't be serious. Who does that?

"Take your truck?" I say. "I can't do that."

"Why not? I'm offering."

I raise an eyebrow, considering. He's about my age, maybe a couple of years older. He's taller than me, the kind of taller where you can wear fancy heels on a date, but don't have to stand on your toes to kiss.

Kiss? Right. Like I'd know anything about that.

What I read in books and magazines doesn't count.

My eyes travel across his broad shoulders, down to his slim waist, and quickly back to his face.

Get a grip, Rell. Look at his eyes, not his body. You're the one who's acting creepy about this.

His green eyes widen when I meet them.

Oh, great. He knows I've been checking him out.

His uniform is hardly stylish, but he makes it work. Wisps of sun-streaked hair peek out from the edges of his cap.

My stomach flips. *He's cute. How did I miss this?*

Oh, yeah. The boxes.

Focus, Rell!

I swallow and point. "That truck?"

"Yeah. The Datsun with the surf racks. Don't laugh. It's paid for."

I feel the blush rise. "No! I mean, it's great—"

He laughs again. "Relax. I'm just teasing. It may not look like much, but it runs well. You can drive a stick, right?"

My heart sinks.

"No."

"Good, because it's an automatic. You have no excuse."

His eyes are full of mischief. This is too easy. Nothing involving my stepmonster is ever easy. I'm missing something.

"Why are you getting involved? This isn't your problem."

He flicks his stylus against his tablet. "I'm from Lauele, born and raised. Watanabe Global is a major sponsor of the new International Abilities Surf Camp."

"I think they're announcing some kind of partnership with Get Wet Prosthetics tonight," I say.

"Get Wet started the International Abilities Surf Tournament. Jay Westin—you know Jay?"

"No."

"He's a close friend. I've surfed with him since boogieboard days. The surf camp is Jay's idea. He wants to make it easy for kids with disabilities to learn to surf."

"That's amazing," I say. "I don't know much about the camp at all."

"When I left Lauele this morning, the crew from Get Wet was already busy setting up. They're probably waiting on this stuff."

"Regina's text said I had to get the boxes delivered before noon."

He reaches out and pats a box. "Take my truck and get your boxes delivered. If makes you feel better, I'm not helping you; I'm helping my friend, Jay."

There's something wrong with this. Finally, I see it.

"But if I take your truck, how will you get home?"

"Me? Bus. With stops, it's only a four hour trip."

My mouth drops. *I can't let him do that.*

Laughter bubbles out of him like water from a fountain. "I'm not taking the bus, Rell. I'll drive the Mini Cooper home and meet you later. We'll trade. I'm off in a couple of hours."

He pauses, waiting for me to agree.

I stand in the sunshine looking at the stacks of boxes. I so want to leave them. I'm tired of Regina's passive-aggressive crap.

"Of course, if you have another option..." he says.

All those boxes.

He's right. Leaving the boxes would only hurt the auction, not Regina. The truck's old and worn, but it should do the trick. As weird as this is, I don't think it's a scam.

Okay. I'm doing it.

I fumble in my purse. "I don't have a lot of cash with me—"

He pushes my hand away from my wallet.

"Nonsense," he says. "I'm not taking your money." He crosses his arms and frowns. "Stop trying to make this complicated, Rell. It's very simple. You need to get those boxes to Lauele. I have a truck. It's cool."

I throw up my hands. "This is insane."

He laughs. "Insane is trying to shoehorn those boxes into a Mini Cooper. It's really no big deal. I'm happy to help. C'mon. Let's finish up the paperwork, load the truck, and get you on the road."

Chapter 2

BACK AT THE RENTAL OFFICE, he runs around the counter and brings up the forms on a monitor.

"Where are you staying? Waikiki? I know it's not in Lauele. There aren't any hotels out there."

"We're staying somewhere close. It's the private residence of someone my stepmother knows." I grab my phone and pull up the address. "It's called Hale O Ka Poliahu."

"No way. You know Poliahu?"

I blink, wondering at his tone. "Uh, no. I think she's someone my stepmother met while skiing in Switzerland. When news got out about Watanabe Global sponsoring the auction for the surf camp, Poliahu offered us her home. She said staying there would be easier than driving back and forth across the island."

"She's right. Lauele is not a tourist-y kind of place. Not a lot of services out there. But, wow. You hit the jackpot. Poliahu's estate is legendary."

"You know it?"

He shakes his head. "By reputation only." He hits enter a few times as the screen flashes. "The house sits upcountry in the mountains above Keikikai Beach. It's usually empty. I can't remember the last time Poliahu was home."

The printer under the counter whirls, spitting out the rental contract. "Okay. One Mini Cooper Convertible. Two day rental. Aw, seems like a shame to fly all this way and only stay two days."

"Believe me, two days with my family is long enough."

He pauses, then lightly touches my hand. "I'm sorry," he says.

I shrug. "It is what it is. It's fine."

With a highlighter, he marks up the contract. "Since it's a corporate rental, here's where the collision insurance and extra driver fees are waved. Be sure to bring it back full, or we'll have to charge you extra for the fuel. Initial here, here, and here. Sign there. I just need your driver's license, and we're done."

I really don't want to hand him my license, but I have no choice. Reading the signs posted all over the office, I realize why the reservation's under R. Watanabe and booked under Regina's account. This is the moment when he tells me I can't rent a car at all. One last calculated humiliation by Regina, I'm sure.

Maybe he'll tell me how to catch the bus.

I keep my finger over my birthdate as I slide my license across the counter, but when he picks it up, he sees it anyway.

"Hey! Today's your birthday! hauʻole la hānau."

I blush.

Again.

"Thanks," I mumble. "Is this a problem?"

He double-checks it. "For a regular rental, you're underage. We make exceptions for corporate rentals."

Hallelujah!

I let the air I was holding out in a rush.

He hands my license back with a sympathetic smile. "It's a silly rule. Most of the guys who work here are under 25, and we drive the cars all the time."

He throws me the keys from his pocket and grabs the keys to the Mini off the rack. We walk back through the rental lot to his truck parked in shade of a big monkeypod tree. He opens the door for me, and I climb in.

"Don't worry. It's rusty and a little dinged up, but my truck's safe. Just make sure you brake extra hard and pump 'em a bit before you stop."

"What!"

"Kidding, kidding! The brakes are fine. Man, you make teasing too easy." He slams the door and the whole cab rattles. I start the engine. Warm air blasts from the vents. I look for the button to roll down the widows.

He taps on the glass and points.

It's a hand crank.

I roll the window down.

Literally.

It takes forever.

The whole time he's grinning at me.

"Good," he says when the window's open. "I wasn't sure if you knew what that was. There's no air-conditioning, so you'll want to keep the windows rolled down. Just think of it as driving a convertible with a roof." He pats the hood. "Meet me at the boxes."

I adjust the rearview and figure out how to put it in gear. When I'm at the far side of the parking lot, I surreptitiously test the brakes.

No problem. The truck's bigger than what I'm used to, but it handles well.

I pull up next to the boxes and leave the truck idling. It doesn't take long to load them. Rather than stick my bag next to me, I slip it in the back behind the cab and in front of the boxes.

For a moment, I stand there a little dazed and overwhelmed. I'm not quite sure how all this came together.

"Know where you're going?" he asks.

I hold up my phone. "I've got the address. Google Maps should get me there."

He holds up a finger. "I almost forgot. Wait just one sec."

He dashes back inside and comes back with a business card and a lei made of shiny black seeds. "Here's my phone number. Call if you have any problems. I can leave work early if you need me."

"My number is—"

He wiggles his phone. "Got it off the paperwork. I'll text when I get back to Lauele this afternoon."

I look at the neatly stacked boxes and shake my head.

"Is this what they mean by the aloha spirit?"

He gives me a look like he's not sure where I'm going with this. "Isn't this just doing the right thing? That's universal, no?"

No. But thank goodness I'm in Hawaii.

"I don't even know your name," I say.

He holds out his hand. "Jerry Santos."

I take it. It's warm and strong and slightly rough.

"Rell Watanabe."

He grips my hand tighter and pulls me a little closer. He places the lei around my neck. "Aloha, Rell," he says, pecking me on the cheek. "Welcome to Hawaii."

Chapter 3

"You're late."

When I step out of the truck, I ignore my stepmonster for a moment and take in the view. From the driveway, I can see all the way down the mountainside to the beach and out to sea. Waves that look like squiggly lines roll to the sand. If I squint, I can see surfers riding to the shore. The air is chilly, far chillier than I ever imagined Hawaii would be. I puff out a breath, expecting to see it turn to frost like it does back home in winter, but it doesn't.

"What happened to the convertible you insisted on? Don't tell me you'd rather drive this—" I don't have to look. I know how her mouth twists over these words —"whatever it is."

I turn to her and force a smile. "Hi Regina. It's nice to see you again."

She snorts, but keeps her eyes from rolling. "Those boxes don't belong here. I told you to take them to the venue. That means the place where the auction is being held, not the house where we're staying. I'll try not to use such big words in the future."

"I know what venue means, I just—"

She sighs. "It's hard for you to think of others, I know, but please remember we're guests here. No doubt that jalopy is leaking oil on Poliahu's beautiful driveway."

"If it's leaking oil, I'll scrub it."

"With what? Your toothbrush? Honestly, Rell, if you'd use your brain for once —just move the truck. Don't be so dramatic."

The front door crashes open, and Zel and Ana come tumbling out, chasing a gray tabby.

"Get him!" Zel shrieks.

"I got the rope. You tie the noose," Ana shouts.

Noose? No way. I didn't hear that right.

Zel lunges for the cat, but misses. "I told you I'm not doing the noose again, Ana. You have to learn how to tie it yourself."

"But you know what happened last time, Zel. You do it."

"No."

The cat starts left, then jukes right, fleeing between Ana's legs.

"You're letting him get away!" Zel says.

"Anastasia! Drizella!" Regina shouts. "I told you to leave that filthy animal alone. You'll get fleas."

The cat escapes over a rock wall and disappears under a bush.

"Aw, Mom," they chorus. "You never let us have any fun."

Good grief. My stepsisters are monsters.

"Enough. I am not getting held up in customs again because you two have fleas."

Zel pouts and scratches her arm. "It wasn't fleas, it was—"

Regina holds up her hand. "Don't argue. You want fun? Fine. Go change. Rell's taking you to the beach."

What?

"Me?"

"Yes, you. You're already dressed for it in those ragged shorts and t-shirt. I hope you didn't embarrass yourself by wearing that on the plane."

Zel snickers. "I bet she wore that on the plane."

Ana says, "Not in first class!"

Brats!

I look at my cut-offs and t-shirt. "What's wrong with my clothes?"

"Rell, the real question is what's right?" Regina snips. "They're hardly couture. They're fine for house cleaning, I suppose, although I don't really know."

"Or going to the beach," Ana says.

"You promised fun, Mom," Zel says.

I look at the twins. Growing up under Regina, they really didn't stand a chance.

It's not their fault.

I can play nice.

"You really want me to take them to the beach?"

Regina says, "Yes. But first move the truck and sign the papers."

"What papers?"

"Why must you question everything I say? Get a move on. You haven't got all day."

She spins on her heel and heads to the house.

"Girls, let's go. Mommy has lots to do. Unlike Rell, Mommy's busy, busy, busy. A lollygagger, that's what Rell is. But she's here now to take care of you."

"Is lollygagger French for nanny?" asks Zel.

"No, dummy," says Ana. "She's not our nanny. She's old Papa Watanabe's daughter."

"But he's dead."

"Yeah," says Ana, picking at a scab on her arm. "He's worm food now."

"So if she's not our new nanny, why is she here?" Zel asks.

Ana shrugs. "I dunno. Maybe she wants something."

"My new iPhone? She can't have that."

Regina grabs each of the twins by the arm and hisses. "Rell is nothing for you to worry about. She wants nothing; she gets nothing. She's just here for a couple of days, one night only, then she's going back to school, and you'll never see her again. Now go change!"

She marches them to the door and shoves them into the house. Pausing on the threshold, she points to the truck and then to the street before slamming the door hard enough to rattle the glass.

I close my eyes. "Two days is an eternity."

"Meow?"

I bend down and look under the bushes. "Kitty-kitty," I say. Gray fuzz peeps out at me. "It's okay, sweetie. They've gone. I won't let them hurt you."

"Prraow?"

I hold out my hand, and the cat slinks over and rubs against me. I pick her up, and she melts, her purr vibrating so deeply in her chest that it tingles against my shoulder.

"At least somebody's happy to see me."

The cat snuggles deeper, warming me until I'm no longer shivering. I need to get my jacket out of my bag.

A red cardinal swoops by, flitting from branch to branch in the tree above me.

"Look at you! You're gorgeous," I say.

He preens and trills.

I laugh. "Now you're just showing off." He bobs his head and shakes his tail.

A monarch butterfly lands on the roof of the truck, the black and orange patterns of his wings blurring in the sunlight like—

"Oil!"

I put the cat down and hurry to park on the street.

Jerry's truck runs fine, but I'm not taking a chance.

I only have one toothbrush.

Chapter 4

I SET THE PARKING BRAKE, grab my jacket from my bag in the back, and walk slowly up the driveway. I hesitate, then enter the house through the servant's side door.

"Hello?" I call.

My stepmonster answers from the dining room. "We're in here," she sighs, "Waiting on you, as usual, Rell. But take your time. It's not like we've other, more important things to do."

In the dining room, at one end of a long dining table sits three men, two in crisp aloha shirts and khakis and one in a three-piece wool suit and tie. There are stacks of papers piled high on the table and several pens lined up next to an empty chair.

Regina nervously hovers, fidgeting with her pearls.

I narrow my eyes. She's never nervous.

On the table are official-looking stamps, seals, and ink pads. Behind the men on the buffet table are more file boxes stuffed with millions of folders.

Except for the warm wood furnishings, everything is in shades of white. White gardenias float in crystal bowls, their scent cool and clean. Snowy linens cover the table.

Even wearing my jacket, I shiver. Somehow the beautiful room comes off as cold as a mountain peak. The vibe is Hawaiian-Eskimo, something weirdly anti-tropical. Looking out the window, I half-expect to see a snow-dusted coconut tree.

At the far side of the room in front of a fireplace are two chairs and a table arranged for a cozy tête-à-tête. The fireplace is big enough to roast an ox.

We need a fire to warm things up. Heaven knows we have enough paper here to burn down the house.

Twice.

Regina places her palm on the back of a chair and raps her ring against it, the sound like a judge's gavel.

"Sit here, Rell. Let's get started."

I pull out the chair. It's heavier than it looks and slides awkwardly along the thick carpet.

I sit, and the man in the three-piece suit turns to me. "Rell, we've met before—"

"When I was twelve. I remember."

He continues as if I'm invisible. "My name is Michael Lucius. I'm an attorney with Lucius, Griffin, and Melton. These are my associates, Avery Me'e and Mark Andrews. Do you know why you're here?"

"No."

"Yes, you do," Regina says. "It's your birthday."

"You remembered! Wait. Are you throwing me a surprise party? Is that why you brought me to Hawaii?"

"No."

"You're teasing. My surprise party is the luau tonight! I knew the charity auction couldn't be real."

Regina's lips press into a thin white line.

Awesome. Now if I can just get her eye to twitch...

I say, "Oh, no. Did I ruin the surprise?"

The corner of her eye jumps.

Yes!

"Rell, not everything is about you. The auction tonight has nothing to do with your birthday."

Of course not. I know better than to expect a party. But the surf camp doesn't make sense. Charity's not Regina's thing.

I wink. "Got it. No birthday luau."

Regina takes a deep breath. "You're here to sign papers, that's all."

"And deliver boxes. Don't forget that part."

She squints and pinches the bridge of her nose. With any luck, I've given her a migraine.

"That's enough," she says. "No one likes a drama queen. You sign papers every year on your birthday."

Yeah, in the school secretary's office. It's no big deal.

This feels like a big deal.

"Not in Hawaii," I say.

"You're complaining about a trip to Hawaii? Unbelievable. Nothing I do makes you happy. You even disliked the convertible."

"Yeah, thanks for arranging that. So thoughtful."

Regina throws her hands in the air. "See? Do you see what I deal with? Clearly, this is why we're here today, gentlemen."

Mr. Lucius delicately coughs. "If I may? Rell, it's exactly as your stepmother said. You're here to sign a paper. The process today is much like what's happened in the preceding years, but with a little more formality. Mr. Andrews is a notary. As Regina is your guardian, Mr. Me'e and I will serve as witnesses to your signature. Everything is in order."

Mr. Andrews nods and holds up his notary seal. "I need to see your driver's license for my records. We all know who you are, but contracts are contracts. We must obey the law."

For the second time today, I hand a stranger my ID and watch as he copies information from it. Stamp, stamp, sign, double-sign, date, and he's done.

"As a Notary Public, I certify that the young lady in front of me is Rell H. Watanabe," he says.

"Thank you, Mr. Andrews," says Regina. "Let's get on with it."

Chapter 5

As I slide my driver's license back into my wallet, Jerry's business card falls out.

"What's that?" Regina asks.

"Nothing," I say, tucking it back in as my heart beats wildly. "Just a card from the rental place."

To hide my reaction, I reach for the stack of papers nearest me. "Do I have to sign all of these?"

Mr. Lucius chuckles. "No, my dear. That would take hours. We've simplified it for you. You just have to sign one document." He takes the papers from me and flips to the back where a post-it flag sticks out. "We only need your signature here. I've already dated it."

I pick up a pen and scan the page.

"Mr. Me'e and Mr. Lucius already signed the witness lines," I say.

"Of course. Unlike you, they are sensitive about wasting other people's time," Regina says. "Sign and let these good people get on with their day, Rell."

Her tone is annoyed, but her face is eerily blank.

Something's off.

I flip a couple of pages.

"What am I signing?"

Regina rolls her eyes, but her facial expression doesn't change. "I told you. Papers that allow me to continue to pay for your schooling. You want that, right?"

I turn and look up at her. "Smile," I say.

"What?" she sputters.

No change.

"Smile."

"You ungrateful little—"

No change.

"Are you upset with me?" I ask. "I really can't tell if you're mad or happy or sad—"

The penny drops.

Her face has been Botox'd to the max. I peer closer. *That's a new nose. The flab under her chin has definitely been tightened, too.*

She's not happy or sad. She's annoyed as always, but plastic surgery has taken care of both the wrinkles and the emotion. Even her skin looks waxy.

Whatever.

I turn back to the document.

"Mr. Me'e, does signing this paper allow me to graduate high school in the spring and start college in the fall?"

Mr. Lucius shoots him a look and says, "This is not a negotiation."

Negotiation? All I've asked is a simple yes/no question.

Mr. Me'e says, "It allows—"

Regina snaps, "Do you want me to pay your tuition or not? That's what it comes down to, Rell. Sign it, and things go on exactly as they have before."

"It that correct, Mr. Me'e?"

Mr. Me'e says, "Signing will—"

"Yes," says Mr. Lucius. "If you sign the document, Regina can continue to pay for your schooling."

"There are other options," Mr. Me'e says.

"Yes, she can be homeless. She can get a GED. She can get a job as fry cook. Or she can complete her education in comfort. It doesn't matter to me. I try to do a good thing, and it's turning into a mess. Typical. Sign or not, but stop wasting everyone's valuable time, Rell," Regina says.

"But with all these papers, it seems like—"

Regina shakes her head as she reaches over and snatches the pen out of my hand. "I'm sorry, gentlemen. This has been a colossal waste of time. Apparently, Rell feels the need to read each and every scrap of paper before signing."

Wait a minute.

"I just want to know—"

"We told you, but, as always, you're not listening. You're complaining that I brought you to Hawaii instead of letting you stay at school and sign the papers there." She turns to Mr. Lucius. "You're right. I should've anticipated this. She was always such a difficult, suspicious child."

"I am not."

"See?" Regina says.

Mr. Me'e says, "Do you want me to explain—"

"Lucius," Regina interrupts, "contact her school this afternoon and tell them next month's tuition and dorm fees can't be paid."

"Yes, Regina."

Mr. Me'e starts to speak, but Regina stops him again.

"She's stubborn and foolish, Mr. Me'e." Regina waves her hand at all the mountains of paper. "There's no way Rell can read through everything before the payments are due. As you know, without her signature, my hands are tied when it comes to disbursing funds on her behalf."

Mr. Me'e says, "That's true, however—"

Regina cuts him off again. "I appreciate your concern for her welfare, even if she doesn't. Your heart is in the right place, Mr. Me'e, but if Rell insists on being uneducated and out on the street, it's her choice."

Mr. Lucius stands. "I think we're done here today, gentlemen."

Regina shakes Mr. Lucius's hand. "Thank you again. I'll be in touch. Rell, see them out. It's the least you can do."

Regina pivots and exits the room.

I look at the document.

Sign or be homeless and uneducated.

I'm not going to cry. She can't make me cry.

Life doesn't have to be like this.

Next year, I'm going to college. I'll get out from under Regina's thumb. I'll scrub dishes and wait tables if I have to.

But first I have to graduate from high school.

The pages blur, but I manage to pick up a pen, find the signature line, and scrawl my name across it.

The men stand up. Mr. Me'e sighs as he picks up the papers. Regina rushes back into the room.

"She signed?"

Mr. Me'e holds it up.

"I want a copy of that for my records. Several copies, in fact," Regina says. "Put the original in the vault."

"Avery?" Mr. Lucius says.

Mr. Me'e places the signed paper in his briefcase and locks it. "Consider it done. I'll have the copies delivered tomorrow."

"Mommy," says a voice, "I thought Rell was taking us to the beach."

Zel and Ana stand in the doorway, wearing the most hideous swimsuits I've ever seen, all ruffles and bows.

With their frizzy hair, they look like overdressed poodles at a clown convention. *Ridiculous.*

The stress gets to me, and I can't help it.

I laugh.

"Mom!" yips Ana. "What's wrong with Rell?"

Yips. Like a poodle.

I throw my head back and howl.

"Nothing, dear. She's just deliriously happy to see you." Her tone is angry, but Regina's face doesn't change.

Oh, man. She has resting witch face. And she did it on purpose.

I almost fall out of the chair.

Mr. Lucius reaches for the pitcher on the sideboard. "Maybe a glass of water would help?"

Laughter burns the anger and sadness away. I feel much better.

"No," I say. "It's okay. I'm fine."

Snort, giggle.

I swallow hard.

Get a grip, Rell. Keep it up and the next thing you know you'll be locked away in an insane asylum.

I rub my eyes and take a breath. "Those boxes need to get to the *venue*. The rental car guy told me that's at a pavilion above Keikikai Beach. Is that a good place for the girls to swim?"

"Yes. It's one of the best family beaches on the island," Mr. Me'e says.

I open my mouth and a hiccup escapes. "Excuse me. That red-eye flight was long. But flights are cheaper after midnight, right?"

The barb goes right over Regina's head. I've been dismissed and forgotten like yesterday's dishes.

It's not worth a sigh.

"Zel and Ana, let's give Regina some peace and quiet so she can get her work done before the party. It's beach time. Not even paperwork can ruin a day at the beach."

Chapter 6

THE GIRLS DON'T SAY anything until after they climb in truck, and we're heading down the mountain to the beach.

"Ana says you're not our new nanny."

"No, Zel, I'm your big sister," I say.

"Stepsister," Ana says.

I shoot her a look. "Right. Stepsister. I know it's been a long time since we've seen each other. I think you guys were just four—"

"If you're not our new nanny, why are you taking us to the beach?" Zel asks.

"Don't you want to go to the beach? It's fun."

Ana shrugs her shoulders. "Whatever."

"Whatever," says Zel.

"Your mom told me to take you to the beach."

"Whatever," Ana says again. "But remember, just because you're driving, you're not the boss of us."

"Yeah. The last nanny thought she was the boss of us," Zel says.

"Nanny Bossy didn't last long," Ana says, staring out the window. "We Nair'd her."

"Nair'd her?" I ask.

"In her shampoo."

"You didn't!" I gasp.

Zel nods. "We did. Now she's Nanny Baldo."

Ana scrunches up her face. "More like Nanny Patches."

I give them another look. "So how bossy was she?"

Ana turns to me. "She wanted us to pick our clothes up off the floor."

"And read books."

"And took away our candy."

"We NEED our candy."

"So don't try to take it," Ana says.

"Okay," I say and try not to scratch my suddenly itchy head.

When we hit the highway that circumnavigates the island, I turn right and follow the signs to Lauele. The ocean peeps through the ironwood trees on the left, but it's not until we come to a two-story building with a big sign saying Hari's on the front that the view really opens up.

Across the street from Hari's is a beach pavilion with a sign that reads Keikikai Beach. Big delivery trucks fill the parking lot. In a grassy field people are setting up a big event tent and an on-site catering kitchen.

"Must be the place," I say, pulling into the parking lot.

Zel points to the big banner across the front of the tent: International Abilities Surf Camp Charity Auction & Luau.

"You think?"

Ana rolls her eyes. "You're right, Zel. She's too stupid to be our nanny."

"Hey!"

They jump out of the truck and start heading toward the beach.

"Zel! Ana! What about all the boxes?"

Without stopping, they wave at me.

"Not our problem," Zel says over her shoulder.

"That's why you're here," Ana says.

"And your truck smells like old feet!" Zel shouts.

I scramble out of the truck. I almost forget, but at the last minute I grab my purse off the seat and whip it over my head and across my body. The girls are striding across the sand now. "Zel! Ana! Get back—"

"Jerry, you can't park here."

I whirl around.

Nobody's there.

"What?" I say.

I hear a tongue click and a sigh. "Down here."

I peer over the hood of the truck. "Oh. Sorry, I didn't see you."

Near the license plate, a tiny man with a clipboard adjusts his hat and frowns. "Why are you driving Jerry Santos's truck? Where's Jerry?"

"I—"

"Never mind. You have to move it. We need the entire parking lot for the event tonight."

"But—"

"Eh, Luna. Check out the back. The wahine brought the boxes we've been waiting for." Two thick brown hands reach over the side of the truck and lift out a box.

The guy with the clipboard grins. "Why didn't you say so? Hui! Eh, gangies! Come kokua!"

In an instant, one by one the boxes begin to rise out of the truck and float toward the tent.

What the what?

I walk around the front of the truck and into a scene from *Willy Wonka*. A fireman's brigade of men no taller than three feet are unloading the boxes and handing them down the line and into the tent.

The one lifting the boxes out of the back taps the side of the truck. "Eh! Das the last one," he says. "All pau!"

I peek into the back to check, but when I turn around to thank them, they've disappeared.

The first guy rips something from his clipboard and holds it out. "Your receipt."

I glance at it. "Menehune Inc.?"

He grins. "We're Local 808. No job too big or small. We specialize in rock walls. I'm Luna. You a friend of Jerry's?"

"Sort of."

"Ah," he nods. "That kind of friend."

"No!" Heat pinks my cheeks. "He just lent me his truck. That's all."

He cocks his head. "Oooh! You're THAT kind of friend."

I adjust my bag over my shoulder and glare. "I don't know what you're talking about."

"Relax, titah. I'm just joking with you. You work for Watanabe Global, right?"

"Sort of. I'm Rell."

"Ah-ha! I thought I recognized that smell."

"What?"

I fight an impulse to sniff my arm pit. Instead I surreptitiously rub my cheek on my shoulder and breathe deeply.

Flowers and laundry detergent.

This guy's nuts.

He flicks his wrist. "Nothing. You remind me of your mother."

"You knew my mom?"

"Oh, yeah. She was a Mahope. The Mahopes go way back in Lauele. You never know?"

I shake my head. "No."

"Your family owns land around here. It's just mauka of the land where they want to build the surf camp. See?" He points uphill. "That's where the road will go. You seen the designs, yeah?"

I shake my head. "I don't know anything about the project."

"Well, go park Jerry's junkalunka truck in front of Hari's store—he won't mind—and come to the tent. We'll show you everything."

"Thanks, but I can't. The twins took off down to the beach, and I need to keep an eye on them."

Luna whistles. "Makani!"

"Yeah, Luna?" a voice answers.

"Girls. Beach. Now."

"On it!"

I don't see Makani, but I hear feet thunder across the pavement. A heartbeat later, little puffs of sand rise from the beach.

Luna smiles. "No worries. Makani will keep an eye on them."

My stomach clenches. "I don't know Makani."

"No worries. He's like the wind. He'll make sure they don't get into trouble."

"I think I better—"

He taps the side of the truck. "I need you to move this first. After you park the car, go into Hari's store. Tell him Luna wants a sprunch. Put it on my tab."

"Luna, you sly dog. Tell Hari yourself. Don't let this guy fool you, Rell," says a voice behind me.

"Jerry! Don't spoil my fun," Luna says.

My heart skips.

Jerry!

He startled me.

That's it.

That's all.

It has nothing to do with his deep surfer's tan or eyes like green beach glass.

Right.

Jerry holds out his hand. Reflexively I hold mine out, too. He drops keys into my palm.

"I hoped I'd find you here. Your rental car's across the street at Hari's. Are my keys still inside the truck?"

"Yes."

"I'll get my truck out of Luna's hair."

"Thanks so much for loaning it to me. I couldn't have done this without you."

"No problem." He opens the door and climbs in the cab.

I grab the open window before he can shut the door. "Hey. You said you were involved with the surf camp. Luna was just going to show me the plans. Wanna come see?"

Inside, I groan.

That sounds desperate. Needy. Guys hate that.

"I'd love to. Be right back."

I watch as Jerry backs up and parks across the street next to an orange Mini. I can't stop smiling.

"Oh, yeah," says Luna. "Totally a friend like that."

Chapter 7

WHEN JERRY JOGS BACK, he's holding a hideous ruffled floral beach wrap. "I think this belongs to you."

I want to die.

"Actually, I think it belongs to one of my stepsisters." I quickly stuff it in my purse. "I really should go check on them."

"Makani's with them," Luna says. "They're fine."

I hesitate.

Jerry comes to my rescue. He jumps up on the rock wall separating the grass from the sand and scans the beach.

"Luna's right. The girls are fine. See for yourself."

He reaches down and pulls me up next to him. He puts a hand on my shoulder and leans close as he points toward the ocean. His aftershave reminds me of cedar and cinnamon.

I breathe deeply.

And a touch of clove.

I shake my head.

This is ridiculous, Rell. You're acting like a lovesick puppy. Knock it off.

Jerry mistakes my headshake for a no.

"Can't see them? Look a little more to the right."

He leans closer until his breath kisses my cheek.

Wintergreen mint.

All I have to do is turn my head, and we'll be kissing for real.

Ah! Focus! Ana and Zel. Where are they?

I follow Jerry's arm as it points out along a lava outcrop. The girls are still close to the main beach, splashing in a shallow tide pool. A few feet away, a medium-sized yellow dog approaches them, wagging its tail.

A dog.

The girls wanted to hang a cat.

This can't be good.

I step away from Jerry, so I can think.

"I see Ana and Zel, but I don't see Makani," I say.

"He's out there. Guaranteed," Luna says.

"Makani's a dog?" I ask.

Luna cocks his head. "A dog? No, Makani's a—"

"She's talking about 'Ilima," Jerry interrupts.

"'Ilima? Who's 'Ilima?" I ask.

"That yellow poi dog next to the girls is named 'Ilima. Between 'Ilima and Makani, the girls are in good hands. There's no need to worry about them," Jerry says.

"Everyone keeps telling me that I don't have to worry because Makani's out there, even though I can't see him. Are you telling me now that 'Ilima's a lifeguard? She'll jump in and rescue the girls if they get swept out to sea?"

"'Ilima's 'Ilima," Luna says, scratching his head. "Makani's Makani. I'm Luna. He's Jerry. You're Rell. Why is this so confusing?"

Jerry laughs and jumps down from the wall.

"It's not, Luna. The reef's scary when you're not from Lauele. Rell just wants to make sure the girls are safe."

"Didn't we just say so?" Luna says.

"Yes, but she needs to understand things for herself." Jerry jerks his head toward the tent. "If 'Ilima's here, Uncle Kahana is, too. Why don't you come in and meet him? He can show you the plans. It will just take a minute, and then we'll walk down to Piko Point."

"Piko Point?"

He points towards the girls again.

"Piko Point is at the end of the lava outcrop. From there I can show you where the surf tournament's held and tell you all about the surf camp."

From the ground, Jerry reaches up and places his hands along my waist. Without thinking I lean down and put my hands on his shoulders as he lifts me off the wall. On the ground, I have to look up a little to see his eyes. I know with just a little stretch, our lips would meet.

Cedar, cinnamon, cloves, and wintergreen mints.

Jerry clears his throat and smiles as he releases me, taking a half a step back.

"We are friends," sings Luna. "Friends, friends, friends! We are friends."

I turn toward him, but Luna's gone.

"What's that all about?" Jerry asks. "Why is he singing an old Cecilio & Kapono song?"

"Who knows," I say. "He's a little—"

"Strange?" Jerry raises an eyebrow.

I roll my eyes. "I was going to say quirky."

"You don't know the half of it," Jerry says, taking my hand. "C'mon. Let's check out the tent."

Chapter 8

INSIDE THE TENT, a young woman with long hair piled on top of her head is smoothing tablecloths over a row of tables. Head down, she says, "Stack the brochures on the end, Luna. I want people to see the full list of auction items before they come in to bid." She looks up. "Oh, Jerry! I thought you were Luna."

"He's around here somewhere, Nalani. I just saw him," Jerry says.

"Luna!" Nalani shouts. "I need—"

"Already pau, Nalani!" says Luna's voice.

I turn, and a table that I swear wasn't there when I walked in is now next to the door and covered with artfully swirled stacks of brochures.

"What about the flowers?" Nalani says, placing her hands on her hips.

Like magic, a vase filled with purple bougainvillea appears.

"And pens!" Nalani says.

A woven basket of pens quivers next to the vase.

Nalani cracks her gum. "Why do I have to remind you buggahs about everything?"

"You're welcome," says Luna, but I can't tell if it's coming from under a table, behind the stacks of boxes, or outside the tent.

She cracks her gum again and smiles at us. "Who's your friend?"

Jerry says, "This is Rell Watanabe."

"Hi," I say and hold out my hand.

"As if." She ignores my hand and kisses my cheek. "Aloha, Rell. Strangers shake. 'Ohana honi—kiss."

"'Ohana? You mean family?"

"Don't look surprised. The word 'ohana existed long before *Lilo and Stitch*. And, yeah. We're second cousins on your mother's side. The last time I saw you, you were busy eating sand on Keikikai Beach."

"Ew!"

She shrugs. "It's what babies do. You don't remember coming to Lauele?"

"No."

Nalani puts her arm around my shoulders. "It was a long time ago. If your mother was still alive, I'm certain you would've been back many times. Let me get Uncle Kahana. He'll want to meet you."

"I have an Uncle Kahana?"

"Oh, honey! Everyone has an Uncle Kahana. There he is," she says. "E hui! Uncle Kahana! Someone to see you."

At the far end of the tent, in front of a massive stage, a slightly built elderly man in a faded t-shirt and worn board shorts turns toward us. He raises his brown arm and waves.

"Send 'em over, Nalani. It's too far for an old broke 'okole man to walk all the way over there."

Nalani gives me a little nudge, and Jerry and I thread our way through the tables.

Panic bubbles.

I have an Uncle Kahana.

People I don't know call me family.

My mother's family was from Lauele.

I give Jerry a side-glance.

I have to know.

"Are we related?" I whisper.

He pauses for a minute, considering. "Calabash cousins for sure. My great-great grandfather's aunty was hānai to your fifth cousin's mother, and she married my third cousin's nephew, so yeah, we're 'ohana."

Family.

My heart sinks.

"You know what calabash means, right?" Jerry says.

"No."

"It's an old Hawaiian idiom. Basically, it refers to all the people who make sure you never go hungry as well as the people you feed. It's less about sharing physical blood than sharing experiences and responsibilities."

I feel a sharp tug on the bottom of my shirt. When I reach back, I feel Luna's thick hand squeeze mine.

"Don't worry," he whispers. "Calabash cousins can *date*."

I spin around, but all I see is the edge of a tablecloth settling against the floor.

"Did you say something?" Jerry asks.

"Me? No."

I hear a giggle, and then Luna's voice sings, "Friends, friends, friends."

"It's just Luna singing again," I say.

"Luna. What a pest!" Jerry says.

"So, we're calabash cousins, but not blood."

"Right," he says.

Calabash. The butterflies settle. It might not make a difference to him, but it does to me.

Wait a minute.

I touch his arm. "Is that why you lent me your truck?"

Jerry shakes his head. "Of course not. I didn't know you were 'ohana until I saw Luna talking with you. One of his quirks is he only talks with family."

"But I'd never met him before. How could he possibly know me?"

Jerry shrugs. "I don't know. But no one outside of family ever sees him or his crew."

Luna giggles again. From somewhere around my knees, he sing-songs, "First comes love, then comes marriage, then comes Rell with a—"

I smack the tabletop.

"Cockroach?" Jerry asks. "They get pretty big in Hawaii."

"It's nothing."

Luna giggles again.

Imp.

"Close," says a voice in my ear, "but not quite."

Chapter 9

IT DOESN'T TAKE us long to reach the far end of the tent where Uncle Kahana is standing next to a table with an architect's model.

"Uncle Kahana, this is—"

"Rell Watanabe." He leans over and kisses my cheek. "You look like your mother."

It's so unexpected that I have to catch my breath.

"You knew my mother?"

"Of course. And your father. And your grandparents—"

"Yeah, Uncle Kahana is real old," says Jerry.

Uncle Kahana narrows his eyes. "Don't you have cars to park?"

"Nope."

"You sure? I hear you college boys are good at that."

"The best! We learned from old futs like you."

Uncle Kahana snorts and wags his finger. "One of these days, Jerry, if you're lucky, you'll get to be as old as me."

"I hope so, Uncle, I hope so."

"But for now, Jerry, let me show Rell the surf camp. It's because of Watanabe Global that it's possible." Uncle Kahana motions for me to come closer. "This is why we're here."

The model shows six cabins connected by paved trails with ramps and handrails. Near the parking lot are outdoor showers, racks for storing surfboards, and a covered pavilion with cooking facilities. Uncle Kahana opens one of the cabins like a dollhouse.

"Four beds in each cabin's main room with a separate space for aides or camp counselors. No bunk beds. Everything's extra-wide for wheelchairs, and the bathrooms have rails and chairs in the showers. The goal is to allow campers to live as independently as possible."

"You should see the zip lines and towers. Awesome," Jerry says.

"That's not until Phase Two, when we add the obstacle courses for strength and agility training." Uncle Kahana shoots me a glance. "You know about the tournament?"

I shake my head. "I don't know anything. Tell me."

"When the Abilities Surf Tournament went international and got corporate sponsorship, Jay and Nili-boy came up with the idea to add a summer surfing camp. When they started, the whole thing was sponsored by Get Wet Prosthetics and some grants, but frankly they can't do it without the support of businesses like Watanabe Global. This camp is going to be life changing."

I run a finger over a cabin. "It's a camp for kids who want to become pro surfers?"

Uncle Kahana's head snaps toward me. He frowns and opens his mouth, but doesn't speak. I look up from the model and catch his eyes. He reads something in my face and softens.

"The camp is for more than just kids, Rell. Adults, too."

"But the goal is to win the competition, right? It's a surf tournament."

Uncle Kahana chuckles quietly. "No. The goal is to heal. When bodies, minds, hearts, and souls are healed, they have a desire to test themselves. Competition is the natural result, that's all. You've been to Piko Point?"

Jerry says, "Not yet. She just got off the plane this morning."

"Take her, Jerry. Tell her. It will all make sense then." He cocks an eyebrow at me. "You surf?"

I smile and echo Jerry. "Not yet."

He pats my arm. "No worries! With a name like Rell, you'll be a natural."

Chapter 10

AT THE EDGE of the sand near the showers, Jerry stops. He steps out of his shoes and pulls off his socks.

"No shoes," he says. "Only tourists walk on beaches in shoes."

"We're supposed to carry them?"

He takes my shoes from me and sets them next to his on top of the short rock wall.

"You want me to leave my shoes here? Are you nuts? I only have one other pair. Someone will steal them."

He looks at me, amused. "This is Lauele. Nobody'll bother them. Promise."

I step off the walkway and onto the sand. It's warm on the top and cooler underneath as it squishes between my toes. There's a light breeze coming off the ocean. It's not enough to chop the water, just enough to keep things from getting too hot. At Keikikai Beach, the water is bathtub calm and clear as glass. A little ways down the beach, a young mother is splashing with her toddler, but other than them, the beach is empty.

"Where is everyone?"

He cuffs my shoulder. "It's Friday afternoon. Most people in paradise work for a living."

"I mean, where are the girls?" Panic rises. "I don't see them."

Jerry shades his eyes. "There. Walking out to Piko Point. They're on the Nalupuki side."

I follow his arm to the lava outcrop stretching out to sea. On the far side I see waves splash as they hit the rocks. This side is calm. The other is wild. I have a vision of the girls tumbling into the rough water, followed by my head on Regina's wall.

I shift my weight and run.

"Rell! Wait!"

At the start of the rocks, Jerry catches my arm, forcing me to stop.

"Slow down. Makani's with them, remember? They're just exploring."

"I have to get out there."

"Okay, but don't run. You're barefoot, remember? Parts of the reef are slippery. Other spots are sharp. Let's go slow. Step where I step."

His hand travels down my arm to grab my hand.

"We have to wade just a bit to get to the first rock. It won't get higher than your knees, promise. But keep your eye on the water. You never want to turn your back to the ocean."

I tell myself it's the shock of the water that makes me squirm and not the feeling of holding a boy's hand.

Good grief.

Maybe an all-girls prep school isn't everything it's cracked up to be.

We step out of the ocean and onto the lava. It's rough and rippled like water and dotted with pockets of salt, but it feels warm under my toes.

I raise a hand to my eyes and peer out toward the point. The girls are sitting down near a big saltwater pool, watching something in the water. 'Ilima is sitting a few yards away, chewing her tail.

"It's easy," Jerry says. "But watch where you step. It's low tide, so there might be some wana exposed."

"What's that?"

"It looks like a black ball of spikes. It's a sea urchin. Nothing to worry about, but you really don't want to step on one."

"It's like a sea cactus?"

Jerry snorts. "Good one. Just don't let them hear you say that."

"Wana are sensitive?"

His eyes twinkle. "Totally!"

When we get near the girls, I hear them arguing.

Ana says, "It's a killer snake."

"You're lying," Zel says.

"I saw a video about it. One bite from a sea snake, and you're dead before you get back to shore."

"Nuh-uh."

"Put your foot in the water and wave it around if you don't believe me."

"You do it."

"Hi girls," I say.

Ana looks up. "Let's make Rell do it."

"Yeah. Rell, put your foot in the water."

"So a sea snake can bite it? That's not very nice."

Ana's eyes flit to Zel. "There's no snake," she says.

"We just want to know how cold the water is," Zel says.

Jerry squats down next to the girls. "Put your own hand in the water. Rell can't tell you if it's cold."

"Who're you?" Ana asks.

I say, "This is Jerry."

"Is he your boyfriend?" Zel asks.

I shoot Jerry a look.

Why? Why do I do this? He's not my boyfriend. I don't have to check with him to see if he agrees.

"No," I say evenly. "But he is my friend. We drove to the beach in his truck."

"Ugh. That old thing? You need a better truck," says Zel.

"Yeah, your truck smells like seaweed."

"And stale burritos."

My face turns purple.

Let a wave take me now.

Please.

I can't look at Jerry.

The girls are beyond rude.

Jerry throws his head back and laughs.

"Of course it smells like seaweed and burritos. It's a surf truck."

Zel and Ana's eyes bug out of their heads.

"Are you crazy?" Ana says.

"Or just weird?" Zel says as she stands.

She moves toward a rock the size and shape of a basketball perched near the edge of the biggest tide pool.

"Careful!" Jerry says. "That rock is called Pohaku. It's part of an ancient fishing shrine. Be respectful, and don't get too close."

"What?"

"Stay away from that rock," Jerry says. "It's not something you touch or play with."

"Come on, Ana," says Zel. "Let's leave the love birds alone."

"Yeah, love birds." Ana rises and makes kissy noises as she walks over to another tide pool. "Ooo! A crab! Let's catch it!"

Jerry stands. "Charming. Your sisters?"

I sigh. "Stepsisters."

"Wicked little demons, aren't they?"

"I don't really know. I haven't seen them in years. But you're probably right."

The water in the saltwater pool is deep, but I can see all the way to the bottom and through a large archway that leads to black water.

"Is there a sea snake?"

He shrugs. "It's possible, but highly unlikely. Sea snakes are really rare in Hawaiian waters. I've never seen one. It was probably an eel."

I bend down and run my fingers along the surface of the water. "It's colder out here than near the shore."

"Right off the point is deep water. There's a channel between us and the other side. That's what makes Nalupuki a great surfing beach."

Beneath my fingers, the water stirs. A thin rope peeks from a crevasse, then shoots out to wind between my fingers. I'm too surprised to jerk my hand away.

"What's that?"

Jerry gasps. "It's a baby snowflake eel. They're usually really shy. I've never seen one do this. It's like he's happy to see you."

More fish rise from the bottom and head to the surface. I see yellow tangs and purple damsel fish, striped sergeant majors, and others I don't recognize. I pull my hand out of the water.

"They must think I have food," I say. "Do people come out here and feed them?"

The look on Jerry's face is odd. It rolls through different expressions until it lands on something between sheepish and puzzled.

"Nobody I know," he says.

I stand and look at the strip of sand off to the right. Just past it is the hillside from the architect's model.

"That's where the surf camp is going?"

Jerry nods. "Yeah. That's Kaulupali land over there. Your family owns a few acres just above it. Uncle Kahana is gifting some of his Kaulupali land to Jay's foundation to use for the surf camp. Come out to the very edge of the lava with me, and I'll tell you the whole story."

"There's a mystery?" I tease. "A deep, dark secret?"

But when Jerry reaches for my hand to help me over a slippery patch, I see the pain in his eyes.

"There's a reason for the surf tournament and the camp." He sweeps his arm out over the bay.

"It all began here during our freshman year of high school."

Chapter 11

OUT AT THE very edge of the lava outcrop, the waves splash against the rocks, sending a fine mist toward us. In the water just off the point, a guy on a green surfboard and a girl on a cream one wait for the next set. The guy waves at Jerry.

"Santos!" he shouts. "Where's your board?"

"Home," Jerry says.

"Brah! Better hurry. Kids will be out of school soon," calls the girl.

"Can't," Jerry says.

"You snooze, you lose! The waves wait for no one," says the guy.

Like magic, a gentle swell forms off the point. The surfers swing their legs onto their boards and paddle into position where the wave suddenly builds four feet higher.

"Chee-hoo!" the guy calls.

"Laters, Jerry!" says the girl.

Jerry's eyes are on the surfers as they head to shore.

"You surf here a lot?"

He nods, but doesn't look at me. "From the time we could walk, we were in the ocean. Like I said, the International Abilities Surf Tournament, Get Wet, the surf camp—it all begins here."

He tugs my hand until our shoulders touch.

"Our freshman year, Jay Westin and I were competing in a surf tournament. Jay was the favorite." His lips twist wryly. "In those days, Jay was always the favorite. When the heat started, we all raced from the beach, paddling to get to the sweet spot just there," he points, "right where those surfers were. The waves were bigger that day. We were jockeying for position when someone yelled, 'Fin!'"

I look back to the beach and shiver.

It's so far.

"But it was just a dolphin, right?"

"No. Sharks. I saw them."

"Them?"

"Two. One the size of Jaws and the other his littler brother. Jay was out farther than the rest of us. From Piko Point, the shark fins made a beeline to him and disappeared."

"They left?"

Jerry shakes his head. "They dove. Sharks ambush. The biggest one rocketed from the bottom and came up underneath Jay's board, knocking him off and into the water. I saw the other one circling below."

I squeeze his hand. I have no words.

"When Jay came up for air, he shouted at us to go—to head back to shore."

"But you didn't."

"I couldn't. I knew he'd never leave me. I heard sirens and jet skis start up on the beach. I tried to paddle toward Jay. I thought if I could get him up on my board, we'd be okay. I knew help was coming, but before I could get there— "

He swallows and presses his lips tight, the horror of that day as fresh as a minute before him.

"The smaller shark bit Jay."

"You saw that?"

"Yeah. In all its technicolor glory. Red blood in blue water looks purple. Seafoam turns pink. Bone is whiter than white." Jerry reaches down and touches his shin a few inches above his ankle. "It ate his foot."

"My—"

I can't even say it.

Jerry tugs my hand until I look him in the eye.

"Jay lost his foot, but more importantly, he lost himself that day. Before the attack, being in the ocean was like breathing to him. People think losing a limb is about what someone can or can't do, but that's the smallest part of it."

"Jay Westin. You said he started Get Wet Prosthetics?"

Jerry nods. "That came later. After it happened, Jay filled his empty surfing space with hate. It took a lot of time, but the ocean eventually healed him—body, mind, heart, and soul. He figured out how to surf again. To forgive himself."

"Himself?"

"You sound surprised."

"But it's the shark who took his foot."

"It's complicated." Jerry rubs his face. "Anyway, Jay and his cousin Nili-boy started Get Wet Prosthetics to help others reconnect with the lives they were meant to live." He gestured toward the beach. "This camp is the next step. Watanabe

Global is doing a lot of good by supporting the auction. That's one reason why I helped you."

"One?"

Jerry presses his shoulder against mine. "Don't push it," he says.

I watch the surfers pull out of the wave and head back out.

"After what you saw, you still surf?"

"Every day I can. Rain or shine, big waves or glass."

I look at the waves crashing against the lava and think about pink foam and white bone.

"I'd never get in the water again."

"You only say that because you've never surfed."

"What about sharks? They're still out there."

Jerry gives me a side-glance. "We worked it out. It's all cool now."

"What—"

Bark, bark, bark, BARK, BARKBARKBARK!

Chapter 12

WE WHIRL around in time to see the girls rocking the round stone perched on the edge of the biggest tide pool. 'Ilima's dancing around them, her jaws snapping like a shark.

BARKBARKBARK.

"Come on, Ana! One more push, and we'll get it in the water!"

"No!" shouts Jerry as he lurches toward them. He slips on the lava and falls to his knees. "Stop it! You don't know what you're doing!"

The stone starts to tip.

"Girls," I say as I scramble around Jerry.

'Ilima leaps and bites one of Ana's ruffles, tugging the back of her suit off her hips.

"Eeee!" Ana shrieks. "I'm being attacked!"

The stone tumbles.

Zel pumps her fist. "Yes!"

'Ilima releases Ana's suit and rushes to the edge of the tide pool. As the stone sinks to the bottom, big silver bubbles rise like jellyfish and pop at the surface. 'Ilima collapses on the lava, raises her head, and howls.

"Stupid dog," Zel says, marching over. "Nobody bites my sister but me!"

She swings her foot, kicking 'Ilima squarely in the ribs.

'Ilima's howl turns into a yelp. She leaps to her feet, saltwater dripping off her chest. Pinning her ears back, she growls.

"Zel! Ana! Don't move!" I say.

"That dog pantsed me!" Ana says, pulling her suit up over her butt. "Kick it again, Zel!"

"Ana, are you hurt? Let me see."

I spin her around, but she covers her backside with both hands.

"Don't! You're as pervy as the dog."

There's not a mark on her.

Zel draws back her foot again. "Don't you growl at me, crazy dog. I'll kick you again."

"No, you won't!" I grab each of them by the arm. "Stop this right now!"

It's not until I turn back to Jerry that I see the tears in his eyes. He's kneeling at the edge of the pool, staring at the bottom in shock.

"Jerry?"

No response.

"Jerry, your knee is bleeding. Are you okay?"

At the sight of blood, the girls still.

He raises his eyes from the water and looks at the girls. "Why?" Tears spill down his cheeks. "That was a sacred 'aumakua stone. A guardian of this place for hundreds of years. People come here to pray, to meditate, to leave offerings. I told you it's an ancient shrine. I told you to leave it alone."

Zel scrunches up her face. "It's just a stupid rock."

Ana says, "Yeah. If it's so important, why did people leave it here?"

'Ilima lowers her head and growls deeper.

Jerry stands and pulls his shirt over his head, tossing it on the ground. The sunlight glistens on his surfer's broad shoulders and trim waist.

"Go," he says. "Get them out of my sight."

His hands move to his belt.

Ana pulls her arm out of my grasp.

"You're not the boss of us," she says.

Jerry unbuckles his belt and moves to the top button of his cargo shorts. "Leave before I'm tempted to use my belt to do more than hold up my pants."

"I'm tell—ow!" Ana says when I grab her by the ear.

"You can't—ow, ow, ow!" chants Zel.

I twist their ears a little harder.

"I'm not your nanny. I'm your big sister and that does make me the boss of you! We're going home. Now."

Ana and Zel try to plant their feet, but I twist relentlessly and force them to stumble back to the beach.

I hear a splash and look over my shoulder. Jerry's pants are on the ground near the big saltwater pool. His feet sink below the surface.

After what the girls did, he'll never speak to me again.

Goodbye, Jerry's feet.

Zel realizes I'm distracted and tries to pull away, but I grip harder.

"Stop it, Rell! You're hurting me!"

"Good."

At the rock wall near the showers, I let go of the girls long enough to grab my shoes.

Jerry's shoes.

I run my fingers over them.

Goodbye, Jerry's shoes.

It's been real.

I turn on the shower and rinse my feet.

"Into the water," I say.

"No."

"It's too cold."

"We'll shower at home."

"You're not getting sand in the car and making more work for Jerry. Rinse."

"No."

Oh, yes. Yes, you will.

I grab ruffles.

"Let go!"

I twist for a better grip.

"Hey!"

"Rinse the sand off your feet or I'll dunk your whole body under the spray," I say.

"You can't make us."

"You're not the boss!"

I yank, pulling their legs into the spray.

"Cold, cold, cold!" they shriek.

"Good," I say.

"Ha! Fooled you. It's not that bad."

"Yeah, we wanted to anyway!"

"Let's get really wet and soak the car!"

"Yeah! Water's way worse than sand."

Out the corner of my eye, I spot 'Ilima limping around the showers and slinking behind the trash cans.

She's following us.

That can't be good.

"Let's go," I say.

'Ilima trails us all the way past the event tent and across the street to the rental car. I unlock it and push Zel toward the backseat.

"It's too small," she whines.

"Complain to your mother."

"It's too hot," Ana says.

"Get in."

"I want to sit up front."

"No, I want to," Zel says.

I grit my teeth. "You both get in the back right this minute or so help me, I'll leave, and you can walk."

"I hate you!" Ana says.

"Right back at ya," I say.

"I'm telling Mom," Zel says. "She'll punish you for being mean to us."

I count to three, then slide the driver's seat all the way forward. "Get in."

They grumble, but finally climb in. When I get in, I feel their knees and feet pushing against my back.

They want to be that way? Fine.

I turn all the air conditioning vents toward me and start the engine.

"Hey! What about us?"

"Can we put the top down? It's hot."

"No. Be quiet."

"I want a drink."

"Me, too."

"Let's go in the store."

"No," I say.

"Come on, Rell. Buy us a drink."

"It's hot, and we're thirsty."

I adjust the mirrors. "You can get one at the house."

"You're so mean, Rell."

"Mom was right about you."

When I put the car in reverse, 'Ilima steps out of shadows to watch us leave. I roll down my window.

"I'm sorry," I tell her. "I hope your ribs are okay. I won't let them hurt you again."

"What's Rell saying?"

"She's apologizing to the dog!"

"That dog attacked me!"

"It should be put down!"

"She's crazy. I can't believe Mom sent us with her."

'Ilima locks eyes with me.

My eyes dim like I'm going to faint. I take a deep breath and try to shake the ringing out of my ears.

I smell sandalwood and lemonade.

'Ilima tips her head to the side and chuffs.

The taste of lemons fills my mouth, sweet and sour and a little salty, just the way Mama used to make it.

In an instant, I'm three years old again, running through the backyard sprinklers. Mama says, "Rell! Time for lunch, sweetheart."

Mama?

"What are we waiting for?" Ana whines.

"It's so hot!"

I swallow, and the memory's gone.

When I look back, 'Ilima isn't there.

"Mom is so going to hear about this," says Zel.

"Uh-huh," says Ana.

Chapter 13

I'M SO angry that I don't consider parking on the street when I get to the estate and pull all the way to the back of the house. I grab my purse from the seat next to me, throw the keys inside, and hold the door open for the girls. They climb out acting stiff and sore, like I forced them to ride twisted like pretzels in a box. A door opens, and Regina stalks out.

"My precious," she says, throwing her arms wide.

"Mommy!" the twins shout and rush to her, crocodile tears falling like rain.

"My lambkins! What's wrong? Are you hurt?"

"Mommy, Rell yelled at us."

Regina's jaw clenches as her eye starts to twitch. "I'm sure it was just a misunderstanding. Rell knows better than to yell at you."

"Regina—"

"And Mommy, we were thirsty, but she refused to let us drink!"

"What! In this heat?" Regina pulls the girls close. "That's cruel, Rell, even for someone as thoughtless and uncaring as you."

"She made us ride in the back without air conditioning!"

"That's not all! She twisted our ears! Look!" Ana flips back her hair.

Regina looks at Ana's ear, then Zel's.

"Oh, my babies! Your ears are all red and swollen!"

"Regina—"

Regina rises to her full height and squares her shoulders. "I am so disappointed in you, Rell. I wish I could say I was shocked, but I'm not."

"The girls pushed—"

She holds up her hand. "I don't want to hear it. Clearly, this is my fault. I thought if you spent some time with your sisters, you'd love them as much as they love you. I thought you'd decide you missed us and would want to be part of the family again. But I see my hopes were misplaced. Your father was right about you."

Her words stop me cold.

Victory shines behind her eyes. She's daring me to ask.

I won't give her the satisfaction.

It's a stare-down until one of us blinks.

She holds out her hand. "Keys," she says.

I blink.

"What?"

She wiggles her fingers. "Give me your keys. After the way you've behaved, you're not going anywhere."

"But the auction—"

"I don't want you anywhere near the auction. You've proven you can't be trusted. You'll spend the night in your room."

"I—"

Faster than a snake, Zel reaches out and tugs my purse off my shoulder.

"Got it, Mommy! Her keys are inside."

"Give that back!" I reach to swipe it from her, but Regina sweeps Zel protectively behind her.

"Don't you touch her. You've done enough damage."

Zel unzips my purse and pulls out my phone. "We got her cell, too!" she crows.

"Give me Rell's phone," says Ana.

"Why?"

"I want to send text messages to her friends."

"She doesn't have any friends," says Zel, pushing buttons. "Oh, man! Her phone's locked! We can't text from it."

"Let's throw it in the toilet!"

"Yeah!"

"Come back here," I say and move towards the door. Regina blocks me.

"Run along and get ready, dears."

"But we don't want to go to the auction."

"Bor-ring!"

Regina pats their heads. "You're not going to the auction, sillies. That's for grownups. I've arranged for all the good girls to spend the night at the fabulous Princess Party at Disney's Aulani Resort."

"Rell's not a grownup," Zel says.

"She's not a good girl either," snickers Ana. "At the party, I'm going to be Jasmine."

"No, I am!"

"Too late. I called it."

"You're Olaf!"

"Olaf isn't a princess!"

The girls bicker all the way into the house.

They still have my phone!

I better not find it in the toilet.

Regina says, "We need to talk."

I scowl. "I've nothing to say to you."

"Then listen." She steps close, so close I can see the makeup spackled under her eyes. "We can do things the easy way or the hard way. It doesn't matter to me. If you want to keep going to that fancy school, you'll do what I say. Otherwise, I'll cut your funding, and you'll be out on the street."

"Why can't I go to the auction?"

"Because I said so. This deal is bigger than you know. You've proven that you can't handle taking two little girls to the beach. There's no way I'm letting you near something this important."

"Funding a surf camp for disabled people is big? That makes no sense, Regina. What's your angle?"

"No imagination. That's what your father said about you. Rell wears her heart on her sleeve, he said. There's no way she could ever play poker."

"Regina—"

"Get your things. I'll show you to your room. In the morning you can drive yourself to the airport."

Oh, no.

My bag.

In my mind, I clearly see it in the back of Jerry's truck.

She sees the look on my face. Her eyes widen like it's *her* birthday.

"You don't have it?"

"It's—I think I left it in the back of the truck."

"You have no clothes."

"No."

Regina throws her head back and cackles. "No car, no phone, no clothes! How utterly perfect. There's no way for you to go now."

Chapter 14

ON MY WAY to a tiny room just off the kitchen, I discover the laundry room. After Regina and her entourage leave, I toss my clothes in the washer and take a long, hot shower. Wrapped in a fluffy towel, with no one else around, I pour myself a glass of guava juice, make a peanut butter sandwich, and scrounge up a bag of chips. Shivering, I take them outside to sit in the twilight while my clothes dry.

Damp hair hanging down my back, I sit on a chaise lounge on the patio and sigh. Even though the sun has gone down, it's far warmer outside than in the house. Regina must have the air conditioning cranked. I could almost see my breath when I got out of the shower.

My dinner sits next to me on a small side table.

I need to eat. That iffy breakfast burrito on the plane was hours ago.

I take a bite of sandwich, but I can't swallow past the lump in my throat.

Accentuate the positive, Rell. Don't let Regina get you down.

Bright side: At least I'll have clean clothes for the plane ride home.

Clean clothes. Big whoop.

I force the down the bite of sandwich and wipe my eyes on a corner of the towel. Time to suck it up. Only babies cry. Big girls pull up their panties and problem solve.

Even if their panties are still in the dryer.

Identifying the problems is always the first step in dealing with Regina.

Problem one: car keys. I'll search the house. I doubt Regina took them with her.

Problem two: my phone. There's got to be a landline for the house. Find it and call Jerry.

Problem three: Jerry's number. I need my purse. It has Jerry's business card.

Problem four: find a phone book or computer. Call the rental company. Somebody there can give me Jerry's cell.

Call his work?

Gee, Rell, that's not stalkerish at all.

Oh, Jerry.

What would I even say? Sorry my wicked stepsisters pushed your special rock into the ocean? Hope you were able to get it out?

Unbelievable.

I can't forget the look on his face.

I should've stayed and helped him instead of running away like an idiot.

He'll wonder why I'm not at the party.

He'll think I'm mad at him or something.

Who am I kidding? He'll be relieved I'm not there.

I look at my sandwich and soggy chips and wrinkle my nose. *I bet they're having dinner now. Luau food like roast pork and fresh pineapple.*

Bright side: peanut butter's okay. A little sticky. Filling. The bread's fresh.

Hey, another one: The surf camp will be built. That's a good thing, right?

But it makes no sense. Why would Regina care about a surf camp? There's no margin in it.

Jerry—

Stop it. Just stop it.

A guy like that probably has a girlfriend. The way Luna talked, probably several *friends.*

Cedar, cinnamon, cloves, and wintergreen mints.

The sunlight on his bare shoulders when he took off his shirt.

Should've kissed him when I had the chance.

Just one dance at the party. Is that so much to wish for? It's my birthday, for crying out loud.

I'm not going to cry.

Not going to.

Dang it!

Through the tears, I see a star peeking over the mountain top.

The first star.

No candles on my birthday cake. Heck, no birthday cake! I'm not wasting this chance.

"Starlight, star bright; first star I see tonight; I wish I may; I wish I might; have the wish I wish tonight."

I close my eyes and wish.

"Woof."

I whip open my eyes. In the shadows on the far side of the patio is a yellow dog. "'Ilima?"

She limps towards me until she is standing in a pool of moonlight. I rise from my chair and lean forward, one hand clutching my towel, the other outstretched.

"Hey, girl. What're you doing here? That's a long walk from the beach. How're your ribs?"

She sits and cocks her head at me. Her tongue drops out of her mouth as she pants.

"Thirsty? Be right back."

In the kitchen I fill a bowl full of cool water and bring it out to the patio.

I set it next to her. "Here you go."

She glances at it, then bats it away with her paw.

"You don't want it?"

Her eyes lock like laser beams on my sandwich. She smacks her lips.

"Sandwiches aren't for dogs."

She whines and lies down, resting her head on her paws. Her eyes never leave my sandwich.

"Really? You like peanut butter?"

"Woof!" She sits up, ears forward.

I shrug. "Okay."

I tear off a chunk and toss it to her.

She catches it mid-air and gulps it whole.

"Careful! You keep eating like that, you'll choke."

Her ears droop as her body shakes, quivering in the moonlight. The air fills with the scent of sandalwood and lemons. Sparkles of silver light cascade down her body like glitter as she bows her head. I hear chanting or drums—a rhythmic beating that pulses like ocean waves against the shore. A gust of wind swirls around the patio, blowing the bag of chips to the ground.

"'Ilima?"

The high, clear note of a conch shell echoes against the house, a wall of sound so loud I cover my ears.

"'Ilima, what's going on?" I shout. "We better get inside."

Her limbs and torso elongate as she rises.

Before me stands a beautiful Hawaiian woman.

"'I—'I—'Ilima?"

"Woof," she says.

I step back and almost trip over my own feet. My heart is pounding. I can't get enough air to breathe, let alone scream.

The woman laughs, and it is the sound of wind chimes and beach glass. "Relax," she says, rolling her shoulders and neck. "I'm just playing with you." She touches her ribs and grimaces. "Although I could've done without the kick in the ribs. What's the matter with those two? Are they retarded?"

Reflexively, I say, "Don't say retarded. People aren't retarded."

She smiles without showing her teeth. "My mistake. It's tough to keep up with your human terms; they change so often. What should I say?"

"Intellectually disabled or differently abled."

This conversation is surreal. I shake my head to clear it, but the woman is still there.

"Are they?" she says.

I blink. "What?"

"Intellectually differently abled?" she says.

"No." I cock my head to the side. "At least I don't think so."

"Ah. Just plain mean, then. Good. That makes this easier." She stares at the rest of the sandwich still in my hand. "You going to finish that?"

"Uh, no. Knock yourself out," I say as I hand it to her.

Her fingers brush mine.

Oh, man. She's real.

'Ilima the woman takes dainty bites, but finishes the sandwich as fast as a dog.

"Oh, that's better," she says. "Changing form always makes me hungry!" She points to the glass of guava juice. "May I?"

"Be my guest."

Like I'm going to say no.

She drains the drink in one great swallow. "Umm, that's good," she says.

She sees me watching her.

She deliberately raises the empty glass to her lips.

She raises an eyebrow.

And takes a bite.

Glass crumbles and falls to the ground.

What the?

She chews.

Crunch, crunch, crunch.

She smiles, this time showing her teeth. There are little bits of glass clinging to her lips.

The world starts to dim. There's a buzz, buzz, buzzing in my ears.

This time I really do faint.

Chapter 15

WHEN I COME TO, I'm lying on the chaise lounge. 'Ilima is holding out a glass of water.

"Don't worry. It's a new one from the kitchen. I didn't even lick it."

I sit up too fast. The blood rushes from my head.

Don't faint. Don't faint.

It's all over if I faint.

'Ilima puts a hand on her hip and waves the glass near my face.

"Take it. Drink. Trust me. It's all going to be okay. I promise."

The water is cold against my tongue as I gulp it. When it hits my stomach, I feel more awake.

"Better?"

I nod.

"Good." She holds out her hand and pulls me to my feet. The towel starts to fall, but I catch it and wrap it tighter against my chest.

"Jerry, huh?" She circles behind me. "A girl could do a lot worse."

She snorts bitterly. "Many have."

She prods my back.

"Tall, but not too tall. Slender, almost willowy."

She runs her fingers through my hair.

"Good girl," she says with a snicker.

Is she petting me?

I bite my lip.

Don't lose it, Rell. Don't laugh.

"Nice hair. You've given me a lot to work with."

"Work how? What're you going to do with me?"

"Give you a birthday present, of course. What did you think was going to happen?"

"I have no idea."

She faces me again. "Look," she says, holding up a mirror.

"Where did—"

But then I see the girl in the mirror, and it doesn't matter where the mirror came from.

"That can't be me!" I say.

'Ilima smirks. "Of course it is."

"It can't be."

"How do you know? Have you ever seen the real you?"

It's me, but a me I've never seen before.

I'm wearing a silk floral shift tied over my shoulder. My hair is swept high and to the side with cascading curls. The smell of the gardenias in my hair mixes with the twisted lei of tiny white flowers around my neck.

I reach up to touch them.

"Pikake," she says. "A kind of jasmine. Don't touch or they'll brown."

My makeup is subtle. Just a few sweeps of mascara on my eyelashes, a kiss of blush along my cheekbones, and a light coral lip stain. My skin looks radiant. Dangling from my ears are simple gold drops in the shape of the flowers in my lei. On my feet are thin leather flip flops that show off my newly manicured toes. A glance at my fingers shows the same finishing touch.

Oh, no.

I reach down and run fingers over my shins.

Smooth as a baby's bottom.

'Ilima smirks. "Pits, too. I'm guessing your razor is in your bag."

"How—"

"Granted, Jerry probably would have preferred you in the towel, but let's not throw ourselves at him anymore that we already have, shall we?"

"Why—"

"So you can go to the party and dance with your beau. That's what you wanted, right?"

I turn sideways in the mirror. "But this—"

"You were expecting a poufy blue dress and impractical heels? Mainlanders," she scoffs. "No sense of style."

"How—"

She lowers the mirror and tsks. "Good grief, child. Speak in complete sentences. I know you can."

She raises the mirror again, holding it in front of me like a wish.

"See? Perfect. Jerry is waiting. You want to go or not?"

I swallow.

"Yes."

"Good."

"But I don't have my car keys—"

A car pulls into the driveway and beeps its horn.

"Gecko," she says. "Hawaii's version of Uber or Lyft. Much better than your Mini Cooper pumpkin coach, even if we had the keys. Come along, Rell. We don't have all night."

As I get in the car, the driver doesn't say a word, just twitches nervously. In the rearview mirror I see that his eyes are slit like a reptile's. He sees me watching and quickly slips on a pair of dark glasses. His fingertips are odd, too big and puffy for his hands. Before I can look further, 'Ilima pushes the door closed and stands outside the car twiddling a finger at me. I roll down the window.

"Here's the deal: The car and driver will be waiting for you as soon as you step back into the parking lot. No need to call. The driver will only bring you back here, so don't bother trying to get to the airport or someplace crazy like that. You kiss that boy, the one you wished on, the car won't come. In fact, if you kiss him, you'll go back to standing in a towel with wet hair dripping down your back. Transitions are funny. The towel may shrink a little, too, so keep that in mind."

I reach through the open window and touch her arm. "Thank you, 'Ilima. It's a wish come true."

She lifts my hand off her arm and gives it a little squeeze. "I'm not a fairy godmother, Rell. I don't grant wishes; I pay my debts. That's all this is."

"Who are you?"

"Don't look a gift horse in the mouth." She sees the look on my face and softens. "It's your birthday, Rell. Go have fun."

Chapter 16

THE TENT at Keikikai Beach glows like a candle. As we pull up, I hear live music; guitars and ukuleles strum as a velvety voice caresses a melody filled with Hawaiian vowels. The driver takes me all the way to edge of the red carpet where a perky young man in a blue aloha shirt opens my door and presents me with his hand.

"Aloha!" he says. "Do you need parking assistance?"

"Um," I mumble as I exit the car.

"No," croaks the driver.

As soon as I'm standing on the edge of the carpet, the driver hits the gas. The valet barely has time to get the door closed.

"Whoa!" yells the valet. "Where's the fire?" He turns to me. "Are you okay?"

I take a deep breath. "Yes. Thank you."

"That guy's crazy. Do you know him?"

"No. He's a hired driver."

He pulls out a cell phone. "Which company?"

"Gecko."

"Gecko? Never heard of them." He raises an eyebrow. "You sure he's legit?"

I stifle a laugh. "He was provided by my—"

By my *what*? My dog? I shudder. 'Ilima's not my dog. Definitely not my fairy godmother, either. My gift horse? I bite my lip to keep from laughing.

The valet's eyebrow goes higher.

I'm taking too long to answer.

I cover my hesitation with a cough.

"Oh, excuse me. Sorry, got a frog in my throat. The driver was sent by my, um, *benefactor*. He came highly recommended."

The valet holds out his phone. "You should report him. There's no excuse for that."

"I will."

Although I don't think a dog who isn't a dog is going to care very much.

The valet wiggles his phone.

Oh, no. He's still waiting for me to make the call.

"Thanks, but I'll call later," I say. "No need to spoil the evening."

He slips his phone back into his pocket and holds out a hand. "Your invitation, miss?"

Invitation?

Crap.

I'm not carrying a purse. I run my hands down my sides, but the shift has no pockets. I hold out my empty hands, give a weak smile, and shrug.

His eyes do a quick sweep from head to toe, assessing. He must like what he sees, because he smiles and says, "It's okay. Just tell me your name so I can have it announced."

Double crap!

"That's not necessary," I stammer. I try to step past him, but he takes a step sideways, forcing me to stay on the edge of the red carpet.

"I know it sounds silly, but it's an old-fashioned tradition the organizers are insisting on."

This is the last thing I need.

"I don't want to bother everyone," I say. "After all, I'm late. The event has already started."

"It's not a bother. Look, other people are waiting to be announced."

I peek around him and see a short queue of guests lined up at the top of the red carpet. At the archway leading into the tent stands a seven foot mountain of a man in silver brocade livery. Two teenage boys in loincloths block the doorway with crossed wooden staffs topped with white cloth balls.

At the giant's nod, a couple hands a gilt-edged card to him. He regards it for a second, then nods again. The couple steps forward, the staffs are uncrossed and whisked aside, and another man in a loincloth and a short feathered cape softly blows on a conch shell. As the echo dies, the giant announces the couple's names and ushers them in. Once the couple enters the tent, the wooden staffs are crossed again, and the whole thing starts over.

I sigh.

Only Regina would insist on something so pompous and ridiculous.

Inside the tent, nobody seems to be paying much attention to the guests' arrivals. The music doesn't pause, and I can see people talking as they wander between the tables filled with auction items.

Maybe it's no big deal. Even if he announces me, it's unlikely Regina will hear it.

"Your name, miss," the valet prods. "Tell me quick, and it will be over before you know it."

Fine. Here goes nothing.

"I'm Rell," I say. "Rell Watanabe."

The valet jumps back. "Rell Watanabe! I'm so sorry, Ms. Watanabe! Your driver should've brought you to the special VIP entrance! Let's get you right to the front!"

He gestures frantically to the giant. VIP, he mouths. BIG TIME!

The giant looks startled, but bows to the couple next in line, executes a snazzy military turn, and starts toward me.

I want to die.

My cover's blown before I can even get into the party.

I look at my feet still on the edge of the red carpet.

Should I step back onto the parking lot? How long will it take for the car to return and whisk me away?

I lift a foot and hold it over the pavement as I scan the parking lot. I spot the Gecko car barreling towards me. While I can't see his eyes through his dark sunglasses, I can feel his lizard's gaze lock onto my foot, the heel of my flip-flop perilously close to touching the road.

Go or stay?

One shot, one dance. That was my wish.

I risk looking back. The giant is almost to me when another man sidles next to him.

"It's okay, Moki," he says. "The lady is with me."

The mountain pauses mid-stride. "You sure, Jerry?"

"I got this. Thanks, guys," Jerry says and holds out his arm.

The valet nods and moves to the next car at the curb.

When I slip my hand into the crook of Jerry's elbow, he tucks it tight. From the corner of my eye, I see the Gecko car swerve away.

"Okeydokey," says the mountain. His eyes widen when they meet mine. "Wow, laulau, Jerry. She's cherry like a '57 Chevy. You're a lucky man."

He snaps off a salute. "Ma'am."

One complicated three-step about-face and he's striding back to the archway.

I feel the laughter Jerry's fighting to stifle as it rumbles in his chest. He turns and leads me away from the red carpet.

"Cherry like a '57 Chevy?" I say. "Really?"

He shoots me a look. "It's a compliment."

"Cherry like a classic car?"

"Moki works in a body shop straightening fenders all day. To him, something particularly fine is cherry." Jerry takes my hand off his elbow and twirls me around, giving a low whistle.

A potted hibiscus lining the walkway twitches.

I snatch my hand away. "Women are not dogs to be whistled at."

'Ilima pops into my head.

Maybe some of us are.

Can't think about that now.

Jerry cocks his head to the side, a slow smile pulling at his lips. "Moki's right.

You look cherry—like you stepped out of an ad from the 1960s."

"You and that wolf-whistle belong in the '60s."

"This is Lauele. Sometimes there's not much difference."

"Cherry and Jerry, sitting in a tree, k-i-s-s—" sings a voice from the behind the potted plant.

"Knock it off, Luna!" I hiss.

"What?" Jerry asks.

"Nothing," I say.

I hear Luna giggle as his footsteps retreat.

Chapter 17

JERRY LEADS me around the back of the tent to the area near the makeshift kitchen. There's an open doorway, and we pass through it and into the main tent. As I look around, I realize we're standing behind the stage.

Wires and cables run everywhere. Off to the side is an audio mixing board and monitors, the dials bouncing to the rhythm of the band playing on stage. Standing behind the loudspeakers that are pointed toward the crowd, it's surprisingly quiet backstage.

Jerry says, "Don't worry. This is one of the servers' entrances. You really didn't want to be announced, did you?"

I shake my head. "My stepmonster didn't want me here tonight."

"No! Not want you? Impossible." He clutches my hand to his chest like a B movie hero.

My heart leaps.

Chill out, Rell. He's joking.

'Ilima's right. I can't make this too easy.

I pull away.

"You mean the impossible boxes at the airport weren't a big enough clue that I'm not the favorite daughter?"

"They did make me wonder."

A waiter with a loaded tray rushes through the door. "Excuse me," he says. "Pupus coming through!"

"Oh, sorry," I say and step aside.

The waiter rolls his eyes at me. "The party's on the other side of the stage, people. This area is for staff only. If you love birds want a little privacy, head to the beach."

"Lighten up, Renten," Jerry says. "No act."

Renten sniffs. "Some of us are working, Jerry. Don't you have cars to park?"

Jerry stamps his foot and fakes a charge. Renten squeals and quickly rounds the stage.

"Yeah, that's what I thought," Jerry calls.

Cedar, cinnamon, cloves, and wintergreen mints.

I lace my fingers so I can't reach out and run my fingers through his hair.

Do I really need the car to bring me back to Poliahu's? Maybe walking home wouldn't be so bad.

Maybe I don't have to go back there at all.

I glance at my dress.

I'm on borrowed time.

But how short could that towel be?

Naked and in public, Rell. Keep that in mind. Do not kiss him!

When Jerry turns to me, his wide grin fades when he sees the look on my face.

Awesome!

I probably have crazy stalker woman tattooed on my forehead.

"Rell—"

"I'm sorry, Jerry." The words rush out like a train wreck.

He purses his lips. "You say that a lot."

He's got great lips. Soft and pillowy and firm like—

"Rell?"

"What? Oh. Sorry."

"Stop saying that. I'm the one who's sorry about how I behaved at Piko Point."

I look down, confused.

Piko Point?

He tips my chin up. "You don't have anything to apologize for."

He's talking about the rock.

This conversation is going to suck.

I take a breath.

"No, I do. I was supposed to be watching Ana and Zel. I'm responsible for the disrespectful and disgraceful way they pushed—"

He places a finger against my lips. Warmth spreads like butterscotch from the pit of my stomach to the ends of my toes.

"Shhhhh. I was there, too," he whispers. "It's not your fault."

"But the rock?"

"I got it back where it belongs. I actually think Pohaku enjoyed the swim."

He brushes a strand of hair from my cheek. My knees go weak. Those lips look so soft.

"...'Ilima?" he asks.

Crap. I missed something.

"'Ilima the dog?" I say.

It's his turn to look confused. "Yeah, the yellow dog at Piko Point. I haven't seen her. That sister of yours—"

"—stepsister—" I say.

"—Ana—" he says.

"—Zel—" I say.

"—whatever. One of those demons kicked 'Ilima really hard. I went to check on her later, but I couldn't find her. Uncle Kahana says she's missing. Have you seen her?"

"Uh, no," I say, eyes wide and face blank.

I should get an Oscar.

On stage, the song ends. The room applauds. Someone calls, "Hana hou! Hana hou!"

I raise an eyebrow at Jerry.

"It means they want more."

The singer says, "Ah, mahalo plenny, everyone. On behalf of Uncle Tiko, Uncle Butchie, and the rest of the band, I want to thank Get Wet Prosthetics for having us here tonight."

"Hana hou, Tuna! Hana hou!"

The singer turns to the band. "You guys wanna do one more?"

"Shoots," says the bass player. "Let's do *Ahe Lau Makani*."

Back into the microphone, Tuna says, "One last song. Everybody out on the dance floor. Shake some loose change out of your pockets for the surf camp. Uncle Butchie, take us home."

The lead guitarist counts off. "One-two-three, one-two-three." The band swings into the intro.

"Is that a waltz?"

"Yeah," says Jerry.

"That's going to get everyone dancing? Not *YMCA* or *Boot Skootin' Boogie* or—"

"This is Lauele, remember?"

Through a seam in the backdrop, I see people grab partners and head to the area in front of the stage. Young, old, and everyone in between shuffle in modified boxed-steps.

In the soft glow of lantern light, it's magical.

Jerry takes my hand, the challenge clear in his eyes.

"No way. You waltz?" I say.

He puts his left hand on my waist. "Don't worry. I'll be gentle."

"Ha!" I put a hand on his shoulder. "Try to keep up."

We sway for a couple of beats, then his palm gently presses me backward, and we're off. He leads me in a few simple steps, and I follow with ease.

"You've done this before," he says.

"Six years of dance lessons."

"I thought you went to a fancy all-girls school."

"Yep. That means I can lead, too. Need a few pointers?"

He pulls me closer. "Oh, no, babe. We're just getting started."

He lengthens his stride, and we glide and swoop, my heart pounding one-two-three, one-two-three. He spins me in double-time, and I keep my eyes glued to his face, the one thing in sharp focus as the rest of the world whirls by. He pulls me tighter to his chest. I inhale cedar, cinnamon, cloves, and wintergreen mints.

One-two-three, one-two-three.

Ocean waves. Sand between my toes. Sunlight and tradewinds caressing my hair.

One-two-three, one-two-three.

Stepping over tide pools at Piko Point. Yellow tangs and snowflake eels. Feathery corals and translucent fins.

One-two-three, one-two-three.

As the song reaches the chorus, he signals for a dip.

One-two—

CRASH.

We tumble to the floor, the strands of my lei tangling between us.

Chapter 18

"Rell! Are you okay?"

I feel a tug on my foot. I try to lift my leg, but my flip-flop is caught on a cable. As I kick it off, I realize my dress is riding high on my thighs. I quickly sit up and tug the hem down.

"Oh, yeah," I mutter. "This is much more practical than high-heels and poufy skirts. Bloody 'Ilima!"

"'Ilima? She's here?"

"No, she didn't get in the Gecko car with me."

"Rell, look at me. I need to check your eyes. Did you hit your head?"

"No. Just injured my pride." I gather my flip-flop and slip it back on. "Are you okay?" I ask.

He rolls to his side and props his head in his hand. "It feels like the scrape on my knee might be bleeding again."

"Oh, Jerry! I'm—"

He shakes his head. "Nope. You're not allowed to say that anymore. The tragedies of the world aren't your fault."

"Tragedies of the world?" I grin.

He sits up and bumps my shoulder with his. "I meant comedies of the world. If it makes you feel better, you can take the blame for the trip. See you next fall."

"But you were leading!"

"I accept your apology," he says.

I punch his shoulder.

"Abuse! Abuse!"

"Right."

He laughs and wiggles his fingers menacingly. "Tickle retaliation!"

"Don't you dare—"

"Here's your mic, Ms. Watanabe."

Three people enter backstage and stand by the audio board.

"Call me Regina," says my stepmonster. "Like Cher or Beyoncé."

"Oh, like in that movie—"

"I have no idea what you're talking about," she says in a voice icicle cool. "There's only one Regina."

Regina?

"Eep!" I squeak and dive under the stage. Jerry hesitates for a split second, then slides next to me.

"They can't see us here," he whispers.

I'm too afraid to do more than nod.

Regina and Mr. Lucius stand near the stage stairs. An audio tech fiddles with Regina's mic. At the audio board he says, "Can you give me a little test?"

Regina says, "Test one, two, three."

Mr. Lucius says, "Eeney, meenie, miny, mo."

The audio tech watches the dials and frowns. "Mr. Lucius, could you repeat that please?"

"Catch a tiger by the toe."

The audio tech pats his pockets and looks around. "Your battery is low. I'm going to have to get a new one from the truck. Be right back."

As he disappears outside, Regina puts her hand on her hip. "The incompetence of these islanders is stunning."

I feel Jerry bristle.

Sorry, Jerry. My stepmonster's a jerk.

"A few more hours," Mr. Lucius says, "and it will all be over. Once the deal's done, you don't have to stay on this rock."

Regina lowers her voice. "The bribe worked?"

"There are no bribes, Regina. Only meaningful campaign contributions."

Jerry and I exchange a glance. He pulls his phone out of his pocket and hits record.

"And was our contribution meaningful?"

"Very. Once the permits for the surf camp's access road and utilities are filed with the county, the planning commission will be forced to approve our development behind it. It's just a matter of paying the filing fees. We're prepared to cover whatever doesn't get raised tonight."

From her purse, Regina pulls out some lipstick and starts smearing it along her lips. "Don't be too hasty, Lucius. Let them sweat and be grateful when we save their project. Public gratitude now will make it impossible for anyone to believe they didn't know about the eighty story high-rise we're building on the property behind them."

Jerry sucks in his breath so fast, I'm afraid they'll hear us. He holds the phone closer to them.

Mr. Lucius says, "Marketing is ready to go. Did you see the mock-ups of the sales campaign? We're positioning it locally as bringing jobs and technology to a blighted economy."

"Technology? That sounds expensive," says Regina.

"We're donating a few computers and upgrading the internet connection to the high school. That's it."

"Because we care," Regina says.

"Of course."

I want to smack the smirk right off his face.

"In the Euro and Asian markets we're positioning the development as the perfect island escape—a real life Bali Hai. We've already shot the beauty scenes of the beaches for the media campaigns." He sighs. "But have you thought this through, Regina? Do you really want an ugly, low budget surf camp of cripples to be the first thing your clients see?"

Regina laughs, and it's the sound of nails on a chalkboard and the last wormy apple as it falls off a tree.

"You're funny, Lucius. The camp is never going to be built. With my development, taxes and land values are going sky high. My analysist predicts that most of the land will be in foreclosure in less than five years. I'm going to own all of Lauele."

"I still don't understand, Regina. Other than the beach, there's nothing here. The only store or restaurant for miles is Hari's."

She puts away her lipstick and rubs her lips together. Her mouth is shiny and red, like she's chewing glass.

"The first thing I'm going to do is knock down that ugly convenience store across the street and build a nice, modern natural foods kind of place."

"The lot's too small. You won't have parking."

"We'll raze the beach pavilion and expand the parking lot on this side. Once everything's private, there won't be a need for public works anymore."

Mr. Lucius holds up his hand. "The beach laws are ridiculous in Hawaii, Regina. You have to allow public access—even through private land."

"People won't come if the entire area's gated. We'll keep the riffraff out. Even the beaches will belong to the Bali Hai tenants."

"I don't think we can make that—"

"You can and you will. Increase our campaign contributions if necessary," she snaps.

Waving a black box and cord, the audio tech slips through the doorway. "Got a whole new set-up right here, Mr. Lucius."

"About time," mutters Regina.

The audio tech replaces Mr. Lucius's mic and pack.

"Let's test again," he says.

"If he hollers, let him go," Mr. Lucius says.

"Perfect." He places the old set next to the audio board. "Regina? Can you give me one last check?"

"Eeney, meenie, miny, mo."

Chapter 19

ABOVE US, the waltz fades. As the applause dies, the band scurries down the stairs and exits backstage. A woman's voice says, "Mahalo, gang. Before we get started with the auction, Uncle Kahana wants me to introduce someone who has become dear to our hearts: Regina Watanabe. Aunty Regina!"

"Aunty Regina?" Regina hisses. "Cow, I'm not related to you. These people!"

"Mic-ay on-ay," whispers Mr. Lucius. "Smile!"

Regina's fake smile doesn't reach her eyes.

Maybe it's not Botox.

As the woman exits stage right, Regina and Mr. Lucius climb the stairs and enter stage left. The audience is still applauding when the woman stops backstage and bends down.

"Howzit, Jerry," she says.

"Hey, Tuna," he says. "This is Rell."

"Aloha, Rell. I like your lei. Don't stay under the stage too long. Get plenny spiders. Laters, gangies." She waves with just her thumb and pinky outstretched as she heads outside.

I turn to Jerry, eyes wide in the darkness. "How—"

He shrugs. "It's Tuna. We used to call her Tunazilla when we were kids. Voice of an angel, body of a linebacker. She just knows things."

Above us, Regina begins speaking.

"As you know, Watanabe Global has deep roots in this community. From the first moment I heard about the International Abilities Surf Tournament and its goal of expanding into a surf camp, I knew this project was exactly aligned with everything Watanabe Global stands for. Its value is immeasurable—"

"My father would never have torn down a community for money," I say. "She's going to ruin Lauele."

"There won't be a Lauele," Jerry says.

"This is my community, too. I've got to stop her."

"Rell—"

I grab Jerry's cell phone, crawl out from under the stage, pick up the abandoned mic set, and switch it on. There's enough juice in the batteries to make the needles bounce.

Suck it, Regina!

I hold the mic next to Jerry's phone and press play.

Nothing.

I press again.

Nothing.

I look closer.

Locked!

"Jerry, what's your password?"

"Ua mau ke ea o ka 'aina i ka pono."

"What?"

"Just hand me my phone."

Jerry stands next to me, flicking his fingers over his phone screen.

"Ready," he says.

"Let's do this!"

The file starts to play, but nobody can hear it over the loudspeakers.

"The battery's too weak," Jerry says. "Cut the other mics and boost it through the board."

I pull down the audio faders for Regina and Mr. Lucius's mics, cutting her off mid-sentence.

This is for you, Mama.

For you and our 'ohana.

I twist a dial and bring up the volume on the mic I'm holding above the cell phone.

"Is this better?" my voice booms over the loudspeakers.

"Rell?" shouts Regina from the stage.

Over the speakers, Regina's recorded voice says, "The camp is never going to be built. With my development, taxes and land values are going sky high. My analysist predicts that most of the land will be in foreclosure in less than five years. I'm going to own all of Lauele."

Chaos explodes.

The audio tech comes flying backstage. "What are you guys doing?" he shouts. "Get away from that equipment!"

Jerry steps in front me. "Just listen, Darin! The whole thing is a scam."

"Jerry—"

"LISTEN!"

Darin pauses.

Regina's voice says, "We'll keep the riffraff out. Even the beaches will belong to the Bali Hai tenants,"

Darin mouth drops. "Oh my—"

Regina and Mr. Lucius come flying backstage.

"Stop this immediately!" shrieks Regina. Her lipstick's smeared in a long red streak across her chin. Her hands go to her hair. "I demand that you give that illegal recording—"

"Fake illegal recording," shouts Mr. Lucius. "This is a fraudulent attempt to malign my client!"

Darin stands next to Jerry, blocking access to the cell phone.

"Play that again, Jerry," he says. "I wanna know which politician we're impeaching."

Regina spots me cowering behind the guys.

"This is all your fault, Rell! When I get through with you—"

I turn and flee.

Chapter 20

My foot barely touches the asphalt in the parking lot before the Gecko car screeches up. The valet runs up, but I'm faster. I fling open the door and jump into the backseat.

"Rell!" shouts the valet, "Is it true? Is Watanabe Global planning to build a huge—"

"Yes!" I say. "Sorry!"

I slam the door shut.

"Hit it!"

The driver snaps my head back as he accelerates out of the parking lot, smoke billowing behind.

The whole way to the house, I shake.

I stare out the windows at the empty beaches and modest homes that line the main road. The moon shines over the ocean, the light reflecting off coconut trees and hibiscus hedges as we speed by. I burn each image into my brain, trying to create a lifetime of memories in just a few minutes.

I can never come back.

None of this is real. It's all a giant chess match to get a high-rise development approved in Lauele. My father's company is planning to turn sleepy Lauele into an exclusive version of Waikiki. Regina never planned to support the surf camp. She just wanted the infrastructure permits approved so she could build her high-rise condominiums.

They must hate us.

I hate us.

Even if Jerry convinces people that I had nothing to do with it, there's no way I can show my face around here again.

Goodbye, Jerry.

It's probably best we never kissed.

The driver doesn't bother pulling into the driveway. He just whips up next to the gate and slams on the brakes. The locks on the backdoors pop open when I touch the door handle.

"Thanks," I say as I swing my legs and step outside. "I appreciate—"

SLAM!

The door rips out of my hand as the car takes off like a cockroach when the kitchen light comes on.

"Hey!" I'm so angry, I step out of my flip-flops and fling them after the car.

They miss by a mile.

Story of my life.

"Happy eighteenth birthday to me. It's all downhill from here."

Chapter 21

ALL THE LIGHTS are on in the house. It should be cheery and bright, but it feels cold and sterile. I shut the front door and blow on the decorative glass pane set in the middle. Mist coalesces, the patterns as delicate as a snowflake.

That's frost, I swear.

Inside the house is the faint scent of smoke. As I walk through the entry, I hear wood crackle and snap. I follow the sounds to the dining room and discover a roaring fire in the fireplace. Two white wingback chairs flank the fire on either side. Between them is a small table overflowing with a coffee service and trays. 'Ilima the woman is sitting in the chair to the right, a teacup and saucer balanced in her lap.

"Back so soon?" she says. "He must not have been a very good dancer."

"Can you get me to the airport?"

She takes a sip from her cup and watches me over the rim. "Where are your shoes?"

"Really? That's what you're concerned about?"

She shifts and curls her feet beneath her. "Come sit by the fire. Poliahu loves the cold, but she's mindful of the comfort of her guests." She gestures to the coffee service. "There are cookies, cake, sandwiches. Have a bite of something. Your blood sugar's low."

"How would you know?"

"Your smell."

"That's ridiculous."

She shrugs. "It's true. You haven't eaten a meal in hours. Your body tells me it's hungry by the sickly-sweet smell that's coming off you in waves."

"It's probably the flowers you're smelling."

"Nope. It's you. I've learned a lot about humans living with Kahana."

"You and Uncle Kahana?"

"Get your mind out of the gutter. It's not like that." She takes another sip, her eyes never leaving me. "Sit," she says. "You're making me nervous."

When I sit down, she hands me a plate of cookies and a teacup. "Liliko'i biscuits. I think you call them passion fruit cookies. Hold out your cup, and I'll pour."

"That's okay. I don't like tea or coffee," I say.

"Good, because this is hot chocolate." When she tips the pot, the chocolate pours out as rich and thick as molten lava. She fills my cup only halfway. "So you can dunk," she says.

"What—"

"Uh-uh. No talk. Eat."

I'm too tired and hungry to argue.

The cookie is crisp like shortbread with a thin layer of passion fruit jam on the top. I dunk one into the hot chocolate, and it clings to the cookie like a hug.

I gently blow, then bite.

Ohhhhh," I moan. "I forgive you everything."

She grins like the Cheshire cat drinking cream. "Eat, child. We'll talk later."

I'm not sure how long I sit there, but when I'm done, the platters are empty. Little pies filled with coconut pudding, rolled pastries filled with cream and candied pineapple, tiny sandwiches filled with watercress and cucumber—I eat them all.

"More?" 'Ilima says.

"I couldn't."

She wrinkles her nose. "Well, at least you don't stink of hunger anymore." Setting her cup down, she sits forward and leans close.

"Bali Hai," she says. "The name isn't even Hawaiian."

"I didn't know about the development."

"But now you do." 'Ilima leans back in her chair. "Regina's bringing modern jobs and prosperity to backward Lauele."

"No, she's not."

"Are you sure? You're Rell Watanabe of Watanabe Global."

"My mother was a Mahope. This is my 'ohana."

'Ilima's eyes narrow. "'Ohana is an easy word to say when you'll get on a plane tomorrow."

I rock back in my chair. 'Ilima's words sting as harshly as if she'd slapped me.

Oh, come on! What am I supposed to do?

"I'm only eighteen!" I say.

She picks up her cup and takes a sip. "Yes, you're not a child any longer," she says.

"You mean I'm responsible?"

"When you claim the privileges of 'ohana, you also accept the responsibilities."

Jerry's words pop into my head.

"No one goes hungry," I say. "That's what you're getting at?"

'Ilima smiles.

"Jobs feed people. You think the jobs are important. You think what I did tonight to stop the development was wrong."

'Ilima takes another sip, her eyes never leaving my face.

I take a deep breath.

"I know you're powerful. You can probably turn me into a frog or something. But I don't agree. Jobs are not more important than people. There is more to life than money. Regina may still find a way to build her high-rise, but I'm going to do everything I can to make sure it's not on my mother's land in Lauele."

'Ilima's eyes crinkle. "A frog? Is that how you see yourself?"

"I...no," I say.

"Say ribbit."

"No!"

'Ilima's mouth quirks. "C'mon. I want to hear you say ribbit."

"I'm not going to say it."

"Why?"

"Because I'm not a frog!"

"Because you're not a frog. I wonder, Rell, if I held up a mirror in the moon-light now, would you recognize the real you?"

Seriously?

We're back to mirrors and moonlight?

Shoot me now.

'Ilima takes one look at my face and bursts into laughter.

"Ah, child. Clearly, you're not made for poufy dresses, even if you don't realize that yet."

"Is Bali Hai the reason you did all of this?"

"Oh, no. That's merely a bonus."

Bonus?

The fire crackles. 'Ilima reaches out with the poker and pushes a log deeper into the flames.

"That's better. Nice and hot," she says. "You danced with the boy."

"Yes."

"But you didn't kiss him."

"No."

Her eyes gleam. "Then where are your shoes?"

I take a deep breath. "Out in the middle of the street."

"Why?"

"I threw them at the car."

"Why?"

"Because the driver almost ran me over when I was getting out."

'Ilima sits back and bites her lip. "You left my birthday gift in the street?"

I rise. "I'm sorry. That was thoughtless. You've been very kind to me. I'll go get them now."

She crosses her legs and rests her head against the chair. "There's no need," she says, "since you've shown me you've no use for my gifts."

I flinch as wet hair tumbles down my back. In my hands is a washcloth. One side of my body is warm from the fireplace, the other is freezing.

Freezing because I'm naked.

I flip the washcloth, pulling it this way and that, trying to cover all of my bits and pieces, but it's no use.

'Ilima rolls her eyes. "Modern humans are so uptight. You would've thanked me if you'd kissed him."

I step behind my chair. "Where are my clothes?"

"Where did you leave them?"

"In the dryer."

"Then that's where you should check."

I spin around and head to the laundry room.

Bloody, bloody dog!

As I put on my clothes, I hear her chuckling. Yanking my shirt over my head, I storm back into the dining room.

"You think this is funny?"

"Are you mad because I didn't fold and iron your clothes?" She sniffs. "I'm not your maid."

"Or my fairy godmother. You said that. Who are you? Why are you doing this to me?"

'Ilima stands. In the flickering of the firelight, she grows, filling the space around her until her head brushes the ceiling. "I do things to achieve my own purposes," she says. "I pay my debts and collect those owed to me. This night isn't over."

Chapter 22

THE FRONT DOOR swings open with a force that shatters the glass pane in the center.

"RELL! You will come here this instant!"

The last word is a hiss no human can make.

I have just enough time to see 'Ilima shrink back into a dog and curl up beneath a chair before my stepmonster stalks into the room.

"Traitor!" she shrieks. "After all I've done for you. I paid for your schooling, your room and board, and the clothes on your back!"

She grabs a vase from the sideboard and throws it at me. I duck, and it shatters against mantel. "No more! Do you hear me? No more!"

I square my shoulders and pull my head high. With nothing left to lose, she has no power over me.

"Go back to the hell you crawled from, Regina! I don't need you or your money."

"Oh, no? Your fancy school has been cancelled. You have nowhere to go."

"I can stay with the headmaster and his family. I've done it before during the holidays. They won't mind. I can stay with them until I get a job and can pay my own way."

Regina cackles. "You think you stayed with the headmaster's family because they liked you? No, Rell. I paid them to take you in. They don't care about you. You're just a paycheck to them."

"I don't believe you. When I fly home—"

"You won't."

"What?"

Regina grins and my blood chills. She wags her manicured finger at me and speaks so softly I can barely hear her. "You're not going back to school, Rell. You're not well. After the way you treated your sisters today and the lies you told at the auction, well, it's obvious you're a very troubled girl. I have a very special place in mind, a place that will heal your damaged mind. It's a lockdown facility in Taiwan. We'll reassess after the second or third round of electric shock therapy, but the doctors are very keen on some new brain surgery techniques they'd like to try."

My mouth goes dry.

"You wouldn't."

She crosses her arms. "I already have."

"You can't."

"I can. I did."

Her phone beeps, and she glances at the text message.

"The medical crew is on its way. I just received confirmation of straight jacket restraints and meds to make you compliant. See for yourself."

She holds out the phone, but when I move to take it, she yanks it away.

"You really think I'd give you my phone? That's your problem, Rell. You think everyone is as stupid as you."

"No. She thinks everyone is as kind as she is," says Uncle Kahana from the doorway. He steps to the side. "Watch out, Avery. There's glass on the floor here."

Mr. Me'e walks into the room, a folded paper in his hands. "Hello, Rell. Remember me?" he says.

I nod.

"What are you doing here? You work for me!" Regina says.

"I quit."

"You can't quit. I have your firm on retainer. Nobody treats me like this." She punches buttons on her cell phone. "I'm calling Lucius right now."

"Knock yourself out," Mr. Me'e says.

"And I'm calling the police! You are all trespassing!" Regina flounces to the other side of the room. "Lucius? I need you immediately!"

Uncle Kahana says, "Is she always like this?"

Mr. Me'e nods.

"I think the surf camp dodged a bullet."

'Ilima thumps her tail.

"'Ilima! I've been looking for you everywhere!" Uncle Kahana says.

'Ilima chuffs.

"Fine," says Uncle Kahana. "We'll talk about it later."

Mr. Me'e hands me the paper. I unfold it. It's the paper I signed in this very room so many lifetimes ago.

"Rell, I didn't make copies of this document like Regina and Mr. Lucius wanted. That's the original. You have no idea what you signed, do you?"

"Something that allows Regina to pay for my schooling. If I don't sign these papers every year, she can't pay my tuition. I don't earn enough cleaning the school kitchen to pay for more than half my board."

Mr. Me'e sighs. "That's what I was afraid of. Rell, those papers you signed every year were your consent—your permission—for Regina to continue to act as your legal guardian."

"Isn't that what I said?"

"No." He turned to Uncle Kahana. "It's as I suspected. She really doesn't understand."

Uncle Kahana comes to me and kneels at my feet. He takes my hands in his and looks me in the eye.

"Rell, when you signed those papers every year, you told the courts that you wanted Regina to be in charge of you and your estate. Your father set his will up so you could choose. Regina was not your guardian until you chose her."

In an instant, I'm twelve years old. Daddy is dead. The house is full of somber people wearing black. Regina and Mr. Lucius take me into Daddy's office. Regina hands me a brochure with pictures of horses and smiling girls.

"Wouldn't you rather be there? Look at this school."

I can't think. The black lace on my dress is itchy, and my shoes pinch.

Mr. Lucius says, "All you need to do is sign right here, Rell. You can be there tomorrow."

I pick up the pen and scrawl my name.

I blink back the tears. "All these years I could've had another guardian? But no one wanted me!"

Mr. Me'e says, "That's not true, Rell. Lots of your father's friends and family wanted you. Your mother's family, too. Before anyone had a chance to talk with you, you disappeared. When people pushed, Mr. Lucius just showed them the paper you signed naming Regina as your guardian. Regina forbade anyone from contacting you at school."

"Rell, lots of people have been waiting for this day," Uncle Kahana says. "Do you know why?" I shake my head. "Today you turned eighteen. You no longer need a guardian. Anyone who wants to contact you can."

I can't breathe.

Mr. Me'e nods. "I have a stack of birthday cards in my car dating back to when you turned thirteen." He looks down. "But I didn't give them to you because you signed that paper today giving Regina power of attorney over you and your estate."

"This paper makes her the boss of me?"

"Yes. And your estate."

My head is spinning. It's too hot near the fire.

"You said my estate. What's my estate? Money? Did Daddy leave me enough to finish school? Is there enough for me to go to college?"

Mr. Me'e and Uncle Kahana exchange a look.

"Rell," says Uncle Kahana, "your estate is Watanabe Global."

Mr. Me'e nods. "You control the whole thing."

Chapter 23

Sirens wail in the distance, getting closer as they climb the mountain. It's either the police coming to arrest Uncle Kahana and Mr. Me'e or the Taiwanese doctors with straightjackets and needles coming to take me away.

Before I can say anything, Regina rushes back across the room, waving her cell phone at me.

"I hope you're satisfied. Lucius is filing so many charges against all of you, you won't see daylight for a century."

"You planned to steal my mother's land and build high-rise condos on it. You were going to raise the taxes so high, people would beg you to buy them out for pennies on the dollar," I say.

"Rell—" Regina says.

"You were never going to build the surf camp," I say. "You just wanted the permits. But the joke's on you, Regina. Because of what you said tonight, the auction was never held. Without the auction, there aren't any funds to pay the fees."

"You see what I mean, gentlemen? Rell is delusional. She thinks there's a big conspiracy. The truth is, as a show of good faith, Watanabe Global just paid the fees for the surf camp's permits. Everything is in order."

"Not quite." I stand and hold out the paper. "Do you see this, Regina? It's the paper I signed this afternoon. It's the only copy."

Regina lunges at me.

I yank the paper away.

"Did you really think I'd let you touch it? That's your problem, Regina. You think everyone is as evil as you."

I wad up the paper and toss it into the fire.

"NOOOO!" Regina screams, pushing me aside and plunging her hands into the flames.

"Grrrr," growls 'Ilima as she shoots out from under the chair and chomps down on Regina's arm.

Regina screams and pulls her charred hands out of the flames.

Uncle Kahana grabs a bowl filled with floating gardenias and dumps the water over Regina's hands.

Regina falls to her knees, sobbing.

'Ilima retreats under the table, spitting and rubbing her tongue along the carpet.

All of this goes on, but I never take my eyes off the charring ball of paper until there is nothing left but ashes.

Chapter 24

I'M SITTING on Poliahu's front steps when Jerry walks up and sets my bag down beside me.

"Thanks," I say.

"I was going to give you your bag earlier, but you left in such a hurry."

He tosses a pair of flip-flops at my bare feet.

"I found these out in the road. I think they belong to you."

As I bend to put them on, he kneels at my feet.

"Allow me." He cups my heel in his hand and slips the strap between my toes. "Perfect fit. They must be yours."

"Because they wouldn't fit anyone else?"

He laughs. "Don't be silly. Slippahs fit everybody. That's why they're the official non-shoe of Hawaii." He nudges my leg. "Scoot over."

I slide over so he can sit next to me, and we watch as the EMTs load Regina into the ambulance.

Bright side: they got to use some of the sedatives she ordered for me.

Waste not, want not.

"Where are the twins?" Jerry asks.

"Aulani. They're enjoying a Disney Princess Sleepover Party. I'll pick them up tomorrow."

"What're you going to tell them?"

I sigh. "I don't know. That's tomorrow's problem."

"You're staying here alone?"

I shake my head. "No. Once Regina's on her way to the hospital, Mr. Me'e is taking me to a hotel in Waikiki."

"Or you can stay with me."

I look at him.

"I mean, with my family. My mom said to ask you. She's worried."

"'Ohana," I say.

"Of course."

"Calabash."

Jerry puts his arm around my shoulders. "Calabash," he says.

Uncle Kahana comes over and pecks me on the cheek. "Happy birthday, Rell."

"Thanks."

"I'll see you tomorrow. Come on, 'Ilima. Let's go home."

'Ilima rises slowly from the lawn, limping a little.

"Hey, what happened to you?" Uncle Kahana says.

She chuffs and jumps into his car.

"Kicked in the ribs?" Uncle Kahana says. "Who?"

'Ilima sits up on the front seat and locks eyes with me through the windshield.

In my head I hear her voice: *I pay my debts and collect those owed to me.*

I shiver.

No matter what, I need to make sure I'm never on 'Ilima's bad side.

"Cold?" says Jerry, pulling me closer.

I bury my nose in his shirt.

Cedar, cinnamon, cloves, and wintergreen mints.

"Rell?"

I raise my chin and capture his lips. At first, they're soft with surprise, but firm enthusiastically as our kiss deepens.

Cedar, cinnamon, cloves, and wintergreen mints.

And something a whole lot more.

He breaks the kiss and takes a deep breath. I snuggle back down, and he rests his chin on my head.

"I know who I am," I say.

"Oh? Is this a game? Am I supposed to guess?"

"I'm Rell Watanabe."

"Nice to meet you, Rell. I'm Jerry."

"And I know what I want."

I feel him hold his breath.

"I'm afraid to ask," he says.

I sit up and look him in the eye.

"I want to build a surf camp."

TATAU

Uncle Akumu has tattoos. Big, thick *pe'a* lines shout his ancient Samoan genealogy as they crisscross his thighs. On his arms he carries his own story. There's Aunty Lani's name surrounded by vines and *pua fiti*. There's a manta ray and turtle, a bullet with RIP for cousin Ikaika, and something I can't make out that's covered in swirls and shark teeth that rolls over his shoulder and down his back. When I ask Uncle about it, he just says some things are better remembered than displayed.

Uncle Akumu is cool.

When I tell Bishop I want tattoos like Uncle Akumu, he frowns.

"No, you don't," he says. "The church forbids *tatau*."

But I do.

I say, "I want to be just like Uncle Akumu."

"No, Kiliona," he says. "You want to be like Jesus. Does Jesus have tattoos?"

Of course I want to be like Jesus. We sing songs about how we want to be like Jesus in Primary as He looks down from His poster. Sister Sinaloa says Jesus knows everything, like if you asked Him for help with your math homework, He'd know all the answers.

But Jesus also tells you to figure it out for yourself.

Read.

Ponder.

Pray.

I read, ponder, and pray, but I still don't know the answers.

When I ask Uncle Akumu for help, he laughs his great booming laugh. He takes my math paper off the counter and wraps his arms around me.

"Math is hard," he says and rubs my head. "Good thing you smart."

He sits next to me and shows me how six times five is thirty. How eleven divided by seven is one, remainder four, and how two goes into eight four times. Pretty soon my homework's done. Tomorrow when Mrs. Tui calls on me, I'll have the answers.

Jesus knows all the answers to all my questions, but Uncle Akumu helps me get my homework done.

That's why I want to be like Uncle Akumu, tattoos and all.

Maybe Jesus is really like Uncle Akumu, only we can't see His tattoos under His red robes.

Maybe Bishop never looked.

INFESTATION

On a lava outcrop surrounded by ocean on three sides, 'Ilima in the shape of a yellow poi dog picked her way to Piko Point. Waves hissed along the edges, filling nooks and crannies with what would become pockets of salt in the sun.

To the west, a makau moon descended over the sea, guiding wanderers through the dreamlands of Pō.

To the east, wispy clouds thickened against the pali rising above Lauele, O'ahu. *Rain in the morning*, 'Ilima thought with a glance at the sky. *But rain or shine, tourists will still come. When you're on vacation, all days are beach days. Pohō, that.* She flicked her tail. *Surely, Kalei will understand.* She sighed. *Or not. Niuhi like to paddle their own way.*

Each step toward Piko Point took her farther from the beach pavilion and the two-lane highway hugging the coast. Across the highway were Hari's convenience store and the second story apartment where 'Ilima and Kahana, her human companion, lived. Hari's was the place to buy rainbow shave ice, musubi, or rock salt plum; a place where old futs like Kahana nursed cold drinks on the lānai, playing games of remember when.

Drenched in moonlight, 'Ilima paused, observing stars, winds, and currents. *All systems go.* She shook from nose to tail, rolling her head and twisting her shoulders. It felt good to leave the human world behind, if only for an hour or two. She licked her lips; the reef's tang of limu and old fish blood tickled the back of her throat.

As she breathed in the salted night air, an offshore breeze carried the scent of stale cooking oil, kiawe smoke, and teri beef—the ghost of one of Hari's plate lunch specials. *Food!* 'Ilima's eyes widened. *I should've brought Kalei something. Pork laulau, chicken adobo—something, anything. Food is the quickest way to a shark's heart.* She snorted. *Well, food or sex, and that's not happening, not even in times as desperate as these.*

Leaping over a puddle and ignoring a cast-off crab shell, 'Ilima continued to the large tide pool at the end of Piko Point. The pool had a hidden tunnel leading through the reef and out to the great blue deep. It was the traditional port for Niuhi sharks transitioning from sea to land and the easiest place to meet.

Her ears drooped as she considered her strategy. *Playing messenger isn't Kalei's thing, but maybe I can convince him.* She lifted her head and perked her ears. *Whatevers. If he says no, I'll find another way. He's not my last hope.*

Her tail wavered. *Unless he is.*

At the edge of the tide pool sat Pōhaku, a light grey basalt rock the size and shape of a big beach ball and the unofficial go-between of humans and the ancient sea-dwelling po'e o nā mo'olelo. As 'Ilima approached Pōhaku, she spotted a dark shape lounging in the water.

"Marco!" A sudden splash sent ocean spray bitter as a sea urchin up her nose. She shifted to her human form with a sneeze.

"Kalei!"

"No, you're supposed to say 'Polo,'" Kalei mocked, splashing her again.

"Uoki, Kalei! I mean it! That water went up my nose." 'Ilima dabbed her face with the edge of the yellow kīkepa her human shape wore and sneezed again.

"Bless you," he laughed. "Or whatever it is humans say."

"Bless you or gesundheit." 'Ilima sniffed and dropped her kīkepa. "At least that's what Kahana says."

"Gesundheit. What a strange word." In his human form, Kalei climbed out of the tide pool and stood dripping in the moonlight, water shedding like pearls off his skin.

"Pants!" 'Ilima said.

"You're such a prude. Too long among humans, you."

"Pants or I'm leaving. Now."

"A malo. We'll split the difference." Kalei wrapped a length of cloth around his loins and hips, snugging it tight. "You're late."

"I couldn't get away. Kahana was watching an old kung fu movie."

"You're lucky I had decent company and stayed." He jerked his thumb to the stone. "Pōhaku's been filling me in on all the Lauele gossip."

'Ilima inclined her head to the stone. "Aloha e Pōhaku. It's good to see you."

As a stone-bound being, Pōhaku spoke in thoughts that rose in their minds like bubbles in a lava lamp. ALOHA E 'ILIMA, he replied. IT'S GOOD TO BE SEEN.

Leaving his feet dangling in the water, Kalei sat on the edge of the pool and eased back against Pōhaku. "So what's the big— auwī! What the—?" He rubbed his shoulder and peered at the stone. "Eh, Pōhaku! You're covered in kūpe'e!" One by one, he began plucking the sea snails, popping them like berries between his fingers. "Auwē," he tsked. "So many! Kahana's slacking in his duties. 'Ilima must not be letting him out of the house again."

'Ilima crossed her arms. "I have no control over what Kahana does. Humans don't listen to me."

IT'S NOT KAHANA'S FAULT. KŪPE'E MOVE SO FAST.

Kalei smirked. "Snails *are* faster than old men. Probably smarter, too."

EVERYTHING'S RELATIVE, Pōhaku thought, his words thick like guava jelly. DANGER. PLEASURE. EVEN SPEED AND SIZE.

"Spoken like a stone," Kalei said, tossing crushed kūpe'e to fish. "There. All better now." He gave Pōhaku at pat.

MAHALO E KALEI, the thought a warm orange kite rising in the sky. BUT TOMORROW THEY'LL BE BACK. The image of storm clouds and broken string.

"Don't be so glum!" Kalei said, brushing the last fragments of shells and meat from his fingers. "No worries, Pōhaku. The future takes care of itself."

"Spoken like a shark," 'Ilima muttered.

Kalei stilled, his focus drawn to 'Ilima like a red lehua floating in the sea. "A Niuhi, you mean."

'Ilima cocked her head. "Isn't that what I said?"

Kalei gave her a sly look and whistled. "Come, 'Ilima," he called, slapping the ground next to him. "Sit."

"Watch it." 'Ilima's eyes narrowed.

"So sensitive, eh Pōhaku?"

IT'S A MATTER OF PERSPECTIVE, Pōhaku thought.

Kalei's smile held too many teeth. "She knows what I mean."

"Let's pretend I don't," 'Ilima said.

"Just what I said, *come sit with me*." 'Ilima didn't move. "Don't believe me?" Kalei held out his hands and spread his arms wide. "There's plenty of room to cool your feet." He slapped the ground again. "Come. Sit. Lean against Pōhaku with me. He won't mind."

I WON'T.

"See?"

'Ilima shook her head. "I'll sit over here, thanks." She carefully lowered herself, tucking her kīkepa under her knees.

"Don't trust me?"

"After all we've been through?" 'Ilima rolled her eyes. "Trust isn't the issue."

He frowned. "Sounds like it is."

"No." She paused to smooth the fabric. "Ever look in a mirror?"

"Whatever for?"

"In your human form, Kalei, you're Mr. Aloha come to life, all rippling muscle and so deliciously 'ono, women—and a few men—can't resist. You're used to people coming on to you that way. But I'm not a woman. Not really."

"You're not a dog, either, but not even Kahana recognizes that." He flashed his teeth. "Admit it. You like soft couches and kibble."

She curled her lip. "Careful, Kalei. I still have all my teeth."

"Oh, good," he said, "something to look forward to."

'Ilima smiled, but it didn't reach her eyes. "As handsome as your human form is, it's not what interests me."

"Your loss."

She took a deep breath. "I need your help. We have a problem."

"*We* have a problem? You got a gecko in your pocket, 'Ilima?"

She stiffened her spine. "Yes, *we*."

He narrowed his eyes. "Aren't you the one always saying Niuhi belong in the water?"

"It concerns everyone, land and sea," she said.

"A human problem, then?"

"Yes."

Kalei crossed his arms and shifted his weight. "Why me? Does your human problem have a biting solution?"

"I'm not sure."

"But it's not off the table?"

'Ilima shrugged.

"Excellent," Kalei said. "Tell me more."

As she gathered her thoughts, 'Ilima's eyes swept the shadowy shoreline and the night-empty beaches of Nalupuki and Keikikai. With everyone safely in bed, no porchlights welcomed or lit the way home. Slipping her tongue between her lips, she tasted Lauele's hopes and dreams as they journeyed across the water, fleeing dawn and the bustle of day. *Things are different in the dark,* she thought. *Quieter. Simpler.*

"Times are changing," she said.

Kalei rolled his eyes. "How profound. I expected more from you, 'Ilima."

"I'm talking about the pandemic."

"*Pan*demic?"

"Yeah. Worldwide."

"Here? In Lauele?"

'Ilima nodded. "The past year or so."

He shook his head. "I remember *epi*demics." Kalei kept count with his fingers.

"Venereal disease, a gift from Cook's crew. Then cholera, influenza, mumps, measles, whooping cough, smallpox, leprosy—it's hard to keep track. Human sickness ebbs and flows like a tide."

"Yeah, back when disease came by ship. Airplanes are much faster. Now the whole world gets sick at once. Modern disease is no tide," 'Ilima said. "It's tsunami."

"But there weren't more offerings. I would've noticed. Remember the 1800s?" Kalei mused. "Back then bodies were stacked four deep on the docks waiting for canoes to take them out beyond the reef."

'Ilima shrugged. "Modern diseases don't always kill. At least, not everybody." She leaned against a rock, settling deeper onto the damp lava. "Remember Kalaupapa?"

"Of course. Ever try leprosy?" Kalei shuddered. "Ugh. *Chewy.*"

With a sigh, 'Ilima swept her long, dark hair into a bun and knotted it on the top of her head. "Can you at least try to think about something other than your stomach for once?"

"You're in a mood," Kalei said. "Kahana buy you a flea collar again?"

She ignored the barb. "To stop the pandemic from spreading, humans declared the entire world Kalaupapa. Everybody had to stay in one place. Nobody could leave."

Kalei laughed. "But rats don't stay in one place."

"This time they did. Human governments forbade travel."

"*Forbade?* And people listened?" Kalei reached down and rubbed Pōhaku. "Eh, Pōhaku, you hear that? We're back to the old days of kapu! Chiefs decree and people obey. Get ready! Kahana's going to put you back on temple hill."

AN OFFERING OF POI WOULD BE NICE. THREE-DAY OLD AND THICK AS YOUR FINGER.

"With pua'a smokey and hot from the imu," Kalei said. "None of this fake banana leaf-wrapped crockpot—"

"Enough, you two," 'Ilima snapped. "The past is past. Humans are not going back to kapu laws."

Kalei rested his head against Pōhaku. "But you said governments *forbade.* That's a big word. What happened to democracy?"

She shrugged. "Extraordinary times, extraordinary measures. But it happened. Just last month Kahana and I walked Waikīkī from Kahanamoku to Kaimana on *sand.* There wasn't an ABC beach mat or umbrella in sight. You really didn't notice?"

"No," Kalei said. "But I'd starve before swimming near Waikīkī. Too sunscreeny. Almost as bad as Hanauma Bay."

LIKE COCONUT CREAM FLOATING ON ICE WATER, Pōhaku thought.

"Vile bilge water, you mean," Kalei grumbled. "That stuff only smells like coconut—fake coconut. It tastes pilau and sticks to your teeth."

"And for a whole year you didn't notice it was gone, Kalei?" 'Ilima said.

He shrugged. "Told you. I stay away from tourist places. Most Niuhi do. It's better for everyone."

'Ilima pinched the bridge of her nose. "You're probably right. But trust me. Because of the travel kapu, there was no sunscreen or masses of people on the beaches. The 'āina and kai rested. But it's all changing again." She swallowed and looked him dead in the eye. "There's a vaccine, Kalei. The travel kapu is lifting. People are buzzing. They're tired of staying home. A swarm is forming. It's the start of a new perpetual mosquito season."

"So?" Kalei broke eye contact and flicked a crab into the water. "Tourists are always coming. They flock to hotels in Waikīkī and Kō Olina or to short-term rentals in Kailua and Hale'iwa. They stay for a week, maybe ten days, and go home. They leave their money and reduce the tax burden—or so I hear. It's a bit of a trade-off, of course, but they stay in their lanes and we stay in ours. We don't see them if we don't want to."

"Tskah," she scoffed, "There are no lanes anymore. Today five rentals, Wranglers and passenger vans, pulled into the parking lot at Keikikai, one right after the other."

"Oh. Lost on their way to Waimea?"

"No. They meant to come here."

Kalei sat up. "Why?"

"Because they can. They unloaded snorkel gear, boogie boards, and beach umbrellas. They climbed all over Piko Point—"

"How—" Kalei interrupted.

"Social media," 'Ilima said. "Heard of it?"

Kalei rolled his eyes. "I'm vaguely familiar."

"You have no idea, do you?" 'Ilima sighed.

"Like you said, *let's pretend I don't.*"

"Fine. Cell phones—"

"I know phones. 'Reach out, reach out and touch someone,'" he sang.

"That's 1970s phones. Now they're pocket-sized and people carry them everywhere."

"So they can reach out and touch someone?" he teased. "*Everywhere?*"

"People don't carry phones to talk—"

"Then what's the point?" Kalei asked. "Better off carrying a rock."

HEY. Pōhaku's indignation fizzed like soda poured over ice. I'M RIGHT HERE.

'Ilima rubbed her eyes and pinched the bridge of her nose. "I know you're not this naive, Kalei."

"Who me? I'm just a shark," he said. "What do I know about posting photos or video?"

"Uh-huh. So you know social media's the world's new party line. Everybody's connected, all the time."

"*Connected*. Sounds sexy," he purred.

"Get your head out of the gutter," 'Ilima sniffed.

"You're telling me social media's not about sex?"

"It's about being *special*. Everyone's trying to show off new and exotic—"

"Exotic." Kalei grinned, teeth gleaming in the moonlight. "I'll show you *exotic*."

'Ilima squeezed her eyes tight. "Can I just get through this, please?"

Kalei waved a hand. "I'm listening."

"Remember when insider guidebooks became a thing?" 'Ilima said. "*Island Secrets Revealed, Hawaii's Hidden Gems?*"

"Yeah. What idiot came up with that? There's no place to get decent sashimi without standing in line anymore," Kalei groused.

"Those were books. You had to go find books. With social media, access to knowledge is instantaneous. Think of a dead whale's scent trail multiplied by a billion. All the scavengers, local *and* global, immediately know where and when things happen."

"Okay."

"Okay? *Okay?!*" 'Ilima fumed. "Just a few days ago some lōlō with a cell phone stumbled onto Lauele, raved about the pristine reef and beaches on Insta-Snap-Book, and now we're infested with tourists. *We have a problem*."

"And you want me to bite someone? Is this why we're talking?"

"Argh!" 'Ilima splashed water at him. "This very afternoon, a tourist was sitting at one of the tables at the beach pavilion, eating a poke bowl—"

"You mean a bowl of poke," Kalei interrupted.

"No!" shouted 'Ilima. "A poke bowl! It's not the same thing!"

"Okay. Weird distinction, but okay."

"Kalei, there's a difference between a bowl of poke and a poke bowl that I need you to understand." 'Ilima took a deep breath. "As I walked by, the tourist stuck his chopsticks in the rice at the bottom of his bowl and started clapping his hands at me, shouting, 'Shoo! Get out!' When I turned to look at him, he stood up and waved his arms. 'Get away, you homeless, flea-bitten mutt! Get away from my poke bowl!' Shocked, I just stared. I wasn't anywhere near his poke bowl. And that's when he threw a water bottle at me and tried to chase me off the beach. This beach, Kalei. *Our* beach!"

"Oh. So you need help getting rid of a body. Why didn't you say so?"

"No!" 'Ilima inhaled and counted to three. "No. I didn't hurt him."

Bemused, Kalei asked, "Why? Are you going soft in your old age? Too many puppy snuggle-wuggles with Kahana? Is this about needing me to scratch behind your ears with my sharp shark teeth?"

'Ilima jumped up.

HERE IT COMES, Pōhaku thought, his words splattering like lava from a vent.

As fire flashed along her limbs and steam sizzled from the sea-drenched rock beneath her, 'Ilima's womanly body stretched taller than a coconut tree. She leaned down and hissed with the roaring sound of thunder in the surf. "This is why I can't have a normal conversation with you, Kalei. Of course, I didn't hurt him. It was *daylight*, near the showers by the pavilion at *Keikikai beach*."

Kalei smothered a yawn. "You've killed for far less."

"Argh!" she growled as lightning struck the ocean from a clear blue sky. "This. This is why I choose a dog form." In the blink of an eye, 'Ilima shrank back to normal human-size. She stood at the edge of the tide pool and counted wavelets until she could speak without shrieking. "Times. Have. *Changed*."

"You keep saying that," Kalei said. He stood and reached high over his head, twisting his back and stretching. "Ugh. No TV. No plates of sashimi and wasabi. No bowls of poke or poke bowls—whatever they are. No moonlight swim with a tasty wahine. I can't believe I came ashore and transformed for this."

'Ilima hung her head. "Tell me how you'll feel when Keikikai bay is covered with tourists doing yoga on SUP boards. Or when Piko Point reeks of human blood from the skinned knees of people climbing over slick lava rock. Or—" She paused and raised her eyes to his. "Or maybe it's different for you. Ocean-born, you can go to the northern islands or Respite Beach. But this is my *home*. It used to be *our* home. Look at what happened to Pōhaku. If Kahana hadn't gone and dug him up, he'd still be forgotten in a landfill."

IT'S TRUE, Pōhaku thought. THE MODERN WORLD IS UNKIND TO THE STONE-BOUND.

'Ilima held her fingers like a camera frame and walked toward Kalei. "Can you imagine what would happen if I'd snapped that tourist in half like I wanted to? Me, in all my glory, all over the world in seconds?" She dropped her hands. "At least humans can wrap their heads around a big shark."

Kalei flexed his muscles. "More big than Jaws?" He laughed. "They couldn't handle *that*."

'Ilima sat back down and crossed her legs. "I thought about asking you to cruise up and down the beaches, Kalei, but people are stupid. Seeing you wouldn't keep them away or even out of the water; it would just bring more looky-loos. We can't have the chaos your last shark attack caused."

"What chaos? There wasn't any chaos," Kalei said.

"Of course there was. The guys with the hukilau nets."

"Oh. You mean the last attack that made the news," Kalei said.

'Ilima sat up. "What?"

"Nothing." Kalei waved his hand. "Insignificant."

"Kalei."

"What?"

"You can't go around biting people," 'Ilima said.

"Technically, it wasn't a bite." He shrugged. "No body, no crime."

'Ilima massaged her temples. "You're giving me a headache."

"I had a good reason," he said.

He did.

"No doubt," she said. "But that's my point. Whatever you did or didn't do—*don't tell me*—it didn't keep people away."

"So we do something more public. Use one of those phone camera-thingies," he said.

'Ilima looked away and watched the waves break over the edge of the reef. Onshore, a rooster crowed. A glance at the mountains told her dawn was just three hours away. *I'm running out of time.* She said, "Kalei, shark attacks spark shark hunts. Tourism associations sponsor bounties. Our ocean ecology is still trying to recover from the last one." She shook her head. "No. Revealing ourselves isn't the answer. We need a different solution."

Kalei stood with his back to Pōhaku and watched an 'iwa bird fly out to sea. A lone car drove along the two-lane highway, blasting Jawaiian music as its headlights lit up lauhala trees.

"Okay," he said. "The problem is too many tourists are coming, but you don't want me to bite anybody or cruise up and down the beach." He looked down his nose at her. "Right?"

'Ilima sighed. "Right."

"Too bad, so sad." He raised a hand and started counting off options. "We can't take out the road. They'll just build it back again. We can't buy the land and fence it off. Kahana already owns most of Lauele, but the beaches are open to everybody."

"That's the problem," 'Ilima said. "We can't keep them out."

"Humans obey human laws."

"Thank you, Captain Obvious," snorted 'Ilima.

"We need them to change their laws," Kalei said.

"Kapu laws are dead. Democracy, remember? Why are we going in circles? Is this a shark thing?"

"I'm brainstorming. What are humans afraid of?" Kalei mused.

Pōhaku thought, SUCH TINY LITTLE CREATURES.

"Yeah," said Kalei as he scratched his arm. "With such big mouths and appetites." He regarded the moon as it dipped closer to the horizon, stars shining like broken glass through the marine haze. He turned to her. "'Ilima, why come to me? I don't see how anything sharky is going to fix this."

"I said I needed *you*."

"Uh-huh."

"You. Your access to your father's ear."

Pōhaku's laughter tickled like champagne. An image of the great ocean god Kanaloa's ear swelled in their minds.

"Ew, Pōhaku!" 'Ilima groaned. "Did you have to show us hair *and* wax?"

Kalei sighed. "You want me to bring this problem to the mighty Kanaloa."

"Yes. It affects everybody."

"Biting someone's safer," he said. "Kanaloa might decide *you're* the problem."

"I know," 'Ilima said, picking at a salt pocket. "I wouldn't come to you if I had another way."

"You'll owe Kanaloa personally."

"I know."

"And me."

'Ilima rolled her eyes. "Believe me, I *know*. I also know nothing surprises Kanaloa."

"So why—"

"You know why, Kalei." 'Ilima paused. "Kanaloa likes to be *asked*."

"He likes to be owed," Kalei said.

"That, too."

"Me, too," he said with a crooked grin.

'Ilima sighed.

Kalei rubbed his chin and slicked back his hair. "I just don't know what you expect Kanaloa to do."

"I don't either. Something. Anything. Nature finds a way."

Kalei paced. "A hurricane? Sink a bunch of boats? Stop the tradewinds?"

"None of that keeps tourists away," 'Ilima said. "It's our people that get hurt with those kinds of natural consequences—think of salt in taro patches and shredded banana leaves."

Kalei threw up his hands. "Like that matters. In Lauele they don't fear famine anymore. There's no respect for shadows and teeth."

AN ITCH NO ONE CAN SCRATCH, Pōhaku thought.

"More kūpe'e, Pōhaku? Did I miss one?" Kalei asked.

NATURALLY, IT'S THE LITTLE THINGS THAT MEAN SO MUCH. An image formed in their minds.

'Ilima and Kalei exchanged a look.

"Can he?" 'Ilima asked.

"He's a god, right?" Kalei said. "Go big or go home."

"What doesn't kill you makes you stronger," 'Ilima said.

"Oh, I hope not. Stronger humans? Next, they'll want my teeth," Kalei said.

HUMANS ARE JUST NIUHI WITH DENTAL PLANS. The image of a shark flossing his teeth.

"Brave words when I can just roll you over the edge, Pōhaku," Kalei said.

LIKE THE BUTTERFLY WINGS OF A STINGRAY, Pōhaku's laughter drifted through their minds.

'Ilima waved her hand, dismissing the image. "Kalei, I need an answer. Will you speak to Kanaloa?"

He worried his lip for a bit, then nodded. "Fine. I'll do it." As Kalei leaped into the water, he called, "You better pray Father Dear is in a good mood."

"If prayer were all it took, I wouldn't have involved you. Mahalo e Kalei," 'Ilima called as a shark fin slipped through the tunnel and headed out to sea. Walking over to Pōhaku, she laid her hand on the stone. "Think it will work?"

Pōhaku's slow thoughts billowed like a sail in the wind. This time, they tasted of hope.

TWO WEEKS LATER, the parking lot at Keikikai was full of broadcast vans and reporters, each jockeying for the best position. Behind yellow tape cordoning off the beach, hazmat-suited techs gathered samples from the ocean and tide pools along Piko Point. From their balcony above Hari's, old man Kahana and 'Ilima in the shape of a yellow poi dog enjoyed the show.

"Smell that?" Kahana asked.

'Ilima wagged her tail, ears forward.

"Yeah, it's hard to miss. Hari's got the kiawe coals sizzling. Hulihuli chicken and kalbi. Bet he sells so many plates to the news crews he runs out of mac salad."

'Ilima whined.

"Nah, sistah. No worry. He'll save some for us."

'Ilima poked her head between the railing's bars. *All the better to see you with, my dear.*

Kahana gestured to the guy swinging a Geiger counter along the sand. "Eh, think he's gonna find Myrna's wedding ring?"

'Ilima cocked her head at Kahana and chuffed.

"Oh, right. Geiger counters are for *radiation*. My bad." Kahana hitched up his shorts. "Ho, those guys in the suits must feel like manapua in a steamer. Too bad they can't just jump in the ocean and cool off." He leaned against the banister and shook his head. "So weird. Never seen anybody sick from *snorkeling*. When they rolled the ambulances the first time, I was spearfishing, the Chang kids were jumping off rocks, and Nili-boy was also in the water. Kanani—her auntie's cousin's daughter works at the health department, yeah? Anyway, Kanani said those poor buggahs didn't dare leave their hotel bathrooms for five days. Barely made their flights home."

'Ilima shrugged.

"Ruins your whole vacation." Kahana paused. "Or maybe *runs* is your whole vacation," he chuckled.

'Ilima rolled her eyes.

"C'mon. That was funny."

'Ilima's ears drooped.

"Everyone's a critic," Kahana said with a sigh. "I'm just glad it wasn't Hari's mac salad." He held up his phone. "Check it. #HariOnolicious is trending. Gotta love news crews. They're all about the buzz."

'Ilima refused to look.

"Fine. Be like that." Kahana slipped his phone in his pocket as an ice blue Prius pulled into the parking lot. "There she is. That's the one I was telling you about."

'Ilima's ears perked.

Kahana pointed with his chin to the woman climbing out of the car. "Yeah, the one in the green shirt. She's from UH Manoa. Sharp. She told me yesterday it's something in the ocean that's making people sick."

'Ilima whined.

"I dunno. It only affects people who aren't from Lauele. Her theory is if you're local, there's something in your guts—your na'au, yeah—that kills whatever it is that makes others sick." Kahana snickered. "She thinks it's all the poke and limu we eat from the reef, but you and I know it's all the fried noodles and chicken katsu everybody orders from Hari's."

'Ilima yawned and stretched.

"Yeah. *Whatevahs*," Kahana said. "Nili's got a new job. He's supposed to hang out at the pavilion and parking lot and warn folks heading to the beaches about the snorkel-trots. Has an official shirt and everything. Word's getting out. Snorkel-trots aren't fatal." He paused. "They think."

Kanaloa, 'Ilima thought. *Nature found a way.*

"The health department's going to leave the crime scene tape and put up signs, but you and I can still go anytime. Nili said."

The woman in the green shirt beeped her car, tossed her keys in a bag, and pulled out a tablet. Kahana shifted his weight. "Akamai, that professor. She'll figure it out. No matter how hard, people always find a way," he mused.

It's the little things, 'Ilima thought.

Kahana pulled out his phone again and punched some buttons. "Posted!" He smiled. "Now everybody knows how lucky we are. #Blessed, yeah?"

MAVERICK'S

I t's not like I'm stupid.

I lean my bike against the convenience store, far away from the aban-doned cars near the gas pumps. Grandad would be furious if he knew what I was doing—too risky, he'd say. But he's never been an eleven-year-old girl stuck in the mountains above Heber with her brothers and Grandad for three long years.

Free at last.

I jimmy the backdoor like Matt taught me and enter through the employee entrance, not the big glass storefront where anyone can see.

I know better than to expect things like Ding Dongs and slushies. I have no hope for Bic Lighters, Pepperoni Stix, or batteries.

But every girl deserves ChapStick.

I want things my brothers don't scavenge, like notebooks and pens. Maybe some magazines. Toilet paper would be heaven.

This store is heaven.

I remember it.

Only good things come from Maverick's.

The dead body is a bummer.

The smell hits me first. I swallow hard to keep last night's rabbit stew down, but it's a near thing. I find a push broom in the utility closet and use it to sweep the bones aside, scrunching arms and legs together until there's a clear path to the door.

I don't look closely. Male, female, it doesn't matter. In jeans, sneakers, and a hoodie, dead is dead—and this one's been dead since the beginning.

You don't get beef jerky-light unless you've had all the moisture sucked right out of you. Only Thirst does that. The hollow-husked bodies it leaves behind are straight out of a horror flick.

I am Legend.

The Road.

Contagion.

28 Days Later.

At any moment—

Stop.

Just stop.

Now is not the time to think about Grandad's movie collection. Being off the mountain and back in Heber is messing with my head. Heber's small town, but it's not quite BFE.

But today it could be.

I open the office door and slip into the store. It's obvious critters and the elements have finished what looters started. What's left of the glass in the front wall is hazy, a milk-blind, cataract white.

The hood of a Chevy Impala stands stalled half-way to the Cheetos aisle, guarding barren shelves designed for chili-lime sunflower seeds, BBQ corn nuts, and special edition Milky Ways. Florescent blue and orange puddles pool under the drink station, but there's so much dust, the floor's no longer sticky. Raccoon prints and mice droppings run along the countertops.

As I pass the Impala, I don't look to see if the driver's still in the car.

I've gotten good at not looking.

I don't know what's worse: the death stench wafting from the office or the sinus-scalding odor of carnivore pee. Something big like a bear marked the store as his territory. I listen, but don't hear wuffle-snorts of warning or movement.

Maybe it's gone.

I hold my breath for a couple of heartbeats and get ready to drop my backpack. If a bear decides to eat me, there's nothing I can do except run and hope he'll be more interested in my pack than me.

Stay or go?

Go is safer. Avoid confrontation. Live to fight another day.

The bear would've eaten me by now.

I'll stay. Just another moment or two to make sure that there's nothing left to scavenge besides dented shelving units and rusting Impala parts.

Nobody needs shelves or car parts.

At the compound, Grandad has tons and tons of storage racks stocked floor to ceiling, everything hidden underground with solar lighting and custom ventilation.

Three years ago, we arrived at Grandad's in the middle of the night. The ink not dry on his learner's permit, Matt white-knuckled Mom's Suburban up the mountain passes and through snow packed deeper than the running boards.

Standing on his porch, Grandad looked at us kids and sighed. "Your father is a fool," he said. "But at least I raised your mother right. There's beans and macaroni waiting. Get your gear. Tomorrow we set snares and start practicing with the bows."

In the morning, KSL showed video of National Guard units leaving Camp Williams, headed out to enforce a state-wide quarantine to stop the spread of Thirst. But by then Thirst had gone airborne, spreading coast to coast and from Peru to Canada. Nobody's sure who blew the dam at Deer Creek, flooding Provo Canyon, or who took out highway 40 at the Mayflower exit, cutting Heber off from Park City two days later—at least we never heard. Grandad said it was country folk who knew the city hoards would come. A week later we watched the Salt Lake riots and the Provo inferno on TV until KSL stopped broadcasting.

The country folk were right.

In the mountains, winter settled in.

Three years last fall, and we still have plenty of salt, fuel, tools, game, and clean water. Grandad says his plan worked. Even the garden's doing well.

But scrub oak leaves are tough on your bum.

I walk around the counter, pulling at drawers and tipping over the save a penny cup, searching for a forgotten pen or magazine.

That's when I see them: three cougar cubs nestled under empty cigarette racks.

Behind two sleeping balls of fluff, a set of bright blue eyes peek at me; a mouth yawns wide. It blinks twice, then bristles like water in a hot skillet. Ears pinned and tail twitching, as it hisses and chirps like a bird.

I want to hug it and squeeze it and name it Fred.

Instead I back slowly and don't run until I reach the office door.

Outside, my first clue is my bike is missing.

The second is the arm that wraps me in a strangle hold; the third is the hand that covers my mouth.

"Told you I saw a girl," says a man. "Told you."

"Shut-up, Cleet. Can't you see I'm busy here?" says the man throttling me. His b.o. is enough to choke a moose. Not even the lingering scent of campfire smoke dampens it.

He leans into me, his rotten tooth and dog crap breath rushing against my cheek. He lets go of my mouth just long enough to strip away my backpack and pulls me tight until his ribs dig into my shoulder. "You, missy. I got you. You know that, right?"

His hand covering my mouth tastes like wood ash and gasoline. I try to hold my breath and nod at the same time.

"We got your bike, and we got your pack. Now we got you."

I hold still, still as a deer in the bush. Grandad taught me that.

"Show her the knife, Cleet."

Cleet comes around my side, a too-skinny dude in a ratty biker jacket, waving a twelve-inch bowie knife. It's the kind of knife that Dan calls a Texas toothpick and Jerry calls a letter opener. He walks up close and holds the blade against my face, the point just under my eye. He's breathing hard and fast.

"See this, bitch? See it? Wanna feel it?"

If I kick him in the nads, he'll drop like a sack of potatoes, the knife forgotten with the glass on the asphalt. I almost raise my knee to do it, but I remember Grandad's words.

I wait.

Cleet presses the knife, and I feel the skin under my eye split.

"I'm gonna do it, Butch. I'm gonna cut her eye and squish it like a grape."

Blood starts to trickle. I feel more than hear Butch's sigh, his chest expanding against my shoulders, the great gush of fetid air falling over my face like a cloud of gnats.

If Cleet's crappy knife or Butch's trench mouth gives me an infection, I'm gonna be pissed.

To stretch the Neosporin, Grandad's partial to swiping cuts and scrapes with alcohol on a cotton ball. *Lots* of alcohol. His way burns like hellfire and no scuff is too minor. Fight infection before it starts is his mantra. I pray every day that Bobby finds more ointment.

Butch shakes his head. "Take a chill pill, Cleet. Let's not damage the merchandise, capisce?"

Cleet pouts. "You said the next one's mine."

"Cleety, I'm not saying we're not going to have us some fun. But be smart. Park City pays top dollar—"

Cleet brightens. "This little bitch is our ticket?"

Butch plays it cool. "Mebbe. But her value goes down if you snick her eye out quicker than a snot rocket."

I watch the madness dim in Cleet, banked like a fire against a cold winter night. It won't take much for the ember to flare into a raging wildfire, but for now the promise of trade is enough for him to pull the knife away. "Hear that, bitch? We gonna have fun!" He hocks a loogie from deep in his sinuses and spits. It spiderwebs across my nose.

"Damn you, Cleet," roars Butch, flinging his hand off my mouth. "You almost got me!"

I feel warm goo slide off my nose, cross my lips, and drip from my chin.

I think about still water, about clouds over the reservoir, about the cougar kits in the convenience store, about anything at all except what's oozing down my face. Grandad has prepared me for this and much worse.

I hope there's still rabies vaccine in the med cache. I think I'm going to need it.

"Ugh! You gross son of a bitch! It's running down her neck and onto my arm!"

Cleet giggles.

I want to reach up and grab Butch's greasy hair and whip him over my shoulder, but I don't.

Patience, I tell myself. You're still okay.

"Sweetheart," says Butch, "we can do this the easy way or the hard way."

Hard, I think. Please be the hard so I can bite your fricken nose off and shove it—

Butch tightens his arm against my throat. "The hard way's my favorite," he says as he licks the side of my face.

I make a mental list.

• Hammer fist.

• Primary target.

• Go noodle, then twist, turn.

• Finish with a round house kick to Cleet's head or maybe step into his circle, take his knife, and gut him like a fish.

So many options.

Cleet giggles again. "You said hard."

Wait. I have to wait.

Butch sighs again. "Get a zip tie, knucklehead."

Cleet steps out of my view.

Zippers swish open.

A can of soup clunks to the ground and rolls near my feet, bumping against a large shard of glass.

With no easy way to grasp it, I file the glass under last resort.

The can, however, is just the right size for brain bashing.

Butch shifts his weight, impatient. "C'mon, dumbass. I ain't dancing with her all day. Get me a tie."

"Ain't got none," says Cleet.

"Check the side pocket."

"Nope."

"Then get me a rope or something."

Cleet says, "All we gots is your shirt. You want me to cut it?"

"Are you shitting me? Cut my shirt?" says Butch.

"You know, into strips. We can tie her."

I feel Butch shake his head. "You are the dumbest mother f'er. What about her pack?"

Cleet picks it up. "Right. I'll cut it. That'll work."

Butch is so angry he forgets he's holding me. As his body relaxes, my brain shouts *Now! Throw your head back, break his nose, rake his shins with your boot heel, turn and jab him in the Adam's apple.*

Run.

But I don't know how many Butches and Cleets there are or where they're camped. If I run, someone will chase. Someone may find, and I can't risk that.

Grandad's rules. The life of the one for the many. Always.

I force myself to be still like a deer, like a rabbit, like a mouse.

"No, you idiot! Don't cut it. Open her pack and see what she's got," snarls Butch.

There's not much. It's not a real backpack, just the one I used for school once upon a time. I carry it light, so things are easy to find.

When Cleet shakes it, a multi-tool, a LifeStraw, a baggie of elk jerky, a lighter, a roll of duct tape, and a metal water bottle tumble out.

"Duct tape. Bingo," says Butch.

Bingo, I think. *Just like Grandad said.*

Butch gives my whole body a shake to tell me he means business. "Put your hands in front," he says. "Don't try anything funny. Cleet? Do her."

When Cleet comes to wrap my wrists, he sees something in my eyes. Or maybe it's something he doesn't see. Whatever the reason, he doesn't hesitate to punch me square in the jaw. "What're you looking at?" he says.

It's my wake-up call.

I let my head snap back and roll my shoulders forward. My spine sinks. *Weak, weak, weak,* I think. *Beaten. Cowed.*

I whimper, the first sound I've made since I ran out of the store.

"Hey! What did I tell ya about the merchandise?" snaps Butch.

"She's gettin' uppity."

"She's eighty-five pounds soaking wet. I think we can handle her."

"I cut you once, bitch. I'll cut you again," says Cleet.

I tremble and close my eyes.

He snorts, satisfied, and winds tape around my wrists so tightly my fingers start to tingle.

"Do her ankles, too," says Butch.

When he's done, Butch releases me. I take my first non-b.o.-tainted breath in ages. The air is sweeter than peaches.

"Sit down." Butch shoves me against the wall, and I slide to the ground, trying to avoid bits of glass and road rash on my elbows. I taste blood from the punch. A tooth feels loose when I poke it with my tongue. None are broken, though. My lips start to swell, but at least he didn't hit my nose.

I like my nose.

I spot my bike, dumped at the base of the chain link fence and useless with its tires slashed.

Now I know it's just the two of them.

They have no need for a solitary bike and no reason to keep it for trade.

Clan-less.

It's a wonder they've survived this long.

Cleet opens the jerky bag and starts gnawing. "Umm," he drools, "teriyaki."

"No way."

"Way."

"Gimme that." Butch swipes the baggie and inhales. "Garlic." He takes a bite. "Sugar, red pepper, salt. Where'd you get spices, girlie? You got people? You got supplies and shit?" He kicks at my pack. "This ain't survival. This is day-tripping. Where's your stash, bitch?"

"Butch." Cleet hands him my water bottle like it's the Holy Grail. He's taken off the top and caught a good whiff.

Butch buries his nose. "Tequila." He turns to me. "What's a kid in the middle of Heber doing with tequila?"

"Gimme," says Cleet. "That jerky made me thirsty."

"Wait a minute. I want an answer."

"Disinfectant," I mumble. "Germs."

"Bullshit," says Butch. He raises his foot to kick me.

"Trade!" I scream. "Samples for the buyers."

Butch nods. "The liquor store on the far end of town was empty. You people took it all, didn't ya? You got it hidden somewheres, probably with all the smokes in town, too. Profiting off people's needs." He kicks me in the ribs, and I hear something pop. "I hate sons of bitches like you."

I breathe through my nose, counting the beats as my lungs fill, praying I don't barf as pain radiates like a nuclear bomb.

One last chance.

"Don't drink it," I say.

"Oh, honey. Wouldn't think of it." Butch takes a healthy slug. "Whoowee, that's good. Here Cleet, wet your whistle."

Cleet takes a long, deep swallow.

Butch grabs it back. "Slow down, son. Somebody's got to be the designated driver."

Cleet titters like a woodpecker, the tequila revving his madness to blow.

Butch rocks his head back like he's downing shots instead of guzzling from a water bottle. He smacks his lips and sucks his teeth. "Damn, that's good. I'm betting blondie's family is squirreled away in the hills nearby. They'll pay dearly, won't they, sweet'ums? Hell, they'll probably thank us. It's not like they have a use for booze and cigarettes." He shakes the half-empty bottle in my face. "Ever drink it?"

I shake my head no.

"Speak up," he snaps.

"No," I whisper. "Grandad calls it the devil's drink."

"Ha! He's right. We're a couple of demons, Cleet and me." He lifts the bottle to his mouth and misses, splashing a little down his front.

Cleet tries to grab it, but Butch won't let him. "C'mon, Butch! You said we was going to have fun."

Butch laughs. "You're right. Here. Drink up. There's plenty where that came from."

Cleet drains it and holds the bottle upside down. "Oops. All gone." He grins and collapses in a heap.

Butch staggers over. "C'mon, asshole. Get up."

Cleet doesn't move. A fine sweat beads on his brow, leaving a sheen on his ashen cheeks.

It's not until his lips turn blue and he starts to shake that Butch falls down, too.

In the heat of the afternoon it doesn't take long for the foam to dry on their lips and chins.

When their bladder and bowels release, I know it's time.

I lean back and scoot up the brick wall until I'm standing. Raising my arms high over my head, I bring them swiftly down while forcing my wrists apart. The duct tape splits as my elbows slide past my hips, just like I'd practiced with Grandad.

Hands free, it's nothing to rip the tape from my ankles and repack my stuff. When I find the lid, I screw it on the empty water bottle and stuff it back into my bag.

I'll have to be extra careful until I can refill my metal bottle from Grandad's special barrel.

But there's still a lot of duct tape on the roll.

On my shoulders, the pack feels too light.

The evening shadows stretch to the roadside; I've been gone too long. Matt's probably on his way to find me.

I check my bike—even though the tires are trashed, the rims are unbent and everything else looks good. New tires aren't a problem; Grandad has them stacked high and deep in the mechanic room.

It will take longer pushing the bike, but I decide I'll walk it along Main to

Arby's, our meeting place in town. Matt can throw it in the back of the buckboard and haul it the rest of the way home.

I give the parking lot a last glance and decide to take the knife. It's clunky, but Jerry will think it's funny, especially if I can find paper and write letters for him to open.

I almost chuck the can of soup into the bushes. Cream of Celery? Really, people? But as Grandad says, waste not, want not. It's still a fine brain basher.

As I move off, I spot Mama Cougar across the street, slinking along the porch of Timber Ridge Dental. When she realizes I've seen her, she drops the rabbit she's carrying and yowls, the sound of fingers on a chalkboard and a goose on a grave. Her kits answer like banshees.

Live humans make her nervous.

I look at the meat I'm leaving and smile.

It's a good day to be a cougar.

NANA'UE

Maiden
Kinohi Loa

In the murky, silver-coined depths of the reef, the lesser ocean god Kamoho'ali'i lurked. In the shape of an octopus or curl of a wave, he watched for a decade, waiting for lelekawa, that moment each day when I fearless leapt from the rocky shore of Kuiopili on the island of Hawai'i and sliced deep into the ocean, splashless and perfect.

It took him a year from our marriage to confess his ten year obsession. He told me I'd caught his eye when I was still slender as pili grass, slipping eel-like through the currents and swimming circles around my cousins. Admiring the bold way I trapped sunlight in my lungs diving for conch and lobster, he waited for me to grow round in hip and strong of limb.

The young are fearless. The aged know better.

But looking back, I couldn't have known that the rogue wave that swept me off the bluff and into the sea a year ago was sent by the handsome stranger who rescued me, Kamoho'ali'i himself.

Safe again on shore, I collapsed, heaving. Forehead against the sand, water gushed from my nose as I coughed the sea from my lungs. My long hair clung to my face and body like jellyfish tentacles.

Ugly, but alive.

Blinking away the salt, when I turned my head the first thing I noticed was the shape of his instep, how it curved to his ankle, the pale under-sole stark against the darkness of his skin. I followed his leg all the way to his face where the sunlight framed a halo around his head.

"What is your name, woman?" he asked, his voice resonating like the downbeat of a pa'u drum.

"Kalei," I stammered.

"Kalei." He smiled. "You will be my wife."

My sister rushed to my side. "Kalei! Are you all right?" As her hands searched for bruises, our cousins ringed close.

"I'm fine," I choked. "Thanks to—"

But he was gone.

When the moon turned, it brought both the Makahiki season and the stranger to our village. Head raised, he approached our chief with a basket of ulua so fresh that the gills still fluttered.

Charmed, Chief Palinui welcomed him to our celebration. Each night for a month the stranger returned bearing gifts from the sea and easily won every competition, dazzling us with his skill at wrestling, spear throwing, and kōnane. A master of riddles and puns, he also enthralled us with stories of great ocean voyages and ancient battles.

Each morning, as dawn streaked palest pink on the horizon, he would beg Palinui's permission to leave. Once granted, he hopped into his weathered canoe with its threadbare sail and disappeared over the horizon. Each morning Palinui's permission to leave came more reluctantly.

All Makahiki he never spoke to me, but I felt his eyes caressing my shoulders, hips, and thighs, the heat of his gaze hotter than Pele's fires. His return during sunset was the reason I lost count in the oli and faltered in my dance, and the reason I was beaten by the kumu hula for dishonoring the gods.

While Mother hid her face in shame, the stranger only laughed, saying, "Nothing so beautiful could ever be offensive."

Annoyed, the kumu hula again raised the bamboo switch, but Father said mildly, "It's only practice, Kumu. Tomorrow at the ceremony her hula will be a perfect offering to the gods."

"There can be no mistakes," the kumu hula growled. "The eyes of the gods are everywhere. Offended gods spare no one."

"I will watch," said the stranger, "and when it is perfect, we will marry."

Before Father could answer, Palinui shouted, "Ho'omaika'i! Our village needs strong and clever men."

With the barest shake of his head, Father stopped Palinui from giving me to the stranger right then and there. "But we must not presume," the chief said.

Father stepped forward. "During Makahiki you proved yourself a worthy competitor, but my daughter requires more than someone who can throw a spear or answer a riddle. What do you offer?"

The stranger held out his arms. "All that I have is hers."

My uncles chuckled and nudged each other. Uncle Lohe whispered, "A battered canoe, an empty fish basket, and the malo around his waist. Our Kalei will have everything!"

A warm body next to mine, I thought. *Rain and lehua blossoms.*

"Especially if she wants to wrestle." More stifled laughter.

"No land, no people, no way," muttered Uncle Pono.

Father tilted his head and crossed his arms to shush the village. Mother placed her hand on my shoulder. *This is what's real,* her touch said. *Our family always protects its own.*

Softer than a feather cloak, Mother's words enveloped me. "You hold out your arms and say that all you have is hers, but I see nothing that will fill the bellies of my daughter or her children," she said to the stranger.

"Food? Is that what concerns you? Food is nothing," the stranger said, turning to the sea. "Fish," he called. "Come."

The surface of the sea roiled like lava in Halema'uma'u crater as an ahi leaped like a dolphin from beyond the reef to the shore. We stood transfixed as the great fish flopped against the sand, his scales shimmering in the twilight as he pushed himself ever closer to the stranger.

Cousin Alama raced to sink his dagger deep into the fish's eye. "Uncle!" he called, "This ahi is as big as four men!"

Palinui said, "Surely such a fisherman will keep his family and village fed!"

Father drew breath to speak, but Palinui didn't pause. "If you agree, my wedding gift will be the portion of land that juts into the sea and a newly planted taro field. In exchange for this fish, the village will build a hale for you and your bride."

"I thank you for your offer," said the stranger. "Be sure to carve a fine fatty slice of the belly for yourself, my chief."

"You will be one of us?"

"When Kalei offers her perfect hula to the gods, I will marry her and live among you."

My stomach trembled. Fear and excitement are much the same.

"As you speak, let the gods hear," said Palinui.

Father took one look at the village's joy in the fish and closed his mouth. Later, when he walked me to the women's sleeping house, he said, "This is unusual."

"He is very sure of himself," I said.

"If you are opposed—"

"He is handsome. And capable." I wrapped my long hair into a bun and tied it on top of my head.

"You want him?"

"There is something exciting between us," I said.

"I know. The whole village knows. I just wish—"

"You worry that he is a stranger. We don't know his people."

Father stopped before the hale door. "Exactly. Chief Palinui wants him, but he isn't the one marrying him. He just thinks of fish, Kalei. Palinui believes if the stranger marries you, when famine roams, it will never call our people home."

"And you don't?"

"He came from the ocean during Makahiki. What's to stop his return?"

"Love," I said.

My father nodded. "I hope that will be enough." He hugged me tight. "Think about it. If you are unsure—at all—do not dance perfectly tomorrow."

"Father!"

"I mean it."

"The gods—"

"Will understand," he said, brushing his lips against my forehead. "Sleep on it."

The next night I stood in the torch light, the line of my neck graceful as a palm tree, my arms reaching out to the sea in the form of Hiki'aka calling her lover home.

With the last 'uwehe, my ti leaf skirt slowed and came to rest against my thighs. Heart pounding as the oli faded into the darkness, I slipped to my knees and kept my eyes to the lauhala mat.

Chief Palinui stood. "It is done."

"Perfectly," sighed the kumu hula.

"Come, Wife," said the stranger, taking my hand and bringing me to my feet.

I didn't dare meet his eyes. "What is your name?" I whispered.

He paused. "Call me Nalukai."

Startled, I looked up. His brown face was unlined, as smooth and as perfect as water in a calabash bowl. *Nalukai? Ocean Wave is an odd name for one so young.*

When I look back at that moment, I cry. Nalukai wasn't an ocean wave; he was a tsunami.

A year later, I was round as breadfruit with his child when he finally told me. I knew something was odd in the way he arose every day from our sleeping mats, flinging off the kapa sheets just before dawn, and disappearing in his canoe until sunset. He always returned with fresh fish, 'opihi, or sea urchins—as Palinui hoped —his nets so full, he fed the entire village.

As the baby turned in my 'ōpū, Nalukai returned one evening carrying great armfuls of crisp green limu harvested from the reef, salty-cold and tasting of the wild sea.

But with our child nearly here, the honeymoon was over.

"Kalei, my love, I have to leave you," Nalukai said.

"Oh? Does Father need you? Is the taro ready for the imu?"

"Put your weaving down, Kalei. My father needs me, not yours. I've tarried too long."

"We're going to your family? That's wonderful!" I looked at my baskets of half-finished kapa and lauhala leaves, twists of coconut husks and kukui nuts, hoping that I had enough time to create fine gifts for his parents. "When do we leave?"

He placed his hands along my cheeks and tilted his head down to mine. Foreheads touching, we honi, our breath mingling and becoming one in our lungs. "Forgive me," Nalukai whispered. "I didn't mean to love you."

"Nalukai, you're such a tease. How many canoes are we taking?" I trailed a finger down this arm. "We can't leave until I make lei and pack gifts of poi and salt. Does your mother prefer roasted crabs or dried 'opae? Oh! Just think of her excitement at our baby."

He smiled, but it didn't quite reach his eyes. "Our baby." He caressed my belly, and I felt it kick, strong and sure against his palm. "Kalei, I have a confession. Nalukai is only one of my names. My parents call me Kamoho'ali'i."

I slapped at him, no more serious than a child. "Oh, Nalukai! If you want to role play, fine. Call me Hiki'aka, and I will dance—"

He caught my wrists and held them to his chest. "Kalei. Look at me."

I thought of the fish, of his leaving and returning, of his confidence and ease with the chief, and his casual conversations about gods and their pleasures. The space behind my heart burned. I shook my head.

"Kalei." The voice of a god. I had to obey.

In that moment I thought I understood what I had lost, but no one can imagine Milu's pit who has not fallen in, and I wasn't even close to the underworld.

Not yet.

"No," I pleaded.

"Our child will be different."

"No."

"He will be dual-natured. Like me, he will be able to change his form. He will be a shark who walks on land. You will have to protect him."

I tried to pull my hands away, but Nalukai held them tight. I raised my shoulders to block my ears from the awful truth, but like all gods, he was relentless.

"Hear me, Kalei. Our child will incite fear and jealousy. The chief will see him as a weapon. The priests will want him for their temples. Others will kill him simply for being different."

Deep in my womb our child rolled, stretching like an octopus until I thought my skin would split, spilling him out into the world in a sea-tide of blood and water.

I shuddered and held my breath until the pain passed. "Nalukai, our child comes."

He tipped my chin to so our eyes met. "To keep him and the others safe, you must never feed him meat—none of any kind. Only taro, banana, and sweet potatoes—things rooted in the land. You must teach him to be humble. Your lives depend on it."

"Our lives? But you'll—"

He shook his head and raised my captured hands to his lips. Gently, he blew on my knuckles, his cool breath shattering me like stones. "No. The only way our child lives is if I return to my father, the great ocean god Kanaloa. It must be now, before the child is born. A child such as this is forbidden by kapu. If I know of his existence, I must kill him."

I bit my lip, but the word slipped out bitter as 'awa. "Why?"

"Why?" he mocked. "Why? Because. That's all you need to know."

"The great Kanaloa decreed." I snatched my hands from his and pulled them to my hair, working swiftly to unbind turtle shell combs and cowry shells. Nalukai watched with hooded eyes. "What you haven't said is that Kanaloa's kapu means death for you, *Nalukai,* if you fail to carry it out. It's your life or our child's."

He sat back. "You love me that much? You'd rather I killed our child than leave?"

I shook my head; combs tumbled to my lap as hair fell like water across my face. "Your leaving on the eve of our child's birth will have the village gossips whispering. Is that what you want?"

He sighed, and his god's breath shook the hale. "The choice is yours, Kalei," he said. "I stay and slaughter all our children as they come. Or—"

Freed at last from a wife's knots, my hair cascaded down my back, brushing the floor like a maiden's. "Go," I said, dropping the hibiscus flowers I'd worn over my left ear into his lap.

He brought the love token to his face, rasping delicate petals against his chin before tossing them one by one into the fire. The flames flared as they ignited, the taste of hibiscus ashes thick in the smoke. He stood. "I watched you," he said, "for a decade in the sea. I waited because I loved you."

"No," I said, watching the last petal curl and blacken. "You really didn't."

I never saw him again.

Sometimes in my darkest hours I wish that I had chosen differently. The aged know what the innocent cannot.

Grandfather
Hānau

SWADDLED AND OILED CLEAN, my daughter Kalei held her newborn son to her breast. "No," she said.

"Kalei," said her mother, my wife.

"No."

"Kalei," I said. "You know he doesn't belong to us. Look at his back. He belongs to the gods."

"The gods?" Her face twisted in the candlelight. "The gods gave him to me. He's mine."

Her mother touched Kalei's brow. "No fever," she said. "That's good." She lifted Kalei's wild hair away from her face and ran her fingers through it, smoothing the snarls and pulling bits of rubbish from the strands. The fire snaps as my wife hummed, working her way down to the ragged ends. "Shall I braid it for you?" she asked.

"Leave it," Kalei said. "I'll never bind my hair again."

"The baby," I said, reaching for him. "Give him to me. It's time."

"This is his father's responsibility," Kalei said.

"She's right," said her mother. "Nalukai should be the one to do it."

I sigh. "His father isn't here. As the grandfather the kuleana falls to me. You know the law."

Kalei turned the baby in her lap and laid his stomach against her knee. She lifted away the swaddling to expose his back. "Look how tiny it is. It's less than the length of my little finger."

"He'll be crippled. Weak. The village cannot bear this burden."

"He grows strong. His appetite is good."

I shake my head. "An open wound in his back will fester."

"It doesn't bleed," she said. "I think it will heal."

"It's a lifetime of pain and suffering. Is that what you want?"

"Let me try," Kalei begged. "I will keep it covered."

"How?"

"He'll wear a cape."

"The villagers—"

"We'll tell them he has his father's kapu—a kapu that requires his back and shoulders to be hidden from the sun."

"Chiefs have kapu. Is that why Nalukai left during the day?"

"Yes."

My daughter raised the baby to her shoulder and rocked him. She smoothed the swaddling over and over, but didn't look at me. This is how I knew she was lying.

She said, "I'll rub his skin with coconut oil and bathe him at night in the sea. No one will ever know."

"People always find out."

"But by then he won't be a sickly infant. He'll be strong. I will call him Nana'ue. He'll be a fisherman like his father."

I frown. "You don't name a child who is about to be returned to the gods."

"Naming is also a responsibility of the father," said my wife.

"He is mine." This time she met my eyes. "I decide."

"Where is his father?"

Kalei shrugged. "Somewhere at sea."

Grandfather
Pa'i Punahele

FIVE YEARS LATER, my daughter Kalei stood outside the men's eating hale, holding Nana'ue's hand.

I reach for Nana'ue. "It's time," I say.

Nana'ue's father should be here to greet him as he moves from the eating house of women and babies to the world of men. He should be the one to bring him to his place on the lauhala mat. He should be the one to slip him the choicest bits from the platters and calabashes, but the kuleana again falls to me as Nana'ue's grandfather.

Inwardly, I sigh. Nana'ue was a pale and spindly child, barely able to carry two coconuts. Damaged. The gods gave us laws for a reason. I should've returned him to the sea.

Kalei bent to adjust the bottom of Nana'ue's kapa cape. "You remember the rules?" she asked him.

Nana'ue nodded. "Taro and bananas. Sweet potatoes and luau leaves. Breadfruit, bananas, and coconut."

"No meat. Ever."

"Yes, Mama."

In the men's eating hale, for a skinny and sickly child, Nanaʻue was ravenous. Next to me on the lauhala mat he ate all the bananas and more than a chief's share of poi.

"What's that?" he asked, pointing the succulent and glistening platter.

"Roast pig," I said.

"Meat." His face fell.

My brother Lohe picked at a fish bone. "Eh, Nanaʻue, why so sad?" he asked.

"My mother says I must not eat meat."

"That's not meat, it's pork," Lohe teased. "Food of the gods. Women can't eat pork. Men can."

"I can't," Nanaʻue said.

"You're with the men now, right?" Lohe said. "Men eat meat." He handed him a rib; the succulent flesh shiny with fat.

Nanaʻue looked at me. I couldn't fail him again.

"Eat it," I said.

I watched as my grandson eats like a man and grows big and strong.

Mother
ʻŌpio

ONE DAY NANAʻUE brought a massive koa log from the rainforest down to the shore. "I am making a canoe," he said. "Father had his own canoe."

My eyes swept my son from feet to head. *How tall he is and strong,* I thought. "And you are very like your father," I said.

Nanaʻue's smile blinded the sun.

All morning he worked, carving a deep groove down the length of the log. When it was ready, he built a fire and tucked coals into the groove. Each time he bent to add more coals, his cape slipped.

"Oh, this stupid thing!" he said, flinging it away.

"Nanaʻue!"

"I know. Just give me a minute."

"What happened to your back?"

"What?" He looked over his shoulder, twisting this way and that.

"Stand still." I knelt and examined the slit along his spine. *Was it bigger? And what were those boney ridges along the edges?* I ran a finger along them.

Nanaʻue laughed. "That tickles!"

"You felt that?"

"Yes. It makes my mouth tingle!"

"Nana'ue, have you eaten—"

"Yes! But I'm starving. Do you have any breadfruit?"

"You're hungry?"

"All the time. Let's eat, Mother."

"I don't—"

He swung his cape over his shoulders and turned to face me. "It's all right. Once I have my canoe, I'll never be hungry again."

Whistling, he sharpened his adze.

Grandfather
U'i

I WAS heating stones for the imu in the cooking shed when Lohe hurries over. "Have you seen 'Ama?" he asked

"He went fishing with the boys."

"They're back, but he's not with them. They said 'Ama headed down to Kuiopili to dive for lobster. I was hoping he'd brought his catch to you for the imu."

"I haven't seen him." We looked toward the point just in time to see Nana'ue paddling his canoe to shore. "Nana'ue! Where have you been?"

"Near Kuiopili. I was diving for lobster." He held up two fine fat ones, their claws waving angrily in the air.

"Did you see 'Ama?" Lohe asked.

Nana'ue shook his head. "No."

"He wasn't there?"

"No. I was alone." Nana'ue beached his canoe, dragging it above the tide line. He moved slowly, as if in great pain. His 'ōpū was distended, and when he brought me the lobsters, I saw that his neck was bruised and swollen.

"Are you okay?" Lohe asked.

"Yeah. Just a little tired," he said.

Nana'ue handed me two full baskets, more than enough lobster to feed the village. "For the evening meal," he said.

"That much diving is hard work. You must be hungry." I broke two bananas from the stalk hanging in the cooking shed.

"No, thank you," Nana'ue said.

"What? Since when do you pass up bananas?"

"I think I'm going to lie down for awhile."

"You better. You must be sick if you're not hungry!" Lohe teased.

"My stomach hurts. I think it's something I ate."

"Go rest," I said. "But if you see your cousin 'Ama, tell him his father is looking for him."

Nana'ue burped. "Okay," he said, walking along the path to the men's sleeping hale.

Mother
'Ike

'AMA.

Mahi.

Nalani.

Ehu.

Nohea.

Five children swallowed whole by the ocean in a single year. No one dared to fish or swim or even comb the reef. No one except Nana'ue. Without the fish he caught in his canoe, hunger would've stalked the village when the taro crop failed.

"It's a shark," said Uncle Helewa. "And a big one."

Father shook his head. "A shark doesn't hunt like this."

"Nana'ue," said Chief Palinui, "what do you think?"

I watched my son sit taller when the chief addressed him. *He's so big and strong,* I thought. *He's a man grown. He's settled. He knows who he is. He's not so anxious all the time.*

"I agree with my grandfather. It's not a shark. We would've seen signs—my fish traps would've been empty or a hooked ahi would've come up half-eaten. I've seen nothing that hints to a big shark in the area."

"No seals have washed ashore with bite marks. The dolphins still settle each night in the bay," said Father.

Uncle Pono raised his chin. "Were they stolen, perhaps? Is some village kidnapping our children for offerings or slaves?"

The priest shook his head. "All of our neighbors are our friends. They are family. They are as concerned as we are."

"But no children are missing from their villages," said Chief Palinui.

"That we know of," said Uncle Lohe.

"Maybe someone should visit them," said Nana'ue. "Learn about their children. Get to know them better. See what they may be hiding."

"Yes," said Chief Palinui. "That's a good idea, Nana'ue. Priest? What say you?"

"It's a sound idea. It's always easier to trust those with whom you've shared meat and poi."

"We must keep the villages united against this threat," said Uncle Helewa.

Chief Palinui stood. "It is decided, then. Nana'ue and 'Umi, you'll leave tomorrow. Nana'ue, travel to the east; 'Umi, to the west. Ask questions, but be gracious. We don't want to provoke a war with baseless accusations. I know you can do this."

Nana'ue beamed.

Grown. And how like his father he is. Full of aloha and pride, I reached out and placed my hand on his back.

Through the cape I felt it.

The sharp edge of a shark's tooth.

Nana'ue reached back and captured my hand, squeezing it tight. "Just think, Mother," he said, torchlight dancing along his skin, "There will be so many new people. So much poi and meat."

CLOSE ENCOUNTERS

An oil slick of rotting fish guts and slaughterhouse blood stretches out behind the dive boat for a quarter mile or more. Immersed in the Dive Master's pre-encounter briefing, shark cages prepped and waiting, nobody even looks up as a zodiac roars alongside and a twitchy man with an AK-47 boards.

Nobody except Captain 'Aukai.

Captain 'Aukai charges out of the wheelhouse, hands flapping.

The gun goes boom.

Blood and brains spatter the wheelhouse wall like a Rorschach ink blot. Captain 'Aukai's body tumbles over the railing, hitting the water like just another bucket of chum tossed overboard by the deckhand.

Twitchy-with-the-Gun has everyone's full attention now.

Standing in her wetsuit with the rest of her tour group, Claire wants to hide from the unnatural way the Captain's body moves in the ocean, tugged this way and that like a rag doll in a washing machine. But she knows showing any fear will draw Twitchy-with-the-Gun's attention like blood in the water, so she presses her lips tight and watches as piece by piece, the Captain disappears inside dark shadows ringed with teeth.

It doesn't take long.

As the last ghost of blood dissipates in the sea off the Australian coast, the Dive Master crosses himself. On the back of his hoodie is the great white shark logo and tagline of the dive charter: Close Enough to Count Teeth.

Twitchy casually—too casually—slings his AK-47 over his shoulder like Huck

Finn's fishing pole and barks something the First Mate. Claire doesn't know the words, but the meaning is clear.

Mine.

All mine.

Over Claire's shoulder, a German lady tosses her wedding ring. It bounces along the deck and rolls along smooth planks to rest against Twitchy's combat boots. He smirks and kicks it overboard, screaming something incomprehensible.

The First Mate holds up his hands, speaking rapidly.

"What's he saying?" asks a Brit. "Anyone know what he wants?"

"Nyaope," whispers the Dive Master.

"Nyaope? Drogen? Ist er hoch auf Drogen?" asks a voice in the back.

"Ja, Drogen—drugs, heroin," says the Dive Master. "He sees the cages and thinks we work for the syndicate. The First Mate is telling him he's made a mistake —we're a dive company offering shark encounters—but he's not listening."

Twitchy stomps along the deck, cursing and shaking his fist, sweat rolling down his face and staining the collar of his flak vest. His pants pockets and gun belt bulge with extra mags. There are only two of them, Twitchy and the man waiting in the zodiac, but the AK-47 makes the numbers irrelevant.

Twitchy whirls, raising the rifle off his shoulder, and fires into the air.

A voice shrieks.

Twitchy's eyes lock on target.

The girl is young, no more than fifteen, with long hair swept up in braids cascading down her back and pink manicured nails peeking from the sleeves of her too big wetsuit.

Twitchy points at her and then at his feet.

Come.

"No," says the Dive Master, stepping forward.

Twitchy grins as he spins the rifle, cracking the butt against the Dive Master's forehead.

The Dive Master drops to his knees.

Twitchy doesn't look back, just steps over him and whistles to his partner.

The zodiac roars to life and pulls alongside the dive boat's gangway.

Twitchy points at the girl, then the zodiac.

A woman in a ball cap pushes the girl behind her.

Twitchy raises his rifle.

Claire looks toward shore.

Two miles or more.

She calmly zips her wetsuit, lowers her head, and charges.

Wrapping him in a bear hug, her momentum carries them both over the railing and into the water.

Bubbles like silver coins burst around them.

Holding her breath, Claire pushes Twitchy away.

Twitchy flounders, air exploding from his mouth as he screams, the weight of his ammo, boots, and flak jacket dragging him down.

As she rises to the surface, Claire only has time to see the first shark nose him just before the second takes off his head.

It's everything the dive charter promised.

IN THE TWENTY AND FOURTH YEAR OF THE JUDGES

Crossing the storehouse, Lady Adina motioned to baskets of dried leaves. "Warm bellies make better soldiers, Quartermaster Liminhi. Have hot yerba mate brought to the sentries throughout the night."

Quartermaster Liminhi made a tick on his scroll. "I'll have one of the serving girls grind leaves after dinner. A banked fire with a caldron of water should be all we need. One person can manage it."

"Assign at least two. It's a long night to tend a fire alone."

"Yes, my Lady. Tortillas to the sentries again at moonset?"

"Filled with leftover stew, I think."

"Very good." Quartermaster Liminhi's stylus swooped and dashed.

Lady Adina paused near drying racks stacked deep with squash. Bending, she counted pumpkins. "A new shipment is coming tomorrow. Let's roast these few dozen with turkey and coypu. Make sure the cooks reserve the seeds. We'll bake them in the morning bread."

Quartermaster Liminhi nodded. "I'll set aside a few handfuls to roast in lard and lime juice."

Lady Adina raised an eyebrow. "And finish them with a sprinkling of salt and chili?"

Quartermaster Liminhi pointed to his spice chest. "Dried chili pods and salt from the coast."

"You're thinking of my husband."

"It's his favorite snack, and as you've said—"

"—an army fights on its stomach. Yes, let's surprise him. He could use a treat."

"I'll have them ready this afternoon."

"My Lady," a voice called.

Lady Adina turned to see her handmaiden fidgeting in the doorway. "Naama, what is it?"

"The scouts have captured a spy on the outskirts of camp."

"So?"

"It's a woman," Naama said, "wearing a Moriantonite cloak. I think she's hurt."

Lady Adina dusted her hands and gathered her skirts. "Fetch my medicine basket and meet me at the guardhouse. Quartermaster Liminhi, I think we're done here."

"Yes, Lady Adina. Shall I send a girl to you with hot water for the wounds?"

"Good thinking. Perhaps a bit of bread, too. If the woman is from the Moriantonite camp, spy or not she's walked a long way."

Approaching the barricades, Lady Adina's eyes swept over the shade canopy and the wind break made of woven willow branches. Next to the remains of a fire, water gourds were full and basic sanitation needs were met. It wasn't plush, but as far as prisons went, it wasn't bad. Some of the prisoners stood up. The guards snapped to attention.

"At ease, soldiers," she said. "Who is in charge?"

"Lieutenant Samuel, my Lady."

"Hey, sweet cheeks!" called a bearded Moriantonite from behind the fence. "Why the sad face?"

"It's because she has a Lehi boy for a husband!"

"Sugar lips! Come here and let us show you what a real man can do."

"Here kitty, kitty!"

"You can scratch my back anytime."

A guard tossed the contents of a latrine bucket over the fence. "If you're going to talk filth, you might as well smell as foul as your words," he snarled. The prisoners scattered, shaking their cloaks and shoes.

Holding her ground, Lady Adina scanned the crowd. "A woman was brought here. Where is she?"

"The spy?" The sentry tipped his head toward the guardhouse. "With the Lieutenant for questioning, my Lady."

"Hear me, soldier. Under no circumstance is that woman to be kept with the other prisoners."

"But—"

A grizzled guard shoved him. "Yes, my Lady. I'll make sure she's nowhere near those dogs."

"Thank you—?"

"Hamson, my Lady. I fought alongside your husband against the Lamanites in the first Amalickiah campaign."

Lady Adina nodded a respectful half-bow. "My husband remembers those who fought with him in that bloody campaign as true men of God. Thank you, Hamson. I know I can count on you."

"My Lady, it is a privilege."

From the guardhouse someone shouted. "Who is your contact, whore? What secrets are you passing to our enemies?"

"Lieutenant Samuel?" Lady Adina asked.

The seasoned soldier's eyes grew grim. "Yes. Newly appointed."

Something crashed against a guardhouse wall.

"And overly enthusiastic, I think. Thank you, Hamson. I'll take it from here." Lady Adina strode to the guardhouse and threw open the door. Huddled in a corner was a woman, shoulders shaking and face hidden by her ragged shawl. Lieutenant Samuel stood over her, a whip high over his head. An overturned table and chairs littered the room. Two soldiers flanking the door raised spears and bared teeth as Lady Adina entered the room.

"There's no need for that," Lady Adina said mildly. "Put your weapons down." Her handmaiden ran up, a large basket held against her chest. "Ah, Naama. There you are. Let's see to our patient, shall we? Thank you, soldiers. That will be all."

"My Lady," Lieutenant Samuel said, "I don't think you understand—"

"Oh, I think I do, Lieutenant," Lady Adina said, flapping her hands at them. "You and your men can wait out there. We'll call if we need you."

"But this woman is a—"

"Whore and a spy? Yes, we heard." The Lieutenant opened his mouth to speak, but she cut him off. "Your interrogation tactics are fascinating, Lieutenant. I'll make sure to mention them to the Captain."

"Lady—"

"Oh, no need to thank me. I'm happy to pass that news along." Her hand cupped his elbow. "But now it's our turn to attend to the prisoner. This is women's work, and you and your men are far too important." She ushered him out the door. "Go on now. We'll take it from here."

Naama shut the door. "Deftly done, my Lady," she said.

"My husband will hear about this. Whips? Spears? Ridiculous. I doubt she can stand in her condition. Look at her."

"Now what?"

Lady Adina sighed. "We do what must be done." She turned to the woman huddled in the corner. The woman flinched. "It's okay," she soothed, "The men have gone. I won't let them hurt you—even if you are a spy, which I sincerely doubt." She bent down. "What's your name, sister?"

The bundle of rag, blood, and bone stirred. "My master calls me Simcha."

"Simcha. That means joy in the old tongue, doesn't it?" Lady Adina touched her on the shoulder. "You must have made your master very happy."

"Only blood makes him happy," Simcha said.

Lady Adina and Naama traded glances. Naama shook her head. "I knew of a man like that," she said. "My master stoned him to death."

Lady Adina pursed her lips. "Enough, Naama. Fix the chairs." She smiled. "I am Lady Adina, and this is Naama, my handmaiden. Take a moment to catch your breath, Simcha, while we straighten the table and chairs." She stood. "I think we'll all be more comfortable off the floor."

"My Lady," called a young voice from behind the closed door. "It's Zissel. Quartermaster Liminhi sent me with hot water and bread."

"Thank you. Come in Zissel."

The door creaked open. Zissel gasped. Lady Adina turned from setting the table upright in time to see Simcha's shawl fall from her face. One eye was swollen shut. Her nose was off-center, her lips mashed bloody.

"Lieutenant Samuel?" Naama asked.

"No," Lady Adina said. "Those bruises are older. Zissel, don't stand there with your mouth open. Come in and shut the door."

Zissel kicked the door closed and scrambled to set the water jug, basin, and bread on the table.

Lady Adina knelt next to the woman. "Simcha, let me see."

"No," Simcha murmured.

"I'll be gentle." With the lightest touch, Lady Adina felt along Simcha's cheekbones and jaw. "Bruised, but in place. Your nose, however, is broken. It's going to hurt when I set it, but if I don't you won't be able to breathe properly."

"It doesn't matter. Leave it."

"Your husband won't like it if you snore all night."

"A non-existent husband is the least of my worries."

"Good. You haven't lost your sense of humor. Naama, take a cup from my basket, fill it with willow bark and hot water, and let it steep. Can you swallow, Simcha?"

"I don't know."

"What else is hurting?"

"All of me. My ribs. I can't breathe."

"Let me fix your nose."

"No."

"Just let me touch it, okay? I won't do anything—"

Crunch.

Simcha rocked back and howled.

"There. That's better," Lady Adina said.

"Is everything all right, my Lady?" Lieutenant Samuel called though the door.

"Everything is fine, Lieutenant."

"But the woman—"

"Is breathing much better now. Thanks for your concern."

"You said," Simcha gasped, "you wouldn't do anything—"

"I meant anything that would make it worse. It's better, right?"

Simcha gingerly placed fingers along the sides of her nose. Cautiously, she drew air into her lungs. Finally, she nodded. "Better. But it still hurts."

"The willow bark tea will help. Who did this to you?"

"My master. He is a man of much passion."

"Hmmm," Lady Adina said. "Is that what they're calling it these days?"

Simcha looked to the floor.

Lady Adina bit her lip. "It's okay. You're safe. Can you raise your arms?"

"No," Simcha said.

"Zissel," Lady Adina said, "help me stand her up. Let's get her in a chair."

"Can't." Simcha gestured to her feet.

Lady Adina lifted Simcha's hem. Her feet were a raw and bloody mess, full of thorns and scrapes from traveling over rough terrain. "Where are your shoes?"

"He took them after he beat me so I couldn't run away. But that didn't stop me." She held up ragged palms. "I crawled the last mile. I was coming to your camp when the scouts found me."

"Naama, hand me the jar of salve, the green one, please," Lady Adina said. "Wet the rag a bit. I'm going to have to clean these wounds before binding them."

Simcha waved her hands. "This doesn't matter. What matters is my message."

"You'll be more comfortable clean."

"No—"

"I'll be more comfortable with you clean," Lady Adina said.

"If I don't get my message to him, none of us will ever be clean again."

Lady Adina rinsed out her rag. "What message?"

Simcha shook her head. "I'm not telling. I'll speak my truth to him and no one else."

"Brave words for a captured spy."

"You know I'm not a spy. And I'm not a whore like those soldiers said. I love my people. I hate what my master is doing to them."

"This is going to sting a bit."

Simcha sucked air around her swollen lips, but didn't cry when ointment was smoothed over raw flesh.

"The willow bark tea is ready, my Lady," Naama said.

"Ready to try a sip?" Lady Adina held the clay cup to Simcha's lips. "This will ease the pain."

"Why are you helping me? Those soldiers wanted to beat me."

"Soldiers see what they expect, not what's in front of them. They cannot imagine a woman in Morianton clothing being anything but a spy. I see something more."

"Maybe I'm a spy trying to trick you into taking care of me."

"Crawling over thorns and breaking your nose? I don't think so."

"You trust too much," Simcha said.

"I trust just enough," Lady Adina said. "I listen to the still, small voice. He tells me what to do."

"And what does this small voice say about me?"

"That you've been ill-used. Beaten. But God has brought you to us for a reason." Tears welled in Simcha's eyes and spilled, running streaks of clean down her bruised and dusty cheeks. "Sister, why are you here?" Lady Adina asked.

"My master—"

"Who is your master?"

"Morianton."

Naama dropped the bread she was preparing. "She is a spy!"

"Naama—"

Naama jumped toward the door. "Her master is Morianton!"

Simcha's head dropped to her chest, her sobs louder and messier.

"Hush, Naama." Lady Adina raised Simcha's chin. "Morianton did this to you?"

Simcha nodded.

"Why?"

"His meat was cold."

The women blinked. "His meat was cold?" Zissel asked. "What do you mean his meat was cold?"

"He likes it hot, you see, so the head cook waits to pull it from the fire. From the kitchens I run with the platter. But this day, although he'd called for the meat, Morianton kept strategizing with his officers. I stood while they spoke and watched as the meat juice pooled on the platter, cooling until a thin skin of grease congealed. I trembled, waiting for the moment when he reached to fill his plate. He lifted a portion, then paused, the gravy thick and pasty. His first blow knocked the tray out of my hands. The second struck my jaw. I don't remember the others except for his grunts. His kicks caught me here." She ran a hand along her ribs.

Lady Adina lightly brushed the rag over Simcha's cheeks. "When did they take your shoes?"

Simcha shrugged. "I woke in my tent without shoes or water. I prayed for deliverance." She met Lady Adina's eyes. "Morianton owned my body. But my soul belongs to God. I knew what I had to do. That night I left."

"Through an armed camp?"

"The night watch was asleep. I walked by the light of the stars until I came to the river. A voice told me to head upstream. I walked, each step a prayer that I would be in time. That someone would believe me. When I could no longer walk, I crawled. But God was with me in the darkness. Or so I thought until the scouts found me and the soldiers brought me here."

"You must have felt like you'd leaped from the fire into the frying pan," Lady Adina said.

Simcha nodded. "When the lieutenant tipped the table and chairs, my belief faltered. Had I come so far to be whipped like a dog? I felt God had abandoned me."

"And now?"

"And now I think maybe this was God's plan all along." Simcha's smile didn't reach her eyes. "I heard it all, of course. That's why I'm here. Morianton plans to flee and take possession of the land northward."

Lady Adina eyes widened. "He means to unite his people with Bountiful." Her thoughts raced. "If he's successful—"

"All liberty is lost," Simcha said.

"Naama, where is my husband this morning?"

"In counsel with Teancum and the First Guard, my Lady."

"Please tell him there is someone he needs to meet. Now. Don't take no for answer. Bring the entire council, if you can."

"Right away, Lady Adina." Naama turned and flung open the door.

"What's wrong?" Lieutenant Samuel barked.

"Oooooo, are you going to get it!" Naama laughed. "Your spy is our savior!"

"Stupid girl—"

"Yeah, tell that to Captain Moroni," Naama called as she raced past. "He's going to be here soon."

"Captain Moroni is your husband?" Simcha asked.

"Yes."

"He'll hear my words."

"Of course."

"I won't be hung for a spy."

Lady Adina laughed. "Hardly. You are our honored guest."

"This is God's hand. I see it now. Everything led to this."

"We owe you a great debt, Simcha. More than you know. People will bless your name and thank God for your sacrifices. Let's get you into a chair. Honored guests don't huddle on the floor. There, that's better. Don't forget your willow bark tea. Tell me, do you like roast pumpkin seeds? They are my husband's favorite snack. Zissel, run to the Quartermaster and tell him we're going to need more. A triple batch, at least."

GAMBLE

Under the hazy glow of a streetlight, Tyche the Goddess of Chance taps her stiletto heel, careful to keep her sequined dress clear of alleyway grime. We're a long way from Fifth Avenue, but Tyche always looks like she stepped out of a high-class department store window or salon.

Me, not so much.

A hand on her hip, she says, "Jace, honey, it ain't complicated. You hold the dice. You think of the girl—"

"—Lydia," I say. "Her name is Lydia."

"Yeah, whatever. You think of Lydia. You shake the dice twice for luck, pucker your lips, blow 'em a kiss, then chuck 'em nice and easy. The roll tells you all you need to know."

"That's it?"

"That's it."

Above us, light shines through the curtains of the second story window in a brownstone apartment. I can just make out the curve of Lydia's body propped unnaturally in a chair and the shapes of the skin-suited Idylwyrn thugs hovering around her. There's no sign of Harlan Fairfox of the Unseelie Court, but once the Feywilde portal opens, all bets are off.

I can't lose Lydia again.

I can't.

Standing in the shadows below the fire escape, Tyche slips the dice into my palm and says, "You'll rescue the girl—or not. That's up to you. But hurry. My dice and I are headed to Monte Carlo to fleece a whale."

I hold the dice up to the light. They don't look like much, just two six-sided cubes, each side numbered one through six; the wood so old, the edges and corners are rounded. I rub my thumb along dots burned black and deep. Against my skin, the dice are smooth, warm—

Alive.

I swallow.

Tyche tousles and primps her hair, fluffing and smoothing perfection. For a moment, the scent of jasmine and winter musk covers the smell of cat piss and fried onions. "C'mon," she says, flapping a hand at me. "Shake 'em like you mean it. Tick-tock, big guy. I ain't got all night. Neither do you."

"I thought they'd be different," I say, tilting them this way and that. "I dunno, Ty. They remind me of Cracker Jack prizes. Where's my baseball card and Bazooka gum? Where's the comic strip with the corny joke?"

"Seriously, Jace?"

"Don't get mad. I'm just surprised your famous dice are these shoddy chunks of wood marked with charcoal. Why not ivory or gold or—"

"Or what, genius? Diamonds and jade? Because valuable things only come in shiny packages, right?" She gives me the once over, drinking in my too-long legs, sleeveless hoodie, and fire-licked face.

I try not to flinch. "All I'm saying is I expected something else. Something substantial," I say.

Her eyes narrow. "My dice are carved from a branch of the Tree of the Knowledge of Good and Evil, you moron. Of course they're wood," she says. "Of course they're worn. They're older than—"

"What? Dirt? Dirt's nothing, Ty. Dirt's yesterday. Now if you'd said older than time—now that's old. And, I gotta say, a little cliché, even for you."

She rolls her eyes. "Puh-leeze," she says, reaching into her evening bag for a pack of Virginia Slims. She shakes out a cigarette and lights up.

Tyche smokes when she's pissed. Pissed is good. Pissed is off-balanced and right where I want her.

She drops her lighter and snaps the bag shut. "Those dice are plenty valuable, Jacie. Trust me," she says, pulling smoke deep into her lungs.

"I do, Ty. I trust you and your word more than you know." Wiggling my fingers, I watch the dice dance. It's the biggest gamble of my life.

Tyche bites back a sigh. "Stop gloating," she says. "It's annoying."

"I'm not gloating."

"You won, okay? Do you need to hear it? Fine. Jace won. A mortal beat me. There. I said it. I don't know how, but you did."

"I won because you think losing is an option. It isn't. I did what I had to do to beat you, Ty. I'll do anything to save Lydia." I give the dice a quick shake in my palm, then hold them tight as I brush my knuckles against my lips. "With these dice, I can't lose. I know it."

She grins like Erinyes, curdling the blood in my veins. "You think because you roll them, you're guaranteed the result you desire? You flatter me," she says and bobs her head. "That takes way more mojo-juice than I've got. The dice don't let you choose, you know. They don't influence destiny. They just reveal it."

The tip of her cigarette glows as smoke wafts toward me. Menthol. I hate menthol. It's fake. Chew gum or smoke, people. You're not fooling anyone. Wrinkling my nose and fanning my face, I say, "Seven is six and one, two and five, three and four. Those are good odds. Much better than one and one."

Tyche closes her eyes and inhales until a long line of cigarette ash crumples and falls. I've pushed her to her limits, but she opens her eyes and answers me civilly enough.

"Mortal odds have nothing to do with it. With these dice, there are only two options. Roll a seven and you'll know bursting through the door will rescue the girl. Rolling snake eyes means—"

"I die if I try. Yeah, you've made that clear."

She sticks out the tip of her tongue. With nails the color of oysters, she daintily picks a speck of tobacco and flicks it into the darkness. "So do it already," she says. "Chop-chop."

I shake my head. "There's no need. Regardless of the dice, I'm going in. I won't let Harlan Fairfox or his cronies take Lydia through the portal."

"Seems to me, knowing if you're going to die if you attack now would lead a person—a *smart* person—to make a different choice."

I shrug.

For a second it I think she might flick her cigarette at me, but instead she says, "You looking for a cherry on top? Fine. Here you go: more time doesn't change destiny or fate, Jace—they're inevitable. Roll 'em. You'll see."

"Stop rushing me. I won my roll fair and square," I say.

She closes her eyes and blows smoke through her nostrils like a yogi searching for peace. "Yes," she says "You did. Every being Seen and Unseen knows I pay my gambling debts, Jace. You want to know if you'll rescue the girl? Toss the dice. I don't care either way."

Another deep drag takes the burn down to the filter. By the nicotine stains on her fingertips, the Goddess of Chance loves her smokes. Maybe goddesses don't worry about cancer or taxes or death.

She reaches into her bag again, this time conjuring lipstick the color of pomegranate blood. She smirks as she tints her lips. "Tell you what, Jacie. If you roll snake eyes, I'll take you to Monte Carlo. You'll get a kick out of my whale—arms dealer, drug lord, empire built on prostitution and child trafficking—there's something special about winning evil money."

I think about the kidnapped woman in the apartment above and what will happen to her—to us—if I don't succeed.

It's not a happy thought.

Tyche purses her lips, then lights another cigarette. Feigning boredom, she blows a smoke ring. "Fish or cut bait, Jace."

I clench my hand into a fist, squeezing the dice tight. "No."

"No? What do you mean, no?" This time she flicks ash at me. "Roll. The. Damn. Dice. Jace. That's the whole point of winning them. You're being ridiculous."

I shake my head, lift the leather lace from around my neck, and pull my medicine bag out. Without looking, I open it and dump in the dice, letting them rattle and come to rest next to a four-leaf clover and a dried mole's ear. Pulling the strings tight, I tuck the bag back under my hoodie. "You bet me a roll of your dice, Tyche, but you didn't say when I had to do it."

Tyche's ennui vanishes in a heartbeat. "You wouldn't dare!" she says.

It's my turn to grin. "Oh, I dare, Ty. I'm risking it all on the fact that if I enter the apartment with your dice and lose, you'll lose even bigger."

"Give me back my dice!"

"When I'm done. That's the deal."

"Oh, you're done, Jace. You're so done." Talons sprout from fingernails, teeth lengthen, wings erupt from shoulder blades. Her voice growls with all the hate and heat of Hades. "Roll my dice now or I'll feed your liver to Cerberus. The Furies will knit stockings from your entrails."

I wag a finger at her. "Not so fast. A bet's a bet, right? The dice are mine until I roll."

She snaps the cigarette at my face.

I lean to the left.

The cigarette passes harmlessly over my shoulder.

I've had flames flung at me before—my scars prove it. A lit cigarette is nothing. She should know better. I beat her once before, didn't I?

Deep breath.

"Tyche, I need you to listen. I'm not wasting my roll on something I already know: this *is* the time to rescue Lydia. If they take her through the portal, she's gone forever. Every minute she spends in Feywilde is a year or more here. Losing is not an option. So, if you ever want your precious dice back, it's not just me who's going against Harlan Fairfox, it's *we*."

Her wings unfurl.

Car alarms go off.

Our eyes lock. We both know whomever blinks first, loses.

"You sure you want to play, little man?" she says. "These stakes are way out of your league. Last chance. Roll or I'll take them from you."

"You can't."

"Watch."

"To be clear then, by taking back the dice before I roll, you acknowledge that the great goddess Tyche is *welshing* on our bet?"

I'm all in.

She stands there, blinking, a fireball in one hand, her beaded Gucci bag in the other.

I go for the throat.

"Of course, it doesn't have to be just you and me against Harlan Fairfox, Ty. I'm sure you've plenty of powerful friends to invite to our rescue party. The more the merrier—and the more likely you'll get your dice back."

I quirk my eyebrow and smile.

It takes her only a second that feels like an eternity to snuff out the fireball and fold back her wings. "Fine!" she hisses. "I'll call in my markers. But when this is over, it's still not over."

Raising her head to the moon and howling a curse, she vanishes, leaving only the afterglow of a rude gesture to scorch the hair off my arms.

Guess luck's not such a lady after all.

In the apartment above, I hear voices as more lights flick on. Tyche and her reinforcements better be quick. I touch the dice through the medicine bag around my neck and stare at the window.

Lydia, I'm coming.

Losing is not an option.

NIGHTWALKER

(MEMOIR)

T he moon was full or nearly so; it flooded my second story window and dripped down the walls to puddle on the polished cement floor. Drenched in moonlight, I lay in my bed breathing in the rich scent of plumeria and hibiscus flowers growing outside a mid-campus dorm at The Kamehameha Schools.

I couldn't sleep.

The evening trade winds had long faded away leaving the night air heavy and humid. I rolled over, kicking off bedsheets that clung to my legs like octopus tentacles. It was the second night of an eight-day high school band camp, and as an upperclassman assigned to a freshman dorm, it was my night to keep tabs on the fifteen freshmen girls on my floor.

It was easier than it sounds.

Perpetually endowed by revenue from Princess Bernice Pauahi Bishop's crownlands, The Kamehameha Schools are private schools for Native Hawaiians with their main campus located high on a ridge above Honolulu, Oahu. Like most elite prep schools with facilities and faculty that rival small colleges, competition for admittance is fierce, but tuition at Kamehameha is unimaginably subsidized, and most students receive full scholarships. Because of this, students are constantly reminded that it's a gift to attend and that the line waiting for their coveted spot is long and eager. Typical teen hijinks are simply not tolerated. Summer band camp was no exception.

I know that crushes a lot of male sleep-away camp fantasies, but after two fourteen-hour days of brutal rehearsals, much of it in the hot sun, all freshmen girls wanted was to crawl into bed at lights out, praying they'd make it through the rest of camp. Being on duty as an upperclassman mainly meant handing out Band-Aids for blisters, aloe for sunburns, and keeping an eye out for heatstroke and homesickness. The night I was on duty, I kept my door cracked so I could hear if anyone needed anything.

Easy.

Click. Slap, slap, slap.

I sat up. It was the unmistakable sound of a door opening and rubber slippahs flip-flopping down the hall.

I slipped on my glasses and peered at my watch. 1:23 am. *Wonderful. Sunburn, heatstroke, or homesick? Probably a dehydration headache.* I sighed. *Tylenol and Gatorade to the rescue.* I rolled out of bed and pulled my door wide.

Each dorm room had a large transom window set above its door that allowed light to spill into the inner hallway. Heavy beams of moonlight fell like water through the transoms, cascading through the inky darkness like God's own spotlights. From the far end of the hall to my right, someone approached.

Slap, slap, slap.

The door on my left swung open; Maile, the flute section leader, rubbed her eyes and scowled. "Somebody sick?"

I shrugged. "Headed this way. Not fast. Probably not a puker."

We glanced toward the communal bathroom across the hall from us.

Slap, slap, slap.

The steps grew louder, closer, and we could see a dark shadow breaking the beams of light as it traveled down the hallway.

Slap, slap, slap.

"Stupid freshmen. They never drink enough." Maile craned around me. "Hey," she hiss-whispered down the hall. "Are you sick or do you just have to pee?"

Slap, slap, slap.

The shape was only one doorway, one beam of light away.

All of the hair, fine and downy-soft, rose along my arms. My scalp prickled. "Eh," I called, "who's there?"

Slap, slap, slap.

Right in front of us.

But no one was there.

Unwavering, the footsteps passed, stomping down the stairs to the main floor. We heard the crash bar on the main door collapse, the door lurch open, and felt the night rush in, running like fingertips through our hair, caressing our bare legs as the building breathed. We didn't hear the footsteps continue down the sidewalk, just the sound of the heavy metal door resettling in its frame. Once again, the building held its breath.

In the stillness, the taste of fresh coconut burned in the back of my throat.

Maile and I exchanged just one look, then turned back into our rooms. This time, I shut my door tight and said a little prayer for those who walk the night.

Maile and I never spoke of what we'd seen, just held each other's eyes a moment too long as the hall lights went out each night after floor prayer, both secretly grateful it was some other upperclassman's turn to keep watch.

Later, I heard stories from boarders who called that dorm home all school year long. It's the ghost of a pregnant student who hanged herself in the 1960s, 1920s, 1890s; it's *'aumakua* visiting from Hilo, from Lihue, from Kahului; it's a prank; it's a dream; it's the haunting of an ancient *kahuna* priest bound to stones stolen from his *heiau* temple's altar and used to build the dorm's retaining wall— everyone knows unscrupulous foreigners reused finished stones after the Hawaiian gods fell.

None of those stories felt right.

I once dared to ask our *kahu*, the resident campus chaplain. He smiled and fiddled with his rosary as he told me that over the years, many people had seen unusual things in that dorm. When called, he'd come to them in the middle of the night with prayers and ti leaves, saltwater and aloha. He believed whatever walked these halls was harmless, and like all souls deserved kindness.

"E ho'okikaha me ka maluhia," he said. Let it wander in peace.

BALCONY HOUSE
HAT TRICK
(MEMOIR)

The signs lie.

Standing at the trailhead to Balcony House at Mesa Verde in Colorado, I thought I knew what I was getting into. When I bought tour tickets for my family and our friends the Bradshaws the day before, the signs at the visitor's center warned me about the 100 plus stairs I'd have to climb down and the rickety 32' wooden ladder I'd have to scale—not to mention the assorted smaller ladders and uneven steps carved into the rock that I'd have to ascend.

It's no secret that I'm not comfortable on ladders. Heights I can handle as long as I'm not somehow suspended in mid-air. Tall buildings? No problem. Ski lifts? No way. Zip lines? See ya.

Truth be told, I'm not fond of stairs either. I figure if modern people are supposed to climb more than a single flight of stairs at a time, God would not have allowed the invention of escalators and elevators.

Unfortunately, over the years I've also evolved into more of a sedentary *cool, can I see it on Netflix?* person than the gung ho *let's shoot our own documentary on site and live off rehydrated mac and cheese for a week* person I used to be.

Some might say I'm lazy. I think of it as growing old enough to afford air conditioning and appreciate room service.

I knew going into it that this trip was supposed to be a throwback to the good old days when our two families camped and hiked together and made s'mores around the campfire with the kids—although this year we were staying in a hotel with indoor plumbing, hot water, and real beds and the only kids with us were our two seventeen-year-old caboose babies.

Everyone was jazzed. We'd traveled a long way to see the ruins of the Pueblo cliff dwellings on Memorial Day weekend, the first weekend of the year that the tours opened. None of us had ever been here. And while the thought of hanging off a cliff and swinging in the breeze made my stomach queasy, there are some things you just have to suck up and do.

Like a good sport, I bought the tickets, swapped out my rubbah slippahs for tennis shoes and socks, and slathered on sunscreen.

The whole night before I psyched myself for the climb up the 32' ladder. I had a plan—look straight ahead and keep climbing like a machine. Don't stop. Don't look down. Don't look up. Just do it.

I got this.

I think.

But then during the topside orientation the perky ranger holds up her hat. "And then near the end of the tour, you'll crawl through the tunnel."

What the what? Tunnel? Nobody said anything about a tunnel. There were no signs at the visitor's center about crawling through a freaking tunnel.

"The tunnel is as wide as my hat. It's 12 feet long and gets wider in the middle, then narrows back down to 18 inches. I want you to understand that once you put your foot on the tall ladder and start to ascend, there's no going back. We all go up and out through the tunnel."

Oh, baloney. No way the ADA would let that fly in a national park. There's got to be a handicap by-pass or something.

A tall dude raises his hand. "Why not?"

Ranger Perky chirps, "It's not safe to go backward. You have to go forward. There really is no going back." She waves her hat around. "Don't worry. Everyone here can fit. Trust me. Things squish—you just have to make them."

Oh, no. Obviously, as an anorexic park ranger she's never wrestled her lumps and bumps into spanx shapewear. Trust me. Things definitely do NOT compress or squish as much as everyone hopes. Doesn't she know that in the olden days women wore corsets to get an 18 inch waist?

My corset days were looong in the rearview.

Fudge.

"Let's go!" she says.

"I'm out," says Tall Guy. "I'll wait here."

I open my mouth and turn to my husband.

He just looks at me and shrugs his shoulders.

I close my mouth and look around.

Seriously, who's wider than me? I can't be the only chunky monkey on this tour. That guy? Am I bigger than that guy? I mean around the middle. He looks one can shy of a keg. Anybody else? Not her. She's smaller than me. Her, too. Him,

him, her—all shopping the plus section, but smaller than me. Oh, no. Am I really the biggest person here? Did the ranger see me when she said everyone could fit through her hat? There're a lot of people here, and I was standing way in the back. What happened to all the geriatric people I saw at the visitor's center? Where are the folks with the walkers and canes? Why does everyone here look like a triathlete?

I bite my lip.

I say to my teen daughter, "I don't think I can fit through an 18 inch hole."

She pats my shoulder. "Mom, she said everyone could fit. Besides, that guy over there is bigger than you. Just go after him."

I eye Keg Dude. Maybe he's fatter, maybe not.

He's oddly unconcerned.

Of course. He's a dude.

He pulls a granola bar out of his pocket and starts munching.

He sees me watching him and waves. "The ranger said no food on the trail, so I'm eating this now. Don't want to attract scavengers to the archeological site."

Perhaps this info should make me feel better, but all it really does is make me afraid that he and I are both in denial. The whole tour is supposed to be an hour. Who carries snacks for an hour hike?

As we head down the trail, I whisper to my friend, "I'm not sure I can do this." She's known me from college, from before the kids and late night ice cream runs, when my skinny jeans were truly skinny and my waist was the same circumference as my current thigh.

She pats my arm. "We can do hard things."

She's thinking I'm afraid of the ladder and heights. Yes, we can do hard things, but not impossible things. Camels and eyes of needles come to mind.

We start down the 100 stairs. Desert heat radiates off the metal bolted into the side of the cliff. The stair edges are slick with wear, and I hold the rail in a sweaty death grip, certain that I'll slip and bounce down the cliff.

On second thought, that would solve a lot of things. I consider loosening my grip, but then I imagine myself in a broken heap of blood and bones at the bottom and realize I'd probably chip my teeth on the way down and would have to go to the dentist.

I hate the dentist.

I hold a little tighter and creep down a little slower.

After lulling me with a gentle walk, eventually we turn a corner and come face to face with the 32' ladder, the point of no return.

I glance at my friend. "We can do hard things," she says again.

Yes, we can. We can bear children. We can sit through hours of piano recitals, soccer games, and debate tournaments and finish science fair projects at 3 am. We can cook Thanksgiving for 60 people and figure out what to get our MILs for Mother's Day.

We tell our daughters to face their fears. I glance at mine with her long limbs and athlete's grace. Will she ever listen to me again if I chicken out?

A small part of my brain recognizes the brilliance of this strategy. I'm so freaked out about the tunnel that climbing a ladder is no big deal.

Mostly.

At the top, there are a few more turns, and then a narrow passageway I squeeze through to get to the first big room. It's dark. I can't see with my sunglasses. I suck it in to get around the last bit.

I made it through the tunnel!

Woot!

Except it's not the tunnel. Apparently, the tunnel is much smaller and farther along the trail.

The Ranger is nattering on about kivas and rainwater, but all I'm thinking about is the evening news where the lead story tonight will be about the daring rescue attempt to pull a wide load out of a narrow shaft.

Rescuers knock down a 1200 year old wall. Pueblo people weep at another westerner's desecration of their ancestral homeland.

Helicopters and cranes are involved.

Conservationists cry that the cost to historic antiquities is too high, so they advocate simply cementing me in place.

Environmentalists claim that leaving my body to rot will pollute the natural eco-system and cause an explosion in the rat and insect population. They advocate removing me in pieces.

Exercise gurus stand at the entrance and shout at me to do isometrics until the bacon grease and butter finally melts off my derriere and they slid me out like birthing the world's biggest baby.

Stuck in the tunnel there is nowhere to pee. For days.

I'm encased in a tight tunnel, underground, buried in a grave.

In the dark with the spiders, worms, and rats.

And snakes.

This is much, much worse than hauling myself up a freakishly tall and rickety wooden ladder.

Don't ask me what Ranger Perky says about the ruins or history or culture. I don't hear anything except the sighs of everyone about to be inconvenienced by my chocolate-loving body. Small children are about to be traumatized. Their therapy bills alone are going to break the bank.

I'm puffing hard before we even get there.

At the tunnel, I realize it's a bunny-sized hole in a man-made wall. My friend who weighs what she did in high school, nonchalantly stops, drops, and slithers in.

I feel my daughter press against my back.

I can't see Keg Dude. Did he climb the ladder? Is he even here or did he wisely chicken out?

I don't know.

Prescription sunglasses—on or off? Too dark to see with them, too blind without them. Screw it. I leave them on. No place to put them that won't get squished. On my face is the safest bet.

I bend down and firmly banish a nightmare memory of the last time I tried on spanx.

With my friend in front, I figure I can grab her ankle and use pressure to communicate through Morse code that things are not right. I'm pretty sure three long squeezes, three short squeezes, and three long squeezes are S.O.S. Like Lassie, she'll go for help—after all her family is still behind me, trapped on the other side of the tunnel from hell. She'll be motivated to work hard to see them again.

Maybe they'll get a helicopter ride. They'd like that.

I'm grateful my daughter's behind me. She won't be afraid to shove, pinch, or push whatever gets stuck. She won't be dainty. She's an uber fit jockette with a teenager's natural abhorrence of both public humiliation and her parents.

If I were Catholic, I'd cross myself and say a final Hail Mary. Instead I console myself with the famous Hawaiian chant, no make A, no make A. No matter what. No. Make. A.

I wiggle through the first part and almost weep with joy to discover how open the middle section is.

Behind me my daughter shrieks. "Oh, gross! Somebody spit in the tunnel! Mom! Watch where you're going!"

"I don't care," I say. "I'm wearing my sunglasses. I can't see in the dark."

"Did you crawl right through it? I bet you did!"

The only thought I have is to wonder how much spit reduces friction.

I see the light ahead. The opening at the end is narrower than what I've already slithered through. I try not to think of corks and bottles. I fight the urge to try to swing my legs around so I can go out feet first—there's no way I can do that. I have a quick flash of being stuck and folded like a taco. It's not pretty.

My knee grinds on a stone. I feel skin tear and blood well. I twist my shoulders and finally go for the least graceful but quickest exit I can do.

As I plop out onto the ground, my friend looks at me with the oddest expression on her face. I stumble to my feet.

My daughter pops out behind me. "See, Mom, told you you'd fit."

I'm breathing hard, much harder than I should for such a little thing.

Later, safely in the parking lot, my husband of thirty years hugs me. "That was rough. I didn't want to say anything, but I know that hike hit all of your buttons."

Oh, yeah. Heights. Climbing. Underground. Small spaces. Tight spaces. Darkness. Fear of public humiliation. Shame for a once athlete's now lack of physical fitness.

Good times.

We can do hard things.

This is the part of a story where the heroine sees the error of her ways, knows she can accomplish great things, and decides to change her life by going on an exercise and diet program. The story ends with her successfully running a marathon in the fall and dedicating her life to eradicating adult couch potatoes and enforcing ADA rules at national parks.

But sadly, this isn't fiction, at least not today.

Pass me the remote.

And the chips.

Turn up the AC. Mama needs a nap.

PERSONA NON GRATA

The doorbell won't stop, not for God or love or money. I open the door just wide enough to scowl at the woman on my front porch. She's not alone, but doesn't know it.

I've rehearsed this moment over and over, but seeing her in the flesh, I realize this is going to be harder than expected.

"Go away, Maggie," I say. "There's nothing here for you."

"Kiki, wait! Don't shut the door."

Maggie hasn't slept, and it shows. Since last Wednesday, I've watched her TV persona rotate between national press conferences and HallelujahNet, Salt Lake City's streaming megachurch channel.

On TV, in her televangelist power suits and sensible shoes, she stands next to her camera-ready husband, Reverend Phil. She cradles a picture of their missing daughter as he calls upon viewers to unite in a Power Hour of Prayer.

On my porch, she's wearing oversized sunglasses, sweats, and a hoodie pulled low.

Incognito.

But I know the real her.

She whips off the glasses. "Please. I'm begging. You've got to help me."

I cross my arms. "I don't have to do—"

"I know we've had our differences—"

My jaw drops. "*Differences*? Is that—"

"—but Celeste is your family, too!"

My eyes narrow. "As I recall, you and Phil made it very clear that I am *not* family. Admit it; you erased me from the photo albums. That's cold, Mags, even for you."

Maggie bites her lip so hard it bleeds.

"Kiki," she says, "please."

"I'm not in the family albums, am I?"

She dumps her glasses in her purse. "How would you even know something like that?"

I shake my head. "I know things, Maggie. You know I do. That's why you're here."

"I'm here because blood is thicker than photos," she says.

I sigh. We haven't spoken in nearly twelve years, but I know my sister well. If she's here, she's beyond desperate. I state the obvious. "Phil doesn't know you're here." Maggie shakes her head. I glance up and down the street. "No reporters? No media?"

"No. I told the Reverend—"

"You call Phil *the Reverend*?"

"Only in public. Things—"

"Oh. So I'm public?"

"No, you're—" Maggie pauses.

I put my hand on my hip. "Well, which is it? Family or public?"

Maggie finally tastes blood on her lips and digs in her purse for a crumpled tissue. "It's complicated."

"Ya think?"

"Look, be mad at me. Hate me. But I know you love Celeste."

"And the Right Reverend Phil?"

"Fuck Phil," Maggie spits, spraying bright red droplets. "His way isn't working."

I throw the door wide. "Well, if it's fuck Phil, come on in."

As Maggie crosses my threshold, I grab salt from a nearby bowl and surreptitiously reset the warding. Stuck outside, there's an immediate wave of frustration from the invisible beasties trailing Maggie.

I swallow a snort of laughter. *Tough titty said the kitty. My house, my rules.*

They howl, but I just grin and shut the door. Nothing's coming in that's not invited, that's for damn sure.

Gran's ghost slips to the door, presses her eye to the peephole, and gives me a thumbs up. She points at Maggie, and I turn in time to see her aura leap, shining brighter and taller.

It's a good sign.

How much brighter, how much more herself would Maggie be if she could stay free of those beasties for an hour, a week, a month? I can lock them out of my house, but Maggie will always call them back. She can't banish what she doesn't recognize.

"How does it feel to be home?" I say.

"This was Gran's house, then yours. Never mine."

It's my turn to bite my lip.

Her eyes wander. "You changed the carpet for stone."

"Stone's easier to clean."

"Gran never let anybody wear shoes in the house," Maggie says.

"Yeah, well, now you don't have to worry about it."

"Painted, too."

"Lots of things change," I say.

"Hmmm," she says.

Maggie stands in the front parlor where I do my client readings. It's tasteful, but I admit it aligns with certain expectations. The table is shrouded in a long purple tablecloth embroidered with mystical suns, moons, and stars. It's flanked by a couple of heavy high-backed chairs. Dozing under fringe-trimmed silk are tarot and oracle decks. More for atmosphere than anything else, Gran's old Ouija board lies propped against candles and leather bound books. Along the far wall is a bookcase filled with baskets of empty drawstring bags and collections of crystals, oils, and herbs.

And the odd skull or two.

"Have a seat," I say.

I don't have to see her face to know Maggie closes her eyes, says a prayer, and counts to ten before turning to me. "I'm sorry. I can't—"

"The kitchen, then. It's fine."

Disappointed, Gran throws up her hands and leads the way down the hall. She knows she won't be part of the spectacle there.

Nestled at the back of the house, the kitchen is bright and sunny. Herbs in pots line windowsills. On open shelves are canning supplies, a pickle crock, and jars of spices labeled cinnamon, ginger, and star anise. Beside the open-hearth fireplace are Gran's knitting basket and rocking chair. In the middle of the room is a big farm table with a bowl of red apples on a hand-crocheted doily.

The kitchen is another kind of stage, but one Maggie associates with childhood, not parlor tricks. As she draws closer to the room, I feel relief wash over her like a waterfall. The farm table and benches worn smooth remind her of Gran's Sunday towers of mashed potatoes, gravy, biscuits, and ham.

I see the farm table and remember the day I lovingly washed Gran, the shroud linens sheer and damp, sticking to the table as I rubbed potions deep into her skin. When I asked what to dress her in, Gran said since she was meeting God, it ought to be her Sunday best. When I asked whether to serve cake or cookies, Gran said it didn't matter to her. The dead don't eat.

Memory is a funny thing.

Halfway to the kitchen, I pause to consider my cards and crystals. I don't need them—no real witch does, but clients do. Regular folks need tangible things to shuffle and caress; it's what makes the ephemeral corporal, the magic real. To my clients, our time together is not about me; it's the cards.

In truth, all I do is tell them what they already know.

But Maggie doesn't believe in trappings or tricks. I nod to myself. Cards would only get in the way; she'd ignore or dismiss them.

As Maggie sits in the kitchen, bathed in lemon-yellow sunlight, inhaling fresh basil and mint, when I speak, I want her to know it's me and not cards or crystals.

Belief is always a choice.

I walk into the kitchen empty-handed, grab the cutting board and knife from the counter, and sit across the table from Maggie. With her back to the hall and fireplace, she's looking down at her lap and worrying her lip raw.

"Here," I say, pushing the board towards her. "Apples and cheese. Eat something. You're too pale."

"You cut the skins off."

"So?"

"That's how Celeste likes them, remember? When she'd come here, you'd always spoil her by cutting off the skins." Maggie reaches out, but doesn't pick up a slice.

"Skins can be bitter."

I glance down the hallway and spot a shadow hovering near the door to the guest room. I shake my head at it, but it doesn't retreat.

Stubborn.

Fine. But eavesdroppers seldom like what they hear.

Maggie's hand still wavers over the apples and cheese.

"Oh, for hell's sake!" I snag the unsliced half of apple and bite. "See? No poison."

Maggie lifts an apple slice and takes the tiniest nibble.

I choose my words carefully. "I don't know what you want from me, Mags. The police are looking for Celeste. Hell, the whole country is looking for her. I have nothing to offer. In fact, I'm a dangerous influence. I'll lead her straight to hell. Just ask Phil."

"Kiki—"

"And that's another thing. Twelve years! You don't get to call me Kiki. Only family calls me Kiki. Call me Janet, just like the UPS guy and the lady who does my taxes."

Names have power.

"Okay, *Janet*. Or should I call you *Madam Janet*?"

A sliver of apple sticks in my teeth. "No," I say, "Her Serene Celestial Royal Highness will do." I take a bite of cheese to keep myself from saying something I'll regret.

Maggie takes another nibble, then shoves the whole slice into her mouth. "Janet," she mumbles around the apple, "Janet, Janet—Janet is the name on your driver's license. That's not who I need. I need Auntie Kiki."

"Auntie Kiki is dead."

"Don't be like that."

"That's what Phil told her," I say.

Maggie nods. "She cried when he told her, cried and cried until he said you'd gone to heaven to play with Jesus."

I snort and roll my eyes.

"Phil made a game of it. He'd send her outside to watch the clouds, saying good girls could see Auntie Kiki playing the harp. She never did, of course."

"That's sadistic, even for a self-righteous son of a bitch like Phil."

Maggie dabs at her lip. "Phil was right, though. She only cried for a couple of days. The young are resilient. They bounce."

"I didn't bounce."

"No," Maggie says. "You remember, don't you? You remember it all. How Kiki was her first word. Not Mama or Dada. *Kiki*. How she loved digging in the garden with you. Tarrwots, remember? She called them tarrwots."

"Of course I remember. Tarrwots and green knees." I don't dare blink. No matter what she says, I will not cry. I'm done with tears.

Maggie leans forward. "And after her dinner, remember how she smelled fresh from her bath?"

"Like marigolds and starshine."

"Remember how she snuggled when you read her a story and how she loved thunder and lightning, but only if she was with you?"

"Yeah."

"You two had a connection. It was like you could read each other's minds. You always knew what she was thinking and feeling. When she needed a snack. When she needed a cuddle. When she needed to be brave. In some ways, she was more your daughter than mine."

"Celeste is *your* daughter, Maggie. None of this is on me."

"But do you remember how it was? How tight you were?"

"Yeah, I remember. I remember it all. I remember how Phil took Celeste away from me. And how you didn't stop him."

She shrugs. "I'm not going to lie. It was easier without you around."

I open my mouth to say all the words that will end this right here and now, but I don't. Ending it now won't actually end it. Eventually, Maggie will be back, seeking the answers she can't find anywhere else.

But I can't let her think I'm a pushover, either.

I raise an eyebrow and say, "Sister, if this is how you kiss and make up, you need to leave. Now."

Lost in memory, she says, "Without Auntie Kiki, Mama reads the stories. Mama dries the tears."

I can't believe my ears. I say, "That's the most selfish, asinine thing you've said in a lifetime of assholery. There is always enough love to go around."

She snaps back to the present. "It wasn't selfish to keep her safe."

"From me?" I cross my arms. "You've been drinking Phil's Kool-Aid too long."

"Get over yourself, *Janet.* There are real dangers in the world. You're just Phil's excuse." From her purse, she pulls out a toy. I snatch it.

"Miss Kitty!" I turn the cat over and over. "Miss Kitty! I thought you burned."

"No. Toby Tiger burned. Phil never noticed the difference." She slips another pale apple slice between swollen lips. "While he raged, I hid Miss Kitty in a shoebox. I couldn't give her back to Celeste, even though she cried longer for Miss Kitty than for you." Maggie tilts her head. "How does that make you feel?"

"Now you're just being a bitch."

"Maybe, maybe not. It took me a long time to realize the problem wasn't Miss Kitty." She pauses to crumble a bit of cheese between her fingers. "Or you," she sighs. Keeping her eyes on the cheese, she says, "The day Phil pronounced you dead, Celeste was supposed to be napping. Phil heard her giggling, so he went into the room to...to...to *redirect* her. She was sitting up in bed, laughing and clapping as Miss Kitty danced over her head. Phil swore the toy was possessed—and you'd given it to her. But it wasn't a spell you cast or a devil you summoned." She looks up. "It was Celeste. She's like you."

I slowly smooth Miss Kitty's fur and work hard to keep my tone neutral. "I'm sure Phil beat the devil out of her."

Maggie sighs. "He didn't have to. Kids don't remember."

"The hell they don't."

She shakes her head and brushes cheese crumbs from her fingertips. "Celeste doesn't remember you or Miss Kitty flying or the imaginary friends she used to talk to. Trust me. A mother knows."

"Uh-huh. Well, if you know so much, why come to me?"

She enunciates like each word is fire on her tongue. "You see what *is.*"

I lean forward. "The news said Celeste was kidnapped, but there was no ransom demand. Do you think she ran away?"

Maggie sighs. "You tell me. I want the truth, whatever it is."

I sit back. "I can tell if she's alive or not, but if somebody's got her, I can't whisk her back home. If she doesn't want to be found, she won't be. I can't actually *do* anything."

Maggie slams her hand on the table. The knife on the cutting board jumps. "All I'm asking is for you to do for your niece what you do for strangers." She opens her purse. "Is it money? How much?"

"How dare—"

She waves a pocketbook at me. "Why, Janet? Why do you have to make everything so bloody hard?"

"Put your money away."

"I'm the one risking the most here!"

I raise my voice. "Put it away! You have no idea what's at stake, Maggie."

"My daughter! My daughter is at stake!"

I breathe in basil, mint, and lavender and count to ten.

Is it enough? I wonder. Is she ready to pick a card and let me read the future she already knows?

I say, "The police? FBI? What do they think?"

She tosses her pocketbook back into her purse and dabs her eyes with a tissue. "They're split. Some think she left on her own; others think she was taken. Her browser history was wiped, but her cell phone and wallet were on her dresser. Nothing suspicious in her text messages. They think—" She looks into her lap and whispers, "They think it might have been someone from the church."

I touch my sister's hand. "You may learn things you'd rather not."

"But at least I'll know."

"And Phil?"

"Fuck Phil."

"Yeah, you said that." I turn Miss Kitty and look her dead in her marble glass eyes. I give Maggie one last out. "In the end, there's no guarantee you'll get her back. Still want to do this?"

"I have to."

Maggie's card is on the table.

Showtime.

I take a deep breath. "Okay. I'll do it."

"Oh, thank God, Ki—I mean, Janet. Thank you."

I gather my will and set a shield around us. I don't want any stray *something* getting in the way of what I'm about to do. Maggie's blind, but not dumb.

I cradle Miss Kitty and think of the young girl who cherished her and the young woman she's become. I think of my sister and what I need to say. I close my eyes, find the soul thread I'm looking for, and *tug*.

"Uuuugggghhhh," I moan.

"What?" Maggie leans in.

My hands start to shake. The memorized words trip off my tongue. "Celeste! By Michael, the Archangel, and all saints past and present—"

"Do you see her? Is she all right?"

I'm not even through the first part.

"Shhhh!" I say without opening my eyes. "Be still. The connection's faint."

"That's good, right? That means she's—"

My eyes pop open. "It doesn't mean anything."

"You talk with the dead—"

"And sometimes the unborn, sometimes the never-born, and occasionally the still living. Hell, trees and butterflies and fishes—even rocks. You're right; Celeste and I have an unusual connection. Over the years, I've been able to sense her, but right now there's something in the way. I need to center and try again."

I wiggle in my seat, clear my throat, and close my eyes. "Celeste! I call upon—"

"What? What's in the way?"

I fling my eyes open. We're never getting through this, and this is the easy part.

"You! You're in the way." I jump up, walk to the rosemary pot, and break off a sprig. I wave it over Maggie's head and around her shoulders, muttering under my breath. Gran sits in her rocker and yawns like it's all too much for words.

But clients are clients.

"Here," I say, thrusting the rosemary at Maggie. "Hold this."

"Why?"

"Just do it. Your negativity is harshing the vibe."

"I'm not holding a frigging twig. This is ridiculous," she says.

"You came to me, remember? And how is this more ridiculous than Phil's Power Hour of Prayer?"

"It just is."

"Take it."

Maggie sets her jaw.

"Take it or I break out the crystals and tarot cards!"

"Fine. I'll hold it. Sheesh."

"And shut up!"

"Okay."

"I mean it. No talking."

Maggie pretends to zip her lip.

I give her the hairy eyeball for a few beats, then sit back down. I need to turn this train down the right track, but Maggie won't be easily lead.

Sisters are the worst.

I tuck Miss Kitty under my chin and take a deep cleansing breath. "Let's both close our eyes and concentrate on Celeste."

Maggie nods and bows her head.

I reset the shield and begin again.

"Celeste! It is I, Auntie Kiki, who summons." I sneaky-peek with one eye. Maggie's eyes are still closed.

Good.

My voice drops an octave, chugging down the track.

"Celeste! Bone of my bone, blood of my blood! By the four corners and two poles, by lightning and wind, summer and spring!" My hands shake first, then my whole body. The bench starts to rattle; the knitting basket tumbles across the floor as air rushes down the chimney. The train's at full speed. My voice raises to a shriek. "I call to you through time and space! Reveal, reveal, reveal!"

I gasp and go stiff as a board.

Miss Kitty tumbles to the floor.

I open my eyes.

Maggie's eyes are round. She's breathing like the last mile of a marathon. "Did you find her?"

I nod. "You don't have to look anymore."

"What?"

"She's gone from you, Mags. She's at peace."

"How do you know?"

I look past Maggie's shoulder to the figure in the hall. Maggie crumbles. "She's here, isn't she? She's standing right behind me. I can feel her. Oh, Celeste, baby, I'm sorry, so sorry. What happened?"

I shake my head. "It doesn't matter. None of it matters now."

"Tell me."

The figure in the hall nods and sweeps her fingers at me. She wants me to tell her mother. I roll my neck, easing the tension. Although I've rehearsed what to say, it still sticks in my throat.

"Celeste snuck out of the house around 2 a.m. She didn't take her phone because Phil put a tracking app on it. She didn't take her wallet because she had no money to spend."

Maggie leans forward. "What was she wearing?"

"What?" I blink. The narrative's broken. "Why?"

"I need to know if you're telling the truth. What. Was. She. Wearing!"

When I look down the hallway, I can just make Celeste out if I squint. She points to her pants, then shirt, and holds up her shoes. I say, "Gray fleece pajama pants with black cats on them, a black t-shirt, pink and grey Vans, no socks." She holds up her wrist. "Oh, and a leather bracelet, with, um, dancing alpacas on it." She shakes her head. "Or maybe llamas." She nods. "Yeah, llamas. I get those two mixed up."

"OhGodohGod, it's her. It's really her. We kept the Vans out of the news reports. I never told anyone about the bracelet. She'd come home with it just the day before." Maggie hiccups and pulls another tissue from her purse. "I thought some boy had given it to her. Told her to take it off before her father saw it."

I open my mouth, but bite my tongue. Some things are better left unsaid.

I tug on my sister's soul thread, sending waves of calm and tranquility. I hope she'll skip this next part, that she'll just accept Celeste isn't coming back and leave. But I know my sister. She's going to want to follow her daughter's story to the bitter end.

Maggie drops the rosemary sprig and blows her nose. Her lip is bleeding again, but she ignores it. "Tell me," she says. "Everything."

I catch the eye of the shadow in the hallway and raise a brow.

She nods.

I know this part, too.

"Celeste was walking along River Road when a white panel van pulled past her and stopped."

"White van?" Maggie looks at the ceiling. "White—Tom? Tom Marco's plumbing truck! Oh my God, TOM? I'll kill that son of a bitch."

I latch onto Maggie's arm to keep her seated. I screw my eyes tight and pinch the bridge of my nose, but I don't know what to say. Tom's not part of the story.

I look down the hall. The shadow is still there. Celeste shakes her head. Nobody, she mouths. It was nobody.

By the fireplace behind Maggie, Gran rocks faster.

I say, "No, it's not Tom. It was nobody—nobody she or anyone knows."

"But—"

I hold up a finger, shushing Maggie before she can speak. It's clear only Celeste can tell the story.

"Give me a second," I say.

I open my mind and invite Celeste in.

Things get wavy as I feel a *push*. There's a snap of electricity that travels from my toes up my spine and lodges in my chest. My heartbeat—*Celeste's heartbeat*—thunders in my veins as adrenaline squish-squish-squishes. Her thoughts are my thoughts, her feelings, my feelings.

Blood calls to blood. We are—as ever—connected.

And then from my mouth, her voice: *"Mom?"*

"Celeste! Is it you?" Maggie grips my arm, her knuckles white.

Pain shoots to my head. This time when I moan, it's real.

"Talk to me, Celeste! Momma's here!"

Celeste says, *"I didn't run when the van pulled over or when he asked me where the nearest gas station was or if River Road meets I-15. By the time I knew to run, it was too late. I woke in the back of the van, blindfolded and gagged."*

Maggie doesn't breathe.

"Momma? He hurt me, Mom. Bad. He called them games, but he always won. He's done this before, many times. I disappointed him. I died too fast."

Like coffin nails on a chalkboard, sound explodes from Maggie's chest, a volcano wail of a mother's soul shredding. Her pain hits me like a blast furnace, spinning my delicate connection out of control.

"Tell me, baby. Tell me so I can find this monster and make him pay!"

I shield hard and search for Celeste. She speaks. *"You can't. He's smart. He never hunts in the same place twice."*

"What does he look like? There's got to be something you can tell us."

"There's nothing. He took my eyes, first thing. He wanted to be the last thing I saw, but I don't remember anything except red. The taste, the sound, the smell of red."

From my mouth, Celeste's voice is flat and hollow, isolated from the pain and horror.

Bodies feel.

Spirits think.

Maggie rocks like a mother with a fussy toddler. "Celeste, honey, where are you?" She calls out to the kitchen. "I need to bring you home so you can rest in peace."

When Celeste paints me a picture of endless desert, I flinch.

A raging bonfire.

Ashes shifted.

Chemicals.

More ashes.

Black liquid swirling down gas station toilets and rest area porta-potties, dumped into irrigation ditches and ponds; Celeste is everywhere and nowhere.

Are trying to kill her? I mentally shout. *I'm not telling her that. No mother deserves that.*

Celeste breaks our connection and leaves it up to me.

I clear my throat. "Celeste says there's no body to bring home. He scattered her ashes."

"Ashes? Where?"

"I'm not sure. The image is, um, dark. In water, I think."

"Oh, God!"

"It's peaceful. I mean, she's at peace. She's good."

"Good? My baby is alone!"

"I don't think she's alone."

Maggie pauses. "You mean Gran's with her? How can that be? Gran was...Gran was—"

"Like me."

"Exactly."

I say, "Of course Gran's with her. Gran's always been with her. Where else would Gran be?"

Behind Maggie's back, Gran rolls her eyes and picks Miss Kitty up from under the table, making her dance three feet off the floor. I give Gran the evil eye until she sets Miss Kitty down. In a huff, Gran passes through Maggie and heads down the hall to Celeste.

Maggie rubs her arms and says, "Is Celeste still here? I felt something cold pass by."

I peek down the hall.

Celeste is gone.

"No," I say. "She's moved on."

"With Gran?"

There's a thump and muffled giggles coming from Gran's old room, my guest room now.

"Yeah. I think Celeste was just waiting to talk with you."

"What happens now?"

I shrug. "She'll transition to a new existence. I can tell you she's joyous and excited at all that's to come. It's not how you wanted it, but trust me, we all go through it. We all leave the nest. Celeste is just transitioning a little sooner than expected."

Maggie abruptly stands. "You don't seem upset."

"It's not news to me."

"You knew?"

"Bits."

Maggie's eyes narrow. "You saw Celeste."

I shrug.

"When?"

I sigh. This part's tricky. I meet Maggie's eyes.

"A few days ago."

Maggie curls around the gut punch I've delivered and sinks back down on the bench. "Days. And you didn't call? We're sisters!"

I tell the truth. "You weren't ready to believe."

Her hand flies to her mouth. "Oh, God. Phil. What do I tell Phil?"

"Fuck Phil, remember? He's the whole reason it's come to this."

Maggie shoves her purse over her shoulder. "You can't blame him."

"Watch me."

She glances at the kitchen clock. "It's almost three. I've got to run." She stands and gathers her purse and tissues. "We're on again at five. Damn it! What am I going to tell the press?"

"Nothing. Celeste will just be a missing girl whose family refuses to engage with them—that's boring. They'll move on to juicer click-bait quick. Promise."

"And Phil's Power Hour of Prayer?"

I stand and square my shoulders. "Again, tell them nothing. Prayers harm no one. We could all use good thoughts and energy sent our way, living or dead."

She slides on her sunglasses. "I can't believe my baby's gone."

When Maggie sniffs, she spies Miss Kitty under her bench. She starts to bend, but I'm faster.

"Miss Kitty stays with me."

Maggie opens her mouth to protest, but I cut her off.

"I think we're done," I say and move toward the front door.

Maggie blows her nose and follows.

As she crosses the threshold, her little beasties wrap their claws around her arms, legs, and spine. One sits on her head like a party hat and whispers in her ear. She draws herself up.

"I don't believe you," she says. "You're just like Gran, a fake, a phony, and a fraud who leads people away from the truth."

I sigh. It's her voice, but the beastie's words. "Wow. A fake, phony, and a fraud. That's a lot of Fs. You're pretty fond of that sound today."

Maggie scowls. The beastie on her head sticks out its tongue. Gran leans over my shoulder, threatening it with a rolling pin. It cowers, its fear goosing Maggie into action. She doesn't know why, but she raises her hood and hides it.

Like that's going to help.

Her beasties are so ridiculous, I grin.

But Maggie doesn't see Gran or the beasties.

She snaps, "It's all a joke to you, isn't it? What kind of person tells someone that her daughter is dead? *Tortured* and dead! A sociopath, that's who. You never loved us. You can't love anything."

"Whatever, Maggie. Remember, you came to me."

"Phil's right. Celeste *was* better off without you. *I'm* better without you."

"Okay."

"You think you know things, so know this," she sniffs. "This was a mistake. You won't see me again."

"Kinda what I'm counting on," I say and shut the door.

Gran watches through the peephole until Maggie's car is out of sight.

"You're sure we'll never see her again?"

Gran nods.

"From your lips to God's ears," I say.

Behind me, applause breaks out.

I turn.

Celeste grins and takes a bite of freshly peeled apple. "Oscar-worthy, Auntie Kiki. That was awesome."

HEPATITIS SEA

(MEMOIR)

Puerto Vallarta, Mexico. Three cruise ships line the harbor, the tail end of a long line of luxury hotels and timeshare condos that frame a crescent-shaped beach. Looming over the others like an unmoored city block, our mammoth ship squats squarely in the middle.

We're on a once-in-a-lifetime extended family vacation.

Yesterday, as I meandered the boardwalk with my aging parents, the rest of our herd went on a jungle adventure whizzing down ziplines a thousand feet in the air, riding burros through crocodile rivers, and eating dubious street tacos.

Devoid of the possibility of death, my family beach day has a tough act to follow.

Armed with cruise ship towels, thirty of us stand on crumbling sidewalk overlooking the shore, ignoring offers of free tequila shots and extra cheap, so cheap almost free tattoos. The weather is beautiful. The sand below is flawless, leveled by a man pulling a board roped over his shoulders like an old-fashioned dry farmer with a plow. At the far end of the beach is an impressive pile of seaweed and driftwood.

Local families dot the beach, but almost no tourists. The air is full of charcoal barbecue and mariachi boom boxes. Volleyballs and Frisbees fly overhead. Growing up in Hawaii, it's the kind of family day at the beach my brother, sisters, and I experienced a million times.

Although, I admit the mariachi music is new.

For the price of a few drinks and snacks, a beachfront hotel graciously allows us to use their cabanas and lounges right on the shore. While some of the older kids hunt down the parasailing man, the younger ones wiggle impatiently as sunscreen is slapped on. They know they have to wait for my brother Kalai and me to give them the green light to jump in the water.

Island-born and raised, Kalai and I stand at the water's edge and consider the sea.

"You said there's a freshwater inlet?" he asks.

I gesture to the left. "About a mile that way. There's a bridge over a causeway that runs into the ocean. People tie up boats there. Lots of tourists."

"Bull shark territory. That's not good." He shakes his head.

"No. That's why we're down here with the locals. Locals know the best beaches, right?"

"Yeah," he says, "plus we *blend*." His eyes linger on my milky legs, and he grins. "Or at least some of us do."

Barefoot, Kalai is six and a half feet tall and blessed with our father's dark Hawaiian complexion. Taking after our mother's northern European roots, I'm slathered in SPF 10,000 and wearing a crappy straw hat.

I swat at his arm. "Yeah," I say. "Keep telling yourself that. You blend like Godzilla on vacation."

"Oh, yeah? What's Spanish for *kaiju*?"

"Why? You gonna stomp sandcastles?"

"Maybe," he laughs.

"Tide's coming in," I say.

He glances back at the beach. "No worries. The kids' towels are above the high-water mark." He looks to the left. "What's a mooring doing there?" he asks.

"Where?"

"That float over there." He gestures with his chin, island-style. "It's anchored. Why put a mooring there?"

"Catamaran?" I guess. "Maybe jet skis," I add as one zooms by.

"Jet skis? Too shallow this close to shore. You'd suck sand right through the intake. Ruin the engine in nothing flat."

Up the beach we watch a cabana boy drive a jet ski all the way to shore, cutting the engine just before beaching it. My brother cringes.

I shrug. "Close to shore is not scary. Not deep. Easy for tourists. Their profit margin must be high enough to cover sand damage."

Kalai nods. We Hawaiians know all about tourists on vacation.

The water laps at our toes. This ocean's not the crystal clear of Waimanalo, but it beats muddy Deer Creek Reservoir any day. I roll my head on my shoulders, loosening up for the plunge.

"Feels good," I say. "Waves are big enough for fun, but not big enough for worry."

Kalai raises an eyebrow. "It's not the size I'm worried about; it's the break. Look at the way the waves suddenly stack and crash."

"Very abrupt. It reminds me of Sandy's. Remember all the ambulances that used to race by the house?" I say.

He chuckles. "Yeah. Stupid tourists. Thought the ocean was a pool." He crosses his arms. "But why is the water so dark past the shore break? It's weird. With all these waves, it can't be a shallow reef. Wonder what's out there."

"Yesterday, when I looked back from the bridge, I saw sand all along the coast —not reef or rock."

"That's good." He waves a hand at the acres of pristine beach. "With this onshore, it should be a sand bottom for a long way out."

"Yeah. Easy on bare feet." I wiggle my toes. There's something different about this sand. I reach down and pick up a handful. It's a little coarser than the beaches I grew up on, but definitely sand, not clay or crushed rock. I let it dribble through my fingers.

The penny drops.

"No shells," I say.

"Too many tourists," Kalai says.

"I mean—"

"We going to do this?" he asks. "The only way to really know is to head out there."

To our right, the first of our big kids is getting strapped into a parasailing rig. Cousins stand in a loose ring, laughing and snapping Instagram photos on their smartphones. The one getting strapped in starts an impromptu recitation of his will, giving away his possessions. A cousin offers the parasailing man more money if he doesn't come back.

I feel Kalai's side-eye again. He says, "We've seen what we can see from shore. Enough already. Let's go."

He takes a couple of giant strides and dives through a wave. I toss my hat above the tideline and follow him out.

In just a few heartbeats we're through the surf break. The water temperature is glorious. We're both treading water, knees tucked high to keep our feet safe from the possibilities of coral, stingrays, and broken glass.

Like the girl in *Jaws*, Kalai gives a sudden chin-snapping jerk in the water. "I can't touch," he says.

"What?" I glance back; we're barely offshore. Uncurling like an octopus, I send a questing tentacle down to the ocean floor.

Nada.

I say the obvious. "Me neither."

"Let me check." He takes a lungful of air and slowly sinks under the waves. I wait, watching for his fingertips and wondering if he's going to grab my ankle. He bobs up and wipes his eyes.

"How deep?" I ask.

He shrugs. "Deep. Twenty feet or more. I never touched."

We tread water, considering.

"It's a shelf," I say. "The whole coastline. They must truck in the sand. It's filtered and screened; that's why there aren't any shell fragments. It's all manmade."

"Explains the moorings so close to shore," he says, "and the dark water."

"Does it explain that?"

"What?"

"That." I point. He spins in a half-circle. "You ever see anything like it?"

He tilts his head as we regard the foot wide line of scummy brown foam that bubbles just past the shore break. It runs along the entire beach for 200 yards in both directions. I feel him give me side-eye, like he's weighing how much to share.

"Once," he sighs. "Near a sewage plant."

Oh, gag.

"This wasn't here yesterday afternoon when I scoped out the beach," I say.

"Yesterday afternoon the tide was going out," he says.

I know that, but I'm in denial. "There was nothing on the beach, not even a brown streak from the foam," I say, ignoring the man with the sand-smoothing boards. "Sewers run 24-7, right?"

"Cruise ships," he says.

"They wouldn't."

He shrugs. "Tide's right."

"There are laws," I say.

He snorts.

"*International* laws," I say.

My pretend naiveté is beneath his contempt, not even worth a headshake as his eyes continue to scan the water. His engineer's mind calculates distances, currents, and ground slope compounded by an algorithm of the capacity of high-rise hotels, cruise ships, and parts per million. By his slight squint and furrowed brow, the numbers aren't good.

I choose instead to concentrate on the vastness of the ocean and the curative properties of salt.

He sighs. "Technically, this area probably qualifies as deep water."

"I can't believe we came all this way to swim in a cesspool!"

"Whose idea was a family Mexican cruise?" he snaps. "I wanted to go to Hawaii, but you wanted to go *exotic*."

"Mexico was less than half the cost of Hawaii," I say.

"Well, you get what you pay for."

I shove water at him.

"Careful. Around here that's assault with a deadly weapon," he says, but his attention is back onshore.

I follow his eyes.

"Here they come," he says, watching as the middle kids shriek and splash, coming out to us through the waves and oogie brown foam.

Kalai turns to me and says, "Okay, it's gross, but we're already out here. We can't tell anyone. If Mom finds out—"

"There's not enough hand-sanitizer or antibiotics in the world." I shudder.

We watch as a nephew runs away from the waves, gets knocked down, rolls a bit, and swallows some water. He retreats up the beach, doubled-over and hacking like a sixty-year-old chain smoker.

Kalai and I wince.

I say, "Dad always said saltwater cures everything. He's fine."

Kalai says, "Yeah."

We both add a silent *probably*.

"Okay," Kalai says, "Here's the plan. Fifteen minutes, then we'll head to the beach. Bored, the kids will follow us in. They aren't island-born like us. They won't want to spend the whole day in the water. We'll leave the beach little earlier than planned to get ice cream or something."

"Beyond this funky water, we've got another problem," I say. "This shelf is a huge drop-off. Deep, murky water filled with nastiness this close to shore is prime shar—"

"Don't jinx it," he says. "You're right, but there are a lot of people in the water." He scans the ocean around us. "Okay, there are a lot of people knee-deep in the water, a few on jet skis, a few parasailing, and just us idiots out past the break," he amends. "But there's no point in freaking out the kids."

"Agreed."

Ten more feet of determined rec-center pool splashing and they're here.

"Hey, kiddo!" I say to my daughter. "You made it!"

"Yep!"

Kalai reaches out and snags his child's arm. "Careful, sweetheart. It's really deep. You can't touch here."

"This is stupid," she says, latching on to him like a barnacle.

My daughter, who'd been calmly treading water next to me, suddenly shrieks, "What? We can't TOUCH?!" She wraps her arms and legs around me in a death grip. "That's it. I'm going back to where I can stand."

"Uh, it's really better if you tread water," I say. "You don't know what you could step on."

"Oh, Mom!" she says in the superior way only twelve-year-old daughters can.

It's obvious to her that I am foolish; nothing would dare nibble on her dainty painted toes, toes that flash like bright little fish in the water.

Snack zone, I think.

I start to drift closer to shore and realize I'm almost to the scum.

Death by shark or cholera. It's a tough choice.

Kalai reads my mind and smirks.

"Who can float the longest?" he says and rolls his shoulders back, lifting his toes to the sun.

His daughter flips on her back for a second, then pops upright, doggy paddling like she's churning butter. "This is stupid. I'm going to get a snack."

"Me, too," my daughter says and abandons me for shore.

He's right; our kids aren't water babies; they're desert rats. Unlike our mother, we won't have to wait until the sun goes down to get our kids out of the water.

Ten minutes later, everyone is drying off; the biggest kids are burying the littlest in the sand, turning her into a mermaid sculpture with seaweed hair.

For the first time in my life, I don't want to get back in the ocean.

A waiter in flawless cool whites appears at my shoulder. "Freshwater shower, Señora?" he says, pointing to the side of the pool deck.

Hallelujah.

At the showers, as I rinse the last of iffy water out of my hair, I wonder where the PVC drainpipe goes. I try to convince myself that there's an elaborate underground sewer system that leads to a modern waste management plant full of shiny pipes and filters.

It doesn't work.

I wrap up in a towel and wander back to a lounge chair in the shade and sit next to my mother. Kalai follows. Mom looks up from her book, startled to find us already out of the water.

"It's okay," I say. "They were done swimming."

Out of habit, she runs her eyes along the shoreline, counting noses. "But why are you and Kalai here? Is it time to go already?"

"No. We just wanted to spend some time with you, Mom."

"I'm just reading. You guys should swim. I know how much you love the ocean."

Catching a waiter's eye, I order two Cokes without ice, hoping the bubbles will kill whatever I feel certain is creeping through my system.

As Mom turns a page, Kalai sits next to me, pulling his baseball cap low. Suppressing a shudder, I flick something brown and shriveled off my thigh.

"Jellyfish?" he drawls, lifting his chin to the water. "I thought I felt something sting out there. Kids notice?" he asks.

"Your daughter did. I told her it was just salt on her sunburn."

He laughs. "Good one," he says.

"Besides, these jellyfish don't leave a mark, just irritate a little." I wiggle in my chair. "I think I still have one inside my suit, though."

He snickers. Brothers are like that.

The waiter brings two icy Cokes in the bottles, and I hand one to Kalai. I push my sunglasses higher on my nose. There's a smudge of sunscreen on the lenses, but like the jellyfish in my swimsuit, I choose to ignore it. When you're from Hawaii and living in the Utah desert, the best day at home rarely beats the worst day at a beach.

"Puerto Vallarta is beautiful," I say, "and this is a locals' beach, but the locals don't swim."

"What?" asks Mom. "Why not? Are the kids all right?"

Kalai and I exchange glances.

"The water's a little...sharky," Kalai says.

"Ah," says Mom. "Good thing the kids are through swimming, then.

My brother and I clink bottles.

"Good one," I say.

RESISTER

When Alicia Brown spotted Reginald "Monty" Montgomery's black Jag roaring through Serenity Circle, she dropped her *Cosmo* next to the emergency bottle of Grey Goose and ran for the coffee pot.

She poured a fresh cup—two Splendas, no cream—just as Monty, Senior Funeral Director and Chairman of the Board, blew into the foyer of Montgomery Mortuary, *One and Done, Our Promise for Over 50 Years*.

"What the hell, Alicia?" he griped, waving his cell phone. "You know Thursdays are golf days. I was just about to birdie on the 8th. I had the Mayor in the palm of my hand."

She held out the mug. "Sorry, Mr. Montgomery, but this can't wait. We've got a Resister."

Monty rolled his eyes and took a healthy slug. "Resisters are Reggie's department. Call him."

"I did, but he's had a minor fender-bender with the hearse."

"With a Resister in the back?"

"No, Reggie couldn't get—"

"Wait. The Resister's *loose*?"

"No, it's okay." Alicia jerked her head toward the morgue. "She's chilling in the cooler. The husband and some guy brought her in."

"Damn it, Alicia! For a second I thought we had a real problem." Monty rubbed his chest. "You know I got a weak heart."

"Sorry, Mr. Montgomery. I called because the situation's a bit delicate."

"Oh?" Monty said, sipping his coffee.

"She's a repeat."

"What?" Monty choked. "We haven't had a two-fer in over a decade. It's right there in our brochure!"

"Technically, she's a three-fer," Alicia said.

"*Three*?" Monty put the coffee down and picked up the paperwork. "What's our exposure? Missing children? Pets?"

Alicia shook her head. "Nothing on the police scanner."

"Doorbell footage? Witnesses?"

"I don't think so. Nothing on the news."

"Hallelujah for small favors. Where's the husband?"

"In the Consolation Room. They've been waiting over an hour. But there's something off about the second guy. He's twitchy. Like he has an ax to grind."

Monty frowned. "You think the husband lawyered-up?"

"I'm not sure."

"JC Penny suit? Scuffed pleather loafers?"

"No, wrinkled khakis and a golf shirt, no logo. He's not one of the regular hearse-chasers."

"Probably a *CSI* wannabe." Monty sighed, scanning pages. "This crapfest just gets better and better."

Alicia hefted the coffee pot. "Refill?"

"No, I better get in there." Monty adjusted his tie. "Straight?"

"Yeah. Turn," Alicia said, running a lint brush across his shoulders. "You're good. No dandruff. Mint?"

Monty popped it into his mouth and chewed. "Thanks. I can't believe Reggie botched this so badly." He snapped the file closed. "I'm taking today's green fees out of his paycheck—that'll teach him."

"Mr. Montgomery, just one more thing—I lit candles, but we're gonna have to steam clean."

"Again? Can't you just—"

"Nope. There's not enough Febreze in the world," Alicia said. "Three times in seven months. Can you imagine?"

"No, and neither can you. Resisters don't happen at Montgomery Mortuary. It's right there on the wall—*one and done.*"

"Of course. Should I call Durfy's? See if they can get a cleaning crew out here before lunch?"

"What do you think? I'm already handling Reggie's mess; I'm not doing your job, too," he said, striding down the hall.

When Monty entered the room, the first thing he noticed was five floral candles burning on the credenza. The second was the strong wave of graveyard stench emanating from the soiled tee-shirt of the man rising from his chair.

Monty held out his hand. "Good morning. I'm Reginald Montgomery. I'm so sorry for your loss."

"Thank you," said the man. "I'm Marcus Palmer."

A trained professional, Monty didn't grimace when the hand he shook had the distinct slime of corpse wax clinging to it, though his stomach lurched and his eyes went straight to the industrial-sized bottle of Purell and box of tissues on the conference table.

"Sorry," Mark said. "This stuff is hard to clean off."

"Not at all, not at all. We see this all the time with the Resistant. It's entirely natural and nothing to be embarrassed about." Monty dropped the file on the table and pumped hand-sanitizer like he believed it actually worked.

Monty nodded to the other man. "Under the circumstances, I think we can dispense with handshaking."

"Good, 'cause I wouldn't shake your hand anyway," he said. "You owe us, Montgomery. Big time."

"Bernie—" Mark said.

"No, Mark. What they did ain't right. We ought to sue."

Monty tossed a handful of tissues in the trash and filled his palm again. "And you are?"

"Your worst nightmare!" snarled the man in the slept-in clothes.

Monty looked at Mark, eyebrow raised.

Mark grabbed the man's arm. "Easy, Bernie," he hissed. "Remember, we want him on our side." Louder, he said, "Sorry, Mr. Montgomery. This is my brother-in-law, Bernard Jamison. He's a little distraught."

"So I see." Monty flipped the file open. "As the deceased's brother—"

"Oh, no, no. Martha was an only child. Bernie's married to my sister, Karen. Karen's watching my kids, Daniel and Grace," Mark said.

"Ah," Monty said. "Well, emotional support—"

Bernie said, "I'm not here for *emotional support,* pal. I keep track of where the bodies *ain't* buried, if you know what I mean."

Monty's eyes narrowed. "Are you a lawyer, Mr. Jamison?"

"Maybe," Bernie said. "Maybe not. You shaking in your boots yet, Mr. Big Shot Undertaker?"

Monty sighed. "Positively shivering," he muttered. "Mark—may I call you Mark?"

"Sure. And he's Bernie."

"Nope. Only my friends call me Bernie."

"Really, Bernie?" Mark said. "You're going there?"

"Fine. He can call me Bernie. Sheesh."

"Excellent. Please call me Monty."

Mark said, "Monty, the lady in the front said you're the guy in charge, the one who makes decisions."

"That's me." Monty pulled out a chair. "Let's sit down and discuss this like friends, shall we? What seems to be the problem?"

"Are you kidding me?" Mark said.

Monty gave him a blank look.

"We paid you good money—" started Bernie.

Monty held up his hand. "Let's just start at the beginning." He turned to the last page in the file. "Your wife, Martha Marie Palmer, maiden name Griswold, died seven months ago, on May 7th."

"That's right."

"The cause of death was acute chlorine gas poisoning." Monty paused. "How extraordinary. An industrial accident?"

"No. She was cleaning. She tripped on the bathmat and hit her head. The Windex fell into the bleach bucket. She never woke up."

"My condolences. It says she wasn't found for ten hours—is that right?"

Mark shrugged. "I was on the couch, watching TV. Martha was cleaning. She was always cleaning. I fell asleep and didn't wake up until morning—late for work and with a stiff neck. I found her when I went to—you know."

"No autopsy?"

"No. I refused, and the coroner agreed since the cause of death was obvious. Accidental acute chlorine gas poisoning. The bathroom door was shut."

Monty turned a page. "There are two receiving dates: one the afternoon of May 7th and another pre-dawn, May 12th. This was the Resister incident?"

"Yeah, the first one. There's been three."

"I'm so sorry. Resisters are very rare. Once in a blue moon."

"Yeah, I read your brochure," Mark said.

"Oh, good!" Monty said.

"Not like there was anything else to do while we waited," Bernie muttered.

Mark shot Bernie a warning look and cleared his throat. "We came to Montgomery Mortuary specifically because of your *one and done* reputation, Monty."

Monty nodded. "*One and done* is what our clients experience when they follow our recommendations. However, bodies are sometimes older than coroners estimate. Sometimes other factors come into play. We typically have a single Resister event every three years or so, well below national average, and never twice. *Three* times is unheard of. It might be a new state record. Martha is highly unusual."

"Yeah, well, the whole thing is hinky," Bernie said.

Monty held up a hand. "We'll get to your concerns in a moment, Bernie. Mark, take me through what happened on the twelfth."

Mark inhaled deeply and stared into space. "It was after midnight. The kids were asleep. I heard a noise in the kitchen. Pots banging, cupboards opening. I thought we had a burglar. I grabbed my gun—"

"Your gun?"

"Yeah, from my nightstand. I went downstairs. When I came into the kitchen, there she was, standing with the fridge open."

Monty nodded. "Eating raw hamburger?"

Mark shook his head. "No."

"Chicken breasts? Resisters lick frozen ones like popsicles."

"No, she was pulling out neighbors' casseroles, saying she needed to check them for cheese since Daniel can't have dairy. Gives him the runs."

Monty's eyes bulged. "What?"

"Yeah, on account he's lactose intolerant. He can't have milk, either, not even on cereal."

Monty waved his hand. "Not that. Martha *talked*?"

"Of course. She wouldn't shut up. Started doing the dishes and whining it's a good thing she's back since I was ruining the kids' teeth. Too many cookies and pies, she said. She asked if I'd signed Grace's permission slip for her fieldtrip. Told me she'd take Daniel to soccer practice tomorrow."

"That's incredible," Monty said, scribbling a note. "I've never heard of a coherent Resister. What happened next?"

"I told her she was dead. She just laughed—"

"*Laughed*?"

"Yeah, she laughed and said she knew, but didn't have time to be dead. Started nagging me about mowing the lawn."

"And then?"

"I'd had enough. I double-tapped."

"Double-tapped?"

Mark held his fingers like a gun. "Yeah. Pow-pow. Double-tap. One in the chest, then one in the head. Double-tap."

Nonplussed, Monty sat there for a second, scanning the file. "You shot her in the *head*?"

"Yeah."

"But she came back twice more?" Monty asked, shuffling papers.

"Well," Bernie drawled, "It was head-*ish*."

"Shut-up, Bernie. You weren't there," Mark said.

"What do you mean, head-*ish*?"

"Tell him," Bernie said.

Mark looked away.

"Tell him," Bernie said again. "He needs to know."

"All right! It was her jaw. The second bullet ran along her jaw and out the back of her throat." Mark glared. "Happy now, Bernie?"

Bernie patted Mark's arm. "It's okay. It's still a double-tap in my book."

"So, not really in the head," Monty said. "That makes sense." He tuned a page. "After the," air quotes, "*double-tap*, what happened?"

"She went down. I ran around the counter and picked her up. She was stunned and didn't kick much. There wasn't any blood."

"No, there wouldn't be. Her heart wasn't pumping."

"I panicked. She started to come around, started making weird noises. I worried she'd wake the kids."

"But the gunshots..." Monty trailed off, then shook his head. "Never mind. Continue, please."

"I threw her into the pantry and braced a kitchen chair under the doorknob. I called the mortuary's after hours number, and not five minutes later, Reggie and his assistant, Barry, roll up in a hearse."

"How fortunate they responded so quickly," Monty said. "Go on."

"Reggie freaked out when he heard about the double-tap. He made me wait in the living room while he and Barry got Martha out of the closet and into the hearse. Reggie said it was all over. But it wasn't. Not by a long shot."

Monty tapped the file. "Mark, the paperwork says you didn't embalm."

"No. Martha and I talked about it, you know, *before*. We think it's important to return to the earth. I made that clear to Reggie at our first consultation. Instead of a headstone, we're planting an apple tree. The kids want to bake pies."

"Well, there you have it. Not embalming is risky, Mark. It prevents—"

Bernie leaned forward. "I know what you'd like us to *think* it prevents, Monty, but we don't believe in embalming or the Easter Bunny because we're not dummies. Embalming's a scam. It's another way to rip-off the bereaved."

Monty exhaled and silently counted to three before speaking. "Bernie, it's not—"

"Don't 'Bernie' me like you're God Almighty or Morgan Freeman, *Monty*. The problem wasn't the lack of embalming; it was the sub-standard temperature of your coolers."

"That's ridiculous. Our coolers are kept at the regulation 38 degrees!"

"Yeah, unless the power goes out and back-up generators fail. The morgue went dark the evening of May 11th, Monty. We know. Barry squealed."

"How dare you. I'm not going to grace that accusation with a response."

Bernie pounced. "And then there's the timing, Monty. The funeral was scheduled for the twelfth, a Saturday. Reggie claimed it was the next available time slot, but really, it was because you charge extra for Saturdays, don'tcha?"

"We try to accommodate—"

Bernie cut him off. "The seventh to the twelfth! Do the math, Monty! Burial within three days is the *law*, and for good reason."

"The three day rule is not law, just a common misconception based on old wives' tales. Resisters don't always rise after the third day."

Bernie went for the jugular. "But Martha did, Monty. She did because you let her body warm up. *One and done*, my—"

"Enough, Bernie," Mark said. "I think Monty understands where we're coming from."

"I hear what you're saying, and I feel for you, but I don't think you understand your culpability in all of this. Embalming makes time, temperature, and all sorts of other things non-issues. Not embalming is highly irregular—"

Mark said, "But so is coming back! Resisters don't happen in places like Farmington, Monty. They happen in places like Haiti or Zimbabwe or—"

"San Francisco!" Bernie said.

"Right!" Mark said. "Weird places. In Farmington, it's not normal for the dead to do laundry."

"Laundry? You didn't tell me that," Bernie said.

"Yeah, well, I found my shirts in the dryer later. It's not important."

"Did she remember the Bounce?"

"Yeah."

"Well, that's Martha for you."

"Gentlemen, let's stay focused," Monty said. "You know why Resisters rise in places like California? Because those places don't *embalm*."

Bernie opened his mouth, but Monty waved his hand, cutting him off. He pointed to the file. "Regardless, Mark signed *here* and initialed *there*, acknowledging the risks involved with his burial plan that were contrary to our recommendations. Really, as awful as this is, this is entirely your fault, Mark. You knew she was a Resister, and yet you still buried her in a cardboard coffin without a vault."

Bernie's fist slammed the table. "Vaults! Another racket, just like metal caskets. I told Mark not to spring for extras, but he caved when Reggie peer-pressured him into renting a special viewing casket for the service. 'You can't have your wife lying in a cardboard box,' Reggie said. 'What will people think?'"

Mark said, "I think Reggie may have been right about that one. Martha's parents would've—"

"Hush. It would've been fine. Nobody would've said boo. But thanks to the mortuary's incompetence, we couldn't have a viewing in the fancy, rented casket. Instead, we had to pay *another* fee to stuff it full of foam padding to muffle any sounds Martha made. A closed casket, no viewing, and we still had to pay the make-up and hair styling fees! It's all a racket."

Monty closed his eyes until his pulse calmed enough for him to speak.

"Martha was prepped the day before, so yes, you had to pay that fee. Remember, everything was fine until Mark blew half her face to smithereens. His initials are next to *decline cosmetic reconstruction* and also here, acknowledging that an open casket is impossible. We did the best we could with what we had to work with."

Monty flipped a few pages and nodded. "Okay. I'll concede the unfortunate power outage contributed to the first Resistance incident. I'll refund you the make-up and hair styling fees."

"Thank you," Mark said.

"However, if you'd followed our recommendations, there absolutely wouldn't have been a second or third time. Knowing she was a determined Resister, it's unconscionable that you didn't at least bury her in a metal casket."

"Nope. Those are on you, too," Bernie said. "Tell him, Mark."

Mark scraped at a bit of corpse wax on his palm and said, "The second time was a night about a month after the funeral. I heard a noise. Thought maybe a dog or a raccoon had gotten into the trash. I went outside with a flashlight." He held up his hands, turning them over and over. "Martha had raked a big pile of leaves and was bagging them. The downstairs windows gleamed where she'd washed them, but there were bits of her fingers floating in the bucket. She'd worn them down to stubs digging herself from her grave. When she saw me, she turned and started to say something, something about the flower beds, I think. It was hard to understand her with her tongue hanging and half her jaw gone."

"I'm sorry you had to see that," Monty said.

Mark tipped his head to the side and examined his cuticles, running his thumb along each nailbed. "I distracted her by throwing the flashlight. I grabbed a Hefty bag and threw it over her head. She struggled, leaves spilling left and right, but I managed to pick her up and get her into the garage. I tied her with Grace's jump rope and stuck her in the freezer, securing the lid with Daniel's bike lock. The kids were getting up soon, and I didn't want them to see her like that."

"Don't forget the roasts, Mark. They never reimbursed you for the roasts," Bernie said.

Monty flipped a page back and forth. "Roasts?"

"Mark had to empty the freezer to make room for Martha. That was good deer and elk meat, ruined by the time you guys got around to picking her up."

"Ah. Here it is. Melted. What a shame." Monty sighed. "Again, I'm sorry for the loss, but this isn't our problem. Mark put his wife in the freezer, not us. If he'd followed our recommendations for a metal coffin or a cement vault, he'd still have plenty of venison for Sunday dinner."

Bernie shook his head. "I disagree. What was he supposed to do? Invited her in to cook breakfast? How unhygienic is that?"

Monty checked his watch and stifled another sigh.

"Besides," Bernie continued, "she didn't come back the second time because of a cardboard coffin. She came back because you broke the law."

"Beg pardon?"

"You didn't bury her six feet deep."

Monty raised his head and looked down his nose. "At Montgomery Mortuary, we take pride in our burials. We use state of the art measuring tools which—*by law*, as you're so fond of saying—are certified and calibrated annually. There is no way we buried her less than six feet."

"Maybe not at first, but your crew still screwed up," Mark said. "Anything less than six feet is considered Resister-depth, and illegal. After Martha's second rising, I had Barry use your fancy tools. We measured the top of the casket at five feet, ten inches. He admitted that the fill dirt settled. You skimped and didn't compact properly. Want to see the pictures?"

Monty cleared his throat. "Dirt settles when cardboard caskets start to decompose. That's why we recommend metal coffins and vaults for peace of mind. I'm sorry, Mark. I feel for you and all that you've been through, but you must recognize you're at fault for both the second and third risings."

Monty turned the file toward Mark. "There's your signature approving the second burial plan with your initials acknowledging that it was against our recommendations and industry best practices. And here's the line item where we gave you a 50% discount on our least expensive wood coffin for the reburial. Half, Mark! That's barely above cost. And here's where we gave you full return credit for the original cardboard casket, even though it was performing exactly as specified. You wanted back to earth, right?"

Mark mumbled something indistinguishable and hung his head.

"And here, here's the invoice that shows, *per your request in lieu of a metal coffin*, we zip-tied her wrists to specially installed eyebolts and used sheetrock screws to secure the lid. We even reinterred her an extra two feet deep at *no* additional charge. We did all of this because we care, Mark. We really care."

Mark raised his head and swallowed. "But the bolts and screws didn't hold. This morning, I was sound asleep when I felt the bed *dip*. There was an indescribable stench, like wet dog rolled in fish guts. I turned to push Duke away and came face to face with—I can't. I just can't." He buried his face in his hands.

"Would you like some water?"

"No. I just want this over. In my mind, I keep hearing Martha try to speak. It sounded like—it's so awful, I can't bear it. I think she was trying to say—"

"What?"

"Snuggle."

Mark burst into tears.

Monty stood up and opened the conference door. "Alicia?" he called. "Bring the Goose."

"Right away, Mr. Montgomery."

Bernie put his arm around Mark.

Mark hiccupped. "I had to touch her. I had to push her away. I leaped out of bed and threw the duvet—"

"Blanket," Bernie said.

"What?" Mark blinked.

"It was a blanket, not a duvet."

"Martha always called it a duvet."

"Martha was wrong."

Mark pressed his palms against his forehead.

Bernie shrugged. "Details. It's my blessing and a curse."

"Damn it, Bernie! You and your details and conspiracy theories! If I hadn't listened to you—"

"Whoa, I saved you hundreds of dollars! You wanna be somebody's death patsy—"

"Gentlemen, let's move on."

Mark said, "I rolled Martha in the duv—*blanket*, and put her in the trunk. I called Karen. Bernie and I drove here. The lady at the front desk called Barry. And here we are."

"You're sure you brought her back without witnesses, missing pets—"

"What?"

"Nothing. I mean, that's wonderful. Well done. Now that she's back, we have two options. Reinter using a metal casket or vault—"

"Nope. We're not falling for that," Bernie said.

"Or," Monty said, glaring at Bernie, "cremation."

"Cremation? Cook her in an oven like a...a..."

"Roast?" Bernie said.

"Shut up, Bernie," Mark said. "You're not helping."

"Geez, somebody got up on the grumpy side of the bed today."

Monty said, "Mark, I know this is hard for you. Martha's a deep Resister, but even she can't come back from cremation."

Bernie chimed in. "What about that guy in India? The one in all the papers last year. The one who ate his neighbor's cat."

"A hoax. Even the hardline Resurrectionists agree that never happened. Trust me, Mark. Cremation is safe and effective."

"When?" Mark asked.

"As soon as this afternoon. We have two already scheduled—that will allow you to split the preheat fees three ways."

"Oh, goodie," Mark said. "More fees."

"You'll need an urn. We have a lovely selection. I'm sure we can find something that will look great on your mantle."

"Hold your horses, Mr. Let's-Cremate-When-We've-Already-Paid-for-a-Plot-and-a-Coffin-and-Rented-a-Fancy-Casket-for-a-Viewing!" Bernie huffed. "You're double-dipping. Amazing. How do you live with yourself?"

Monty said, "Bernie, for the last time—"

Mark held up a hand. "No, I want to hear what Bernie has to say."

"Here's how they get you, Mark. When somebody doesn't let them rip him off with all their fancy add-ons, they induce Resistance by warming the corpse and let it escape right before the funeral, hoping that will scare him into paying exorbitant fees for things he doesn't need. When that doesn't work, they don't bury the coffin deep enough, so the Resister rises again. But if he still doesn't cave, they sabotage the second burial by using substandard zip ties and don't wire the mouth. They've been in the death business long enough to know that eventually the hands are going to pull free from the wrists, and the Resister will gnaw their way out. The new coffin? It's wood all right—*balsa* wood. And now, at the third rising, they try to up-sell again. Cremate the Resister, it's the only way—and at full price when it's less than half its original weight."

Bernie brushed one index finger with the other. "For shame, Monty, for shame."

Monty sat back in his chair.

"That's an interesting story, Bernie, but here's the truth. Montgomery Mortuary's been taking care of the dead for over fifty years. Someday my son Reggie will take over the business my father started. We understand how difficult it is to lose someone. It's even harder to have them come back. That's why we pride ourselves on *one and done*. But unless you take our advice, Mark, Martha *will* come back. She'll keep trying until something stops her. She's not your typical Resister motivated by revenge or a desire for brains. She's motivated by love."

Bernie said, "Love? That's a new one. Mark, maybe it's not such a good thing that Carol wasn't there this morning."

"Bernie! We're not official. The kids don't know."

Bernie zipped his lips and threw away the key. "Your secret's safe with me. But if Martha had found Carol on her side of the bed, maybe she wouldn't be so hot to come back."

"Bernie."

"Yeah, Mark?"

"Just stop. Please."

"Whatever you need, Mark. I'm here for you."

"Monty, how much?"

"Cremation?" Monty pulled a calculator from his suit coat. "There's the base fee plus a third of the preheat. I'll waive the rush and the prep fees."

"Mighty kind of you," Mark said. "Are you throwing in a car wash, too?"

"Ha! You're a funny man, Mark. I'll get you Durfy's number. If anyone can get the smell out of your trunk, they can. Tell 'em Monty sent you, and they'll give you the WIFI password while you wait for free."

"Amazing."

"But back to Martha. Do you want to inter the urn in the grave or do you want a refund credit—twenty percent of the plot's purchase price, less clean up fees?"

"Twenty percent? That's robbery!" Bernie said.

"It's a used grave, Bernie. It's not worth a tenth of the original price, especially since I'm required to disclose that the original occupant was a Resister. People are superstitious. Even Resurrectionists get spooked. I'm doing you a solid here by offering you twenty percent."

"What's the damage? Rock-bottom," Mark asked.

Monty punched a few numbers. "Urn?"

"No."

"What about the ashes?"

Mark thought for a moment. "You got a manila envelope?"

"Yes."

"Let's go with that."

After number crunching, Monty said, "Cremation, including plot credit and original beauty fee refunded, cremains placed in an 11x13 envelope, comes to $8,495.27. That's the best I can do."

Mark paused. "What if I provide the envelope?"

Monty pressed a few buttons on the calculator and squinted at the result. "That'd make it $8,495.12. Doesn't save much. I buy envelopes in bulk."

Mark propped his head in his hands and sighed. "How much to simply rebury Martha in her grave?"

"A metal casket or vault's going to cost more."

"We don't need them. I saw her stubby arms. Her teeth were worn down to nubs. She could barely walk. It's not going to be easy for her to rise again. How much to wire her mouth, bind her arms and legs to her body with layers of Saran wrap, and bury her face down?"

Bernie said, "Perfect! She'll dig the wrong way!"

"You're both mad."

"And what if we filled the casket with plaster?" Mark said.

"Like a cement vault, but *inside*," Bernie crowed. "Brilliant!"

"How much for that, Monty?"

Monty cleared the calculator and muttered, "Reinternment, plus wire and plastic wrap, plus plaster of Paris, plus three days cooler storage, plus time and labor, minus make-up and hair refund. And since I'm feeling generous, minus a 15% frequent flyer discount. Add tax. That's $8,365.53. You save $129.59 over cremation. But I *cannot* recommend this. She'll find a way to come back."

"Of course you don't like it—you lose money," Bernie said. "Mark's a disrupter. He's the Uber and Airbnb of funerals. It's the wave of the future, Monty, and it's coming for you."

"Gentlemen, you're not thinking clearly. Money isn't the issue. It's peace of mind. It's the— "

"What? The law? The law doesn't require embalming or metal caskets or vaults. It doesn't require cremation—not even for Resisters. I want a simple, natural burial for my wife."

"But the risks—"

"No buts," Mark said. "Write it up. I'll sign your waiver again. And I want my duvet back, too."

"Blanket."

"Whatever, Bernie."

Monty grabbed the file and stood. "This your final decision?"

"Yes."

"You're sure I can't change your mind?"

"I'm sure."

Alicia knocked, then entered carrying a tray.

"Thank you, Alicia. Please, help yourselves while I get the paperwork started. Alicia, come with me."

"How'd it go," Alicia whispered.

"Swimmingly. They want to do a pump and dump. And get this—they want to use plaster of Paris."

"What? Three risings and they still didn't go for cremation or a vault?"

"Nope. Not even a metal casket. I was wrong about Reggie botching the upsell. These guys are a goldmine. Bringing her back a third time was genius."

Alicia grinned.

"Make sure Reggie uses the good plastic wrap. Otherwise, it'll be a bitch to chip the body from the plaster."

"Got it. When?"

"Let's schedule number four in a month. Christmases should be memorable."

"The 24th?"

"No, that's staff family time. Make it the 23rd."

"Done."

"And put her in a Santa hat. It'll be our little joke."

"Oh, you're so bad, Mr. Montgomery! You think the fourth time's going to be the charm?"

"Oh, I hope not. The Jag needs new tires."

WE NEED HAWAIIAN KINE VOICES

(AN ESSAY)

I'm five years old, laying on the carpet in our living room in Kahului, Maui. Evening trade winds tiptoe through the lānai door, bathing the house with the scent of Mom's gardenia and naupaka bushes. On top the tv, an animated Santa Claus dances with a big red sack, singing about ashes and soot. My eyes dart to the flimsy cardboard cutout of a fireplace and chimney taped to the wall next to the Christmas tree. Panic bubbles. I can't breathe.

Aiyah!

"Dad!"

He doesn't even look up from the *Honolulu Star Bulletin*. "What?"

"How does Santa Claus come into the house?"

"Down da chimney, lōlō. You deaf or wot? Jes' listen to da song." He turns a page.

I bite my lip. I have to know. "But Dad, Mom bought our chimney at Long's. It doesn't connect to the roof. Plus we no more snow! How da reindeer gonna land da sleigh on top da roof if no get snow?"

He flicks the edge of the newspaper down and peers at me. He shakes his head. "Moemoe time, Lehua. You need your rest."

Tears well. No Santa. No presents. So unfair. Mainland kids get all the good stuffs. I try again. "Dad, fo'reals. Is Santa going skip us?"

Dad presses his lips tight and gives me small kine stink eye. He clears his throat and looks around the room. When he spocks the lānai door, his eyes light up. "You ever seen a house in Hawaii with no more sliding door?"

"No."

He nods. "Maika'i. Every house get sliding doors. Das because in Hawai'i, Santa comes through the lānai door instead of down the chimney. In Hawai'i we invite our guests into our homes like civilized people. We no make dem sneak in like one thief."

I tip my head to the side, thinking. "But what about da reindeer?"

Dad clicks his tongue. "Da buggahs magic, yeah? They no need land. They just hover in the backyard and wait for Santa fo' come back. Mebbe snack on da banana trees. Now go to bed!"

It's not the first time I have to perform mental gymnastics to bridge what I see in movies, tv, and books with my oh, so different reality, but it's one of the most memorable. At school the teachers try to prep us for mandatory standardized testing, tests we island kids consistently score lower on than our mainland peers.

"Class, what does it mean if the trees have no leaves?" Ms. Yamaguchi asks. "Lehua?"

"Uh, da trees stay make die dead?" I say. "Dey nevah get enough water?"

"No! It means it's winter! The correct answer is winter! Coodesh! Pay attention. You kids trying fo' fail?"

Sigh.

It would be many years later, when I am in college in Utah and walking through a virgin snowfall along a wooded path that I finally understand the imagery and symbolism in Conrad Aiken's "Silent Snow, Secret Snow" in ways more profound than no leaves equals cold equals winter.

Which brings me, finally, to my point.

We need diversity in literature. Kids need access to stories that resonate with their experiences, that are full of people they know and love, that show themselves —their fully authentic selves—as powerful, valued, and real. We need Pacific voices raised in song, dance, print, film, tv—all forms of media, some not even invented yet.

I remember the profound impact of hearing Andy Bumatai, Frank Delima, and Rap Reiplinger on the *radio*. Hawaiian music, for sure, all the time, but spoken words, Pidgin words, so fast and funny, just like Steve Martin and Bill Cosby! To this day, my old fut classmates and I can still recite all the words to "Room Service" and "Fate Yanagi."

That's powerful.

And finally, I find them. Words on paper, in libraries, in *books*. Stories by Graham Salisbury, Lois-Ann Yamanaka, Darrell H. Y. Lum, Kiana Davenport, and Lee Tonouchi open my eyes to the possibility of using my history and experiences, *my voice*, to tell stories to an audience that didn't need long explanations about why whistling in the dark is not a good thing, that a honi from Tutu was a given, or that wearing shoes in the house is the ultimate outsider insult.

I could write stories where the burden to bridge is on the mainland, not the islands. I could write stories for kids in Waimanalo, Kona, Hana, Lihue.

But there's a catch. The reality is that there are many more readers outside of Hawai'i nei than in it. Books for niche audiences are a tough sell for traditional publishers who are driven by the bottom line. And while self-publishing or small press publishing is viable for genres like romance, thrillers, and sci-fi, it's next to impossible for middle grade and young adult books who need the vast marketing channels of a traditional publisher to reach schools and libraries.

I try not to let that matter.

On the mainland, I tell people my books are not for everyone. If you don't know the difference between makau and makai, you're probably going to struggle a bit with the language. You'll miss a lot of the in-jokes and clues as to what's really going on with the characters and plot. You'll have to work a lot harder.

But it will be worth it.

Promise.

NIUHI / LAUELE FLASH FICTION

These are flash fiction stories set in the Niuhi Shark Saga (a series of three novels) and the greater Lauele Universe of stories. If you haven't yet read the novels or other stories, you are encouraged to do so, though these stories are still fun without that background.

'ALIKA AND ARNOLD

Tuna burst through 'Alika's bedroom door.

"'Alika! Aunty—"

WHAM!

'Alika's punch landed solidly in her gut. "How many times I wen tell you no come—"

Tuna bent over, one arm on her stomach, the other braced against the door jam. "Banana leaves," she wheezed. "Big bunches of ti leaves. Chicken wire."

'Alika stood there, mouth open and catching flies. "What? What you said?"

"Try look!" Tuna said, pointing toward the window.

Through the jalousies 'Alika could see Uncle Butchie and Uncle Kawika rummaging in the back corner of Tutu's lot.

"This pig more small than last year's," Uncle Butchie said. "At least we no need dig the imu deeper."

"Yeah," said Uncle Kawika. "Not too much rubbish to clear, either."

Uncle Butchie jammed his shovel in the loose dirt. "You saw the banana stalks and ti leaves Myrna wen bring?"

"Yeah, get plenny. Eh, when you like do 'em?" Uncle Butchie asked, tilting his head toward the pig pen.

"Bumbai," Uncle Kawika said. "When 'Alika-dem stay school. I no like him getting all ulukū."

"Arnold," 'Alika breathed. He shoved Tuna aside and raced out of the room.

"Wait!" Tuna puffed. "Arnold's not in the pen!"

Halfway down the hall, 'Alika screeched to a halt. "Where?"

"I left him by the Nakamura's side fence tied to the big coconut tree."

'Alika nodded and turned toward the front door. He gave Tuna one last look as she tried to stand up straight. "Eh, sorry, yeah?" he said as he slipped outside. "But I did tell you fo' knock first."

When 'Alika rounded the corner by the Nakamura's fence, all he saw was Tuna's bike leaning against a coconut tree. "Arnold?" he whispered.

Nothing.

Creeping closer, he spotted some jute twine wrapped around the coconut trunk and disappearing into the hibiscus hedge. "Fo'real, Tunazilla?" he muttered. "This string wouldn't hold a mongoose. Arnold better still be here or I'll whop yo' jaw fo'real."

He ran his fingers along the string and crawled under the hedge to discover a big pig dozing in the shade.

"Arnold!"

Startled, the pig grunted and jumped. Seeing 'Alika, his curly tail whirled like a hula hoop, and he made happy pig snuffle noises as he ran to him.

"Shhhhhhh," said 'Alika as he scratched behind Arnold's ears. "It's good to see you, too, buddy. But we've got to get out of here." With one quick tug, 'Alika snapped the string from the coconut tree and wrapped it around his hand.

What to do? Where to go?

'Alika's eyes landed on Tuna's bike.

But it's a girls' bike, he thought. *No way.*

From the house Tutu's voice called, "'Alika! Your breakfast is getting cold. You better hurry or you going miss the bus!"

"Screw it," 'Alika said. "Sometimes you just gotta hele. C'mon, Arnold."

'Alika threw his leg over the bike seat and pedaled away, Arnold following like they'd done this a million times.

LIZ'S CLOSET

It was exactly the kind of thing Liz hated doing.

Hot.

Dusty.

And guaranteed to make a much bigger mess before it was over. Her mother used to say cleaning closets was a lot like eating an artichoke—to get to the heart, you had to unpeel layers that were never going to ever fit together again.

But it was late November and her New Year's resolution to organize—*get rid of*—all the boys' old baby stuff boxed in the top her closet couldn't be pushed to next year.

Again.

Standing on her tippy-toes, the first box teetered before tumbling over, showering her with bits of desiccated spider and gecko droppings.

"No, no, no!" she shrieked, shuddering as she dropped it. "Ugh! I did not sign up for this! This crap had better not be in my hair!"

She bent forward, shaking her head and running her fingers through her hair. When she was confident that nothing ugi was crawling along her scalp, she whipped her hair into a titah bun and sighed. "Just do it, Liz," she said. "When you're done, you can reward yourself with the last of the butter mochi before the kids get home from school."

The first thing she saw when she opened the box was a long red string of stale firecrackers. She laughed. Paul must've confiscated them from Jay a couple of years ago. The burns on the ceiling and cement floor of the carport were still there.

Fortunately, back then all Jay could get his hands on were firecrackers. Heaven only knew what he would do with grownup fireworks.

The next thing she pulled out made her pause: a pacifier without a nipple. *Zader,* she thought. *Even as a baby he destroyed everything he chewed.*

THE SANDWICH

J on Nainoa sat at the picnic table above Keikikai beach playing with a piece of broken beer bottle. The sharp edge of the glass cut a fresh line in the weathered wood as he carefully traced J.N. over and over and over.

So they'll know I was here, he thought.

If anyone had cared to look, they would've seen the way he deftly shaped the curve of the J and the slash of the N, concentrating so hard that his tongue peeked out from between his lips.

Of course, this was all a lie.

Jon's eyes weren't on his initials; they were on the girl sitting thirty feet away and leaning against a coconut tree.

She was drawing something—what, Jon didn't know. But her pencil flew over her notebook in ways that letters and words never did.

More importantly, she had a lunch sack nestled against her hip.

She's skinny. Bet she doesn't eat it all.

Over by the parking lot was a trash can. Jon'd checked it earlier. It was dry and empty. Nothing ugi to contaminate whatever she threw away.

Jon's stomach growled.

I just have to wait.

The girl closed her notebook, tucking the pencil in the spiral binding. Reaching down, she opened her lunch sack.

It was the biggest sandwich Jon had ever seen.

He could smell it. Ham *and* turkey, plus cheese and veggies, all stuffed into what looked like an entire loaf of French bread.

It was bigger than her head.

It was bigger than Jon's head.

Jon's stomach growled.

"Hush," he whispered, wrapping his arm tight. "Just a little longer."

Turning away so he wouldn't see her eat, Jon scrubbed furiously with the piece of glass, carving his initials thick and deep into the tabletop.

A shadow fell blocking the sun.

Jon looked up.

"Eh," said the girl, "you like half?"

Jon didn't know what to do. Of course he wanted the sandwich, all of it, every bit, but he'd be happy for just one bite, leftovers, *whatevers*. The girl stood patiently, holding out half of her sandwich. Just half was at least eight inches long and dripping with ham, turkey, cheese, and veggies. It was more than Jon had eaten in three days.

She jiggled it. "You can, you know. It's no problem. Here. Take it. I get plenny. Too much." She hefted it toward him.

Jon shook his head. "Nah," he said, "I'm good. I got lunch."

She took a big bite of her half of the sandwich. Bits of lettuce rained down.

His stomach growled.

Chewing, she tipped her head to the side. "Oh yeah? Where?"

Jon looked around. "Right over there," he said, pointing to the coconut tree.

"Uh-huh," she said around the sandwich. "'Cause everybody eats coconut bark for lunch. There's an old sunscreen bottle down by the parking lot. Is that your juice box?"

"You calling me a liar?" Jon said, rising from the picnic table.

She shrugged and took another bite.

I'll show her!

Jon walked to the coconut tree. High in the branches were coconuts. He gave the tree a shake.

Nothing happened.

The girl snorted. From her lunch sack she took out a paper towel and placed it on the picnic table. Setting the unbitten half of the sandwich down, she leaned against table. From her half, she took another bite.

Feeling the weight of her eyes, Jon knew he had no choice. He whipped off his t-shirt and slung it around the tree.

"You're going to stretch it out," she said. He heard a pop and fizz. "I get strawberry soda, too."

"I told you I already have lunch."

"Uh-huh," she said, slurping from the can.

Standing at the base of the tree, Jon looked up.

They're really high, he thought. He shot the girl side-eye. *Still watching.*

It was her smirk that did it.

Winding his t-shirt around each wrist and gripping tight, Jon planted a foot against the tree trunk and jumped. Cupping his feet around the sides, he used his thighs to hold his position as he swung his t-shirt higher up the trunk.

Swing, push, pull, stand, swing—

It was a long way to the top. After the halfway mark, Jon stopped looking down. Almost there, he paused to catch his breath and wrapped his t-shirt tighter around his wrists.

She's right, he thought. *My shirt will never be the same.*

"You know get rats in the tops of coconut trees," said the girl. "Big ones."

"Shut up," said Jon.

"Fo'real." Soda slurp. "I just didn't want you to fall if one jumped on you when you reached for a coconut."

What's with this titah? Normal people just leave part of their sandwiches. They don't talk to me. She's crazy.

Finally at the coconuts, Jon looked closely.

No rat noses or tails. Knew it! She's full of shibai!

Taking a big breath and gripping tightly with his knees, he grabbed the biggest, juiciest coconut and started twisting it free.

"Careful," she called. "Don't overbalance when it buckaloose."

"I know what—"

POP!

The coconut detached from the tree.

"Woah!" Jon yelled as he leaned back.

"Drop it!" she shouted as the coconut came tumbling down.

"I know!" Jon said. "I'm not stupid."

"Coulda fooled me," she muttered.

"What?"

"Nothing."

In two seconds Jon was down the tree. He threw his ruined t-shirt over his shoulder and picked up the coconut, shaking it.

"It's heavy," he said. "Going have plenny water and sweet meat."

"Uh-huh," said the girl. "How you going get 'em?"

"What?"

She waved her hand at his pocket. "All I see is one comb. One *broken* comb. How you going open your lunch?"

Jon gave her stink eye.

I'll figure this out, he thought.

"You get spike?" she asked.

"No."

"Oh, machete? Big screwdriver? Maybe even one butter knife?"

Jon wouldn't meet her eyes.

She soften. "I get it. You're independent. You can handle. You don't need handouts. This isn't that. This is...lunch with friends. I'm Akela. What's your name?"

"Jon."

Akela nudged her sandwich. "Jon, you not going make me eat alone, hah? That's rude."

Jon slid on the bench across from her. "Well, I no like be rude."

"Eh, Jon, you like cookies or chips? I get both."

Akela in the Park

Editor note: This one-act play is an alternate version of "The Sandwich" told from Akela's point of view and with their roles switched.

Act One
Scene One

Exterior beach park, Hawai'i, day.

Two ten-year-olds, AKELA MIRANDA (female) and JON NAINOA (male) are sitting at separate picnic tables at a beach park. There is a coconut tree with at least one coconut on it and a barrel trashcan nearby. AKELA has a hoodie tied around her waist and a piece of broken glass in her hand. JON has a big lunch sack/bag next to him and is drawing in a sketchbook. He has earbuds or headphones and is listening to music. AKELA is scratching her initials into the wooden tabletop while secretly watching JON. One of the contrasts is that JON is drawing on paper while AKELA scratches. AKELA has a vibrant interior life that is shown to the audience, but unknown to JON. In the establishing shots, it's clear she is alone in real life, but talks to, hears, and sees POPS, her deceased grandfather. She knows this is odd and tries to hide it, but some of her actions and words leak through to JON.

POPS
(appears)
Ho, I like the slant of your A, Akela. Sharp, that.

AKELA
(out the side of her mouth)
Go away, Pops.

POPS
Is that any way to talk to your grandfather? I raised you better than that.

POPS
My *dead* grandfather! You know the rules—no talking when people are around.

POPS
Psst. What people? That kid? He's not paying attention to us. Rich kid. Got
headphones and everything. What's he doing here?

AKELA
Dunno. Not my problem.

POPS
His pencil moves all funny kine. He's not doing homework. Letters and numbers
don't move like that.

(peers at JON'S sketchbook)

Wow. You should see this, Akela.

AKELA
(hunches away, continues to carve)

POPS
Akela.

AKELA
(ignores)

POPS
Akela.

AKELA
I'm busy.

POPS
Doing what?

AKELA
Making sure somebody knows I was here.

POPS
By carving your initials in an old buss up picnic table? That's how you're going to
leave your mark?

AKELA
I'm making them deep.

POPS
Uh-huh. No act.

AKELA
What?

POPS
I know what you're really doing. You're spocking out Rich Kid's lunch.

AKELA
I am not.
(Stomach rumbles. Pops and Akela exchange a look. Akela sighs.)

POPS
(Looks in the trash can.)
Dry and empty. Perfect. Nothing pilau to ruin a leftover lunch.

AKELA
Pops, I been watching. I think Rich Kid has a lot of food in his bag. Maybe enough
for me to bring back and share. It sounded heavy when he put it on the table. He's
skinny. He won't eat it all.

POPS
What if he does?

AKELA
(shrugs, miserable)

JON closes his sketchpad and opens his lunch. In AKELA'S imagination, it's the biggest sandwich evah. In reality, it's just a regular sandwich.

POPS
Whoa.

AKELA
That's an entire loaf of French bread!

POPS
It's bigger than his head!

AKELA
(stomach growls)
(sniffs)
Ham *and* turkey! Cheese, veggies...

Interlude where AKELA interacts with the sandwich in her imagination. When she snaps back to reality, JON (headphones off) is standing next to AKELA, holding out half of a regular sandwich.

JON
Eh, you like half?

AKELA
Uh—

JON
Can, you know. It's no problem. Here. Take it. I get plenny. Too much.

POPS
Hmmmm. I know you hungry, Akela, but why is Rich Kid giving you half his sandwich?

AKELA
Nah. I'm good.

JON:
(takes a bite of sandwich)
It's 'ono. Turkey *and* ham. Get mustard, too.

AKELA
No need. I got lunch. Thanks.

JON
Oh, yeah? Where?

AKELA
(Looks around. Points to coconut tree)
There.

JON
Uh-huh. 'Cause everybody eats coconut bark for lunch. There's an old sunscreen
bottle down by the parking lot. Your juice box?

AKELA
(rising)
You calling me a liar?

JON
(shrugs and takes another bite)

AKELA
Watch.

POPS
Akela...

*AKELA walks to the coconut tree. She gives it a shake. Nothing. JON snorts.
POPS rolls his eyes. As AKELA fusses with the coconut tree, JON is watching
and continuing to eat, while pulling things like chips, cookies, etc., out of his
lunch bag and setting parts on a paper towel/napkin for AKELA. He's watching, amused. AKELA takes her hoodie and wraps it around the tree trunk to
help her climb.*

JON
You're going to stretch it out.

AKELA
It's fine.

JON
I'm only saying 'cause my moddah would be plenny huhū if I came home with a
stretched out hoodie.

(Pop/fizz of soda can opening.)

I get soda, too.

AKELA
I told you I already have lunch.

JON
Right.
(slurps from can)

*AKELA stands at the base of the tree, hoodie wrapped around the trunk. She
plants a foot against the tree trunk. Meanwhile, as this exchange continues,
POPS is checking out the lunch and what JON is doing. JON continues to be
oblivious to POPS.*

AKELA
(To POPS, sotto voce.)
That's really high.

(Shoots JON side-eye. He's still watching.)

JON
You know get rats in the tops of coconut trees.

AKELA
What.

JON
Fo'real. Big ones.

AKELA
No way.

JON
Way.

AKELA
You're trying to trick me.

JON
(shakes head)

Just warning. Try not to scream or fall if one jumps on you. He only like lunch, too. Oh, pro tip: twist when you grab the coconut. That way you won't fall when it buckaloose.

AKELA
You the coconut expert now? You gonna show me?

JON
Nah. You got 'em. Your lunch, right? Unless you like some of mine...

AKELA
Pops?

JON
Who's Pops?

AKELA
Nobody.

POPS
(shakes his head)

I dunno, Akela. This guy's not normal. Look at him. He's laying out half his lunch for you. All that food! Who does that? Why doesn't he just wrap up what he doesn't want and leave it on the table? Why he gotta talk, talk, talk?

AKELA
I think...I think he sees me like I see you.

JON
What? You talking bubbles. Of course I see you.

AKELA
Not talking to you.

JON
Then who?

AKELA
Nobody! Myself. I'm trying to figure out the best way—

JON
To get lunch?

POPS
(sighs and makes a coconut fall)

AKELA
(shrieks)

JON
Rat?!

AKELA
Coconut! Look—so heavy. It's full of water—more better than soda—with sweet,
sweet meat!

JON
Awesome. How you going open 'em?

AKELA
I'll—

JON
You get spike?

AKELA
No.

JON
Oh, machete? Big screwdriver?

AKELA
No. I'll—I'll—

(Gives him stink eye. She's defeated but won't admit it.)

JON
You're independent. You can handle. You don't need handouts. I get it. This isn't
that. This is...lunch with friends. I'm Jon Nainoa. You not going make me eat
alone, are you?

POPS
(Starts to talk, but AKELA waves a hand and he disappears)

AKELA
I'm Akela Miranda.

JON
Eh, Akela, you like chips or cookies? I get both.

END SCENE

Hawaiian and Pidgin English Glossary

This glossary is intended to help you better understand the stories in this collection. Many of them use Hawaiian or Hawaiian Pidgin English words that may be unfamiliar to the reader. All of the definitions are provided by the author.

'ahi—Hawaiian tuna fishes, especially yellow-fin tuna
'āina—land, earth
akamai—smart, expert, clever
aloha—love, affection, compassion, mercy, greeting, salutation
'a'ole—no, not, never, none
auwē—interjection to express grief, disappointment, to mourn
auwī—ouch
'awa—a bitter ceremonial drink made of *Piper methysticum* (kava)

buckaloose—comes loose
buggah—pest
bumbai—in time

calabash—extended family and friends
chee—interjection similar to gee

chicken skin—goosebumps; a watchful, eerie feeling
choke—an overabundance, many, too much
confunit—confound it
coodesh—interjection, okay, all right already

diva-lani—the ultimate diva, someone who expects special treatment

ʻeʻepa—extraordinary, a person with miraculous powers, a supernatural being
ʻEwa—a place name west of Honolulu used as a directional landmark

fut—fart, figuratively old
futless—without purpose or direction, blah

gangies—the gang, colloquially friends, sometimes students

hāloa—poetic name for taro, a type of prayer, literally long breath
hammajang—beat up, worn
hanabata—snot, figuratively youthful days
hana hou—do it again, repeat, encore
hānai—foster child, adopted child, to adopt
haole—traditional usage meant anything foreign or strange to a specific person or location; modern usage usually refers to a white person, American and colonial influences, non-Native Hawaiian people or objects, or western thoughts and perceptions
hauʻole la hānau—happy birthday
heah—here
heʻe—octopus
heiau—pre-Christian place of worship, shrine, temple
hele—to go, to come, to walk, to move as in a game
henehene—to laugh at, to ridicule, to tease
hiamoe—to sleep, fall asleep
honi—to kiss (modern usage), to touch noses side-to-side in greeting (former usage)
hoʻomaikaʻi—to thank, to praise, to congratulate, to make acceptable
huhū—mad, upset, to anger, offended
hui—to join, to unite, a club or association, to gather, to get someone's attention
hukilau—a community fishing method using large nets
huli or **hulihuli chicken**—to turn, a type of marinated chicken cooked over coals with frequent turning

imu—underground oven

kai—sea, area close to shore, sea water
kalbi—a type of marinade often used for pork or beef ribs
kanaka—traditionally human being, man, person, modern usage often refers to a Hawaiian or part-Hawaiian individual
kapahaki—mixed up, askew
kapu—sacredness, prohibition, forbidden, special privilege or exemption from normal rules
keiki—child, offspring, descendant, youngster
kiawe—a type of tree often used in barbecuing
kupuna—grandparent, ancestor, relative or close friend of the grandparents' generation
kaukau—to eat, food
ki'i—image, statue, likeness
kīkepa—a length of cloth wrapped under one arm and over the shoulder of the opposite arm
kine—kind, something like or related to something else
koa—a type of hardwood, brave, bold, fearless, a soldier or warrior
kōnane—a deceptively simple ancient strategy game similar to checkers
kukui—candlenut tree or nuts from the candlenut tree used for light, figuratively guide, leader
kuleana—responsibility, stewardship, right, privilege
kumu hula—dance teacher, hula master
kūpe'e—a type of edible marine snail symbolic of hidden knowledge

lānai—porch, patio, balcony
lauhala—pandanus leaf used in weaving
laulau—a package, particularly pork and fish with taro leaves wrapped in ti or banana leaves for cooking, an interjection
lavalava—a rectangular cloth worn like a kilt or skirt, especially in Samoa
lehua—the flower of the 'ōhi'a tree, usually deep red in color, figuratively a warrior, beloved friend, or expert
lelekawa—to jump from a high place into water
li'dis—like this
limu—the general Hawaiian name for aquatic plants, usually referring to edible seaweed
loco moco—a layered dish made of white rice, grilled hamburger patty, and sunny-side fried egg smothered in a brown gravy
lōlō—feeble-minded, crazy

mahalo—thanks, gratitude, to thank

mahalo nui loa nā akua, nā ʻaumakua—Abundant thanks and praise to our gods and ancestors

maikaʻi—good, all right, righteous, well-done

Makahiki—year, annual, an ancient four-month festival beginning about mid-October featuring sports, games, and religious observances

makai—on the seaside, toward the sea, in the direction of the sea, the opposite of mauka

makau—fishhook, sometimes symbolic of disorder

makule—aged, old, elderly

malasada—similar to a raised doughnut without a hole, a Portuguese-inspired pastry that's deep-fried, then rolled in sugar, and often filled with custard, pudding, or jelly

malo—loincloth

maluhia—peace, security, tranquility

manini—small, tiny, stingy

manō—the Hawaiian general name for shark, figuratively a passionate lover

mauka—inland, toward the mountains, the opposite of makai

menehune—a legendary race of small people

moana—ocean, open sea, deep sea

moʻbettah—better, more better

moddah—mother

moemoe—to sleep, to ambush, to lurk

mōlī—Laysan albatross

mout—mouth

na akua, na ʻaumakua—our gods and ancestors

naupaka—a native shrub found in the mountains and near coasts with white flowers that look like matching halves

nei—when following a noun or pronoun, this word indicates affection, i.e., Hawaiʻi nei, beloved Hawaiʻi

nīele—to ask too many questions, to be a busybody

nunui—biggest, grandest, most, greatest

ʻohana—family, relative, kin group

ʻōkole—buttocks, butt, bum

oli—a chant that was not danced to that is often heard at the opening of events, gatherings, and ceremonies

ʻono—delicious, tasty, to relish, to crave

ʻopihi—limpet

'ōpū—stomach, abdomen

pali—cliff, precipice, figuratively an obstacle or haughty
pau—finished, done, completed
pe'a—common name for Samoan traditional male tattoo composed of heavy lines and geometric shapes
piko—navel, umbilical cord, figuratively a blood relative or point of origin
pilau—rot, stench, to stink, putrid
pilikia—trouble of any kind, great or small, a problem, nuisance, bother
plenny—plenty
poi—pounded cooked taro, a cornerstone of the Hawaiian life
poi dog—originally a breed of Hawaiian pariah dog, now extinct. Modern usage generally refers to a mutt or mixed-breed dog, sometimes refers to people with mixed heritage.
poke—to slice or cut crosswise into pieces, the name of a traditional Hawaiian dish made of sliced raw fish (often aku/skipjack tuna) or octopus, Hawaiian salt, seaweed, and inamona (roasted kukui nut relish)
poke bowl—the Westernization and cultural appropriation/commercialization of traditional Hawaiian poke, a raw or cooked fish dish served over rice or noodles and seasoned with various spices, sauces, and condiments
pono—goodness, uprightness, moral, correct or proper, righteous
pōpō aniani—glass ball, i.e., Asian fishing float that has traveled to Hawai'i
pōpolo—small black edible berries, slang for someone with very dark skin
pua'a—pig, pork
pua fiti—Samoan name for plumeria or frangipani flowers
puka—hole, perforation, door
pupule—crazy, insane, reckless

shave ice—similar to a snow cone, very fine slivers of ice shaved from a big block and flavored with fruit syrups
shibai—slang used to call out an over exaggeration or blatant untruth, similar to bull-lie
shishi—to urinate
shoyu—soy sauce
skosh or skoshi—a little bit
slippahs—slippers, i.e., casual two-strap sandals with a toe post, sometimes called flip-flips or thongs
spocking or spoked out—checking out, watching
sprunch—a mix of Sprite and fruit punch

taro—a plant with edible corms that was the basis of Hawaiian agriculture, kalo

tatau—Samoan word meaning to mark, i.e., tattoo

tilly—a pejorative term for behavior that is too timid

titah—sister, sisterly, also tough, rough, butch. Depending on usage, it can be endearing or fight-provoking.

ugi—slang for disgusting, gross, uncouth

uhu—parrot fish

uku—slang for many, tons, too much

ulua—a type of jack fish, figuratively a male sweetheart

ulukū—upset, restless, agitated

uoki—stop, quit

'uwehe—a hula step where one foot is lifted and weight shifts to the opposite foot

wahine—woman, girl

wana—a sea urchin with sharp spines

A REQUEST

If you liked this collection, please take the time to leave a review on the site where you purchased it and/or on one of the social media reading sites like Goodreads. Tell your friends that you enjoyed it. Suggest it as reading for your local book club. This helps others learn more about the book and gets the word out. You're welcome to use the #hemeleinpubs tag, too.

Thank you for your time, and thank you for reading this book!

About the Author

Lehua Parker writes speculative fiction for kids and adults, often set in her native Hawai'i. Her award-winning and best-selling series include the Niuhi Shark Saga trilogy, Lauele Fractured Folktales, and Chicken Skin Stories, along with many other plays, poems, short stories, novels, and essays. Her short stories have appeared in *Va: Stories by Women of the Moana*, Bamboo Ridge, and *Sharks in an Inland Sea,* and her plays performed by The Honolulu Theatre for Youth.

A Kamehameha Schools graduate, Lehua is a passionate advocate of indigenous voices and authentic representation in media. She is a frequent speaker at conferences, schools, and symposiums, and mentors through the Lehua Writing Academy and PEAU Lit. When the right project wanders by, she's also a freelance editor and story consultant.

Now living in exile in the high Rocky Mountains, during the snowy winters she dreams of the beach.

Connect with her on online at lehuaparker.com.

facebook.com/LehuaParker

twitter.com/lehuaparker

instagram.com/lehuaparker

About the Cover Artist

JOE MONSON worked at many different jobs before trying his hand at writing and editing fiction. He co-edits with Jaleta Clegg the LTUE Benefit Anthologies series: *Trace the Stars* (2019), *A Dragon and Her Girl* (2020), *Twilight Tales* (2021), *Parliament of Wizards* (2022), *A Hero of a Different Stripe* (2023), and *Troubadours and Space Princesses* (2024). He has a number of other anthologies, collections, and special projects in various stages of planning and completion.

He has one published short story, and is currently working on the first book in a space opera adventure series, as well as several other shorter and longer works. He collects science fiction and fantasy art, but not as much as Paul (as if that was even possible). Joe lives in the tops of the mountains with his lovely and talented wife, their three amazing children, and their pet library. Learn more at joemonson.com.

facebook.com/joe.monson.editor

twitter.com/JoeMonsonAuthor

amazon.com/Joe-Monson/e/B07KSJHPHP

ADDITIONAL
COPYRIGHT INFORMATION

All stories on this page copyright Lehua Parker, and listed in alphabetical order by title.

- "Akela in the Park" (theatrical script) originally performed by The Honolulu Theatre for Youth in Honolulu, Hawaii in June 2021. This is its first print publication.
- "'Alika and Arnold" originally appeared in this collection.
- "Aunty Mitzy's Helpers" originally appeared in this collection.
- "Balcony House Hat Trick" originally appeared on lehuaparker.com (2017). See https://www.lehuaparker.com/2017/06/06/balcony-house-hat-trick/.
- "Bridges" originally appeared in this collection.
- "Brothers" originally appeared in *Vā: Stories by Women of the Moana* (2021) edited by Sisilia Eteuati and Lani Young.
- "Cardinal Alignment" originally appeared as part of *Thrive 125* (2021) on the Utah.gov website. See https://thrive125.utah.gov/parker/.
- "The Champion" originally appeared in this collection.
- "Close Encounters" originally appeared in *Vā: Stories by Women of the Moana* (2021) edited by Sisilia Eteuati and Lani Young.
- "Doors" originally appeared in *Secrets and Doors: Stories by the Secret Door Society* (2015) edited by Callie Stoker.
- "Found" originally appeared in this collection.
- "Gamble" originally appeared in *Grifty Shades of Fey: Cautionary Tales Uncovering the Dark Side of the Fair Folk* (2020) edited by Michael C. Cluff.
- "Hawaiian on the Inside" (essay) originally appeared on *The New Engagement* website (2017). See https://thenewengagement.com/literature/hawaiian-on-the-inside.
- "Hepatitis Sea" originally appeared in this collection.
- "Ho'oloa'a" originally appeared in this collection.
- "Infestation" originally appeared in *Bamboo Ridge: Journal of Hawai'i Literature & Arts, Issue 122* (2022) edited by Tom Gammarino, Bryan Kamaoli Kuwada, D. Keali'i McKenzie, and Lyz Soto.
- "Introduction: An Inland Sea" (essay) originally appeared in this collection.
- "In the Twenty and Fourth Year of the Judges" originally appeared in this collection.
- "Liz's Closet" originally appeared in this collection.
- "Maverick's" originally appeared in *Apocalypse Utah* (2017) edited by Johnny Worthen and Callie Stoker.
- "Nana'ue" originally appeared in *Vā: Stories by Women of the Moana* (2021) edited by Sisilia Eteuati and Lani Young.

- "Nightwalker" originally appeared in the Sick Pilgrim section of the Patheos website on October 5, 2016. See https://www.patheos.com/blogs/sickpilgrim/2016/10/spooky-pilgrim-strange-but-true-stories-lehuas-tale/.

- "Persona Non Grata" originally appeared in *Wasatch Witches* (2021) edited by Beverly Bernard.

- "Red" originally appeared in a slightly different version in *Old Scratch and Owl Hoots* (2015) edited by C. R. Langille and R. L. Weston.

- "Rell's Kiss" originally appeared as "Rell Goes Hawaiian" in *Fractured Slipper* (2018) from Tork Media.

- "Resister" originally appeared in *They Walk Among Us* (2020) edited by Daniel Cureton and Joni B. Haws.

- "The Sandwich" was originally read at Waiʻanae Intermediate School in Waianae, Hawaii in 2021. This is its first print publication.

- "Tatau" originally appeared in *Dialogue: A Journal of Mormon Thought, Volume 54, Issue 2* (2021) edited by Taylor Petrey.

- "This Once Was a Sea" originally appeared in this collection.

- "Tourists" originally appeared in *Mystery In Paradise: 13 Tales of Suspense* (2013) edited by Lourdes Venard.

- "Voices" originally appeared as by Jace Hunter in *It Came from the Great Salt Lake* (2016) edited by K. Scott Forman.

- "We Need Hawaiian Kine Voices" originally appeared on lehuaparker.com (2018). See http://www.lehuaparker.com/2018/05/18/we-need-hawaiian-kine-voices/.

www.ingramcontent.com/pod-product-compliance
Lightning Source LLC
Chambersburg PA
CBHW021503110726
47899CB00001BA/280